LEE CHILD is British, but after he was made redundant from his job he moved with his family from Cumbria to the United States to start a new career as an American thriller writer. His first novel, *Killing Floor,* won the Anthony Award, and his second, *Die Trying,* won WH Smith's Thumping Good Read Award. All his novels feature the maverick Jack Reacher, and all have been worldwide bestsellers; his most recent is *Persuader.*

Persuader

'With a huge body count, *Persuader* is **ballsy**, **dynamic** and not for the faint-hearted.'
Daily Mirror

'Ass-kicking crime writing at its **most thrilling**, uncompromising best.'
Daily Record

'People who should know better are reading him, secreted behind the dust cover of the new Don DeLillo . . . Reacher knows how to strip a **gun** and how to strip a lady.'
Private Eye

'One of the **best** writers in this genre . . . His hero, Jack Reacher, is on top form . . . Reacher has no doubts about his objective: to rid the world of bad guys. And **nobody does it better**.'
Sunday Telegraph

'Jack Reacher is a seriously **tough** but unbendingly moral loner, a taciturn modern-day Galahad who attracts violence like a magnet . . . **violent** and exciting.'
Irish Independent

'Child is a **consummate** thriller writer: his prose is trim but descriptive, his plots believable, fresh and positively airtight, and here he shows himself a **master** of misdirection.'
Time Out

THE ENEMY
LEE CHILD

BANTAM PRESS

LONDON · NEW YORK · TORONTO · SYDNEY · AUCKLAND

TRANSWORLD PUBLISHERS
61–63 Uxbridge Road, London W5 5SA
a division of The Random House Group Ltd

RANDOM HOUSE AUSTRALIA (PTY) LTD
20 Alfred Street, Milsons Point, Sydney,
New South Wales 2061, Australia

RANDOM HOUSE NEW ZEALAND LTD
18 Poland Road, Glenfield, Auckland 10, New Zealand

RANDOM HOUSE SOUTH AFRICA (PTY) LTD
Endulini, 5a Jubilee Road, Parktown 2193, South Africa

Published 2004 by Bantam Press
a division of Transworld Publishers

A catalogue record for this book is available from the British Library.
ISBNs 0593 051823 (cased)
0593 052021 (tpb)

Typeset in 11/13¼pt Century Old Style by
Kestrel Data, Exeter, Devon.

Printed and bound in Great Britain by
Mackays of Chatham plc, Chatham, Kent.

1 3 5 7 9 10 8 6 4 2

Papers used by Transworld Publishers are natural, recyclable products made
from wood grown in sustainable forests. The manufacturing processes
conform to the environmental regulations of the country of origin.

Dedicated to the memory of Adèle King

THE ENEMY

ONE

AS SERIOUS AS A HEART ATTACK. MAYBE THOSE WERE KEN Kramer's last words, like a final explosion of panic in his mind as he stopped breathing and dropped into the abyss. He was out of line, in every way there was, and he knew it. He was where he shouldn't have been, with someone he shouldn't have been with, carrying something he should have kept in a safer place. But he was getting away with it. He was playing and winning. He was on top of his game. He was probably smiling. Until the sudden thump deep inside his chest betrayed him. Then everything turned around. Success became instant catastrophe. He had no time to put anything right.

Nobody knows what a fatal heart attack feels like. There are no survivors to tell us. Medics talk about necrosis, and clots, and oxygen starvation, and occluded blood vessels. They predict rapid useless cardiac fluttering, or else nothing at all. They use words like *infarction* and *fibrillation*, but those terms mean nothing to us. *You just drop dead*, is what they should say. Ken Kramer certainly did. He just dropped dead, and he took his secrets with him, and the trouble he left behind nearly killed me too.

*   *   *

I was alone in a borrowed office. There was a clock on the wall. It had no second hand. Just an hour hand, and a minute hand. It was electric. It didn't tick. It was completely silent, like the room. I was watching the minute hand, intently. It wasn't moving.

I waited.

It moved. It jumped ahead six degrees. Its motion was mechanical and damped and precise. It bounced once and quivered a little and came to rest.

A minute.

One down, one to go.

Sixty more seconds.

I kept on watching. The clock stayed still for a long, long time. Then the hand jumped again. Another six degrees, another minute, straight-up midnight, and 1989 was 1990.

I pushed my chair back and stood up behind the desk. The phone rang. I figured it was someone calling to wish me a happy new year. But it wasn't. It was a civilian cop calling because he had a dead soldier in a motel thirty miles off post.

'I need the Military Police duty officer,' he said.

I sat down again, behind the desk.

'You got him,' I said.

'We've got one of yours, dead.'

'One of mine?'

'A soldier,' he said.

'Where?'

'Motel, in town.'

'Dead how?' I asked.

'Heart attack, most likely,' the guy said.

I paused. Turned the page on the army-issue calendar on the desk, from December 31st to January 1st.

'Nothing suspicious?' I said.

'Don't see anything.'

'You seen heart attacks before?'

'Lots of them.'

'OK,' I said. 'Call post headquarters.'

I gave him the number.

'Happy New Year,' I said.

'You don't need to come out?' he said.

'No,' I said. I put the phone down. I didn't need to go out. The army is a big institution, a little bigger than Detroit, a little smaller than Dallas, and just as unsentimental as either place. Current active strength is 930,000 men and women, and they are as representative of the general American population as you can get. Death rate in America is around 865 people per 100,000 population per year, and in the absence of sustained combat soldiers don't die any faster or slower than regular people. On the whole they are younger and fitter than the population at large, but they smoke more and drink more and eat worse and stress harder and do all kinds of dangerous things in training. So their life expectancy comes out about average. They die at the same speed as everyone else. Do the math with the death rate versus current strength, and you have twenty-two dead soldiers every single day of every single year, accidents, suicides, heart disease, cancer, stroke, lung disease, liver failure, kidney failure. Like dead citizens in Detroit, or Dallas. So I didn't need to go out. I'm a cop, not a mortician.

The clock moved. The hand jumped and bounced and settled. Three minutes past midnight. The phone rang again. It was someone calling to wish me a happy new year. It was the sergeant in the office outside of mine.

'Happy New Year,' she said to me.

'You too,' I said. 'You couldn't stand up and put your head in the door?'

'You couldn't put yours *out* the door?'

'I was on the phone.'

'Who was it?'

'Nobody,' I said. 'Just some grunt didn't make it to the new decade.'

'You want coffee?'

'Sure,' I said. 'Why not?'

I put the phone down again. At that point I had been in more than six years, and army coffee was one of the things that made me happy to stay in. It was the best in the world, no question. So were the sergeants. This one was a mountain woman from north Georgia. I had known her two days. She lived off post in a trailer park somewhere in the North Carolina badlands. She had a baby son. She had told me all about him. I had heard nothing about a husband. She was all bone and sinew and she was as hard as woodpecker lips, but she liked me. I could tell, because she brought me coffee. They don't like you, they don't bring you coffee. They knife you in the back instead. My door opened and she came in, carrying two mugs, one for her and one for me.

'Happy New Year,' I said again.

She put the coffee down on my desk, both mugs.

'Will it be?' she said.

'Don't see why not,' I said.

'The Berlin Wall is halfway down. They showed it on the television. They were having a big party out there.'

'I'm glad someone was, somewhere.'

'Lots of people. Big crowds. All singing and dancing.'

'I didn't see the news.'

'This all was six hours ago. The time difference.'

'They're probably still at it.'

'They had sledgehammers.'

'They're allowed. Their half is a free city. We spent forty-five years keeping it that way.'

'Pretty soon we won't have an enemy any more.'

I tried the coffee. Hot, black, the best in the world.

'We won,' I said. 'Isn't that supposed to be a good thing?'

'Not if you depend on Uncle Sam's paycheck.'

She was dressed like me in standard woodland camouflage battledress uniform. Her sleeves were neatly rolled. Her MP brassard was exactly horizontal. I figured she had it safety-pinned in back where nobody could see. Her boots were gleaming.

'You got any desert camos?' I asked her.

'Never been to the desert,' she said.

'They changed the pattern. They put big brown splotches on it. Five years' research. Infantry guys are calling it chocolate chip. It's not a good pattern. They'll have to change it back. But it'll take them another five years to figure that out.'

'So?'

'If it takes them five years to revise a camo pattern, your kid will be through college before they figure out force reduction. So don't worry about it.'

12

'OK,' she said, not believing me. 'You think he's good for college?'

'I never met him.'

She said nothing.

'The army hates change,' I said. 'And we'll always have enemies.'

She said nothing. My phone rang again. She leaned forward and answered it for me. Listened for about eleven seconds and handed me the receiver.

'Colonel Garber, sir,' she said. 'He's in D.C.'

She took her mug and left the room. Colonel Garber was ultimately my boss, and although he was a pleasant human being it was unlikely he was calling eight minutes into New Year's Day simply to be social. That wasn't his style. Some brass does that stuff. They come over all cheery on the big holidays, like they're really just one of the boys. But Leon Garber wouldn't have dreamed of trying that, with anyone, and least of all with me. Even if he had known I was going to be there.

'Reacher here,' I said.

There was a long pause.

'I thought you were in Panama,' he said.

'I got orders,' I said.

'From Panama to Fort Bird? Why?'

'Not my place to ask.'

'When was this?'

'Two days ago.'

'That's a kick in the teeth,' he said. 'Isn't it?'

'Is it?'

'Panama was probably more exciting.'

'It was OK,' I said.

'And they got you working duty officer on New Year's Eve already?'

'I volunteered,' I said. 'I'm trying to make people like me.'

'That's a hopeless task,' he said.

'A sergeant just brought me coffee.'

He paused. 'Someone just call you about a dead soldier in a motel?'

'Eight minutes ago,' I said. 'I shuffled it off to headquarters.'

'And they shuffled it off to someone else and I just got pulled out of a party to hear all about it.'

'Why?'

'Because the dead soldier in question is a two-star general.'

The phone went quiet.

'I didn't think to ask,' I said.

The phone stayed quiet.

'Generals are mortal,' I said. 'Same as anyone else.'

No reply.

'There was nothing suspicious,' I said. 'He croaked, is all. Heart attack. Probably had gout. I didn't see a reason to get excited.'

'It's a question of dignity,' Garber said. 'We can't leave a two-star lying around belly-up in public without reacting. We need a presence.'

'And that would be me?'

'I'd prefer someone else. But you're probably the highest-ranking sober MP in the world tonight. So yes, it would be you.'

'It'll take me an hour to get there.'

'He's not going anywhere. He's dead. And they haven't found a sober medical examiner yet.'

'OK,' I said.

'Be respectful,' he said.

'OK,' I said again.

'Be polite,' he said. 'Off post, we're in their hands. It's a civilian jurisdiction.'

'I'm familiar with civilians,' I said. 'I met one, once.'

'But control the situation,' he said. 'You know, if it needs controlling.'

'He probably died in bed,' I said. 'Like people do.'

'Call me,' he said. 'If you need to.'

'Was it a good party?'

'Excellent. My daughter is visiting.'

He clicked off and I called the civilian dispatcher back and got the name and the address of the motel. Then I left my coffee on my desk and told my sergeant what was up and headed back to my quarters to change. I figured a *presence* required Class A greens, not woodland-pattern BDUs.

*   *   *

14

I took a Humvee from the MP motor pool and was logged out through the main gate. I found the motel inside fifty minutes. It was thirty miles due north of Fort Bird through dark undistinguished North Carolina countryside that was equal parts strip malls and scrubby forest and what I figured were dormant sweet potato fields. It was all new to me. I had never served there before. The roads were very quiet. Everyone was still inside, partying. I hoped I would be back at Bird before they all came out and started driving home. Although I really liked the Humvee's chances, head-on against a civilian ride.

The motel was part of a knot of low commercial structures clustered in the darkness near a big highway interchange. There was a truck stop as a centrepiece. It had a greasy spoon that was open on the holidays and a gas station big enough to take eighteen-wheelers. There was a no-name cinder block lounge bar with lots of neon and no windows. It had an *Exotic Dancers* sign lit up in pink and a parking lot the size of a football field. There were diesel spills and rainbow puddles all over it. I could hear loud music coming out of the bar. There were cars parked three-deep all around it. The whole area was glowing sulphurous yellow from the street lights. The night air was cold and there was fog drifting in layers. The motel itself was directly across the street from the gas station. It was a run-down swaybacked affair about twenty rooms long. It had a lot of peeling paint. It looked empty. There was an office at the left-hand end with a token vehicle porch and a buzzing Coke machine.

First question: why would a two-star general use a place like this? I was pretty sure there wouldn't have been a DoD inquiry if he had checked into a Holiday Inn.

There were two town police cruisers parked at careless angles outside the motel's last-but-one room. There was a small plain sedan sandwiched between them. It was cold and misted over. It was a base-model Ford, red, four cylinder. It had skinny tyres and plastic hubcaps. A rental, for sure. I put the Humvee next to the right-hand police cruiser and slid out into the chill. I heard the music from across the street, louder. The last-but-one room's lights were off and its door was open. I figured the cops were trying to keep the interior temperature low. Trying to stop

15

the old guy from getting too ripe. I was anxious to take a look at him. I was pretty sure I had never seen a dead general before.

Three cops stayed in their cars and one got out to meet me. He was wearing tan uniform pants and a short leather jacket zipped to his chin. No hat. The jacket had badges pinned to it that told me his name was Stockton and his rank was deputy chief. I didn't know him. I had never served there before. He was grey, about fifty. He was medium height and a little soft and heavy but the way he was reading the badges on my coat told me he was probably a veteran, like a lot of cops are.

'Major,' he said, as a greeting.

I nodded. A veteran, for sure. A major gets a little gold-coloured oak leaf on the epaulette, one inch across, one on each side. This guy was looking upward and sideways at mine, which wasn't the clearest angle of view. But he knew what they were. So he was familiar with rank designations. And I recognized his voice. He was the guy who had called me, at five seconds past midnight.

'I'm Rick Stockton,' he said. 'Deputy Chief.'

He was calm. He had seen heart attacks before.

'I'm Jack Reacher,' I said. 'MP duty officer tonight.'

He recognized my voice in turn. Smiled.

'You decided to come out,' he said. 'After all.'

'You didn't tell me the DOA was a two-star.'

'Well, he is.'

'I've never seen a dead general,' I said.

'Not many people have,' he said, and the way he said it made me think he had been an enlisted man.

'Army?' I asked.

'Marine Corps,' he said. 'First sergeant.'

'My old man was a Marine,' I said. I always make that point, talking to Marines. It gives me some kind of genetic legitimacy. Stops them from thinking of me as a pure army dogface. But I keep it vague. I don't tell them my old man had made captain. Enlisted men and officers don't automatically see eye to eye.

'Humvee,' he said.

He was looking at my ride.

'You like it?' he asked.

I nodded. *Humvee* was everyone's best attempt at saying

HMMWV, which stands for *High Mobility Multipurpose Wheeled Vehicle*, which about says it all. Like the army generally, what you're told is what you get.

'It works as advertised,' I said.

'Kind of wide,' he said. 'I wouldn't like to drive it in a city.'

'You'd have tanks in front of you,' I said. 'They'd be clearing the way. I think that would be the basic plan.'

The music from the bar thudded on. Stockton said nothing.

'Let's look at the dead guy,' I said to him.

He led the way inside. Flicked a switch that lit up the interior hallway. Then another that lit up the whole room. I saw a standard motel layout. A yard-wide lobby with a closet on the left and a bathroom on the right. Then a twelve-by-twenty rectangle with a built-in counter the same depth as the closet, and a queen bed the same depth as the bathroom. Low ceiling. A wide window at the far end, draped, with an integrated heater-cooler unit built through the wall underneath it. Most of the things in the room were tired and shabby and coloured brown. The whole place looked dim and damp and miserable.

There was a dead man on the bed.

He was naked, face down. He was white, maybe pushing sixty, quite tall. He was built like a fading pro athlete. Like a coach. He still had decent muscle, but he was growing love handles the way old guys do, however fit they are. He had pale hairless legs. He had old scars. He had wiry grey hair buzzed close to his scalp and cracked weathered skin on the back of his neck. He was a type. Any hundred people could have looked at him and all hundred would have said *army officer*, for sure.

'He was found like this?' I asked.

'Yes,' Stockton said.

Second question: how? A guy takes a room for the night, he expects privacy until the maid comes in the next morning, at the very least.

'How?' I said.

'How what?'

'How was he found? Did he call nine one one?'

'No.'

'So how?'

'You'll see.'

17

I paused. I didn't see anything yet.

'Did you roll him over?' I said.

'Yes. Then we rolled him back.'

'Mind if I take a look?'

'Be my guest.'

I stepped over next to the bed and slipped my left hand under the dead guy's armpit and rolled him over. He was cold and a little stiff. Rigor was just setting in. I got him settled flat on his back and saw four things. First, his skin had a distinctive grey pallor. Second, shock and pain were frozen on his face. Third, he had grabbed his left arm with his right hand, up near the bicep. And fourth, he was wearing a condom. His blood pressure had collapsed long ago and his erection had disappeared and the condom was hanging off, mostly empty, like a translucent flap of pale skin. He had died before reaching orgasm. That was clear.

'Heart attack,' Stockton said, behind me.

I nodded. The grey skin was a good indicator. So was the evidence of shock and surprise and sudden pain in his upper left arm.

'Massive,' I said.

'But before or after penetration?' Stockton said, with a smile in his voice.

I looked at the pillow area. The bed was still completely made. The dead guy was on top of the counterpane and the counterpane was still tight over the pillows. But there was a head-shaped dent, and there were rucks where elbows and heels had scrabbled and pushed lower down.

'She was underneath him when it happened,' I said. 'That's for sure. She had to wrestle her way out.'

'Hell of a way for a man to go.'

I turned around. 'I can think of worse ways.'

Stockton just smiled at me.

'What?' I said.

He didn't answer.

'No sign of the woman?' I said.

'Hide nor hair,' he said. 'She ran for it.'

'The desk guy see her?'

Stockton just smiled again.

18

I looked at him. Then I understood. *A low-rent dive near a highway interchange with a truck stop and a strip bar, thirty miles north of a military base.*

'She was a hooker,' I said. 'That's how he was found. The desk guy knew her. Saw her running out way too soon. Got curious as to why and came in here to check.'

Stockton nodded. 'He called us right away. The lady in question was long gone by then, of course. And he's denying she was ever here in the first place. He's pretending this isn't that kind of an establishment.'

'Your department had business here before?'

'Time to time,' he said. 'It *is* that kind of an establishment, believe me.'

Control the situation, Garber had said.

'Heart attack, right?' I said. 'Nothing more.'

'Probably,' Stockton said. 'But we'll need an autopsy to know for sure.'

The room was quiet. I could hear nothing except radio traffic from the cop cars outside, and music from the bar across the street. I turned back to the bed. Looked at the dead guy's face. I didn't know him. I looked at his hands. He had a West Point ring on his right and a wedding band on his left, wide, old, probably nine carat. I looked at his chest. His dog tags were hidden under his right arm, where he had reached across to grab his left bicep. I lifted the arm with difficulty and pulled the tags out. He had rubber silencers on them. I raised them until the chain went tight against his neck. His name was Kramer and he was a Catholic and his blood group was O.

'We could do the autopsy for you,' I said. 'Up at the Walter Reed Army Medical Center.'

'Out of state?'

'He's a general.'

'You want to hush it up.'

I nodded. 'Sure I do. Wouldn't you?'

'Probably,' he said.

I let go of the dog tags and moved away from the bed and checked the night stands and the built-in counter. Nothing there. There was no phone in the room. A place like this, I figured there would be a pay phone in the office. I moved past

19

Stockton and checked the bathroom. There was a privately purchased black leather Dopp kit next to the sink, zipped closed. It had the initials *KRK* embossed on it. I opened it up and found a toothbrush and a razor and travel-sized tubes of toothpaste and shaving soap. Nothing else. No medications. No heart prescription. No pack of condoms.

I checked the closet. There was a Class A uniform in there, neatly squared away on three separate hangers, with the pants folded on the bar of the first and the coat next to it on the second and the shirt on a third. The tie was still inside the shirt collar. Centred above the hangers on the shelf was a field grade officer's service cap. Gold braid all over it. On one side of the cap was a folded white undershirt and on the other side was a pair of folded white boxers.

There were two shoes side by side on the closet floor next to a faded green canvas suit carrier which was propped neatly against the back wall. The shoes were gleaming black and had socks rolled tight inside them. The suit carrier was a privately purchased item and had battered leather reinforcements at the stress points. It wasn't very full.

'You'd get the results,' I said. 'Our pathologist would give you a copy of the report with nothing added and nothing deleted. You see anything you're not happy about, we could put the ball right back in your court, no questions asked.'

Stockton said nothing, but I wasn't feeling any hostility coming off him. Some town cops are OK. A big base like Bird puts a lot of ripples into the surrounding civilian world. Therefore MPs spend a lot of time with their civilian counterparts, and sometimes it's a pain in the ass, and sometimes it isn't. I had a feeling Stockton wasn't going to be a huge problem. He was relaxed. Bottom line, he seemed a little lazy to me, and lazy people are always happy to pass their burdens on to someone else.

'How much?' I said.

'How much what?'

'How much would a whore cost here?'

'Twenty bucks would do it,' he said. 'There's nothing very exotic available in this neck of the woods.'

'And the room?'

20

'Fifteen, probably.'

I rolled the corpse back onto its front. Wasn't easy. It weighed two hundred pounds, at least.

'What do you think?' I asked.

'About what?'

'About Walter Reed doing the autopsy.'

There was silence for a moment. Stockton looked at the wall.

'That might be acceptable,' he said.

There was a knock at the open door. One of the cops from the cars.

'Medical examiner just called in,' he said. 'He can't get here for another two hours at least. It's New Year's Eve.'

I smiled. *Acceptable* was about to change to *highly desirable*. Two hours from now Stockton would need to be somewhere else. A whole bunch of parties would be breaking up and the roads would be mayhem. Two hours from now he would be begging me to haul the old guy away. I said nothing and the cop went back to wait in his car and Stockton moved all the way into the room and stood facing the draped window with his back to the corpse. I took the hanger with the uniform coat on it and lifted it out of the closet and hung it on the bathroom door frame where the hallway light fell on it.

Looking at a Class A coat is like reading a book or sitting next to a guy in a bar and hearing his whole life story. This one was the right size for the body on the bed and it had *Kramer* on the name plate, which matched the dog tags. It had a Purple Heart ribbon with two bronze oak leaf clusters to denote a second and third award of the medal, which matched the scars. It had two silver stars on the epaulettes, which confirmed he was a major general. The branch insignia on the lapels denoted Armor and the shoulder patch was from XII Corps. Apart from that there were a bunch of unit awards and a whole salad bowl of medal ribbons dating way back through Vietnam and Korea, some of which he had probably earned the hard way, and some of which he probably hadn't. Some of them were foreign awards, whose display was authorized but not compulsory. It was a very full coat, relatively old, well cared for, standard issue, not privately tailored. Taken as a whole it told me he was professionally vain, but not personally vain.

21

I went through the pockets. They were all empty, except for a key to the rental car. It was attached to a key ring in the shape of a figure 1, which was made out of clear plastic and contained a slip of paper with *Hertz* printed in yellow at the top and a plate number written by hand in black ballpoint underneath.

There was no wallet. No loose change.

I put the coat back in the closet and checked the pants. Nothing in the pockets. I checked the shoes. Nothing in them except the socks. I checked the hat. Nothing hidden underneath it. I lifted the suit carrier out and opened it on the floor. It contained a battledress uniform and an M43 field cap. A change of socks and underwear and a pair of shined combat boots, plain black leather. There was an empty compartment that I figured was for the Dopp kit. Nothing else. Nothing at all. I closed it up and put it back. Squatted down and looked under the bed. Saw nothing.

'Anything we should worry about?' Stockton asked.

I stood up. Shook my head.

'No,' I lied.

'Then you can have him,' he said. 'But I get a copy of the report.'

'Agreed,' I said.

'Happy New Year,' he said.

He walked out to his car and I headed for my Humvee. I called in a 10-5 *ambulance requested* and told my sergeant to have it accompanied by a squad of two who could list and pack all Kramer's personal property and bring it back to my office. Then I sat there in the driver's seat and waited until Stockton's guys were all gone. I watched them accelerate away into the fog and then I went back inside the room and took the rental key from Kramer's jacket. Came back out and used it to unlock the Ford.

There was nothing in it except the stink of upholstery cleaner and carbonless copies of the rental agreement. Kramer had picked the car up at one thirty-two that afternoon at Dulles airport near Washington D.C. He had used a private American Express card and received a discount rate. The start-of-rental mileage was 13215. Now the odometer was showing 13513, which according to my arithmetic meant he had driven 298

22

miles, which was about right for a straight-line trip between there and here.

I put the paper in my pocket and relocked the car. Checked the trunk. It was completely empty.

I put the key in my pocket with the rental paper and headed across the street to the bar. The music got louder with every step I took. Ten yards away I could smell beer fumes and cigarette smoke from the ventilators. I threaded through parked vehicles and found the door. It was a stout wooden item and it was closed against the cold. I pulled it open and was hit in the face by a wall of sound and a blast of thick hot air. The place was heaving. I could see five hundred people and black-painted walls and purple spotlights and mirrorballs. I could see a pole dancer on a stage in back. She was on all fours and naked apart from a white cowboy hat. She was crawling around, picking up dollar bills.

There was a big guy in a black T-shirt behind a register inside the door. His face was in deep shadow. The edge of a dim spotlight beam showed me he had a chest the size of an oil drum. The music was deafening and the crowd was packed shoulder-to-shoulder and wall-to-wall. I backed out and let the door swing shut. Stood still for a moment in the cold air and then walked away and crossed the street and headed for the motel office.

It was a dismal place. It was lit with fluorescent tubes that gave the air a greenish cast and it was noisy from the Coke machine parked at its door. It had a pay phone on the wall and worn linoleum on the floor and a waist-high counter boxed in with the sort of fake wood panelling people use in their basements. The clerk was on a high stool behind it. He was a white guy of about twenty with long unwashed hair and a weak chin.

'Happy New Year,' I said.

He didn't reply.

'You take anything out of the dead guy's room?' I asked.

He shook his head. 'No.'

'Tell me again.'

'I didn't take anything.'

I nodded. I believed him.

'OK,' I said. 'When did he check in?'

23

'I don't know. I came on at ten. He was already here.'

I nodded again. Kramer was in the rental lot at Dulles at one thirty-two and he hadn't driven enough miles to do much of anything except come straight here, in which case he was checking in around seven thirty. Maybe eight thirty, if he stopped for dinner somewhere. Maybe nine, if he was an exceptionally cautious driver.

'Did he use the pay phone at all?'

'It's busted.'

'So how did he get hold of the hooker?'

'What hooker?'

'The hooker he was poking when he died.'

'No hookers here.'

'Did he go over and get her from the lounge bar?'

'He was way the hell down the row. I didn't see what he did.'

'You got a driver's licence?'

The guy paused. 'Why?'

'Simple question,' I said. 'Either you do or you don't.'

'I got a licence,' he said.

'Show me,' I said.

I was bigger than his Coke machine and all covered in badges and ribbons and he did what he was told, like most skinny twenty-year-olds do when I use that tone. He eased his butt up off the stool and reached back and came out with a wallet from his hip pocket. Flipped it open. His DL was behind a milky plastic window. It had his photograph on it, and his name, and his address.

'OK,' I said. 'Now I know where you live. I'll be back later with some questions. If I don't find you here I'll come and find you at home.'

He said nothing to me. I turned away and pushed out through the door and went back to my Humvee to wait.

Forty minutes later a military meat wagon and another Humvee showed up. I told my guys to grab everything including the rental car but didn't wait around to watch them do it. I headed back to base instead. I logged in and got back to my borrowed office and told my sergeant to get me Garber on the phone. I

24

waited at my desk for the call to come through. It took less than two minutes.

'What's the story?' he asked.

'His name was Kramer,' I said.

'I know that,' Garber said. 'I spoke to the police dispatcher after I spoke to you. What happened to him?'

'Heart attack,' I said. 'During consensual sex with a prostitute. In the kind of motel a fastidious cockroach would take pains to avoid.'

There was a long silence.

'Shit,' Garber said. 'He was married.'

'Yes, I saw his wedding band. And his West Point ring.'

'Class of 'fifty-two,' Garber said. 'I checked.'

The phone went quiet.

'Shit,' he said again. 'Why do smart people pull stupid stunts like this?'

I didn't answer, because I didn't know.

'We'll need to be discreet,' Garber said.

'Don't worry,' I said. 'The cover-up is already started. The locals let me send him to Walter Reed.'

'Good,' he said. 'That's good.' Then he paused. 'From the beginning, OK?'

'He was wearing XII Corps patches,' I said. 'Means he was based in Germany. He flew into Dulles yesterday. From Frankfurt, probably. Civilian flight, for sure, because he was wearing Class As, hoping for an upgrade. He would have worn BDUs on a military flight. He rented a cheap car and drove two hundred ninety-eight miles and checked into a fifteen-dollar motel room and picked up a twenty-dollar hooker.'

'I know about the flight,' Garber said. 'I called XII Corps and spoke with his staff. I told them he was dead.'

'When?'

'After I got off the phone with the dispatcher.'

'You tell them how or where he was dead?'

'I said a probable heart attack, nothing more, no details, no location, which is starting to look like a very good decision now.'

'What about the flight?' I said.

'American Airlines, yesterday, Frankfurt to Dulles, arrived

thirteen hundred hours, with an onward connection nine hundred hours today, Washington National to LAX. He was going to an Armored Branch conference at Fort Irwin. He was an Armored commander in Europe. An important one. Outside chance of making Vice-Chief of Staff in a couple of years. It's Armored's turn next, for Vice-Chief. Current guy is infantry, and they like to rotate. So he stood a chance. But it ain't going to happen for him now, is it?'

'Probably not,' I said. 'Being dead and all.'

Garber didn't answer that.

'How long was he over here for?' I said.

'He was due back in Germany inside a week.'

'What's his full name?'

'Kenneth Robert Kramer.'

'I bet you know his date of birth,' I said. 'And where he was born.'

'So?'

'And his flight numbers and his seat assignments. And what the government paid for the tickets. And whether or not he requested a vegetarian meal. And what exact room Irwin VOQ was planning on putting him in.'

'What's your point?'

'My point is, why don't I know all that stuff too?'

'Why would you?' Garber said. 'I've been working the phones and you've been poking around in a motel.'

'You know what?' I said. 'Every time I go anywhere I've got a wad of airplane tickets and travel warrants and reservations and if I'm flying in from overseas I've got a passport. And if I'm going to a conference I've got a briefcase full of all kinds of other crap to carry them in.'

'What are you saying?'

'I'm saying there were things missing from the motel room. Tickets, reservations, passport, itinerary. Collectively, the kind of things a person would carry in a briefcase.'

Garber didn't respond.

'He had a suit carrier,' I said. 'Green canvas, brown leather bindings. A buck gets ten he had a briefcase to match. His wife probably chose them both. Probably got them mail-order from L. L. Bean. Maybe for Christmas, ten years ago.'

26

'And the briefcase wasn't there?'

'He probably kept his wallet in it, too, when he was wearing Class As. As many medal ribbons as this guy had, it makes the inside pocket tight.'

'So?'

'I think the hooker saw where he put his wallet after he paid her. Then they got down to business, and he croaked, and she saw a little extra profit for herself. I think she stole his brief-case.'

Garber was quiet for a moment.

'Is this going to be a problem?' he asked.

'Depends what else was in the briefcase,' I said.

TWO

I PUT THE PHONE DOWN AND SAW A NOTE MY SERGEANT HAD LEFT me: *Your brother called. No message.* I folded it once and dropped it in the trash. Then I headed back to my quarters and got three hours' sleep. Got up again fifty minutes before first light. I was back at the motel just as dawn was breaking. Morning didn't make the neighbourhood look any better. It was depressed and abandoned for miles around. And quiet. Nothing was stirring. Dawn on New Year's Day is as close as any inhabited place gets to absolute stillness. The highway was deserted. There was no traffic. None at all.

The diner at the truck stop was open but empty. The motel office was empty. I walked down the row to the last-but-one room. Kramer's room. The door was locked. I stood with my back to it and pretended I was a hooker whose client had just died. I had pushed his weight off me and dressed fast and grabbed his briefcase and I was running away with it. What would I do? I wasn't interested in the briefcase itself. I wanted the cash in the wallet, and maybe the American Express card. So I would rifle through and grab the cash and the card and ditch the bag itself. But where would I do that?

Inside the room would have been best. But I hadn't done it

there, for some reason. Maybe I was panicking. Maybe I was shocked and spooked and just wanted to get the hell out, fast. So where else? I looked straight ahead at the lounge bar. That was probably where I was going. That was probably where I was based. But I wouldn't carry the briefcase in there. My co-workers would notice, because I was already carrying a big purse. Hookers always carry big purses. They've got a lot of stuff to haul around. Condoms, massage oils, maybe a gun or a knife, maybe a credit card machine. That's the easiest way to spot a hooker. Look for someone dressed like she's going to a ball, carrying a bag like she's going on vacation.

I looked to my left. Maybe I walked around behind the motel. It would be quiet back there. All the windows faced that way, but it was night and I could count on the drapes being closed. I turned left and left again and came out behind the bedrooms on a rectangle of scrubby weeds that ran the length of the building and was about twenty feet deep. I imagined walking fast and then stopping in deep shadow and going through the bag by feel. I imagined finding what I wanted and heaving the bag away into the darkness. I might have thrown it thirty feet.

I stood where she might have stood and scoped out a quarter circle. It gave me about a hundred and fifty square feet to check. The ground was stony and nearly frozen by overnight frost. I found plenty of stuff. I found trash and used needles and foil crack pipes and a Buick hubcap and a skateboard wheel. But I didn't find a briefcase.

There was a wooden fence at the rear of the lot. It was about six feet tall. I jacked myself up on it and looked over. Saw another rectangle of weeds and stones. No briefcase. I got down off the fence and walked onward and came up on the motel office from the back. There was a window made of dirty pebbled glass that I guessed let into the staff bathroom. Underneath it were a dozen trashed air conditioners all stacked in a low pile. They were rusty. They hadn't been moved in years. I walked on and came around the corner and turned left into a weedy gravel patch with a Dumpster on it. I opened the lid. It was three-quarters full of garbage. No briefcase.

I crossed the street and walked through the empty lot and

looked at the lounge bar. It was silent and locked up tight. Its neon signs were all switched off and the little bent tubes looked cold and dead. It had its own Dumpster, close by in the lot, just sitting there like a parked vehicle. There was no briefcase in it.

I ducked inside the greasy spoon. It was still empty. I checked the floor around the tables and the banquettes in the booths. I looked on the floor behind the register. There was a cardboard box back there with a couple of forlorn umbrellas in it. But no briefcase. I checked the women's bathroom. No women in it. No briefcase in it, either.

I looked at my watch and walked back to the lounge bar. I would need to ask some face-to-face questions there. But it wouldn't be open for business for another eight hours at least. I turned around and looked across the street at the motel. There was still nobody in the office. So I headed back to my Humvee and got there in time to hear a 10-17 come in on the radio. *Return to base.* So I acknowledged and fired up the big diesel and drove all the way back to Bird. There was no traffic and I made it inside forty minutes. I saw Kramer's rental parked in the motor pool lot. There was a new person at the desk outside my borrowed office. A corporal. The day shift. He was a small dark guy who looked like he was from Louisiana. French blood in there, certainly. I know French blood when I see it.

'Your brother called again,' he said.

'Why?'

'No message.'

'What was the ten-seventeen for?'

'Colonel Garber requests a ten-nineteen.'

I smiled. You could live your whole life saying nothing but *10-this* and *10-that*. Sometimes I felt like I already had. A 10-19 was a contact by phone or radio. Less serious than a 10-16, which was a contact by secure landline. *Colonel Garber requests a 10-19* meant *Garber wants you to call him*, was all. Some MP units get in the habit of speaking English, but clearly this one hadn't yet.

I stepped into my office and saw Kramer's suit carrier propped against the wall and a carton containing his shoes and underwear and hat sitting next to it. His uniform was still on three hangers. They were hung one in front of the other on my coat rack. I walked past them to my borrowed desk and dialled Garber's number. Listened to the purr of the ring tone and wondered what my brother wanted. Wondered how he had tracked me down. I had been in Panama sixty hours ago. Before that I had been all over the place. So he had made a big effort to find me. So maybe it was important. I picked up a pencil and wrote *Joe* on a slip of paper. Then I underlined it, twice.

'Yes?' Leon Garber said in my ear.

'Reacher here,' I said. I looked at the clock on the wall. It showed a little after nine in the morning. Kramer's onward connection to LAX was already in the air.

'It was a heart attack,' Garber said. 'No question.'

'Walter Reed worked fast.'

'He was a general.'

'But a general with a bad heart.'

'Bad arteries, actually. Severe arteriosclerosis leading to fatal ventricular fibrillation. That's what they're telling us. And I believe them, too. Probably kicked in around the time the whore took her bra off.'

'He wasn't carrying any pills.'

'It was probably undiagnosed. It's one of those things. You feel fine, then you feel dead. No way it could be faked, anyway. You could simulate fibrillation with an electric shock, I guess, but you can't simulate forty years' worth of crap in the arteries.'

'Were we worried about it being faked?'

'There could have been KGB interest,' Garber said. 'Kramer and his tanks are the biggest single tactical problem the Red Army is facing.'

'Right now the Red Army is facing the other way.'

'Kind of early to say whether that's permanent or not.'

I didn't reply. The phone went quiet.

'I can't let anyone else touch this with a stick,' Garber said. 'Not just yet. Because of the circumstances. You understand that, right?'

'So?'

'So you're going to have to do the widow thing,' Garber said.

'Me? Isn't she in Germany?'

31

'She's in Virginia. She's home for the holidays. They have a house there.'

He gave me the address and I wrote it on the slip of paper, directly underneath where I had underlined *Joe*.

'Anyone with her?' I asked.

'They don't have kids. So she's probably alone.'

'OK,' I said.

'She doesn't know yet,' Garber said. 'Took me a while to track her down.'

'Want me to take a priest?'

'It isn't a combat death. You could take a female partner, I guess. Mrs Kramer might be a hugger.'

'OK.'

'Spare her the details, obviously. He was en route to Irwin, is all. Croaked in a layover hotel. We need to make that the official line. Nobody except you and me knows any different yet, and that's the way we're going to keep it. Except you can tell whoever you partner with, I guess. Mrs Kramer might ask questions, and you'll need to be on the same page. What about the local cops? Are they going to leak?'

'The guy I saw was an ex-Marine. He knows the score.'

'Semper Fi,' Garber said.

'I didn't find the briefcase yet,' I said.

The phone went quiet again.

'Do the widow thing first,' Garber said. 'Then keep on looking for it.'

I told the day-shift corporal to move Kramer's effects to my quarters. I wanted to keep them safe and sound. The widow would ask for them, eventually. And things can disappear, on a big base like Bird, which can be embarrassing. Then I walked over to the O Club and looked for MPs eating late breakfasts or early lunches. They usually cluster well away from everybody else, because everybody else hates them. I found a group of four, two men and two women. They were all in woodland-pattern BDUs, standard on-post dress. One of the women was a captain. She had her right arm in a sling. She was having trouble eating. She would have trouble driving, too. The other woman had a lieutenant's bar on each lapel and *Summer* on her nametape. She looked to be about twenty-five years old and she was short and slender. She had skin the same colour as the mahogany table she was eating off.

'Lieutenant Summer,' I said.

'Sir?'

'Happy New Year,' I said.

'Sir, you too.'

'You busy today?'

'Sir, general duties.'

'OK, out front in thirty minutes, Class As. I need you to hug a widow.'

I put my own Class As on again and called the motor pool for a sedan. I didn't want to ride all the way to Virginia in a Humvee. Too noisy, too uncomfortable. A private brought me a new olive-green Chevrolet. I signed for it and drove it around to post headquarters and waited.

Lieutenant Summer came out halfway through the twenty-eighth minute of her allotted thirty. She paused a second and then walked towards the car. She looked good. She was very short, but she moved easily, like a willowy person. She looked like a six-foot catwalk model reduced in size to a tiny miniature. I got out of the car and left the driver's door open. Met her on the sidewalk. She was wearing an expert sharpshooter badge with bars for rifle, small bore rifle, auto rifle, pistol, small bore pistol, machine gun and sub-machine gun hanging on it. They made a little ladder about two inches long. Longer than mine. I only have rifle and pistol. She stopped dead in front of me and came to attention and fired off a perfect salute.

'Sir, Lieutenant Summer reports,' she said.

'Take it easy,' I said. 'Informal mode of address, OK? Call me Reacher, or nothing. And no saluting. I don't like it.'

She paused. Relaxed.

'OK,' she said.

I opened the passenger door and started to get in.

'I'm driving?' she asked.

'I was up most of the night.'

'Who died?'

'General Kramer,' I said. 'Big tank guy in Europe.'

She paused again. 'So why was he here? We're all infantry.'

'Passing through,' I said.

She got in on the other side and racked the driver's seat all the way forward. Adjusted the mirror. I pushed the passenger seat back and got as comfortable as I could.

'Where to?' she said.

'Green Valley, Virginia,' I said. 'It'll be about four hours, I guess.'

'That's where the widow is?'

'Home for the holidays,' I said.

'And we're breaking the news? Like, Happy New Year, ma'am, and by the way, your husband's dead?'

I nodded. 'Lucky us.' But I wasn't really worried. Generals' wives are as tough as they come. Either they've spent thirty years pushing their husbands up the greasy pole, or they've endured thirty years of fallout as their husbands have climbed it for themselves. Either way, there's not much left that can get to them. They're tougher than the generals, most of the time.

Summer took her cap off and tossed it onto the back seat. Her hair was very short. Almost shaved. She had a delicate skull and nice cheekbones. Smooth skin. I liked the way she looked. And she was a fast driver. That was for damn sure. She clipped her belt and took off north like she was training for Nascar.

'Was it an accident?' she asked.

'Heart attack,' I said. 'His arteries were bad.'

'Where? Our VOQ?'

I shook my head. 'A crappy little motel in town. He died with a twenty-dollar hooker wedged somewhere underneath him.'

'We're not telling the widow that part, right?'

'No, we're not. We're not telling anyone that part.'

'Why was he passing through?'

'He didn't come to Bird itself. He was transiting D.C. Frankfurt to Dulles, then National to LAX twenty hours later. He was going out to Irwin for a conference.'

'OK,' she said, and then she went very quiet. We drove on. We got about level with the motel, but well to the west, heading straight for the highway.

'Permission to speak freely?' she said.

'Please,' I said.

'Is this a test?'

'Why would it be a test?'

'You're from the 110th Special Unit, aren't you?'

'Yes,' I said. 'I am.'

'I have an application pending.'

'To the 110th?'

'Yes,' she said. 'So, is this a covert assessment?'

'Of what?'

'Of me,' she said. 'As a candidate.'

'I needed a woman partner. In case the widow is a hugger. I picked you out at random. The captain with the busted arm couldn't have driven the car. And it would be kind of inefficient for us to wait until we had a dead general to conduct personnel assessments.'

'I guess,' she said. 'But I'm wondering if you're sitting there waiting for me to ask the obvious questions.'

'I'd expect any MP with a pulse to ask the obvious questions, whether or not they had a special unit transfer pending.'

'OK, I'm asking. General Kramer had a twenty-hour layover in the D.C. area and he wanted to get his rocks off and he didn't mind paying for the privilege. So why did he drive all the way down here to do it? It's what, three hundred miles?'

'Two hundred and ninety-eight,' I said.

'And then he'd have to drive all the way back.'

'Clearly.'

'So why?'

'You tell me,' I said. 'Come up with something I haven't thought of myself and I'll recommend you for the transfer.'

'You can't. You're not my CO.'

'Maybe I am,' I said. 'This week, anyway.'

'Why are you even here? Is something happening I should know about?'

'I don't know why I'm here,' I said. 'I got orders. That's all I know.'

'Are you really a major?'

'Last time I checked,' I said.

'I thought 110th investigators were usually warrant officers. Working plain clothes or undercover.'

'They usually are.'

'So why bring you here when they could send a warrant officer and have him dress up as a major?'

'Good question,' I said. 'Maybe one day I'll find out.'

'May I ask what your orders were?'

'Temporary detached duty as Fort Bird's Provost Marshal's executive officer.'

'The Provost Marshal isn't on post,' she said.

'I know,' I said. 'I found that out. He transferred out the same day I transferred in. Some temporary thing.'

'So you're acting CO.'

'Like I said.'

'MP XO isn't a special unit job,' she said.

'I can fake it,' I said. 'I started out a regular MP, just like you.'

Summer said nothing. Just drove.

'Kramer,' I said. 'Why did he contemplate a six-hundred-mile round trip? That's twelve hours' driving time out of his twenty. Just to spend fifteen bucks on a room and twenty on a whore?'

'Why does it matter? A heart attack is a heart attack, right? I mean, was there any question about it?'

I shook my head. 'Walter Reed already did the autopsy.'

'So it doesn't really matter where or when it happened.'

'His briefcase is missing.'

'I see,' she said.

I saw her thinking. Her lower eyelids flicked upward a fraction.

'How do you know he had a briefcase?' she said.

'I don't. But did you ever see a general go to a conference without one?'

'No,' she said. 'You think the hooker ran off with it?'

I nodded. 'That's my working hypothesis right now.'

'So, find the hooker.'

'Who was she?'

Her eyelids moved again.

'Doesn't make sense,' she said.

I nodded again. 'Exactly.'

'Four possible reasons Kramer didn't stay in the D.C. area. One, he might have been travelling with fellow officers and didn't want to embarrass himself in front of them by having a hooker come to his room. They might have seen her in the corridor or heard her through the walls. So he invented an excuse and stayed in a different place. Two, even if he was travelling alone he might have been on a DoD travel voucher and he was paranoid about a desk clerk seeing the girl and calling the *Washington Post*. That happens. So he preferred to pay cash in some anonymous dive. Three, even if he wasn't on a government ticket he might have been a well-known guest or a familiar face in a big-city hotel. So likewise he was looking for anonymity somewhere out of town. Or four, his sexual tastes ran beyond what you can get from the D.C. Yellow Pages, so he had to go where he knew for sure he could get what he wanted.'

'But?'

'Problems one, two, and three could be answered by going ten or fifteen miles, maybe less. Two hundred and ninety-eight is completely excessive. And whereas I'm prepared to believe there are tastes that can't be satisfied in D.C., I don't see how they're more likely to be satisfied way out here in the North Carolina boonies, and anyway I would guess such a thing would cost a lot more than twenty bucks wherever you eventually found it.'

'So why did he take the six-hundred-mile detour?'

She didn't answer. Just drove, and thought. I closed my eyes. Kept them closed for about thirty-five miles.

'He knew the girl,' Summer said.

I opened my eyes. 'How?'

'Some men have favourites. Maybe he met her a long time ago. Fell for her, in a way. It can happen like that. It can almost be a love thing.'

'Where would he have met her?'

'Right there.'

'Bird is all infantry. He was Armored Branch.'

'Maybe they had joint exercises. You should check back.'

I said nothing. Armored and the infantry run joint exercises all the time. But they run them where the tanks are, not where the grunts are. Much easier to transport men across a continent than tanks.

'Or maybe he met her at Irwin,' Summer said. 'In California. Maybe she worked Irwin, but had to leave California for some

37

reason, but she liked working military bases, so she moved to Bird.'

'What kind of a hooker would *like* working military bases?'

'The kind that's interested in money. Which is all of them, presumably. Military bases support their local economies in all kinds of ways.'

I said nothing.

'Or maybe she always worked Bird, but followed the infantry to Irwin when they did a joint exercise out there one time. Those things can last a month or two. No point in hanging around at home with no customers.'

'Best guess?' I said.

'They met in California,' she said. 'Kramer will have spent years at Irwin, on and off. Then she moved to North Carolina, but he still liked her enough to make the detour whenever he was in D.C.'

'She doesn't do anything special, not for twenty bucks.'

'Maybe he didn't need anything special.'

'We could ask the widow.'

Summer smiled. 'Maybe he just liked her. Maybe she made damn sure he did. Hookers are good at that. They like repeat customers best of all. It's much safer for them if they already know the guy.'

I closed my eyes again.

'So?' Summer said. 'Did I come up with something you didn't think of?'

'No,' I said.

I fell asleep before we were out of the state and woke up again nearly four hours later when Summer took the Green Valley ramp too fast. My head rolled to the right and hit the window.

'Sorry,' she said. 'You should check Kramer's phone records. He must have called ahead, to make sure she was around. He wouldn't have driven all that way on the off-chance.'

'Where would he have called from?'

'Germany,' she said. 'Before he left.'

'More likely he used a pay phone at Dulles. But we'll check.'

'We?'

'You can partner with me.'

38

She said nothing.

'Like a test,' I said.

'Is this important?'

'Probably not. But it might be. Depends what the conference is about. Depends what paperwork he was taking to it. He might have had the whole ETO order of battle in his case. Or new tactics, assessment of shortcomings, all kinds of classified stuff.'

'The Red Army is going to fold.'

I nodded. 'I'm more worried about red faces. Newspapers, or television. Some reporter finds classified stuff on a trash pile near a strip club, there'll be major embarrassment all around.'

'Maybe the widow will know. He might have discussed it with her.'

'We can't ask her,' I said. 'As far as she's concerned he died in his sleep with the blanket pulled up to his chin, and everything else was kosher. Any worries we've got at this point stay strictly between me, you, and Garber.'

'Garber?' she said.

'Me, you, and him,' I said.

I saw her smile. It was a trivial case, but working it with Garber was a definite stroke of luck, for a person with a 110th Special Unit transfer pending.

Green Valley was a picture-perfect colonial town and the Kramer house was a neat old place in an expensive part of it. It was a Victorian confection with fish-scale tiles on the roof and a bunch of turrets and porches all painted white, sitting on a couple of acres of emerald lawn. There were stately evergreen trees dotted about. They looked like someone had positioned them with care, which they probably had, a hundred years ago. We pulled up at the kerb and waited, just looking. I don't know what Summer was thinking about, but I was scanning the scene and filing it away under *A* for *America*. I have a Social Security number and the same blue and silver passport as everyone else but between my old man's Stateside tours and my own I can only put together about five years' worth of actual residence in the continental U.S. So I know a bunch of basic elementary-school facts like state capitals and how many grand slams

Lou Gehrig hit and some basic high-school stuff like the Constitutional amendments and the importance of Antietam, but I don't know much about the price of milk or how to work a pay phone or how different places look and smell. So I soak it up when I can. And the Kramer house was worth soaking up. That was for sure. A watery sun was shining on it. There was a faint breeze and the smell of woodsmoke in the air and a kind of intense cold-afternoon quiet all around us. It was the kind of place you would have wanted your grandparents to live. You could have visited in the fall and raked leaves and drunk apple cider and then come back in the summer and loaded a ten-year-old station wagon with a canoe and headed for a lake somewhere. It reminded me of the places in the picture books they gave me in Manila and Guam and Seoul.

Until we got inside.

'Ready?' Summer said.

'Sure,' I said. 'Let's do it. Let's do the widow thing.'

She was quiet. I was sure she had done it before. I had too, more than once. It was never fun. She pulled off the kerb and headed for the driveway entrance. Drove slowly towards the front door and eased to a stop ten feet from it. We opened our doors together and slid out into the chill and straightened our jackets. We left our hats in the car. That would be Mrs Kramer's first clue, if she happened to be watching. A pair of MPs at your door is never good news, and if they're bare-headed, it's worse news.

This particular door was painted a dull antique red and it had a glass storm screen in front of it. I rang the bell and we waited. And waited. I started to think nobody was home. I rang the bell again. The breeze was cold. It was stronger than it had looked.

'We should have called ahead,' Summer said.

'Can't,' I said. 'Can't say, please be there four hours from now so we can deliver some very important news face to face. Too much of a preview, wouldn't you say?'

'I came all this way and I've got nobody to hug.'

'Sounds like a country song. Then your truck breaks down and your dog dies.'

I tried the bell again. No response.

'We should look for a vehicle,' Summer said.

We found one in a closed two-car garage standing separate from the house. We could see it through the window. It was a Mercury Grand Marquis, metallic green, as long as an ocean liner. It was the perfect car for a general's wife. Not new, not old, premium but not overpriced, suitable colour, American as hell.

'Think this is hers?' Summer asked.

'Probably,' I said. 'Chances are they had a Ford until he made lieutenant colonel. Then they moved up to a Mercury. They were probably waiting for the third star before they thought about a Lincoln.'

'Sad.'

'You think? Don't forget where he was last night.'

'So where is she? You think she went out walking?'

We turned around and felt the breeze on our backs and heard a door bang at the rear of the house.

'She was out in the yard,' Summer said. 'Gardening, maybe.'

'Nobody gardens on New Year's Day,' I said. 'Not in this hemisphere. There's nothing growing.'

But we walked around to the front anyway and tried the bell again. Better to let her meet us formally, on her own terms. But she didn't show. Then we heard the door again, at the back, banging aimlessly. Like the breeze had gotten hold of it.

'We should check that out,' Summer said.

I nodded. A banging door has a sound all its own. It suggests all kinds of things.

'Yes,' I said. 'We probably should.'

We walked around to the rear of the house, side by side, into the wind. There was a flagstone path. It led us to a kitchen door. It opened inward, and it must have had a spring on the back to keep it closed. The spring must have been a little weak, because the gusting breeze was overpowering it from time to time and kicking the door open eight or nine inches. Then the gust would die away and the spring would reassert itself and the door would bang back into the frame. It did it three times as we watched. It was able to do it because the lock was smashed.

It had been a good lock, made of steel. But the steel had been stronger than the surrounding wood. Someone had used a wrecking bar. It had been jerked hard, maybe twice, and the lock had held but the wood had splintered. The door had opened up and the lock had just fallen out of the wreckage. It was right there on the flagstone path. The door had a crescent-shaped bite out of it. Splinters of wood had been blown here and there and piled by the wind.

'What now?' Summer said.

There was no security system. No intruder alarm. No pads, no wires. No automatic call to the nearest police precinct. No way of telling if the bad guys were long gone, or if they were still inside.

'What now?' Summer said again.

We were unarmed. No weapons, on a formal visit in Class A uniform.

'Go cover the front,' I said. 'In case anyone comes out.'

She moved away without a word and I gave her a minute to get in position. Then I pushed the door with my elbow and stepped inside the kitchen. Closed the door behind me and leaned on it to keep it shut. Then I stood still and listened.

There was no sound. No sound at all.

The kitchen smelled faintly of cooked vegetables and stewed coffee. It was big. It was halfway between tidy and untidy. A well-used space. There was a door on the other side of the room. On my right. It was open. I could see a small triangle of polished oak floor. A hallway. I moved very slowly. Crept forward and to the right to line up my view. The door banged again behind me. I saw more of the hallway. I figured it ran straight to the front entrance. Off of it to the left was a closed door. Probably a dining room. Off of it to the right was a den or a study. Its door was open. I could see a desk and a chair and dark wood bookcases. I took a cautious step. Moved a little more.

I saw a dead woman on the hallway floor.

THREE

THE DEAD WOMAN HAD LONG GREY HAIR. SHE WAS WEARING AN elaborate white flannel nightgown. She was on her side. Her feet were near the study door. Her arms and legs had sprawled in a way that made it look like she was running. There was a shotgun half underneath her. One side of her head was caved in. I could see blood and brains matted in her hair. More blood had pooled on the oak. It was dark and sticky.

I stepped into the hallway and stopped an arm's length from her. I squatted down and reached for her wrist. Her skin was very cold. There was no pulse.

I stayed down. Listened. Heard nothing. I craned over and looked at her head. She had been hit with something hard and heavy. Just a single blow, but a serious one. The wound. was in the shape of a trench. Nearly an inch wide, maybe four inches long. It had come from the left side, and above. She had been facing the back of the house. Facing the kitchen. I glanced around and dropped her wrist and stood up and stepped into the den. A Persian carpet covered most of the floor. I stood on it and imagined I was hearing quiet tense footsteps coming down the hallway, towards me. Imagined I was still holding the wrecking bar I had used to force the lock. Imagined swinging it when my target stepped into view, on her way past the open doorway.

I looked down. There was a stripe of blood and hair on the carpet. The wrecking bar had been wiped on it.

Nothing else in the room was disturbed. It was an impersonal space. It looked like it was there because they had heard a family house should have a study. Not because they actually needed one. The desk was not set up for working. There were photographs in silver frames all over it. But fewer than I would have expected, from a long marriage. There was one that showed the dead man from the motel and the dead woman from the hallway standing together with the Mount Rushmore faces blurry in the background. General and Mrs Kramer, on vacation. He was much taller than she was. He looked strong and vigorous. She looked petite in comparison.

There was another framed photograph showing Kramer himself in uniform. The picture was a few years old. He was standing at the top of the steps, about to climb into a C-130 transport plane. It was a colour photograph. His uniform was green, the airplane was brown. He was smiling and waving. Off to assume his one-star command, I guessed. There was a second picture, almost identical, a little newer. Kramer, at the top of a set of airplane steps, turning back, smiling and waving. Off to assume his two-star command, probably. In both pictures he was waving with his right hand. In both pictures his left held the same canvas suit carrier I had seen in the motel room closet. And above it, in both pictures, tucked up under his arm, was a matching canvas briefcase.

I stepped out to the hallway again. Listened hard. Heard nothing. I could have searched the house, but I didn't need to. I was pretty sure there was nobody in it and I knew there was nothing I needed to find. So I took a last look at the Kramer widow. I could see the soles of her feet. She hadn't been a widow for long. Maybe an hour, maybe three. I figured the blood on the floor was about twelve hours old. But it was impossible to be precise. That would have to wait until the doctors arrived.

*　　*　　*

44

I retreated through the kitchen and went back outside and walked around to find Summer. Sent her inside to take a look. It was quicker than a verbal explanation. She came out again four minutes later, looking calm and composed. *Score one for Summer*, I thought.

'You like coincidences?' she said.

I said nothing.

'We have to go to D.C.,' she said. 'To Walter Reed. We have to make them double-check Kramer's autopsy.'

I said nothing.

'This makes his death automatically suspicious. I mean, what are the chances? It's one in forty or fifty thousand that an individual soldier will die on any given day, but to have his wife die on the *same* day? For her to be a homicide victim on the same day?'

'Wasn't the same day,' I said. 'Wasn't even the same year.'

She nodded. 'OK, New Year's Eve, New Year's Day. But that just makes my point. It's inconceivable that Walter Reed had a pathologist scheduled to work last night. So they had to drag one in, specially. And from where? From a party, probably.'

I smiled, briefly. 'So you want us to go up there and say, hey, are you sure your doc could see straight last night? Sure he wasn't too juiced up to spot the difference between a heart attack and a homicide?'

'We have to check,' she said. 'I don't like coincidences.'

'What do you think happened in there?'

'Intruder,' she said. 'Mrs Kramer was woken up by the noise at the door, got out of bed, grabbed a shotgun she kept near at hand, came downstairs, headed for the kitchen. She was a brave lady.'

I nodded. Generals' wives, tough as they come.

'But she was slow,' Summer said. 'The intruder was already all the way into the study and was able to get her from the side. With the crowbar he had used on the door. As she walked past. He was taller than she was, maybe by a foot, probably right-handed.'

I said nothing.

'So are we going to Walter Reed?'

45

'I think we have to,' I said. 'We'll go as soon as we've finished here.'

We called the Green Valley cops from a wall phone we found in the kitchen. Then we called Garber and gave him the news. He said he would meet us at the hospital. Then we waited. Summer watched the front of the house, and I watched the back. Nothing happened. The cops came within seven minutes. They made a tight little convoy, two marked cruisers, a detective's car, an ambulance. They had lights and sirens going. We heard them a mile away. They howled into the driveway and then shut down. Summer and I stepped back in the sudden silence and they all swarmed past us. We had no role. A general's wife is a civilian, and the house was inside a civilian jurisdiction. Normally I wouldn't let such fine distinctions get in my way, but the place had already told me what I needed to know. So I was prepared to stand back and earn some Brownie points by doing it by the book. Brownie points might come in useful later.

A patrolman watched us for twenty long minutes while the other cops poked around inside. Then a detective in a suit came out to take our statements. We told him about Kramer's heart attack, the widow trip, the banging door. His name was Clark and he had no problem with anything we had to say. His problem was the same as Summer's. Both Kramers had died miles apart on the same night, which was a coincidence, and he didn't like coincidences any better than Summer did. I started to feel sorry for Rick Stockton, the deputy chief down in North Carolina. His decision to let me haul Kramer's body away was going to look bad, in this new light. It put half the puzzle in the military's hands. It was going to set up a conflict.

We gave Clark a phone number where he could reach us at Bird, and then we got back in the car. I figured D.C. was another seventy miles. Another hour and ten. Maybe less, the way Summer drove. She took off and found the highway again and put her foot down until the Chevy was vibrating fit to bust.

'I saw the briefcase in the photographs,' she said. 'Did you?'

'Yes,' I said.

'Does it upset you to see dead people?'

'No,' I said.

46

'Why not?'

'I don't know. You?'

'It upsets me a little.'

I said nothing.

'You think it was a coincidence?' she said.

'No,' I said. 'I don't believe in coincidences.'

'So you think the post-mortem missed something?'

'No,' I said again. 'I think the post-mortem was probably accurate.'

'So why are we driving all the way to D.C.?'

'Because I need to apologize to the pathologist. I dropped him in it by sending him Kramer's body. Now he's going to have wall-to-wall civilians bugging him for a month. That will piss him off big time.'

But the pathologist was a her, not a him, and she had such a sunny disposition that I doubted anything could piss her off for long. We met with her in the Walter Reed Army Medical Center's reception area, four o'clock in the afternoon, New Year's Day. It looked like any other hospital lobby. There were holiday decorations hanging from the ceilings. They already looked a little tired. Garber had arrived before us. He was sitting on a plastic chair. He was a small man and didn't seem uncomfortable. But he was quiet. He didn't introduce himself to Summer. She stood next to him. I leaned on the wall. The doctor faced us with a sheaf of notes in her hand, like she was lecturing a small group of keen students. Her name badge read Sam McGowan, and she was young and dark, and brisk, and open.

'General Kramer died of natural causes,' she said. 'Heart attack, last night, after eleven, before midnight. There's no possibility of doubt. I'm happy to be audited if you want, but it would be a complete waste of time. His toxicology was absolutely clear. The evidence of ventricular fibrillation is indisputable and his arterial plaque was monumental. So forensically, your only tentative question might be whether by coincidence someone electrically stimulated fibrillation in a man almost certain to suffer it anyway within minutes or hours or days or weeks.'

47

'How would it be done?' Summer asked.

McGowan shrugged. 'The skin would have to be wet over a large area. The guy would have to be in a bathtub, basically. Then if you applied wall current to the water, you'd probably get fibrillation without burn marks. But the guy wasn't in a bathtub, and there's no evidence he ever had been.'

'What if his skin wasn't wet?'

'Then I'd have seen burn injuries. And I didn't, and I went over every inch of him with a magnifying glass. No burns, no hypodermic marks, no nothing.'

'What about shock, or surprise, or fear?'

The doctor shrugged again. 'Possible, but we know what he was doing, don't we? That kind of sudden sexual excitement is a classic trigger.'

Nobody spoke.

'Natural causes, folks,' McGowan said. 'Just a big old heart attack. Every pathologist in the world could take a look at him and there would be one hundred per cent agreement. I absolutely guarantee it.'

'OK,' Garber said. 'Thanks, doc.'

'I apologize,' I said. 'You're going to have to repeat all that to about two dozen civilian cops, every day for a couple of weeks.'

She smiled. 'I'll print up an official statement.'

Then she looked at each of us in turn in case we had more questions. We didn't, so she smiled once more and swept away through a door. It sucked shut behind her and the ceiling decorations rustled and stilled and the reception area went quiet.

We didn't speak for a moment.

'OK,' Garber said. 'That's it. No controversy with Kramer himself, and his wife is a civilian crime. It's out of our hands.'

'Did you know Kramer?' I asked him.

Garber shook his head. 'Only by reputation.'

'Which was?'

'Arrogant. He was Armored Branch. The Abrams tank is the best toy in the army. Those guys rule the world, and they know it.'

'Know anything about the wife?'

He made a face. 'She spent way too much time at home in

Virginia, is what I hear. She was rich, from an old Virginia family. I mean, she did her duty. She spent time on post in Germany, only when you add it up, it really wasn't a hell of a lot of time. Like now, XII Corps told me she was home for the holidays, which sounds OK, but actually she came home for Thanksgiving and wasn't expected back until the spring. So the Kramers weren't real close, by all accounts. No kids, no shared interests.'

'Which might explain the hooker,' I said. 'If they lived separate lives.'

'I guess,' Garber said. 'I get the feeling it was a marriage, you know, but it was more window-dressing than anything real.'

'What was her name?' Summer asked.

Garber turned to look at her.

'Mrs Kramer,' he said. 'That's all the name we need to know.'

Summer looked away.

'Who was Kramer travelling to Irwin with?' I asked.

'Two of his guys,' Garber said. 'A one-star general and a colonel, Vassell and Coomer. They were a real triumvirate. Kramer, Vassell, and Coomer. The corporate face of Armor.'

He stood up and stretched.

'Start at midnight,' I said to him. 'Tell me everything you did.'

'Why?'

'Because I don't like coincidences. And neither do you.'

'I didn't do anything.'

'Everybody did something,' I said. 'Except Kramer.'

He looked straight at me.

'I watched the ball drop,' he said. 'Then I had another drink. I kissed my daughter. I kissed a whole bunch of people, as I recall. Then I sang "Auld Lang Syne".'

'And then?'

'My office got me on the phone. Told me they'd found out by circuitous means that we had a dead two-star down in North Carolina. Told me the Fort Bird MP duty officer had palmed it off. So I called there, and I got you.'

'And then?'

'You set out to do your thing and I called the town cops and got Kramer's name. Looked him up and found he was a XII

49

Corps guy. So I called Germany and reported the death, but I kept the details to myself. I told you this already.'

'And then?'

'Then nothing. I waited for your report.'

'OK,' I said.

'OK what?'

'OK, sir?'

'Bullshit,' he said. 'What are you thinking?'

'The briefcase,' I said. 'I still want to find it.'

'So keep looking for it,' he said. 'Until I find Vassell and Coomer. They can tell us whether there was anything in it worth worrying about.'

'You can't find them?'

He shook his head.

'No,' he said. 'They checked out of their hotel, but they didn't fly to California. Nobody seems to know where the hell they are.'

Garber left to drive himself back to town and Summer and I climbed into the car and headed south again. It was cold, and it was getting dark. I offered to take the wheel, but Summer wouldn't let me. Driving seemed to be her main hobby.

'Colonel Garber seemed tense,' she said. She sounded disappointed, like an actress who had failed an audition.

'He was feeling guilty,' I said.

'Why?'

'Because he killed Mrs Kramer.'

She just stared at me. She was doing about ninety, looking at me, sideways.

'In a manner of speaking,' I said.

'How?'

'This was no coincidence.'

'That's not what the doctor told us.'

'Kramer died of natural causes. That's what the doctor told us. But something about that event led directly to Mrs Kramer becoming a homicide victim. And Garber set all that in motion. By notifying XII Corps. He put the word out, and within about two hours the widow was dead, too.'

'So what's going on?'

'I have absolutely no idea,' I said.

'And what about Vassell and Coomer?' she said. 'They were a threesome. Kramer's dead, his wife is dead, and the other two are missing?'

'You heard the man. It's out of our hands.'

'You're not going to do anything?'

'I'm going to look for a hooker.'

We set off on the most direct route we could find, straight back to the motel and the lounge bar. There was no real choice. First the Beltway, and then I-95. Traffic was light. It was still New Year's Day. The world outside our windows looked dark and quiet, cold and sleepy. Lights were coming on everywhere. Summer drove as fast as she dared, which was plenty fast. What might have taken Kramer six hours was going to take us less than five. We stopped for gas early, and we bought stale sandwiches that had been made in the previous calendar year. We forced them down as we hustled south. Then I spent twenty minutes watching Summer. She had small neat hands. She had them resting lightly on the wheel. She didn't blink much. Her lips were slightly parted and every minute or so she would run her tongue across her teeth.

'Talk to me,' I said.

'About what?'

'About anything,' I said. 'Tell me the story of your life.'

'Why?'

'Because I'm tired,' I said. 'To keep me awake.'

'Not very interesting.'

'Try me,' I said.

So she shrugged and started at the beginning, which was outside of Birmingham, Alabama, in the middle of the sixties. She had nothing bad to say about it, but she gave me the impression that she knew even then there were better ways to grow up than poor and black in Alabama at that time. She had brothers and sisters. She had always been small, but she was nimble, and she parlayed a talent for gymnastics and dancing and jumping rope into a way of getting noticed at school. She was good at the book work too and had assembled a patchwork of minor scholarships and moved out of state to a college in

51

Georgia. She had joined the ROTC and in her junior year the scholarships ran out and the military picked up the tab in exchange for five years' future service. She was now halfway through it. She had aced MP school. She sounded comfortable. By that point the military had been integrated for forty years and she said she found it to be the most colour-blind place in America. But she was also a little frustrated about her own individual progress. I got the impression her application to the 110th was make or break for her. If she got it, she was in for life, like me. If she didn't, she was out after five.

'Now tell me about your life,' she said.

'Mine?' I said. Mine was different in every way imaginable. Colour, gender, geography, family circumstances. 'I was born in Berlin. Back then, you stayed in the hospital seven days, so I was one week old when I went into the military. I grew up on every base we've got. I went to West Point. I'm still in the military. I always will be. That's it, really.'

'You got family?'

I recalled the note from my sergeant: *Your brother called. No message.*

'A mother and a brother,' I said.

'Ever been married?'

'No. You?'

'No,' she said. 'Seeing anyone?'

'Not right now.'

'Me either.'

We drove on, a mile, and another.

'Can you imagine a life outside the service?' she asked.

'Is there one?'

'I grew up out there. I might be going back.'

'You civilians are a mystery to me,' I said.

Summer parked outside Kramer's room, I guessed for authenticity's sake, a little less than five hours after we left Walter Reed. She seemed satisfied with her average speed. She shut the motor down and smiled.

'I'll take the lounge bar,' I said. 'You speak to the kid in the motel office. Do the good cop thing. Tell him the bad cop is right behind you.'

We slid out into the cold and the dark. The fog was back. The street lights burned through it. I felt cramped and airless. I stretched and yawned and then straightened my coat and watched Summer head past the Coke machine. Her skin flared red as she stepped through its glow. I crossed the road and headed for the bar.

The lot was as full as it had been the night before. Cars and trucks were parked all around the building. The ventilators were working hard again. I could see smoke and smell beer in the air. I could hear music thumping away. The neon was bright.

I pulled the door and stepped into the noise. The crowd was wall-to-wall again. The same spotlights were burning. There was a different girl naked on the stage. There was the same barrel-chested guy half in shadow behind the register. I couldn't see his face, but I knew he was looking at my lapels. Where Kramer had worn Armored's crossed cavalry sabres with a charging tank over them, I had the Military Police's crossed flintlock pistols, gold and shiny. Not the most popular sight, in a place like that.

'Cover charge,' the guy at the register said.

It was hard to hear him. The music was very loud.

'How much?' I said.

'Hundred dollars,' he said.

'I don't think so.'

'OK, two hundred dollars.'

'Hilarious,' I said.

'I don't like cops in here.'

'Can't think why,' I said.

'Look at me.'

I looked at him. There was nothing much to see. The edge of a downlighter beam lit up a big stomach and a big chest and thick, short, tattooed forearms. And hands the size and shape of frozen chickens with heavy silver rings on most of the fingers. But the guy's shoulders and his face were in deep shadow above them. Like he was half hidden by a curtain. I was talking to a guy I couldn't see.

'You're not welcome here,' he said.

'I'll get over it. I'm not an unduly sensitive person.'

'You're not listening,' he said. 'This is my place and I don't want you in it.'

'I'll be quick.'

'Leave now.'

'No.'

'Look at me.'

He leaned forward into the light. Slowly. The downlighter beam rode up his chest. Up his neck. Onto his face. It was an incredible face. It had started out ugly and it had gotten much worse. He had straight razor scars all over it. They criss-crossed it like a lattice. They were deep and white and old. His nose had been busted and badly reset and busted again and badly reset again, many times over. He had brows thick with scar tissue. Two small eyes were staring out at me from under them. He was maybe forty. Maybe five-ten, maybe three hundred pounds. He looked like a gladiator who had survived twenty years, deep inside the catacombs.

I smiled. 'This thing with the face is supposed to impress me? With the dramatic lighting and all?'

'It should tell you something.'

'It tells me you lost a lot of fights. You want to lose another, that's fine with me.'

He said nothing.

'Or I could put this place off-limits to every enlisted man at Bird. I could see what that does to your bar profits.'

He said nothing.

'But I don't want to do that,' I said. 'No reason to penalize my guys, just because you're an asshole.'

He said nothing.

'So I guess I'll ignore you.'

He sat back. The shadow slid back into place, like a curtain.

'I'll see you later,' he said, from out of the darkness. 'Somewhere, sometime. That's for sure. That's a promise. You can count on that.'

'*Now* I'm scared,' I said. I moved on and pressed into the crowd. I made it through a packed bottleneck and into the main part of the building. It was much bigger inside than it had looked. It was a large low square, full of noise and people. There were dozens of separate areas. Speakers everywhere.

Loud music. Flashing lights. There were plenty of civilians in there. Plenty of military, too. I could spot them by their haircuts, and their clothes. Off-duty soldiers always dress distinctively. They try to look like everybody else, and they fail. They're always a little clean and out of date. They were all looking at me as I passed them by. They weren't pleased to see me. I looked for a sergeant. Looked for a few lines around the eyes. I saw four likely candidates, six feet back from the edge of the main stage. Three of them saw me and turned away. The fourth saw me and paused for a second and then turned towards me. Like he knew he had been selected. He was a compact guy maybe five years older than me. Special Forces, probably. There were plenty of them at Bird, and he had the look. He was having a good time. That was clear. He had a smile on his face and a bottle in his hand. Cold beer, dewy with moisture. He raised it, like a toast, like an invitation to approach. So I went up close to him and spoke in his ear.

'Spread the word for me,' I said. 'This is nothing official. Nothing to do with our guys. Something else entirely.'

'Like what?' he said.

'Lost property,' I said. 'Nothing important. Everything's cool.'

He said nothing.

'Special Forces?' I said.

He nodded. 'Lost property?'

'No big deal,' I said. 'Just something that went missing across the street.'

He thought about it and then he raised his bottle again and clinked it against where mine would have been if I had bought one. It was a clear display of acceptance. Like a mime, in all the noise. But even so a thin stream of men started up, shuffling towards the exit. Maybe twenty grunts left during my first two minutes in the room. MPs have that effect. No wonder the guy with the face didn't want me in there.

A waitress came up to me. She was wearing a black T-shirt cut off about four inches below the neck and black shorts cut off about four inches below the waist and black shoes with very high heels. Nothing else. She stood there and looked at me

55

until I ordered something. I asked for a Bud, and I paid about eight times its value. Took a couple of sips, and then went looking for whores.

They found me first. I guess they wanted me out of sight before I emptied the place completely. Before I reduced their customer base to zero. Two of them came straight at me. One was a platinum blonde. The other was a brunette. Both were wearing tiny tight sheath dresses that sparkled with all kinds of synthetic fibres. The blonde got in front of the brunette and headed her off. Came clattering straight towards me, awkward in absurd clear plastic heels. The brunette wheeled away and headed for the Special Forces sergeant I had spoken to. He waved her off with what looked like an expression of genuine distaste. The blonde kept on track and came right up next to me and leaned on my arm. Stretched up tall until I could feel her breath in my ear.

'Happy New Year,' she said.

'You too,' I said.

'I haven't seen you in here before,' she said, like I was the only thing missing from her life. Her accent wasn't local. She wasn't from the Carolinas. She wasn't from California, either. Georgia or Alabama, probably.

'You new in town?' she asked, loud, because of the music.

I smiled. I had been in more whorehouses than I cared to count. All MPs have. Every single one is the same, and every single one is different. They all have different protocols. But the *are you new in town* question was a standard opening gambit. It invited me to start the negotiations. It insulated her from a solicitation charge.

'What's the deal here?' I asked her.

She smiled shyly, like she had never been asked such a thing before. Then she told me I could watch her on stage in exchange for dollar tips, or I could spend ten to get a private show in a back room. She explained the private show could involve touching, and to make sure I was paying attention she ran her hand up the inside of my thigh.

I could see how a guy could be tempted. She was cute. She looked to be about twenty. Except for her eyes. Her eyes looked like a fifty-year-old's.

56

'What about something more?' I said. 'Someplace else we could go?'

'We can talk about that during the private show.'

She took me by the hand and led me past their dressing-room door and through a velvet curtain into a dim room behind the stage. It wasn't small. It was maybe thirty feet by twenty. It had an upholstered bench running around the whole perimeter. It wasn't especially private, either. There were about six guys in there, each of them with a naked woman on his lap. The blonde girl led me to a space on the bench and sat me down. She waited until I came out with my wallet and paid her ten bucks. Then she draped herself over me and snuggled in tight. The way she sat made it impossible for me not to put my hand on her thigh. Her skin was warm and smooth.

'So where can we go?' I asked.

'You're in a hurry,' she said. She moved around and eased the hem of her dress up over her hips. She wasn't wearing anything under it.

'Where are you from?' I asked her.

'Atlanta,' she said.

'What's your name?'

'Sin,' she said. 'Spelled *S, i, n.*'

I was fairly certain that was a professional alias.

'What's yours?' she said.

'Reacher,' I said. There was no point adopting an alias of my own. I was fresh from the widow visit, still in Class As, with my name plate big and obvious on my right jacket pocket.

'That's a nice name,' she said, automatically. I was fairly certain she said it to everybody. *Quasimodo, Hitler, Stalin, Pol Pot, that's a nice name*. She moved her hand. Started with the top button of my jacket and undid it all the way down. Smoothed her fingers inside across my chest, under my tie, on top of my shirt.

'There's a motel across the street,' I said.

She nodded against my shoulder.

'I know there is,' she said.

'I'm looking for whoever went over there last night with a soldier.'

'Are you kidding?'

57

'No.'

She pushed against my chest. 'Are you here to have fun, or ask questions?'

'Questions,' I said.

She stopped moving. Said nothing.

'I'm looking for whoever went over to the motel last night, with a soldier.'

'Get real,' she said. 'We all go over to the motel with soldiers. There's practically a groove worn in the pavement. Look carefully, and you can see it.'

'I'm looking for someone who came back a little sooner than normal, maybe.'

She said nothing.

'Maybe she was a little spooked.'

She said nothing.

'Maybe she met the guy there,' I said. 'Maybe she got a call earlier in the day.'

She eased her butt up off my knee and pulled her dress down as far as it would go, which wasn't very far. Then she traced her fingertips across my lapel badge.

'We don't answer questions,' she said.

'Why not?'

I saw her glance at the velvet curtain. Like she was looking through it and all the way across the big square room to the register by the door.

'Him?' I said. 'I'll make sure he isn't a problem.'

'He doesn't like us to talk to cops.'

'It's important,' I said. 'The guy was an important soldier.'

'You all think you're important.'

'Any of the girls here from California?'

'Five or six, maybe.'

'Any of them used to work Fort Irwin?'

'I don't know.'

'So here's the deal,' I said. 'I'm going to the bar. I'm going to get another beer. I'm going to spend ten minutes drinking it. You bring me the girl who had the problem last night. Or you show me where I can find her. Tell her there's no real problem. Tell her nobody will get in trouble. I think you'll find she understands that.'

'Or?'

'Or I'll roust everybody out of here and I'll burn the place to the ground. Then you can all find jobs somewhere else.'

She glanced at the velvet curtain again.

'Don't worry about the fat guy,' I said. 'Any pissing and moaning out of him, I'll bust his nose again.'

She just sat still. Didn't move at all.

'It's important,' I said again. 'We fix this now, nobody gets in trouble. We don't, then someone winds up with a big problem.'

'I don't know,' she said.

'Spread the word,' I said. 'Ten minutes.'

I bumped her off my lap and watched her disappear through the curtain. Followed her a minute later and fought my way to the bar. I left my jacket hanging open. I thought it made me look off-duty. I didn't want to ruin everybody's evening.

I spent twelve minutes drinking another overpriced domestic beer. I watched the waitresses and the hookers work the room. I saw the big guy with the face moving through the press of people, looking here, looking there, checking on things. I waited. My new blonde friend didn't show. And I couldn't see her anywhere. The place was very crowded. And it was dark. The music was thumping away. There were strobes and black lights and the whole scene was confusion. The ventilation fans were roaring but the air was hot and foul. I was tired and I was getting a headache. I slid off my stool and tried a circuit of the whole place. Couldn't find the blonde anywhere. I went around again. Didn't find her. The Special Forces sergeant I had spoken to before stopped me halfway through my third circuit.

'Looking for your girlfriend?' he said.

I nodded. He pointed at the dressing-room door.

'I think you just caused her some trouble,' he said.

'What kind of trouble?'

He said nothing. Just held up his left palm and smacked his right fist into it.

'And you didn't do anything?' I said.

He shrugged.

'You're the cop,' he said. 'Not me.'

59

The dressing-room door was a plain plywood rectangle painted black. I didn't knock. I figured the women who used the room weren't shy. I just pulled it open and stepped inside. There were regular light bulbs burning in there, and piles of clothes and the stink of perfume. There were vanity tables with theatre mirrors. There was an old sofa, red velvet. Sin was sitting on it, crying. She had a vivid red outline of a hand on her left cheek. Her right eye was swollen shut. I figured it for a double slap, first forehand, then backhand. Two heavy blows. She was pretty shaken. Her left shoe was off. I could see needle marks between her toes. Addicts in the skin trades often inject there. It rarely shows. Models, hookers, actresses.

I didn't ask if she was OK. That would have been a stupid question. She was going to live, but she wasn't going to work for a week. Not until the eye went black and then turned yellow enough to hide with make-up. I just stood there until she saw me, through the eye that was still open.

'Get out,' she said.

She looked away.

'Bastard,' she said.

'You find the girl yet?' I said.

She looked straight at me.

'There was no girl,' she said. 'I asked all around. I asked everybody. And that's what I heard back. Nobody had a problem last night. Nobody at all.'

I paused a beat. 'Anyone not here who should be?'

'We're all here,' she said. 'We've all got Christmas to pay for.'

I didn't speak.

'You got me slapped for nothing,' she said.

'I'm sorry,' I said. 'I'm sorry for your trouble.'

'Get out,' she said again, not looking at me.

'OK,' I said.

'Bastard,' she said.

I left her sitting there and forced my way back through the crowd around the stage. Through the crowd around the bar. Through the bottleneck entrance, to the doorway. The guy with the face was right there in the shadows again, behind the register. I guessed where his head was in the darkness and swung my open right hand and slapped him on the ear, hard enough to rock him sideways.

'You,' I said. 'Outside.'

I didn't wait for him. Just pushed my way out into the night. There was a bunched-up crowd of people in the lot. All military. The ones who had trickled out when I came in. They were standing around in the cold, leaning on cars, drinking beer from the long-neck bottles they had carried out with them. They weren't going to be a problem. They would have to be very drunk indeed to mix it up with an MP. But they weren't going to be any help, either. I wasn't one of them. I was on my own.

The door burst open behind me. The big guy came out. He had a couple of locals with him. They looked like farmers. We all stepped into a pool of yellow light from a fixture on a pole. We all stood in a rough circle. We all faced each other. Our breath turned to vapour in the air. Nobody spoke. No preamble was required. I guessed that parking lot had seen plenty of fights. I guessed this one would be no different from all the others. It would finish up just the same, with a winner and a loser.

I slipped out of my jacket and hung it on the nearest car's door mirror. It was a ten-year-old Plymouth, good paint, good chrome. An enthusiast's ride. I saw the Special Forces sergeant I had spoken to come out into the lot. He looked at me for a second and then stepped away into the shadows and stood with his men by the cars. I took my watch off and turned away and dropped it in my jacket pocket. Then I turned back. Studied my opponent. I wanted to mess him up bad. I wanted Sin to know I had stood up for her. But there was no percentage in going for his face. That was already messed up bad. I couldn't make it much worse. And I wanted to put him out of action for a spell. I didn't want him coming around and taking his frustration out on the girls, just because he couldn't get back at me.

He was barrel-chested and overweight, so I figured I might not have to use my hands at all. Except on the farmers, maybe, if they piled in. Which I hoped wouldn't happen. No need to start a big conflict. On the other hand, it was their call.

Everybody has a choice in life. They could hang back, or they could choose up sides.

I was maybe seven inches taller than the guy with the face, but maybe seventy pounds lighter. And ten years younger. I watched him run the numbers. Watched him conclude that on balance he would be OK. I guessed he figured himself for a real junkyard dog. Figured me for an upstanding representative of Uncle Sam. Maybe the Class As made him think I was going to act like an officer and a gentleman. Somewhat proper, somewhat inhibited.

His mistake.

He came at me, swinging. Big chest, short arms, not much reach at all. I arched around the punch and let him skitter away. He came back at me. I swatted his hand away and tapped him in the face with my elbow. Not hard. I just wanted to stop his momentum and get him standing still right in front of me, just for a moment.

He put all his weight on his back foot and lined up a straight drive aimed for my face. It was going to be a big blow. It would have hurt me if it had landed. But before he let it go I stepped in and smashed my right heel into his right kneecap. The knee is a fragile joint. Ask any athlete. He had three hundred pounds bearing down on it and he got two hundred thirty driving straight through it. His patella shattered and his leg folded backwards. Exactly like a regular knee joint, but in reverse. He went down forward and the top of his boot came up to meet the front of his thigh. He screamed, real loud. I stepped back and smiled. *He shoots, he scores.*

I stepped back in and looked at the guy's knee, carefully. It was messed up, but good. Broken bone, ripped ligaments, torn cartilage. I thought about kicking it again, but I really didn't need to. He was in line for a visit to the cane store, as soon as they let him out of the orthopaedic ward. He was going to be choosing a lifetime supply. Wood, aluminum, short, long, his pick.

'I'll come back and do the other one,' I said, 'if anything happens that I don't want to happen.'

I don't think he heard me. He was writhing around in an oily puddle, panting and whimpering, trying to get his knee in a position where it would stop killing him. He was shit out of luck there. He was going to have to wait for surgery.

The farmers were busy choosing up sides. Both of them were pretty dumb. But one of them was dumber than the other. Slower. He was flexing his big red hands. I stepped in and headbutted him full in the face, to help with the decision-making process. He went down, head-to-toe with the big guy, and his pal beat a fast retreat behind the nearest pick-up truck. I lifted my jacket off the Plymouth's door mirror and shrugged back into it. Took my watch out of my pocket. Strapped it back on my wrist. The soldiers drank their beer and looked at me, nothing in their faces. They were neither pleased nor disappointed. They had invested nothing in the outcome. Whether it was me or the other guys on the floor was all the same to them.

I saw Lieutenant Summer on the fringe of the crowd. Threaded my way through cars and people towards her. She looked tense. She was breathing hard. I guessed she had been watching. I guessed she had been ready to jump in and help me out.

'What happened?' she said.

'The fat guy hit a woman who was asking questions for me. His pal didn't run away fast enough.'

She glanced at them and then back at me. 'What did the woman say?'

'She said nobody had a problem last night.'

'The kid in the motel still denies there was a hooker with Kramer. He's pretty definite about it.'

I heard Sin say: *You got me slapped for nothing. Bastard.*

'So what made him go looking in the room?'

Summer made a face. 'That was my big question, obviously.'

'Did he have an answer?'

'Not at first. Then he said it was because he heard a vehicle leaving in a hurry.'

'What vehicle?'

'He said it was a big engine, revving hard, taking off fast, like a panic situation.'

'Did he see it?'

Summer just shook her head.

'Makes no sense,' I said. 'A vehicle implies a call girl, and I doubt if they have many call girls here. And why would Kramer need a call girl anyway, with all those other hookers right there in the bar?'

Summer was still shaking her head. 'The kid says the vehicle had a very distinctive sound. Very loud. And diesel, not gasoline. He says he heard the exact same sound again a little later on.'

'When?'

'When you left in your Humvee.'

'What?'

Summer looked right at me. 'He says he checked Kramer's room because he heard a military vehicle peeling out of the lot in a panic.'

FOUR

WE WENT BACK ACROSS THE ROAD TO THE MOTEL AND MADE the kid tell the story all over again. He was surly and he wasn't talkative, but he made a good witness. Unhelpful people often do. They're not trying to please you. They're not trying to impress you. They're not making all kinds of stuff up, trying to tell you what you want to hear.

He said he was sitting in the office, alone, doing nothing, and at about eleven twenty-five in the evening he heard a vehicle door slam and then a big turbo-diesel start up. He described sounds that must have been a gearbox slamming into reverse and a four-wheel-drive transfer case locking up. Then there was tyre noise and engine noise and gravel noise and something very large and heavy sped away in a big hurry. He said he got off his stool and went outside to look. Didn't see the vehicle.

'Why did you check the room?' I asked him.

He shrugged. 'I thought maybe it was on fire.'

'On fire?'

'People do stuff like that, in a place like this. They set the room on fire. And then high-tail out. For kicks. Or something. I don't know. It was unusual.'

'How did you know which room to check?'

He went very quiet at that point. Summer pressed him for an answer. Then I did. We did the good cop, bad cop thing. Eventually he admitted it was the only room rented for the whole night. All the others were renting by the hour, and were being serviced by foot traffic from across the street, not by vehicles. He said that was how he had been so sure there was never a hooker in Kramer's room. It was his responsibility to check them in and out. He took the money and issued the keys. Kept track of the comings and the goings. So he always knew for sure who was where. It was a part of his function. A part he was supposed to keep very quiet about.

'I'll lose my job now,' he said.

He got worried to the point of tears and Summer had to calm him down. Then he told us he had found Kramer's body and called the cops and cleared all the hourly renters out for safety's sake. Then Deputy Chief Stockton had shown up within about fifteen minutes. Then I had shown up, and when I left some time later he recognized the same vehicle sounds he had heard before. Same engine noise, same drivetrain noises, same tyre whine. He was convincing. He had already admitted that hookers used the place all the time, so he had no more reason to lie. And Humvees were still relatively new. Still relatively rare. And they made a distinctive noise. So I believed him. We left him there on his stool and stepped outside into the cold red glow of the Coke machine.

'No hooker,' Summer said. 'A woman from the base instead.'

'A woman officer,' I said. 'Maybe fairly senior. Someone with permanent access to her own Humvee. Nobody signs out a pool vehicle for an assignation like that. And she's got his briefcase. She must have.'

'She'll be easy to find. She'll be in the gate log, time out, time in.'

'I might have even passed her on the road. If she left here at eleven twenty-five she wasn't back at Bird before about twelve fifteen. I was leaving around then.'

'If she went straight back to the post.'

'Yes,' I said. 'If.'

'Did you see another Humvee?'

'Don't think so,' I said.

'Who do you think she is?'

I shrugged. 'Like we figured about the phantom hooker. Someone he met somewhere. Irwin, probably, but it could have been anywhere.'

I stared across at the gas station. Watched cars go by on the road.

'Vassell and Coomer might know her,' Summer said. 'You know, if it was a long term thing between her and Kramer.'

'Yes, they might.'

'Where do you think they are?'

'I don't know,' I said. 'But I'm sure I'll find them if I need them.'

I didn't find them. They found me. They were waiting for me in my borrowed office when we got back. Summer dropped me at my door and went to park the car. I walked past the outer desk. The night shift sergeant was back. The mountain woman, with the baby son and the paycheck worries. She gestured at the inner door in a way that told me someone was in there. Someone that ranked a lot higher than either of us.

'Got coffee?' I said.

'The machine is on,' she said.

I took some with me. My coat was still unbuttoned. My hair was a mess. I looked exactly like a guy who had been brawling in a parking lot. I walked straight to the desk. Put my coffee down. There were two guys in upright visitor chairs against the wall, facing me. They were both in woodland BDUs. One of them had a brigadier general's star on his collar and the other had a colonel's eagle. The general had *Vassell* on his name tape and the colonel had *Coomer*. Vassell was bald and Coomer wore eyeglasses and they were both pompous enough and old enough and short and soft and pink enough to look vaguely ridiculous in BDUs. They looked like Rotary Club members on their way to a fancy dress ball. First impression, I didn't like them very much.

I sat down in my chair and saw two slips of paper stacked square in the centre of the blotter. The first was a note that said: *Your brother called again. Urgent.* This time there was a phone number with it. It had a 202 area code. Washington D.C.

'Don't you salute senior officers?' Vassell said, from his chair.

The second note said: *Col. Garber called. Green Valley PD calculates Mrs K died approx. 0200.* I folded both notes separately and tucked them side by side under the base of my telephone. Adjusted them so I could see exactly half of each one. Looked up in time to see Vassell glaring at me. His naked scalp was going red.

'I'm sorry,' I said. 'What was the question?'

'Don't you salute senior officers when you enter a room?'

'If they're in my chain of command,' I said. 'You're not.'

'I don't consider that an answer,' he said.

'Look it up,' I said. 'I'm with the 110th Special Unit. We're separate. Structurally we're parallel to the rest of the army. We have to be, if you think about it. We can't police you if we're in your chain of command ourselves.'

'I'm not here to be policed, son,' he said.

'So why are you here? It's kind of late for a social visit.'

'I'm here to ask some questions.'

'Ask away,' I said. 'Then I'll ask some of my own. And you know what the difference will be?'

He said nothing.

'I'll be answering out of courtesy,' I said. 'You'll be answering because the Uniform Code of Military Justice requires you to.'

He said nothing. Just glared at me. Then he glanced at Coomer. Coomer looked back at him, and then at me.

'We're here about General Kramer,' he said. 'We're his senior staff.'

'I know who you are,' I said.

'Tell us about the general.'

'He's dead,' I said.

'We're aware of that. We'd like to know the circumstances.'

'He had a heart attack.'

'Where?'

'Inside his chest cavity.'

Vassell glowered.

'Where did he die?' Coomer said.

'I can't tell you that,' I said. 'It's germane to an ongoing inquiry.'

'In what way?' Vassell said.

'In a confidential way.'

'It was around here somewhere,' he said. 'That much is already common knowledge.'

'Well, there you go,' I said. 'What's the conference at Irwin about?'

'What?'

'The conference at Irwin,' I said again. 'Where you were all headed.'

'What about it?'

'I need to know the agenda.'

Vassell looked at Coomer and Coomer opened his mouth to start telling me something when my phone rang. It was my desk sergeant. She had Summer out there with her. She was unsure whether to send her in. I told her to go right ahead. So there was a tap on the door and Summer came in. I introduced her all around and she pulled a spare chair over to my desk and sat down, alongside me, facing them. Two against two. I pulled the second note out from under the telephone and passed it to her: *Green Valley PD calculates Mrs K died approx. 0200.* She unfolded it and read it and refolded it and passed it back to me. I put it back under the phone. Then I asked Vassell and Coomer about the Irwin agenda again, and watched their attitudes change. They didn't get any more helpful. It was more of a sideways move than an improvement. But because there was now a woman in the room they dialled down the overt hostility and replaced it with smug patronizing civility. They came from that kind of a background and that kind of a generation. They hated MPs and I was sure they hated women officers, but all of a sudden they felt they had to be polite.

'It was going to be purely routine,' Coomer said. 'Just a regular pow-wow. Nothing of any great importance.'

'Which explains why you didn't actually go,' I said.

'Naturally. It seemed much more appropriate to remain here. You know, in the circumstances.'

'How did you find out about Kramer?'

'XII Corps called us.'

'From Germany?'

'That's where XII Corps is, son,' Vassell said.

'Where did you stay last night?'

'In a hotel,' Coomer said.

'Which one?'

'The Jefferson. In D.C.'

'Private or on a DoD ticket?'

'That hotel is authorized for senior officers.'

'Why didn't General Kramer stay there?'

'Because he made alternative arrangements.'

'When?'

'When what?' Coomer said.

'When did he make these alternative arrangements?'

'Some days ago.'

'So it wasn't a spur of the moment thing?'

'No, it wasn't.'

'Do you know what those arrangements were?'

'Obviously not,' Vassell said. 'Or we wouldn't be asking you where he died.'

'You didn't think he was maybe visiting with his wife?'

'Was he?'

'No,' I said. 'Why do you need to know where he died?'

There was a long pause. Their attitudes changed again. The smugness fell away and they replaced it with a kind of winsome frankness.

'We don't really *need* to know,' Vassell said. He leaned forward and glanced at Summer like he wished she wasn't there. Like he wanted this new intimacy to be purely man-to-man with me. 'And we have no specific information or direct knowledge at all, but we're worried that General Kramer's private arrangements could lead to the potential for embarrassment, in light of the circumstances.'

'How well did you know him?'

'On a professional level, very well indeed. On a personal level, about as well as anyone knows his brother officer. Which is to say, perhaps not well enough.'

'But you suspect in general terms what his arrangements might have been.'

'Yes,' he said. 'We have our suspicions.'

'So it wasn't a surprise to you that he didn't bunk at the hotel.'

'No,' he said. 'It wasn't.'

'And it wasn't a surprise when I told you he wasn't visiting with his wife.'

'Not entirely, no.'

'So you suspected roughly what he might be doing, but you didn't know where.'

Vassell nodded his head. 'Roughly.'

'Did you know with whom he might have been doing it?'

Vassell shook his head.

'We have no specific information,' he said.

'OK,' I said. 'Doesn't really matter. I'm sure you know the army well enough to realize that if we discover a potential for embarrassment, we'll cover it up.'

There was a long pause.

'Have all traces been removed?' Coomer asked. 'From wherever it was?'

I nodded. 'We took his stuff.'

'Good.'

'I need the Irwin conference agenda,' I said.

There was another pause.

'There wasn't one,' Vassell said.

'I'm sure there was,' I said. 'This is the army. It's not the Actors' Studio. We don't do free improvisation sessions.'

There was a pause.

'There was nothing on paper,' Coomer said. 'I told you, major, it was no big deal.'

'How did you spend your day today?'

'Chasing rumours about the general.'

'How did you get down here from D.C.?'

'We have a car and a driver on loan from the Pentagon.'

'You checked out of the Jefferson.'

'Yes, we did.'

'So your bags are in the Pentagon car.'

'Yes, they are.'

'Where is the car?'

'Waiting outside your post headquarters.'

'It's not my post headquarters,' I said. 'I'm here on temporary detachment.'

I turned to Summer and told her to go fetch their briefcases from the car. They got all outraged, but they knew they couldn't stop me doing it. Civilian notions about unreasonable search and seizure and warrants and probable cause stop at an army post main gate. I watched their eyes while Summer was gone. They were annoyed, but they weren't worried. So either they were telling the truth about the Irwin conference or they had already ditched the relevant paperwork. But I went through the motions anyway. Summer got back carrying two identical briefcases. They were exactly like the one Kramer had in his silver-framed photographs. Staffers kiss up in all kinds of ways.

I searched through them on my desk. I found passports, plane tickets, travel vouchers and itineraries in both of them. But no agendas for Fort Irwin.

'Sorry for the inconvenience,' I said.

'Happy now, son?' Vassell said.

'Kramer's wife is dead, too,' I said. 'Did you know that?'

I watched them carefully, and I saw that they didn't know. They stared at me and stared at each other and started to get pale and upset.

'How?' Vassell said.

'When?' Coomer said.

'Last night,' I said. 'She was a homicide victim.'

'Where?'

'In her house. There was an intruder.'

'Do we know who it was?'

'No, we don't. It's not our case. It's a civilian jurisdiction.'

'What was it? A burglary?'

'It maybe started out that way.'

They said nothing more. Summer and I walked them out to the sidewalk in front of post headquarters and watched them climb into their Pentagon car. It was a Mercury Grand Marquis, a couple of model-years newer than Mrs Kramer's big old boat, and black rather than green. Their driver was a tall guy in BDUs. He had subdued-order badges on and I couldn't make out his name or his rank in the dark. But he didn't look like an enlisted man. He U-turned smoothly across the empty road and drove Vassell and Coomer away. We watched his tail lights disappear north, through the main gate, and away into the darkness beyond.

'What do you think?' Summer said.

72

'I think they're full of shit,' I said.

'Important shit or regular flag-rank shit?'

'They're lying,' I said. 'They're uptight, they're lying, and they're stupid. Why am I worried about Kramer's brief-case?'

'Sensitive paperwork,' she said. 'Whatever he was carrying to California.'

I nodded. 'They just defined it for me. It's the conference agenda itself.'

'You're sure there was one?'

'There's always an agenda. And it's always on paper. There's a paper agenda for everything. You want to change the dog food in the K-9 kennels, you need forty-seven separate meetings with forty-seven separate paper agendas. So there was one for Irwin, that's for damn sure. It was completely stupid to say there wasn't. If they've got something to hide, they should have just said it's too secret for me to see.'

'Maybe the conference really wasn't important.'

'That's bullshit, too. It was very important.'

'Why?'

'Because a two-star general was going. And a one-star. And because it was New Year's Eve, Summer. Who flies on New Year's Eve and spends the night in a lousy stopover hotel? And this year in Germany was a big deal. The Wall is coming down. We won, after forty-five years. The parties must have been incredible. Who would miss them for something unimportant? To have gotten those guys on a plane on New Year's Eve, this Irwin thing had to be some kind of a very big deal.'

'They were upset about Mrs Kramer. More than about Kramer himself.'

I nodded. 'Maybe they liked her.'

'They must have liked Kramer too.'

'No, he's just a tactical problem for them. It's an unsentimental business, up there at their level. They hitched themselves to him, and now he's dead, and they're worrying about where that leaves them.'

'Ready for promotion, maybe.'

'Maybe,' I said. 'But if Kramer turns out to be an embarrassment, they could go down with him.'

73

'Then they should be reassured. You promised them a cover-up.'

There was something prim in her voice. Like she was suggesting I shouldn't have promised them any such thing.

'We protect the army, Summer,' I said. 'Like family. That's what we're for.' Then I paused. 'But did you notice they didn't shut up after that? They should have taken the hint. Cover-up requested, cover-up promised. Asked and answered, mission accomplished.'

'They wanted to know where his stuff was.'

'Yes,' I said. 'They did. And you know what that means? It means they're looking for Kramer's briefcase too. Because of the agenda. Kramer's copy is the only one still outside of their direct control. They came down here to check if I had it.'

Summer looked in the direction their car had gone. I could still smell its exhaust in the air. An acid tang from the catalyst.

'How do civilian medics work?' I asked her. 'Suppose you're my wife, and I go down with a heart attack? What do you do?'

'I call nine one one.'

'And then what happens?'

'The ambulance shows up. Takes you to the emergency room.'

'And let's say I'm DOA when I get there. Where would you be?'

'I would have ridden to the hospital with you.'

'And where would my briefcase be?'

'At home,' she said. 'Wherever you left it.' Then she paused. 'What? You think someone went to Mrs Kramer's house last night looking for the briefcase?'

'It's a plausible sequence,' I said. 'Someone hears that he's dead from a heart attack, assumes he was pronounced in the ambulance or the emergency room, assumes whoever he was with would have accompanied him, goes down there expecting to find an empty house with a briefcase in it.'

'But he was never there.'

'It was a reasonable first try.'

'You think it was Vassell and Coomer?'

I said nothing.

'That's crazy,' Summer said. 'They don't look the type.'

74

'Don't let looks fool you. They're Armored Branch. They've trained all their lives to roll right over anything that gets in their way. But I don't think the timing works for them. Let's say Garber called XII Corps in Germany at twelve fifteen, earliest. Then let's say XII Corps called the hotel back here in the States at twelve thirty, earliest. Green Valley is seventy minutes from D.C. and Mrs Kramer died at two o'clock. That would have given them a twenty-minute margin to react, maximum. They were just in from the airport, so they didn't have a car with them, and it would have taken time to get hold of one. And they certainly didn't have a crowbar with them. Nobody travels with a crowbar in their luggage, just in case. And I doubt if the Home Depot was open, after midnight on New Year's Eve.'

'So someone *else* is out there looking?'

'We need to find that agenda,' I said. 'We need to nail this thing down.'

I sent Summer away to do three things: first, list all female personnel at Fort Bird with access to their own Humvees, and second, list any of them who might have met Kramer at Fort Irwin in California, and third, contact the Jefferson Hotel in D.C. and get Vassell and Coomer's exact check-in and check-out times, plus details of all their incoming and outgoing phone calls. I went back to my office and filed the note from Garber and spread the note from my brother on the blotter and dialled the number. He picked up on the first ring.

'Hey, Joe,' I said.

'Jack?'

'What?'

'I got a call.'

'Who from?'

'Mom's doctor,' he said.

'About what?'

'She's dying.'

75

FIVE

I HUNG UP WITH JOE AND CALLED GARBER'S OFFICE. HE WASN'T IN.
So I left a message detailing my travel plans and saying I
would be out for seventy-two hours. I didn't give a reason.
Then I hung up again and sat at my desk, numb. Five minutes
later Summer came in. She had a sheaf of motor pool paper with
her. I guess she planned on compiling her Humvee list there
and then, right in front of me.

'I have to go to Paris,' I said.

'Paris, Texas?' she said. 'Or Paris, Kentucky, or Paris,
Tennessee?'

'Paris, France,' I said.

'Why?'

'My mother is sick.'

'Your mother lives in France?'

'Paris,' I said.

'Why?'

'Because she's French.'

'Is it serious?'

'Being French?'

'No, whatever she's sick with.'

I shrugged. 'I don't really know. But I think so.'

'I'm very sorry.'

'I need a car,' I said. 'I need to get to Dulles, right now.'

'I'll drive you,' she said. 'I like driving.'

She left the paperwork on my desk and went to retrieve the Chevrolet we had used before. I went to my quarters and packed an army duffel with one of everything from my closet. Then I put on my long coat. It was cold, and I didn't expect Europe was going to be any warmer. Not in early January. Summer brought the car to my door. She kept it at thirty until we were off post. Then she lit it up like a rocket and headed north. She was quiet for a spell. She was thinking. Her eyelids were moving.

'We should tell the Green Valley cops,' she said. 'If we think Mrs Kramer was killed because of the briefcase.'

I shook my head. 'Telling them won't bring her back. And if she was killed because of the briefcase we'll find whoever did it from our end.'

'What do you want me to do while you're gone?'

'Work the lists,' I said. 'Check the gate log. Find the woman, find the briefcase, put the agenda in a very safe place. Then check on who Vassell and Coomer called from the hotel. Maybe they sent an errand boy out into the night.'

'You think that's possible?'

'Anything's possible.'

'But they didn't know where Kramer was.'

'That's why they tried the wrong place.'

'Who would they have sent?'

'Bound to be someone who has their interests close to his heart.'

'OK,' she said.

'And find out who was driving them just now.'

'OK,' she said.

We didn't speak again, all the way to Dulles.

I met my brother Joe in the line at the Air France ticket desk. He had booked seats for both of us on the first morning flight. Now he was lining up to pay for them. I hadn't seen him for more than three years. The last time we had been together was at our father's funeral. Since then we had gone our separate ways.

'Good morning, little brother,' he said.

He was wearing an overcoat and a suit and a tie, and he looked pretty good in them. He was two years older than me, and he always had been, and he always would be. As a kid I used to study him and think, that's how I'll look when I grow up. Now I found myself doing it again. From a distance we could have been mistaken for each other. Standing side by side it was obvious that he was an inch taller and a little slighter than me. But mostly it was obvious that he was a little older than me. It looked like we had started out together, but he had seen the future first, and it had aged him, and worn him down.

'How are you, Joe?' I said.

'Can't complain.'

'Busy?'

'Like you wouldn't believe.'

I nodded and said nothing. Truth is, I didn't know exactly what he did for a living. He had probably told me. It wasn't a national secret or anything. It was something to do with the Treasury Department. He had probably told me all the details and I probably hadn't listened. Now it seemed too late to ask.

'You were in Panama,' he said. 'Operation Just Cause, right?'

'Operation Just Because,' I said. 'That's what we called it.'

'Just because what?'

'Just because we could. Just because we all had to have something to do. Just because we've got a new Commander in Chief who wants to look tough.'

'Is it going well?'

'It's like Notre Dame against the Tumble Tots. How else is it going to go?'

'You got Noriega yet?'

'Not yet.'

'So why did they post you back here?'

'We took twenty-seven thousand guys,' I said. 'It wasn't down to me personally.'

He smiled briefly and then got that narrow-eyed look I remembered from childhood. It meant he was figuring out some pedantic and convoluted line of reasoning. But we got to the head of the line before he had time to tell me about it. He took out his credit card and paid for the flights. Maybe he expected me to pay him back for mine, maybe he didn't. He didn't make it clear either way.

'Let's get coffee now,' he said.

He was probably the only other human on the planet who liked coffee as much as I did. He started drinking it when he was six. I copied him immediately. I was four. Neither of us has stopped since. The Reacher brothers' need for caffeine makes heroin addiction look like an amusing little take-it-or-leave-it sideline.

We found a place with a W-shaped counter snaking through it. It was three-quarters empty. It was harshly lit with fluorescent tubes and the vinyl on the stools was sticky. We sat side by side and rested our forearms on the counter in the universal pose of early-morning travellers everywhere. A guy in an apron put mugs in front of us without asking. Then he filled them with coffee from a flask. The coffee smelled fresh. The place was changing over from the all-night service to the breakfast menu. I could hear eggs frying.

'What happened in Panama?' Joe asked.

'To me?' I said. 'Nothing.'

'What were your orders there?'

'Supervision.'

'Of what?'

'Of the process,' I said. 'The Noriega thing is supposed to look judicial. He's supposed to stand trial here in the States. So we're supposed to grab him up with some kind of formality. Some way that will look acceptable when we get him in a courtroom.'

'You were going to read him his Miranda rights?'

'Not exactly. But it had to be better than some cowboy thing.'

'Did you screw up?'

'I don't think so.'

'Who replaced you?'

'Some other guy.'

'Rank?'

'Same,' I said.

'A rising star?'

I sipped my coffee. Shook my head. 'I never met him before. But he seemed like a bit of an asshole to me.'

Joe nodded and picked up his mug. Said nothing.

'What?' I said.

'Bird's not a small post,' he said. 'But it's not real big, either, right? What are you working on?'

'Right now? Some two-star died and I can't find his briefcase.'

'Homicide?'

I shook my head. 'Heart attack.'

'When?'

'Last night.'

'*After* you got there?'

I said nothing.

'You sure you didn't screw up?' Joe said.

'I don't think so,' I said again.

'So why did they pull you out? One day you're supervising the Noriega process, and the next day you're in North Carolina with nothing to do? And you'd *still* have nothing to do if the general hadn't died.'

'I got orders,' I said. 'You know how it is. You have to assume they know what they're doing.'

'Who signed the orders?'

'I don't know.'

'You should find out. Find out who wanted you at Bird badly enough to pull you out of Panama and replace you with an asshole. And you should find out why.'

The guy in the apron refilled our mugs. Shoved plastic menus in front of us.

'Eggs,' Joe said. 'Over well, bacon, toast.'

'Pancakes,' I said. 'Egg on the top, bacon on the side, plenty of syrup.'

The guy took the menus back and went away and Joe turned around on his stool and sat back-to with his legs stretched way out into the aisle.

'What exactly did her doctor say?' I asked him.

He shrugged. 'Not very much. No details, no diagnosis. No real information. European doctors aren't very good with bad news. They hedge around it all the time. Plus, there's a privacy issue, obviously.'

'But we're headed over there for a reason.'

He nodded. 'He suggested we might want to come. And then he hinted that sooner might be better than later.'

80

'What is *she* saying?'

'That it's all a lot of fuss about nothing. But that we're always welcome to visit.'

We finished our breakfast and I paid for it. Then Joe gave me my ticket, like a transaction. I was sure he earned more than me, but probably not enough to make an airline ticket proportional to a plate of eggs and bacon with toast on the side. But I took the deal. We got off our stools and got our bearings and headed for the check-in counter.

'Take your coat off,' he said.

'Why?'

'I want the clerk to see your medal ribbons,' he said. 'Military action going on overseas, we might get an upgrade.'

'It's Air France,' I said. 'France isn't even a military member of NATO.'

'The check-in clerk will be American,' he said. 'Try it.'

I shrugged out of my coat. Folded it over my arm and walked sideways so the left of my chest stuck out forward.

'OK now?' I said.

'Perfect,' he said, and smiled.

I smiled back. Left-to-right on the top row I wear the Silver Star, the Defense Superior Service Medal, and the Legion of Merit. Second row has the Soldier's Medal, the Bronze Star, and my Purple Heart. The bottom two rows are the junk awards. I won all of the good stuff purely by accident and none of it means very much to me. Using it to get an upgrade out of an airline clerk is about what it's good for. But Joe liked the top two rows. He served five years in Military Intelligence and didn't get past the junk.

We made it to the head of the line and he put his passport and ticket on the counter along with a Treasury Department ID. Then he stepped behind my shoulder. I put my own passport and ticket down. He nudged me in the back. I turned a little sideways and looked at the clerk.

'Can you find us something with legroom?' I asked him.

He was a small man, middle-aged, tired. He looked up at us. Together we measured almost thirteen feet tall and weighed about four hundred fifty pounds. He studied the Treasury ID

81

and looked at my uniform and pattered on his keyboard and came up with a forced smile.

'We'll seat you gentlemen up front,' he said.

Joe nudged me in the back again and I knew he was smiling.

We were in the last row of the first-class cabin. We were talking, but we were avoiding the obvious subject. We talked about music, and then politics. We had another breakfast. We drank coffee. Air France makes pretty good coffee in first class.

'Who was the general?' Joe asked.

'Guy called Kramer,' I said. 'An Armored commander in Europe.'

'Armored? So why was he at Bird?'

'He wasn't on the post. He was at a motel thirty miles away. Rendezvous with a woman. We think she ran away with his briefcase.'

'Civilian?'

I shook my head. 'We think she was an officer from Bird. He was supposed to be overnighting in D.C. on his way to California for a conference.'

'That's a three-hundred-mile detour.'

'Two hundred and ninety-eight.'

'But you don't know who she is.'

'She's fairly senior. She drove her own Humvee out to the motel.'

He nodded. 'She has to be fairly senior. Kramer's known her for a good spell, to make it worth driving a five-hundred-ninety-six-mile round-trip detour.'

I smiled. Anyone else would have said *a six-hundred-mile detour*. But not my brother. Like me he has no middle name. But it should be *Pedantic*. Joe Pedantic Reacher.

'Bird is still all infantry, right?' he said. 'Some Rangers, some Delta, but mostly grunts, as I recall. So have you got many senior women?'

'There's a Psy-Ops school now,' I said. 'Half the instructors are women.'

'Rank?'

'Some captains, some majors, a couple of light colonels.'

'What was in the briefcase?'

'The agenda for the California conference,' I said. 'Kramer's staffers are pretending there isn't one.'

'There's always an agenda,' Joe said.

'I know.'

'Check the majors and the light colonels,' he said. 'That would be my advice.'

'Thank you,' I said.

'And find out who wanted you at Bird,' he said. 'And why. This Kramer thing wasn't the reason. We know that for sure. Kramer was alive and well when your orders were cut.'

We read day-old copies of *Le Matin* and *Le Monde*. About halfway through the flight we started talking in French. We were pretty rusty, but we got by. Once learned, never forgotten. He asked me about girlfriends. I guess he figured it was an appropriate subject for discussion in the French language. I told him I had been seeing a girl in Korea but since then I had been moved to the Philippines and then Panama and now to North Carolina so I didn't expect to see her again. I told him about Lieutenant Summer. He seemed interested in her. He told me he wasn't seeing anyone.

Then he switched back to English and asked when I had last been in Germany.

'Six months ago,' I said.

'It's the end of an era,' he said. 'Germany will reunify. France will renew its nuclear testing because a reunified Germany will bring back bad memories. Then it will propose a common currency for the EC as a way of keeping the new Germany inside the tent. Ten years from now Poland will be in NATO and the USSR won't exist any more. There'll be some rump nation. Maybe it will be in NATO too.'

'Maybe,' I said.

'So Kramer chose a good time to check out. Everything will be different in the future.'

'Probably.'

'What are you going to do?'

'When?'

He turned in his seat and looked at me. 'There's going to be force reduction, Jack. You should face it. They're not going to keep a million-man army going, not when the other guy has fallen apart.'

'He hasn't fallen apart yet.'

'But he will. It'll be over within a year. Gorbachev won't last. There'll be a coup. The old communists will make one last play, but it won't stick. Then the reformers will be back for ever. Yeltsin, probably. He's OK. So in D.C. the temptation to save money will be irresistible. It'll be like a hundred Christmases coming all at once. Never forget your Commander in Chief is primarily a politician.'

I thought back to the sergeant with the baby son.

'It'll happen slowly,' I said.

Joe shook his head. 'It'll happen faster than you think.'

'We'll always have enemies,' I said.

'No question,' he said. 'But they'll be different kinds of enemies. They won't have ten thousand tanks lined up across the plains of Germany.'

I said nothing.

'You should find out why you're at Bird,' Joe said. 'Either nothing much is happening there, and therefore you're on the way down, or something *is* happening there, and they want you around to deal with it, in which case you're on the way up.'

I said nothing.

'You need to know either way,' he said. 'Force reduction is coming, and you need to know if you're up or down right now.'

'They'll always need cops,' I said. 'They bring it down to a two-man army, one of them better be an MP.'

'You should make a plan,' he said.

'I never make plans.'

'You need to.'

I traced my fingertips across the ribbons on my chest.

'They got me a seat in the front of the plane,' I said. 'Maybe they'll keep me in a job.'

'Maybe they will,' Joe said. 'But even if they do, will it be a job you want? Everything's going to get horribly second-rate.'

I noticed his shirt cuffs. They were clean and crisp and secured by discreet cufflinks made from silver and black onyx. His tie was a plain sombre item made from silk. He had shaved carefully. The bottom of his sideburn was cut exactly square. He was a man horrified by anything less than the best.

'A job's a job,' I said. 'I'm not choosy.'

We slept the rest of the way. We were woken by the pilot on the PA telling us we were about to start our descent into Roissy-Charles de Gaulle. Local time was already eight o'clock in the evening. Nearly the whole of the second day of the new decade had disappeared like a mirage, as we slid through one Atlantic time zone after another.

We changed some money and hiked over to the taxi line. It was a mile long, full of people and luggage. It was hardly moving. So we found a *navette* instead, which is what the French call an airport shuttle bus. We had to stand all the way through the dreary northern suburbs and into the centre of Paris. We got out at the Place de l'Opéra at nine in the evening. Paris was dark and damp and cold and quiet. Cafés and restaurants had warm lights burning behind closed doors and fogged windows. The streets were wet and lined with small parked cars. The cars were all misted over with night-time dew. We walked together south and west and crossed the Seine at the Pont de la Concorde. Turned west again along the Quai d'Orsay. The river was dark and sluggish. Nothing was moving on it. The streets were empty. Nobody was out and about.

'Should we get flowers?' I said.

'Too late,' Joe said. 'Everything's closed.'

We turned left at the Place de la Résistance and walked into the Avenue Rapp, side by side. We saw the Eiffel Tower on our right as we crossed the Rue de l'Université. It was lit up in gold. Our heels sounded like rifle shots on the silent sidewalk. Then we arrived at my mother's building. It was a modest six-storey stone apartment house trapped between two gaudier Belle Époque façades. Joe took his hand out of his pocket and unlocked the street door.

'You have a key?' I said.

He nodded. 'I've always had a key.'

Inside the street door was a cobbled alley that led through to the centre courtyard. The concierge's room was on the left. Beyond it was a small alcove with a small slow elevator. We rode it up to the fifth floor. Stepped out into a high wide hallway. It was dimly lit. It had dark decorative tiles on the floor. The right-hand apartment had tall oak double doors with a discreet brass plaque engraved: *M. & Mme Girard*. The left-hand doors were painted off-white and labelled: *Mme Reacher*.

We knocked and waited.

SIX

WE HEARD SLOW SHUFFLING STEPS INSIDE THE APARTMENT AND a long moment later my mother opened the door.

'Bonsoir, maman,' Joe said.

I just stared at her.

She was very thin and very grey and very stooped and she looked about a hundred years older than the last time I had seen her. She had a long heavy plaster cast on her left leg and she was leaning on an aluminum walker. Her hands were gripping it hard and I could see bones and veins and tendons standing out. She was trembling. Her skin looked translucent. Only her eyes were the same as I remembered them. They were blue and merry and filled with amusement.

'Joe,' she said. 'And Reacher.'

She always called me by my last name. Nobody remembered why. Maybe I had started it, as a kid. Maybe she had continued it, the way families do.

'My boys,' she said. 'Just look at the two of you.'

She spoke slowly and breathlessly but she was smiling a happy smile. We stepped up and hugged her. She felt cold and frail and insubstantial. She felt like she weighed less than her aluminum walker.

'What happened?' I said.

'Come inside,' she said. 'Make yourselves at home.'

She turned the walker around with short clumsy movements and shuffled back through the hallway. She was panting and wheezing. I stepped in after her. Joe closed the door and followed me. The hallway was narrow and tall and was followed by a living room with wood floors and white sofas and white walls and framed mirrors. My mother made her way to a sofa and backed up to it slowly and dropped herself into it. She seemed to disappear in its depth.

'What happened?' I asked again.

She wouldn't answer. She just waved the enquiry away with an impatient movement of her hand. Joe and I sat down, side by side.

'You're going to have to tell us,' I said.

'We came all this way,' Joe said.

'I thought you were just visiting,' she said.

'No, you didn't,' I said.

She stared at a spot on the wall.

'It's nothing,' she said.

'Doesn't look like nothing.'

'Well, it was just bad timing.'

'In what way?'

'I got unlucky,' she said.

'How?'

'I was hit by a car,' she said. 'It broke my leg.'

'Where? When?'

'Two weeks ago,' she said. 'Right outside my door, here on the Avenue. It was raining, I had an umbrella, it was shading my eyes, I stepped out, and the driver saw me and braked, but the *pavé* was wet and the car slid right into me, very slowly, like slow motion, but I was transfixed and I couldn't move. I felt it hit my knee, very gently, like a kiss, but it snapped a bone. It hurt like hell.'

I saw in my mind the guy in the parking lot outside the nude bar near Bird, writhing around in an oily puddle.

'Why didn't you tell us?' Joe asked.

She didn't answer.

'But it'll mend, right?' he asked.

'Of course,' she said. 'It's trivial.'

Joe just looked at me.

'What else?' I said.

She kept on looking at the wall. Did the dismissive thing with her hand again.

'What else?' Joe asked.

She looked at me, and then she looked at him.

'They gave me an X-ray,' she said. 'I'm an old woman, according to them. According to them, old women who break bones are at risk from pneumonia. Because we're laid up and immobile and our lungs can fill and get infected.'

'And?'

She said nothing.

'Have you got pneumonia?' I said.

'No.'

'So what happened?'

'They found out. With the X-ray.'

'Found what out?'

'That I have cancer.'

Nobody spoke for a long time.

'But you already knew,' I said.

She smiled at me, like she always did.

'Yes, darling,' she said. 'I already knew.'

'For how long?'

'For a year,' she said.

Nobody spoke.

'What sort of cancer?' Joe said.

'Every sort there is, now.'

'Is it treatable?'

She just shook her head.

'*Was* it treatable?'

'I don't know,' she said. 'I didn't ask.'

'What were the symptoms?'

'I had stomach aches. I had no appetite.'

'Then it spread?'

'Now I hurt all over. It's in my bones. And this stupid leg doesn't help.'

'Why didn't you tell us?'

She shrugged. Gallic, feminine, obstinate.

'What was to tell?' she said.

'Why didn't you go to the doctor?'

She didn't answer for a time.

'I'm tired,' she said.

'Of what?' Joe said. 'Life?'

She smiled. 'No, Joe, I mean I'm *tired*. It's late and I need to go to bed, is what I mean. We'll talk some more tomorrow. I promise. Don't let's have a lot of fuss now.'

We let her go to bed. We had to. We had no choice. She was the most stubborn woman imaginable. We found stuff to eat in her kitchen. She had laid in provisions for us. That was clear. Her refrigerator was stocked with the kind of things that wouldn't interest a woman with no appetite. We ate pâté and cheese and made coffee and sat at her table to drink it. The Avenue Rapp was still and silent and deserted, five floors below her window.

'What do you think?' Joe asked me.

'I think she's dying,' I said. 'That's why we came, after all.'

'Can we make her get treatment?'

'It's too late. It would be a waste of time. And we can't make her do anything. When could anyone make her do what she didn't want to?'

'Why doesn't she want to?'

'I don't know.'

He just looked at me.

'She's a fatalist,' I said.

'She's only sixty years old.'

I nodded. She had been thirty when I was born, and forty-eight when I stopped living wherever we called home. I hadn't noticed her age at all. At forty-eight she had looked younger than I did when I was twenty-eight. I had last seen her a year and a half ago. I had stopped by Paris for two days, en route from Germany to the Middle East. She had been fine. She had looked great. She was about two years into widowhood then, and like with a lot of people the two-year threshold had been like turning a corner. She had looked like a person with a lot of life left.

'Why didn't she tell us?' Joe said.

'I don't know.'

'I wish she had.'

'Shit happens,' I said.

Joe just nodded.

She had made up her guest room with clean fresh sheets and towels and she had put flowers in bone china vases on the night stands. It was a small fragrant room full of two twin beds. I pictured her struggling around with her walker, fighting with duvets, folding corners, smoothing things out.

Joe and I didn't talk. I hung my uniform in the closet and washed up in the bathroom. Set the clock in my head for seven the next morning and got into bed and lay there looking at the ceiling for an hour. Then I went to sleep.

I woke at exactly seven. Joe was already up. Maybe he hadn't slept at all. Maybe he was accustomed to a more regular lifestyle than I was. Maybe the jet lag bothered him more. I showered and took fatigue pants and a T-shirt from my duffel and put them on. Found Joe in the kitchen. He had coffee going.

'Mom's still asleep,' he said. 'Medication, probably.'

'I'll go get breakfast,' I said.

I put my coat on and walked a block to a patisserie I knew on the Rue Saint Dominique. I bought croissants and *pain au chocolat* and carried the waxed bag home. My mother was still in her room when I got back.

'She's committing suicide,' Joe said. 'We can't let her.'

I said nothing.

'What?' he said. 'If she picked up a gun and held it to her head, wouldn't you stop her?'

I shrugged. 'She already put the gun to her head. She pulled the trigger a year ago. We're too late. She made sure we would be.'

'Why?'

'We have to wait for her to tell us.'

She told us during a conversation that lasted most of the day. It proceeded in bits and pieces. We started over breakfast. She came out of her room, all showered and dressed and looking

91

about as good as a terminal cancer patient with a broken leg and an aluminum walker can. She made fresh coffee and put the croissants I had bought on good china and served us quite formally at the table. The way she took charge spooled us all backwards in time. Joe and I shrank back to skinny kids and she bloomed into the matriarch she had once been. A military wife and mother has a pretty hard time, and some handle it, and some don't. She always had. Wherever we had lived had been home. She had seen to that.

'I was born three hundred metres from here,' she said. 'On the Avenue Bosquet. I could see Les Invalides and the École Militaire from my window. I was ten when the Germans came to Paris. I thought that was the end of the world. I was fourteen when they left. I thought that was the beginning of a new one.'

Joe and I said nothing.

'Every day since then has been a bonus,' she said. 'I met your father, I had you boys, I travelled the world. I don't think there's a country I haven't been to.'

We said nothing.

'I'm French,' she said. 'You're American. There's a world of difference. An American gets sick, she's outraged. How dare that happen to her? She must have the fault corrected immediately, at once. But French people understand that first you live, and then you die. It's not an outrage. It's something that's been happening since the dawn of time. It has to happen, don't you see? If people didn't die, the world would be an awfully crowded place by now.'

'It's about *when* you die,' Joe said.

My mother nodded.

'Yes, it is,' she said. 'You die when it's your time.'

'That's too passive.'

'No, it's realistic, Joe. It's about picking your battles. Sure, of course you cure the little things. If you're in an accident, you get yourself patched up. But some battles can't be won. Don't think I didn't consider this whole thing very carefully. I read books. I spoke to friends. The success rates after the symptoms have already shown themselves are very poor. Five-year survival, ten per cent, twenty per cent, who needs it? And that's after truly horrible treatments.'

It's about when you die. We spent the morning going back and forth on Joe's central question. We talked it through, from one direction, then from another. But the conclusion was always the same. *Some battles can't be won.* And it was a moot point, anyway. It was a discussion that should have happened a year ago. It was no longer appropriate.

Joe and I ate lunch. My mother didn't. I waited for Joe to ask the next obvious question. It was just hanging there. Eventually, he got to it. Joe Reacher, thirty-two years of age, six feet six inches tall, two hundred and twenty pounds, a West Point graduate, some kind of a Treasury Department bigshot, placed his palms flat on the table and looked into his mother's eyes.

'Won't you miss us, Mom?' he asked.

'Wrong question,' she said. 'I'll be dead. I won't be missing anything. It's you that will be missing me. Like you miss your father. Like I miss him. Like I miss my father, and my mother, and my grandparents. It's a part of life, missing the dead.'

We said nothing.

'You're really asking me a different question,' she said. 'You're asking, how can I abandon you? You're asking, aren't I concerned with your affairs any more? Don't I want to see what happens with your lives? Have I lost interest in you?'

We said nothing.

'I understand,' she said. 'Truly, I do. I asked myself the same questions. It's like walking out of a movie. Being *made* to walk out of a movie that you're really enjoying. That's what worried me about it. I would never know how it turned out. I would never know what happened to you boys in the end, with your lives. I hated that part. But then I realized, obviously I'll walk out of the movie sooner or later. I mean, nobody lives for ever. I'll *never* know how it turns out for you. I'll never know what happens with your lives. Not in the end. Not even under the best of circumstances. I realized that. Then it didn't seem to matter so much. It will always be an arbitrary date. It will always leave me wanting more.'

We sat quiet for a spell.

'How long?' Joe asked.

'Not long,' she said.

We said nothing.

'You don't need me any more,' she said. 'You're all grown up. My job is done. That's natural, and that's good. That's life. So let me go.'

By six in the evening we were all talked out. Nobody had spoken for an hour. Then my mother sat up straight in her chair.

'Let's go out to dinner,' she said. 'Let's go to Polidor, on Rue Monsieur le Prince.'

We called a cab and rode it to the Odéon. Then we walked. My mother wanted to. She was bundled up in a coat and she was hanging on our arms and moving slow and awkward, but I think she enjoyed the air. Rue Monsieur le Prince cuts the corner between the Boulevard Saint Germain and the Boulevard Saint Michel, in the Sixième. It may be the most Parisian street in the whole of the city. Narrow, diverse, slightly seedy, flanked by tall plaster façades, bustling. Polidor is a famous old restaurant. It makes you feel all kinds of people have eaten there. Gourmets, spies, painters, fugitives, cops, robbers.

We all ordered the same three courses. *Chèvre chaud, porc aux pruneaux, dames blanches*. We ordered a fine red wine. But my mother ate nothing and drank nothing. She just watched us. There was pain showing in her face. Joe and I ate, self-consciously. She talked, exclusively about the past. But there was no sadness. She relived good times. She laughed. She rubbed her thumb across the scar on Joe's forehead and scolded me for putting it there all those years ago, like she always did. I rolled up my sleeve like I always did and showed her where he had stuck me with a chisel in revenge, and she scolded him equally. She talked about things we had made her in school. She talked about birthday parties we had thrown, on grim faraway bases in the heat, or the cold. She talked about our father, about meeting him in Korea, about marrying him in Holland, about his awkward manner, about the two bunches of flowers he had bought her in all their thirty-three years together, one when Joe was born, and one when I was.

'Why didn't you tell us a year ago?' Joe asked.

'You know why,' she said.

94

'Because we would have argued,' I said.

She nodded.

'It was a decision that belonged to me,' she said.

We had coffee and Joe and I smoked cigarettes. Then the waiter brought the bill and we asked him to call a cab for us. We rode back to the Avenue Rapp in silence. We all went to bed without saying much.

I woke early on the fourth day of the new decade. Heard Joe in the kitchen, talking French. I went in there and found him with a woman. She was young and brisk. She had short neat hair and luminous eyes. She told me she was my mother's private nurse, provided under the terms of an old insurance policy. She told me she normally came in seven days a week, but had missed the day before at my mother's request. She told me my mother had wanted a day alone with her sons. I asked the girl how long each visit lasted. She said she stayed as long as she was needed. She told me the old insurance policy would cover up to twenty-four hours a day, as and when it became necessary, which she thought might be very soon.

The girl with the luminous eyes left and I went back to the bedroom and showered and packed my bag. Joe came in and watched me do it.

'You leaving?' he said.

'We both are. You know that.'

'We should stay.'

'We came. That's what she wanted. Now she wants us to go.'

'You think?'

I nodded. 'Last night, at Polidor. It was about saying goodbye. She wants to be left in peace now.'

'You can do that?'

'It's what she wants. We owe it to her.'

I got breakfast items in the Rue Saint Dominique again and we ate them with bowls of coffee, the French way, all three of us together. My mother had dressed in her best and was acting like a fit young woman temporarily inconvenienced by a broken leg. It must have taken a lot of will, but I guessed that was how she wanted to be remembered. We poured coffee and passed things to each other, politely. It was a civilized meal. Like we used to have, long ago. Like an old family ritual.

Then she revisited another old family ritual. She did something she had done ten thousand times before, all through our lives, since we were first old enough to have individuality of our own. She struggled up out of her chair and stepped over and put her hands on Joe's shoulders, from behind. Then she bent and kissed his cheek.

'What don't you need to do?' she asked him.

He didn't answer. He never did. Our silence was part of the ritual.

'You don't need to solve *all* the world's problems, Joe. Only some of them. There are enough to go around.'

She kissed his cheek again. Then she kept one hand on the back of his chair and reached out with the other and moved herself over behind me. I could hear her ragged breathing. She kissed my cheek. Then like she used to all those years before she put her hands on my shoulders. Measured them, side to side. She was a small woman, fascinated by the way her baby had grown into a giant.

'You've got the strength of two normal boys,' she said.

Then came my own personal question.

'What are you going to do with this strength?' she asked me.

I didn't answer. I never did.

'You're going to do the right thing,' she said.

Then she bent down and kissed me on the cheek again.

I thought: *was that the last time?*

We left thirty minutes later. We hugged long and hard at the door and we told her we loved her, and she told us she loved us too and she always had. We left her standing there and went down in the tiny elevator and set out on the long walk back to the Opéra to get the airport bus. Our eyes were full of tears and we didn't talk at all. My medals meant nothing to the check-in girl at Roissy-Charles de Gaulle. She sat us in the back of the plane. About halfway through the flight I picked up *Le Monde* and saw that Noriega had been found in Panama City. A week ago I had lived and breathed that mission. Now I barely

96

remembered it. I put the paper down and tried to look ahead. Tried to remember where I was supposed to be going, and what I was supposed to be doing when I got there. I had no real recollection. No sense of what was going to happen. If I had, I would have stayed in Paris.

SEVEN

GOING WEST THE TIME CHANGES LENGTHENED THE DAY INSTEAD of shortening it. They paid us back the hours we had lost two days before. We landed at Dulles at two in the afternoon. I said goodbye to Joe and he found the cab line and headed into the city. I went looking for buses and was arrested before I found any.

Who guards the guards? Who arrests an MP? In my case it was a trio of warrant officers working directly for the Provost Marshal General's office. There were two W3s and a W4. The W4 showed me his credentials and his orders and then the W3s showed me their Berettas and their handcuffs and the W4 gave me a choice: either behave myself or get knocked on my ass. I smiled, briefly. I approved of his performance. He carried himself well. I doubted if I would have done it any different, or any better.

'Are you armed, major?' he said.

'No,' I said.

I would have been worried for the army if he had believed me. Some W4s would have. They would have been intimidated by the sensitivities involved. Arresting a superior officer from your own corps is tough duty. But this particular W4 did everything right. He heard me say *no* and nodded to his W3s and they moved in to pat me down about as fast as if I had said *yes, with a nuclear warhead*. One of them did the body search and the other went through my duffel. They were both very thorough. Took them a good few minutes before they were satisfied.

'Do I need to put the cuffs on you?' the W4 asked.

I shook my head. 'Where's the car?'

He didn't answer. The W3s formed up one on either side and slightly behind me. The W4 walked in front. We crossed the sidewalk and passed by the bay where the buses were waiting and headed for an official-vehicle-only lane. There was an olive green sedan parked there. This was their time of maximum danger. A determined man would be tensing up at that point, ready to make his break. They knew it, and they formed up a little tighter. They were a good team. Three against one, they reduced the odds to maybe fifty-fifty. But I let them put me in the car. Afterwards, I wondered what would have happened if I had run for it. Sometimes, I found myself wishing that I had.

The car was a Chevrolet Caprice. It had been white before the army sprayed it green. I saw the original colour inside the door frame. It had vinyl seats and manual windows. Civilian police specification. I slid across the rear bench and settled in the corner behind the front passenger seat. One of the W3s crammed in next to me and the other got behind the wheel. The W4 sat next to him up front. Nobody spoke.

We headed east towards the city on the main highway. I was probably five minutes behind Joe in his taxi. We turned south and east and drove through Tysons Corner. At that point I knew for sure where we were going. A couple of miles later we picked up signs to Rock Creek. Rock Creek was a small town twenty-some miles due north of Fort Belvoir and forty-some north and east of the Marine place at Quantico. It was as close as I got to a permanent duty station. It housed the 110th Special Unit head-quarters. So I knew where we were headed. But I had no idea why.

110th headquarters was basically an office and supply facility. There were no cells. No secure holding facilities. They locked me up in an interview room. Just dumped my bag on the table and locked the door and left me there. It was a room I had locked guys in before. So I knew how it was done. One of the W3s would be on station in the corridor outside. Maybe both of them would be. So I just tilted the plain wooden chair back and put my feet on the table and waited.

I waited an hour. I was uncomfortable and hungry and dehydrated from the plane. I figured if they knew all of that they'd have kept me waiting two hours. Or more. As it was they came back after sixty minutes. The W4 led the way and gestured with his chin that I should stand up and follow him out the door. The W3s fell in behind me. They walked me up two flights of stairs. Led me left and right through plain grey passageways. At that point I knew for sure where we were going. We were going to Leon Garber's office. But I didn't know why.

They stopped me outside his door. It had reeded glass with *CO* painted on it in gold. I had been through it many times. But never while in custody. The W4 knocked and waited and opened the door and stepped back to let me walk inside. He closed the door behind me and stayed on the other side of it, out in the corridor with his guys.

Behind Garber's desk was a man I had never seen before. He was a colonel. He was in BDUs. His tapes said: *Willard, U.S. Army.* He had iron-grey hair parted in a schoolboy style. It needed a trim. He had steel-rimmed eyeglasses and the kind of grey pouchy face that must have looked old when he was twenty. He was short and relatively squat and the way his shoulders failed to fill his BDUs told me he spent no time at all in the gym. He had a problem sitting still. He was rocking to his left and plucking at his pants where they went tight over his right knee. Before I had been in the room ten seconds he had adjusted his position three times. Maybe he had haemorrhoids. Maybe he was nervous. He had soft hands. Ragged nails. No wedding band. Divorced, for sure. He looked the type. No wife would let him walk about with hair like that. And no wife could have stood all that rocking and twitching. Not for very long.

I should have come smartly to attention and saluted and announced: *Sir, Major Reacher reports.* That would have been the standard army etiquette. But I was damned if I was going to do that. I just took a long lazy look around and came to rest standing easy in front of the desk.

'I need explanations,' the guy called Willard said.

He moved in his chair again.

'Who are you?' I said.

'You can see who I am.'

'I can see you're a colonel in the U.S. Army named Willard. But I can't explain anything to you before I know whether or not you're in my chain of command.'

'I *am* your chain of command, son. What does it say on my door?'

'Commanding officer,' I said.

'And where are we?'

'Rock Creek, Virginia,' I said.

'OK, asked and answered,' he said.

'You're new,' I said. 'We haven't met.'

'I assumed this command forty-eight hours ago. And now we've met. And now I need explanations.'

'Of what?'

'You were UA, for a start,' he said.

'Unauthorized absence?' I said. 'When?'

'The last seventy-two hours.'

'Incorrect,' I said.

'How so?'

'My absence was authorized by Colonel Garber.'

'It was not.'

'I called this office,' I said.

'When?'

'Before I left.'

'Did you receive his authorization?'

I paused. 'I left a message. Are you saying he denied authorization?'

'He wasn't here. He got orders for Korea some hours earlier.'

'Korea?'

'He got the MP command there.'

'That's a brigadier general's job.'

'He's acting. The promotion will no doubt be confirmed in the fall.'

I said nothing.

'Garber's gone,' Willard said. 'I'm here. The military merry-go-round continues. Get used to it.'

The room went quiet. Willard smiled at me. Not a pleasant smile. It was close to a sneer. The rug was out from under my feet, and he was watching me hit the ground.

'It was good of you to leave your travel plans,' he said. 'It made today easier.'

'You think the arrest was appropriate for UA?' I said.

'You don't?'

'It was a simple miscommunication.'

'You left your assigned post without authorization, major. Those are the facts. Just because you had a vague expectation that authorization might be granted doesn't alter them. This is the army. We don't act in advance of orders or permissions. We wait until they are properly received and confirmed. The alternative would be anarchy and chaos.'

I said nothing.

'Where did you go?'

I pictured my mother, leaning on her aluminum walker. I pictured my brother's face, as he watched me pack.

'I took a short vacation,' I said. 'I went to the beach.'

'The arrest wasn't for the UA,' Willard said. 'It was because you wore Class As on the evening of New Year's Day.'

'That's an offence now?'

'You wore your nameplate.'

I said nothing.

'You put two civilians in the hospital. While wearing your nameplate.'

I stared at him. Thought hard. I didn't believe the fat guy and the farmer had dropped a dime on me. Not possible. They were stupid, but they weren't that stupid. They knew I knew where I could find them.

'Who says so?' I asked.

'You had a big audience in that parking lot.'

'One of ours?'

Willard nodded.

'Who?' I said.

'No need for you to know.'

I kept quiet.

'You got anything to say?' Willard asked me.

I thought: *He won't testify at the court martial. That's for damn sure. That's what I've got to say.*

'Nothing to say,' I said.

'What do you think I should do with you?'

I said nothing.

'What do you think I should do?'

You should figure out the difference between a hard ass and a dumb ass, pal. You should figure it out real quick.

'Your choice,' I said. 'Your decision.'

He nodded. 'I also have reports from General Vassell and Colonel Coomer.'

'Saying what?'

'Saying you acted in a disrespectful manner towards them.'

'Then those reports are incorrect.'

'Like the UA was incorrect?'

I said nothing.

'Stand at attention,' Willard said.

I looked at him. Counted *one thousand. Two thousand. Three thousand.* Then I came to attention.

'That was slow,' he said.

'I'm not looking to win a drill competition,' I said.

'What was your interest in Vassell and Coomer?'

'An agenda for an Armored Branch conference is missing. I need to know if it contained classified information.'

'There was no agenda,' Willard said. 'Vassell and Coomer have made that perfectly clear. To me, and to you. To ask is permissible. You have that right, technically. But to wilfully disbelieve a senior officer's direct answer is disrespectful. It's close to harassment.'

'Sir, I do this stuff for a living. I believe there was an agenda.'

Now Willard said nothing.

'May I ask what was your previous command?' I said.

He shifted in his chair.

'Intelligence,' he said.

'Field agent?' I asked. 'Or desk jockey?'

He didn't answer. *Desk jockey.*

'Did you have conferences without agendas?' I asked.

He looked straight at me.

'Direct orders, major,' he said. 'One, terminate your interest in Vassell and Coomer. Forthwith, and immediately. Two, terminate your interest in General Kramer. We don't want flags raised on that matter, not in the circumstances. Three, terminate Lieutenant Summer's involvement in special unit affairs. Forthwith, and immediately. She's a junior-grade MP and after reading her file as far as I'm concerned she always will be. Four, do not attempt to make further contact with the local civilians you injured. And five, do not attempt to identify the eyewitness against you in that matter.'

I said nothing.

'Do you understand your orders?' he said.

'I'd like them in writing,' I said.

'Verbal will do,' he said. 'Do you understand your orders?'

'Yes,' I said.

'Dismissed.'

I counted *one thousand. Two thousand. Three thousand*. Then I saluted and turned around. I made it all the way to the door before he fired his parting shot.

'They tell me you're a big star, Reacher,' he said. 'So right now you need to decide whether you keep on being a big star, or whether you let yourself become an arrogant smart-ass son of a bitch. And you need to remember that nobody likes arrogant smart-ass sons of bitches. And you need to remember we're coming to a point where it's going to matter whether people like you or not. It's going to matter a lot.'

I said nothing.

'Do I make myself clear, major?'

'Crystal,' I said.

I got my hand on the door handle.

'One last thing,' he said. 'I'm going to sit on the brutality complaint. For as long as I possibly can. Out of respect for your record. You're very lucky that it came up internally. But I want you to remember that it's here, and it stays active.'

I left Rock Creek just before five in the afternoon. Caught a bus into Washington D.C. and another one south down I-95. Then I removed my lapel insignia and hitched the final thirty miles to Bird. It works a little faster that way. Most of the local traffic is enlisted men, or retired enlisted men, or their families, and most of them are suspicious of MPs. So experience had taught me things went better if you kept your badges in your pocket.

I got a ride and got out two hundred yards short of Bird's main gate, a few minutes past eleven in the evening, January 4th, after a little more than six hours on the road. North Carolina was pitch dark and cold. Very cold, so I jogged the two hundred yards to heat myself up. I was out of breath when I got to the gate. I was logged in and I ran down to my office. It was warm inside. The night watch sergeant with the baby son was on duty. She had coffee going. She gave me a cup and I walked into my office and found a note from Summer waiting for me on my desk. The note was clipped to a slim green file. The file had three lists in it. The women-with-Humvees list, the women-from-Irwin list, and the main gate log for New Year's Eve. The first two lists were relatively short. The gate log was a riot. People had been in and out all night long, partying. But only one name was common to all three compilations: *Lt/Col. Andrea Norton*. Summer had circled the name in all three locations. Her note said: *Call me about Norton. Hope your mom was OK*.

I found the old message slip with Joe's telephone number on it and called him first.

'You holding up?' I asked him.

'We should have stayed,' he said.

'She gave the nurse one day off,' I said. 'One day was what she wanted.'

'We should have stayed anyway.'

'She doesn't want spectators,' I said.

He didn't answer. The phone was hot and silent against my ear.

'I've got a question,' I said. 'When you were at the Pentagon, did you know an asshole called Willard?'

He stayed quiet for a long moment, changing gears, searching his memory. He had been out of Intelligence for some time.

'Squat little man?' he said. 'Couldn't sit still? Always shuffling around on his chair, fussing with his pants? He was a desk guy. A major, I think.'

'He's a full colonel now,' I said. 'He just got assigned to the 110th. He's my CO at Rock Creek.'

'MI to the 110th? That makes sense.'

'Makes no sense to me.'

'It's the new theory,' Joe said. 'They're copying private-sector doctrine. They think know-nothings are good because they're not invested in the status quo. They think they bring fresh perspectives.'

'Anything I should know about this guy?'

'You called him an asshole, so it sounds like you already know about him. He was smart, but he *was* an asshole, for sure. Vicious, petty, very corporate, good at office politics, exclusively interested in number one, excellent ass-kisser, always knew which way the wind was blowing.'

I said nothing.

'Hopeless with women,' Joe said. 'I remember that.'

I said nothing.

'He's a perfect example,' Joe said. 'Like we discussed. He was on the Soviet desk. He monitored their tank production and fuel consumption, as I recall. I think he worked out some kind of an algorithm that told us what kind of training Soviet armour was doing based on how much fuel they were eating. He was hot for a year or so. But now I guess he's seen the future. He got himself out while the getting was good. You should do the same. At least you should think about it. Like we discussed.'

I said nothing.

'Meanwhile watch your step,' Joe said. 'I wouldn't want Willard for a boss.'

'I'll be OK,' I said.

'We should have stayed in Paris,' he said, and hung up.

I found Summer in the O Club bar. She had a beer on the go and was leaning on the wall with a couple of W2s. She moved away from them when she saw me.

'Garber's gone to Korea,' I said. 'We got a new guy.'

'Who?'

'A colonel called Willard. From Intelligence.'

'So how is he qualified?'

'He isn't qualified. He's an asshole.'

'Doesn't that piss you off?'

I shrugged. 'He's telling us to stay away from the Kramer thing.'

'Are we going to?'

'He's telling me to stop talking to you. He says he's going to turn down your application.'

She went very quiet. Looked away.

'Shit,' she said.

'I'm sorry,' I said. 'I know you wanted it.'

She looked back at me.

'Is he serious about the Kramer thing?' she asked.

I nodded. 'He's serious about everything. He had me arrested at the airport, to make all his various points.'

'Arrested?'

I nodded again. 'Someone ratted me out for those guys in the parking lot.'

'Who?'

'One of the grunts in the audience.'

'One of ours? Who?'

'I don't know.'

'That's cold.'

I nodded. 'Never happened to me before.'

She went quiet again.

'How was your mom?' she said.

'She broke her leg,' I said. 'No big deal.'

'They can get pneumonia.'

I nodded again. 'She had the X-ray. No pneumonia.'

Her lower eyelids moved upward.

'Can I ask the obvious question?' she said.

'Is there one?'

'Aggravated battery against civilians is a big deal. And apparently there's a report and an eyewitness, good enough to get you arrested.'

'So?'

'So why are you still walking around?'

'Willard's sitting on it.'

'But why would he, if he's an asshole?'

'Out of respect for my record. That's what he said.'

'Did you believe him?'

107

I shook my head.

'There must be something wrong with the complaint,' I said. 'An asshole like Willard would use it if he could, that's for sure. He doesn't care about my record.'

'Can't be something wrong with the complaint. A military witness is the best kind they can get. He'll testify to whatever they tell him to. It's like Willard would be writing the complaint himself.'

I said nothing.

'And why are you here at all?' she asked.

I heard Joe say: *You should find out who wanted you at Bird badly enough to pull you out of Panama and replace you with an asshole.*

'I don't know why I'm here,' I said. 'I don't know anything. Tell me about Lieutenant Colonel Norton.'

'We're off the case.'

'So just tell me for interest's sake.'

'It isn't her. She's got an alibi. She was at a party in a bar off post. All night long. About a hundred people were there with her.'

'Who is she?'

'Psy-Ops instructor. She's a psychosexual Ph.D. who specializes in attacking an enemy's internal emotional security concerning his feelings of masculinity.'

'She sounds like a fun lady.'

'She was invited to a party in a bar. Someone thinks she's a fun lady.'

'Did you check who drove Vassell and Coomer down here?'

Summer nodded. 'Our gate guys list him as a Major Marshall. I looked him up, and he's a XII Corps staffer on temporary detached duty at the Pentagon. Some kind of a blue-eyed boy. He's been over here since November.'

'Did you check phone calls out of the D.C. hotel?'

She nodded again.

'There weren't any,' she said. 'Vassell's room took one incoming call at twelve twenty-eight in the morning. I'm assuming that was XII Corps calling from Germany. Neither of them made any outgoing calls.'

'None at all?'

'Not a one.'

'Are you sure?'

'Totally. It's an electronic switchboard. Dial nine for an outside line, and the computer records it automatically. It has to, for the bill.'

Dead end.

'OK,' I said. 'Forget the whole thing.'

'Really?'

'Orders are orders,' I said. 'The alternative is anarchy and chaos.'

I went back to my office and called Rock Creek. I figured Willard would be long gone. He was the type of guy who keeps bankers' hours his whole life. I got hold of a company clerk and asked him to find a copy of the original order moving me from Panama to Bird. It was five minutes before he came back on the line. I spent them reading Summer's lists. They were full of names that meant nothing to me.

'I've got the order here now, sir,' the guy on the phone said.

'Who signed it?' I asked him.

'Colonel Garber, sir.'

'Thank you,' I said, and put the phone down. Then I sat for ten minutes wondering why people were lying to me. Then I forgot all about that question, because my phone rang again and a young MP private on routine base patrol told me we had a homicide victim in the woods. It sounded like a real bad one. My guy had to pause twice to throw up before he got to the end of his report.

EIGHT

MOST RURAL ARMY POSTS ARE PRETTY BIG. EVEN IF THE BUILT infrastructure is compact, there is often a huge acreage of spare land reserved around it. This was my first tour at Fort Bird, but I guessed it would be no exception. It would be like a small neat town surrounded by a county-sized horseshoe-shaped government-owned tract of poor sandy earth with low hills and shallow valleys and a thin covering of trees and scrub. Over the post's long life the trees would have imitated the grey ashes of the Ardennes and the mighty firs of Central Europe and the swaying palms of the Middle East. Whole generations of infantry training theory would have come and gone there. There would be old trenches and foxholes and firing pits. There would be bermed rifle ranges and barbed-wire obstacles and isolated huts where psychiatrists would challenge masculine emotional security. There would be concrete bunkers and exact replicas of government offices where Special Forces would train to rescue hostages. There would be cross-country running routes where out-of-shape boot camp inductees would tire and stagger and where some of them would collapse and die. The whole thing would be ringed by miles of ancient rusty wire and claimed for

110

the DoD for ever by warning notices fixed to every third fence post.

I called a bunch of specialists and went out to the motor pool and found a Humvee that had a working flashlight in the clip on the dash. Then I fired it up and followed the private's directions south and west of the inhabited areas until I was on a rough sandy track leading straight out into the hinterland. The darkness was absolute. I drove more than a mile and then I saw another Humvee's headlights in the distance. The private's vehicle was parked at a sharp angle about twenty feet off the road and its high beams were shining into the trees and casting long evil shadows deep into the woods. The private himself was leaning up against its hood. His head was bowed and he was looking down at the ground.

First question: how does a guy on motor patrol in the dark spot a corpse hidden way the hell out here, deep in the trees?

I parked next to him and took the flashlight out of the clip and slid out into the cold and immediately understood how. There was a trail of clothing starting in the centre of the track. Right on the crown of the camber was a single boot. It was a standard-issue black leather combat boot, old, worn, not very well shined. West of it was a sock, a yard away. Then another boot, another sock, a BDU jacket, an olive drab undershirt. The clothes were all spaced out in a line, like a grotesque parody of the domestic fantasy where you get home and find abandoned lingerie items leading you up the stairs to the bedroom. Except that the jacket and the undershirt were stained dark with blood.

I checked the condition of the ground at the edge of the track. It was rock hard and frosted over. I wasn't going to compromise the scene. I wasn't going to blur any footprints, because there weren't going to be any footprints. So I took a deep breath and followed the trail of clothes to its conclusion. When I got there I understood why my guy had thrown up twice. At his age I might have thrown up three times.

The corpse was face down in the frozen leaf litter at the base of a tree. Naked. Medium height, compact. It was a white guy, but he was mostly covered in blood. There were bone-deep knife cuts all over his arms and shoulders. From behind I could see that his face looked beaten and swollen. His cheeks were protruding. His dog tags were missing. There was a slim leather belt cinched tight around his neck. It had a brass buckle and the long tail looped away from his head. There was some kind of thick pink-white liquid pooled on his back. He had a broken tree limb rammed up his ass. Below it the ground was black with blood. I guessed when we rolled him over we would find that his genitals had been removed.

I backtracked along the trail of clothes and made it to the road. Stepped over next to the MP private. He was still staring down at the ground.

'Where are we exactly?' I asked him.

'Sir?'

'No question we're still on the base?'

He nodded. 'We're a mile inside the fence line. In every direction.'

'OK,' I said. Jurisdiction was clear. Army guy, army property. 'We'll wait here. Nobody gets access in there until I say so. Clear?'

'Sir,' he said.

'You're doing a good job,' I said.

'You think?'

'You're still on your feet,' I said.

I went back to my Humvee and radioed my sergeant. Told her what was up and where and asked her to find Lieutenant Summer and have her call me on the emergency channel. Then I waited. An ambulance arrived two minutes later. Then two Humvees showed up with the crime scene specialists I had called before leaving my office. Guys spilled out. I told them to stand by. There was no burning urgency.

Summer got on the radio within five minutes.

'Dead guy in the woods,' I told her. 'I want you to find that Psy-Ops woman you were telling me about.'

'Lieutenant Colonel Norton?'

'I want you to bring her out here.'

'Willard said you can't work with me.'

'He said I can't involve you in special unit stuff. This is regular police business.'

'Why do you want Norton there?'

'I want to meet her.'

She clicked off and I got out of my truck. Joined the medics and the forensics people. We all stood around in the cold. We kept our engines running to keep the batteries charged and the heaters working. Clouds of diesel smoke drifted and pooled and formed horizontal strata, like smog. I told the crime scene people to start listing the clothing on the road. I told them not to touch it and not to leave the track.

We waited. There was no moon. No stars. No light and no sound beyond our headlights and our idling diesels. I thought about Leon Garber. Korea was one of the biggest branch offices the U.S. Army had to offer. Not the most glamorous, but probably the most active and certainly the most difficult. MP command out there was a feather in anyone's cap. It meant he would probably retire with two stars, which was way more than he could have ever hoped for. If my brother was right and axes were getting ready to fall, then Leon had already come out on the right side of the cut. I was happy for him. For about ten minutes. Then I started looking at his situation from a different perspective. I worried at it for another ten minutes and got nowhere with it.

Summer showed up before I was finished thinking. She was driving a Humvee and she had a bareheaded blonde woman in BDUs about four feet away from her in the front passenger seat. She stopped the truck in the centre of the track with her headlights full on us. She stayed in the vehicle and the blonde got out and scanned the crowd and stepped into the matrix of headlight beams and made straight for me. I saluted her out of courtesy and checked her nametape. It said: *Norton*. She had a light colonel's oak leaves sewn on her lapels. She was a little older than me, but not much. She was tall and thin and had the kind of face that should have made her an actress or a model.

'How can I help you, major?' she said. She sounded like she was from Boston and not very pleased about being dragged outside in the middle of the night.

'Something I need you to see,' I said.

'Why?'

'Maybe you'll have a professional opinion.'

'Why me?'

113

'Because you're here in North Carolina. It would take me hours to get someone from somewhere else.'

'What kind of someone do you need?'

'Someone in your line of work.'

'I'm aware that I work in a classroom,' she said. 'I don't need constant reminders.'

'What?'

'It seems to be a popular sport here, reminding Andrea Norton that she's just a bookish academic, while everybody else is out there busy with the real thing.'

'I wouldn't know about that. I'm new here. I just want first impressions from someone in your line of work, is all.'

'You're not trying to make a point?'

'I'm trying to get some help.'

She made a face. 'OK.'

I offered her my flashlight. 'Follow the trail of clothes to the end. Please don't touch anything. Just fix your first impressions in your mind. Then I'd like to talk to you about them.'

She said nothing. Just took my flashlight from me and set off. She was brightly backlit for the first twenty feet by the MP private's headlights. His Humvee was still facing the woods. Her shadow danced ahead of her. Then she stepped beyond the range of the headlights' illumination and I saw her flashlight beam move onward, bobbing and spearing through the darkness. Then I lost sight of it. All that was visible was a faint reflection from the underside of leafless branches, far in the distance, high in the air.

She was gone about ten minutes. Then I saw the flashlight beam sweeping back towards us. She came out of the woods, retracing her steps. She walked right up to me. She looked pale. She clicked the flashlight off and handed it back.

'My office,' she said. 'In one hour.'

She got back in Summer's Humvee and Summer backed up and turned and accelerated away into the dark.

'OK, guys, go to work,' I said. I sat in my truck and watched drifting smoke and flashlight beams quartering the ground and bright blue camera flashes freezing the motion all around me. I radioed my sergeant again and told her to get the base mortuary opened up. Told her to have a pathologist standing by, first thing in the morning. After thirty minutes the ambulance backed up onto the shoulder and my guys loaded a sheet-draped shape into it. They closed the doors and slapped on them and the truck took off. Clear plastic evidence bags were filled and labelled. Crime scene tape was wound between tree trunks. It was tied off in a rough rectangle maybe forty yards by fifty.

I left them to finish up by themselves and drove back through the dark to the main post buildings. Checked with a sentry and got directions to the Psy-Ops facility. It was a low brick structure with green doors and windows that might have housed the quartermaster offices way back when it was built. It was set at a distance from post headquarters, maybe halfway to where Special Forces bunked. There was darkness and silence all around it but there was a light burning in the central hallway and in one of the office windows. I parked my truck and went inside. Made it through gloomy tiled corridors and came to a door with a pebble-glass window set in its upper half. The glass had light behind it and *Lt/Col. A. Norton* stencilled on it. I knocked and went in. I saw a small neat office. It was clean and it smelled feminine. I didn't salute again. I figured we were past that point.

Norton was behind a big oak army-issue desk and she had it covered with open textbooks. She had so many on the go that she had taken her telephone off the desk and put it down on the floor. She had a yellow legal pad in front of her with hand-written notes on it. The pad was in a pool of light from her desk lamp and its colour was reflected upward into her hair.

'Hello,' she said.

I sat down in her visitor's chair.

'Who was he?' she asked.

'I don't know,' I said. 'I don't think we'll get a visual ID. He was too badly beaten. We'll have to use fingerprints. Or teeth. If he's got any left in there.'

'Why did you want me to look at him?'

'I told you why. I wanted your opinion.'

'Why did you think I would have an opinion?'

'Seemed to me there were elements in there that you would understand.'

'I'm not a criminal profiler.'

'I don't want you to be. I just want some input, fast. I want to know if I'm starting out in the right direction.'

She nodded. Swept her hair back off her face.

'The obvious conclusion is that he was a homosexual,' she said. 'Possibly killed because of it. Or if not, then with full awareness of it on the part of his attackers.'

I nodded.

'There was genital amputation,' she said.

'You checked?'

'I moved him a little,' she said. 'I'm sorry. I know you asked me not to.'

I looked at her. She hadn't been wearing gloves. She was a tough lady. Maybe her classroom-bound reputation was undeserved.

'Don't worry about it,' I said.

'My guess is you'll find his testicles and his penis in his mouth. I doubt if his cheeks would have swelled that much simply from a beating. It's an obvious symbolic statement, from the point of view of a homophobic attacker. Removing the deviant organs, simulating oral sex.'

I nodded.

'Likewise the nudity and the missing dog tags,' she said. 'Removing the army from the deviant is the same thing as removing the deviant from the army.'

I nodded.

'The foreign object insertion speaks for itself,' she said. 'In the anus.'

I nodded.

'And then there's the fluid on his back,' she said.

'Yogurt,' I said.

'Probably strawberry,' she said. 'Or maybe raspberry. It's the old joke. How does a gay man fake an orgasm?'

'He groans a bit,' I said. 'And then he throws yogurt on his lover's back.'

'Yes,' she said. She didn't smile. And she watched me, to see if I would.

'What about the cuts and the beating?' I said.

'Hate,' she said.

116

'And the belt around the neck?'

She shrugged. 'It's suggestive of an auto-erotic technique. Partial asphyxiation creates heightened pleasure during orgasm.'

I nodded.

'OK,' I said.

'OK what?'

'Those were your first impressions. Do you have an opinion based on them?'

'Do you?' she asked.

'Yes,' I said.

'You first.'

'I think it's bogus.'

'Why?'

'Too much going on,' I said. 'There were six things there. The nudity, the missing tags, the genitals, the tree branch, the yogurt, and the belt. Any two would have done it. Maybe three. It's like they were *trying* to make a point, instead of just going ahead and making one. Maybe trying too hard.'

Norton said nothing.

'Too much,' I said again. 'Like shooting someone, then strangling him, then stabbing him, then drowning him, then suffocating him, then beating him to death. It's like they were decorating a damn Christmas tree with clues.'

She stayed quiet. She was watching me, deep inside her pool of light. Maybe assessing me.

'I have my doubts about the belt,' she said. 'Auto-eroticism isn't exclusively homosexual. All men have the same orgasms physiologically, gay or not.'

'The whole thing was faked,' I said.

She nodded, finally.

'I agree with you,' she said. 'You're a smart guy.'

'For a cop?'

She didn't smile. 'But we know as officers that to permit homosexuals to serve is illegal. So we better be sure we're not letting a defence of the army cloud our judgement.'

'It's my job to protect the army,' I said.

'Exactly,' Norton said.

I shrugged. 'But I'm not taking a position. I'm not saying this

117

guy definitely wasn't gay. Maybe he was. I really don't care. And maybe his attackers knew, maybe they didn't. I'm saying either way, that's not why they killed him. But they wanted it to look like the reason. But they weren't really *feeling* it. They were feeling something else. So they larded on the clues, in a rather self-conscious way.'

Then I paused.

'In a rather academic way,' I said.

She stiffened.

'An academic way?' she said.

'Do you guys teach anything about this kind of stuff in class?'

'We don't teach people how to kill,' she said.

'That's not what I asked.'

She nodded. 'We talk about it. We have to. Cutting off your enemy's dick is as basic as it gets. It's happened all through history. Happened all through Vietnam. Afghan women have been doing it to captured Soviet soldiers for the last ten years. We talk about what it symbolizes, what it communicates, and the fear it creates. There are whole books about the fear of grotesque wounds. It's always a message to the target population. We talk about violation with foreign objects. We talk about the deliberate display of violated bodies. The trail of abandoned clothing is a classic touch.'

'Do you talk about yogurt?'

She shook her head. 'But that's a very old joke.'

'And the asphyxiation thing?'

'Not on the Psy-Ops courses. But most of the people here can read magazines. Or they can watch porn on videotape.'

'Do you talk about questioning an enemy's sexuality?'

'Of course we do. Impugning an enemy's sexuality is the whole point of our course. His sexual orientation, his virility, his capability, his capacity. It's a core tactic. It always has been, everywhere, throughout history. It's designed to work both ways. It diminishes him, and it builds us up by comparison.'

I said nothing.

She looked right at me. 'Are you asking me if I recognized the fruits of our lessons, out there in the woods?'

'I guess I am,' I said.

'You didn't really want my opinion, did you?' she said. 'That was all preamble. You already knew what you were seeing.'

I nodded. 'I'm a smart guy, for a cop.'

'The answer is no,' she said. 'I did not recognize the fruits of our lessons, out there in the woods. Not specifically.'

'But possibly?'

'Anything's possible.'

'Did you meet General Kramer when you were at Fort Irwin?' I asked.

'Once or twice,' she said. 'Why?'

'When did you last see him?'

'I don't remember,' she said.

'Not recently?'

'No,' she said. 'Not recently. Why?'

'How did you meet him?'

'Professionally,' she said.

'You teach your stuff to Armored Branch?'

'Irwin isn't exclusively Armored Branch,' she said. 'It's the National Training Center too, don't forget. People used to come to us there. Now we go to them.'

I said nothing.

'Does it surprise you we taught Armored people?'

I shrugged again. 'A little, I guess. If I was riding around in a seventy-ton tank, I don't suppose I'd feel a need for any more of a psychological edge.'

She still didn't smile. 'We taught them. As I recall General Kramer didn't like it if the infantry was getting things his people weren't. It was an intense rivalry.'

'Who do you teach now?'

'Delta Force,' she said. 'Exclusively.'

'Thank you for your help,' I said.

'I didn't recognize anything tonight that we would take responsibility for.'

'Not specifically.'

'It was psychologically generic,' she said.

'OK,' I said.

'And I resent being asked.'

'OK,' I said again. 'Goodnight, ma'am.'

I got up out of the chair and headed for the door.

'What was the real reason?' she asked. 'If the display we saw was bogus?'

'I don't know,' I said. 'I'm not that smart.'

I stopped in my outer office and the sergeant with the baby son gave me coffee. Then I went into my inner office and found Summer waiting for me there. She had come to collect her lists, because the Kramer case was closed.

'Did you check the other women?' I asked her. 'Apart from Norton?'

She nodded. 'They all have alibis. It's the best night of the year for alibis. Nobody spends New Year's Eve alone.'

'I did,' I said.

She said nothing back. I butted the papers into a neat stack and put them back inside their folder and unclipped the note off the front. *Hope your mom was OK.* I dropped the note in my drawer and handed the file to her.

'What did Norton tell you?' she asked.

'She agreed with me that it was homicide dressed up to look like gay-bashing. I asked her if any of the symbols came from Psy-Ops classes and she didn't really say yes or no. She said they were psychologically generic. She resented being asked.'

'So what now?'

I yawned. I was tired. 'We'll work it like we work any of them. We don't even know who the victim is yet. I guess we'll find out tomorrow. On deck at seven, OK?'

'OK,' she said, and headed for my door, carrying her file.

'I called Rock Creek,' I said. 'Asked a clerk to find their copy of the order bringing me here from Panama.'

'And?'

'He said it's got Garber's signature on it.'

'But?'

'That's not possible. Garber got me on the phone on New Year's Eve and was surprised I was here.'

'Why would a clerk lie?'

'I don't think a clerk would. I think the signature is a forgery.'

'Is that conceivable?'

'It's the only explanation. Garber couldn't have forgotten he'd transferred me here forty-eight hours previously.'

'So what's this all about?'

'I have no idea. Someone somewhere is playing chess. My brother told me I should find out who wants me here bad enough to pull me out of Panama and replace me with an asshole. So I tried to find out. And now I'm thinking maybe we should be asking the same question about Garber. Who wants him out of Rock Creek bad enough to replace *him* with an asshole?'

'But Korea has to be a genuine merit promotion, doesn't it?'

'Garber deserves it, no question,' I said. 'Except it's too early. It's a one-star job. DoD has to bring it to the Senate. That process happens in the fall, not in January. This was a panic move, spur of the moment.'

'But that would be pointless chess,' Summer said. 'Why bring you in and pull him out? The two moves neutralize each other.'

'So maybe there are two people playing. Like a tug of war. Good guy, bad guy. Win one, lose one.'

'But the bad guy could have won both, easily. He could have discharged you. Or sent you to prison. He's got the civilian complaint to work with.'

I said nothing.

'It doesn't add up,' Summer said. 'Whoever's playing on your side is willing to let Garber go but is powerful enough to keep you here, even with the civilian complaint on the table. Powerful enough that Willard knew he couldn't proceed against you, even though he probably wanted to. You know what that means?'

'Yes,' I said. 'I do.'

She looked straight at me.

'It means you're seen as more important than Garber,' she said. 'Garber's gone, and you're still here.'

Then she looked away and went quiet.

'Permission to speak freely, lieutenant,' I said.

She looked back at me.

'You're not more important than Garber,' she said. 'You can't be.'

I yawned again.

'No argument from me,' I said. 'Not on that particular subject. This is not about a choice between me and Garber.'

121

She paused. Then she nodded.

'No,' she said. 'It isn't. This is about a choice between Fort Bird and Rock Creek. Fort Bird is seen as more important. What's happening here on the post is seen as more sensitive than what's happening at special unit headquarters.'

'Agreed,' I said. 'But what the hell is happening here?'

NINE

I TOOK THE FIRST TENTATIVE STEP TOWARDS FINDING OUT AT ONE minute past seven the next morning, in Fort Bird's mortuary. I had slept for three hours and I hadn't eaten breakfast. There aren't many hard and fast rules involved in military crime investigation. Mostly we depend on instinct and improvisation. But one of the few rules that exist is: you don't eat before you walk into an army post-mortem.

So I spent the breakfast hour with the crime scene report. It was a fairly thick file, but it had no useful information in it. It listed all the recovered uniform items and described them in minute detail. It described the corpse. It listed times and temperatures. All the thousands of words were backed by dozens of Polaroid photographs. But neither the words nor the pictures told me what I needed to know.

I put the file in my desk drawer and called the Provost Marshal's office for any AWOL or UA reports. The dead guy might have been missed already, and we might have been able to pick up on his identity that way. But there were no reports. Nothing out of the ordinary. The post was humming along with all its ducks in a row.

I walked out into the morning cold.

The mortuary had been purpose-built during the Eisenhower administration and it was still fit for its purpose. We weren't looking for a high degree of sophistication. This wasn't the civilian world. We knew last night's victim hadn't slipped on a banana skin. I didn't much care which particular injury had been the fatal one. All I wanted to know was an approximate time of death, and who he was.

There was a tiled lobby inside the main doors with exits to the left, the centre, and the right. If you went left, you found the offices. If you went right, you found cold storage. I went straight ahead, where knives cut and saws whined and water sluiced.

There were two dished metal tables set in the middle of the room. They had bright lights above them and noisy drains below. They were surrounded by greengrocer scales hanging on chains ready to weigh excised organs, and by rolling steel carts with empty glass jars ready to receive them, and other carts with rows of knives and saws and shears and pliers lying ready for use on green canvas sheets. The whole place was glazed with white subway tiles and the air was cold and sweet with the smell of formaldehyde.

The right-hand table was clean and empty. The left-hand table was surrounded by people. There was a pathologist and an assistant and a clerk taking notes. Summer was there, standing back, observing. They were maybe halfway through the process. The tools were all in use. Some of the glass jars were filled. The drain was sucking loudly. I could see the corpse's legs through the crowd. They had been washed. They looked blue-white under the lamps above them. All the smeared dirt and blood was gone.

I stood next to Summer and took a look. The dead guy was on his back. They had taken the top of his skull off. They had cut around the centre of his forehead and peeled the skin of his face down. It was lying there inside out, like a blanket pulled down on a bed. It reached to his chin. His cheekbones and his eyeballs were exposed. The pathologist was dissecting his brain, looking for something. He had used the saw on his skull and popped the top off like a lid.

'What's the story?' I asked him.

'We got fingerprints,' he said.

'I faxed them in,' Summer said. 'We'll know today.'

'Cause of death?'

'Blunt trauma,' the doctor said. 'To the back of the head. Three heavy blows, with something like a tyre iron, I should think. All this dramatic stuff is post-mortem. Pure window dressing.'

'Any defensive injuries?'

'Not a thing,' the doctor said. 'This was a surprise attack. Out of the blue. There was no fight, no struggle.'

'How many assailants?'

'I'm not a magician. The fatal blows were probably all delivered by the same individual. I can't tell if there were others standing around and watching.'

'Best guess?'

'I'm a scientist, not a guesser.'

'One assailant only,' Summer said. 'Just a feeling.'

I nodded.

'Time of death?' I asked.

'Hard to be sure,' the doctor said. 'Nine or ten last night, probably. But don't take that to the bank.'

I nodded again. Nine or ten would make sense. Well after dark, several hours before any reasonable expectation of discovery. Plenty of time for the bad guy to lure him out there, and then to be somewhere else when the alarms sounded.

'Was he killed at the scene?' I asked.

The pathologist nodded.

'Or very close to it,' he said. 'No medical signs to suggest otherwise.'

'OK,' I said. I glanced around. The broken tree limb was lying on a cart. Next to it was a jar with a penis and two testicles in it.

'In his mouth?' I said.

The pathologist nodded again. Said nothing.

'What kind of a knife?'

'Probably a K-bar,' he said.

'Great,' I said. K-bars had been manufactured by the tens of millions for the last fifty years. They were as common as medals.

'The knife was used by a right-handed person,' the doctor said.

125

'And the tyre iron?'

'Same.'

'OK,' I said.

'The fluid was yogurt,' the doctor said.

'Strawberry or raspberry?'

'I didn't do a taste test.'

Next to the jars of organs was a short stack of four Polaroid photographs. They were all of the fatal wound site. The first one was as-discovered. The guy's hair was relatively long and dirty and matted with blood and I couldn't make out much detail. The second was with the blood and dirt rinsed away. The third was with the hair cut back with scissors. The fourth was with the hair completely shaved away, with a razor.

'How about a crowbar?' I asked.

'Possible,' the doctor said. 'Maybe better than a tyre iron. I took a plaster cast, anyway. You bring me the weapon, I'll tell you yes or no.'

I stepped in a little and took a closer look. The corpse was very clean. It was grey and white and pink. It smelled faintly of soap, as well as blood and other rich organic odours. The groin was a mess. Like a butcher's shop. The knife cuts on the arms and the shoulders were deep and obvious. I could see muscle and bone. The edges of the wounds were blue and cold. The blade had gone right through a tattoo on his left upper arm. An eagle was holding a scroll with *Mother* written on it. Overall, the guy was not a pleasant sight. But he was in better shape than I had feared he would be.

'I thought there would be more swelling and bruising,' I said.

The pathologist glanced at me.

'I told you,' he said. 'All the drama was after he was dead. No heartbeat, no blood pressure, no circulation, therefore no swelling and no contusions. Not much bleeding either. It was just leaking out by gravity. If he'd been alive when they cut him, it would have been running like a river.'

He turned back to the table and finished up inside the guy's brain pan and put the lid of bone back where it belonged. He tapped it twice to get a good seal and wiped the leaky join with a sponge. Then he pulled the guy's face back into place. Poked and prodded and smoothed with his fingers and when he took his hands away I saw the Special Forces sergeant I had spoken to in the strip club, staring blindly upward into the bright lights above him.

I took a Humvee and drove past Andrea Norton's Psy-Ops school to the Delta Force station. It was pretty much self-contained in what had been a prison back before the army collected all its miscreants together at Fort Leavenworth in Kansas. The old wire and the walls suited its current purpose. There was a giant WW2-era airplane hangar next to it. It looked like it had been dragged in from some closed base and bolted back together to house their racks of stores and their trucks and their up-armoured Humvees and maybe even a couple of fast-response helicopters.

The sentry on the inner gate let me in and I went straight to the adjutant's office. Seven thirty in the morning, and it was already lit up and busy, which told me something. The adjutant was at his desk. He was a captain. In the upside-down world of Delta Force the sergeants are the stars, and the officers stay home and do the housework.

'You got anyone missing?' I asked him.

He looked away, which told me something more.

'I assume you know I do,' he said. 'Otherwise why would you be here?'

'You got a name for me?'

'A name? I assumed you had arrested him for something.'

'This is not about an arrest,' I said.

'So what's it about?'

'Does this guy get arrested a lot?'

'No. He's a fine soldier.'

'What's his name?'

The captain didn't answer. Just leaned down and opened a drawer and pulled a file. Handed it to me. Like all the Delta files I had ever seen, it was heavily sanitized for public consumption. There were just two pages in it. The first was a name-rank-and-number ID sheet and a bare-bones career summary for a guy called Christopher Carbone. He was an unmarried sixteen-year veteran. He had served four years in an infantry division, four in an airborne division, four in a Ranger

127

company, and four in Special Forces Detachment D. He was five years older than me. He was a Sergeant First Class. There were no theatre details and no mention of awards or decorations.

The second sheet contained ten inky fingerprints and a colour photograph of the man I had spoken to in the bar and just left on the mortuary slab.

'Where is he?' the captain asked. 'What happened?'

'Someone killed him,' I said.

'What?'

'Homicide,' I said.

'When?'

'Last night. Nine or ten o'clock.'

'Where?'

'Edge of the woods.'

'What woods?'

'Our woods. On post.'

'Jesus Christ. Why?'

I put the file back together and slipped it under my arm.

'I don't know why,' I said. 'Yet.'

'Jesus Christ,' he said again. 'Who did it?'

'I don't know,' I said. 'Yet.'

'Jesus Christ,' the guy said, for the third time.

'Next of kin?' I asked.

The captain paused. Breathed out.

'I think he has a mother somewhere,' he said. 'I'll let you know.'

'Don't let *me* know,' I said. 'You'll be the one making the call.'

He said nothing.

'Did Carbone have enemies here?' I asked.

'None that I knew about.'

'Any points of friction?'

'Like what?'

'Any lifestyle issues?'

He stared at me. 'What are you saying?'

'Was he gay?'

'What? Of course not.'

I said nothing.

'You're saying Carbone was a fag?' the captain whispered.

I pictured Carbone in my mind, lounging six feet from the strip club runway, six feet from whoever was crawling around at the time on her elbows and knees with her ass up in the air and her nipples brushing the stage, a long-neck bottle in his hand and a big smile on his face. It seemed like a weird way for a gay man to spend his leisure time. But then I pictured the detachment in his eyes and his embarrassed gesture as he waved the brunette hooker away.

'I don't know what Carbone was,' I said.

'Then keep your damn mouth shut,' his captain said. 'Sir.'

I took Carbone's file with me back to the mortuary and collected Summer and took her to the O Club for breakfast. We sat on our own in a corner, far from everyone else. I ate eggs and bacon and toast. Summer ate oatmeal and fruit and glanced through the file. I drank coffee. Summer drank tea.

'The pathologist is calling it gay-bashing,' she said. 'He thinks it's obvious.'

'He's wrong.'

'Carbone's not married.'

'Neither am I,' I said. 'Neither are you. Are you gay?'

'No.'

'There you go.'

'But misdirection has to be based on something real, right? I mean, if they knew he was a gambler, for instance, they might have crammed IOU slips in his mouth or thrown playing cards all around the place. Then we might have thought it was about gambling debts. You see what I mean? It just doesn't work if it's not based on anything. Something that can be disproved in five minutes looks stupid, not clever.'

'Your best guess?'

'He was gay, and someone knew it, but it wasn't the reason.'

I nodded.

'It wasn't the reason,' I said. 'Let's say he *was* gay. He was in sixteen years. He survived most of the seventies and all of the eighties. So why would it happen now? Times are changing, getting better, he's getting better at hiding it, going out to strip joints with his buddies. No reason for it to happen now, all of a sudden. It would have happened before. Four years ago, or

129

eight, or twelve, or sixteen. Whenever he joined a new unit and new people got to know him.'

'So what was the reason?'

'No idea.'

'Whatever, it could be embarrassing. Just like Kramer and his motel.'

I nodded again. 'Bird seems to be a very embarrassing place.'

'You think this is why you're here? Carbone?'

'It's possible. Depends on what he represents.'

I asked Summer to file and forward all the appropriate notifications and reports and I headed back to my office. Rumour was spreading fast. I found three Delta sergeants waiting for me, looking for information. They were typical Special Forces guys. Small, lean, whippy, slightly unkempt, hard as nails. Two of them were older than the third. The young one was wearing a beard. He was tan, like he was just back from somewhere hot. They were all pacing in my outer office. My sergeant with the baby son was there with them. I guessed she was pulling a swing shift. She was looking at them like they might have been alternating spells of pacing with spells of hitting on her. She looked very civilized, in comparison to them. Almost genteel. I ushered them all into my inner office and closed the door and sat down at my desk and left them standing in front of it.

'Is it true about Carbone?' one of the older two said.

'He was killed,' I said. 'Don't know who, don't know why.'

'When?'

'Last night, nine or ten o'clock.'

'Where?'

'Here.'

'This is a closed post.'

I nodded. 'The perp wasn't a member of the general public.'

'We heard he was messed up good.'

'Pretty good.'

'When are you going to know who it was?'

'Soon, I hope.'

'You got leads?'

'Nothing specific.'

'When you know, are we going to know too?'

130

'You want to?'

'You bet your ass.'

'Why?'

'You know why,' the guy said.

I nodded. Gay or straight, Carbone was a member of the world's most fearsome gang. His buddies were going to stand up for him. I felt a little envious for a second. If I got offed in the woods late one night, I doubted if three tough guys would go straight to someone's office, eight in the morning, champing at the bit, ready for revenge. Then I looked at the three of them again and thought, *this particular perp could be in a shitload of trouble. All I'd have to do is drop a name.*

'I need to ask you some cop questions,' I said. I asked them all the usual stuff. Did Carbone have any enemies? Had there been any disputes? Threats? Fights? The three guys all shook their heads and answered every question in the negative.

'Anything else?' I asked. 'Anything that put him at risk?'

'Like what?' one of the older two asked back, quietly.

'Like anything,' I said. It was as far as I wanted to go.

'No,' they all said.

'Got any theories?' I asked.

'Look at the Rangers,' the young one said. 'Find someone who failed Delta training, and thinks he still has a point to prove.'

Then they left, and I sat there chewing on their final comment. A Ranger with a point to prove? I doubted it. Not plausible. Delta sergeants don't go out in the woods with people they don't know and get hit on the back of the head. They train long and hard to make such eventualities very unlikely, even impossible. If a Ranger had picked a fight with Carbone, it would have been the Ranger we found at the base of the tree. If two Rangers had gone out there with him, we'd have found two Rangers dead. Or at the very least we would have found defensive injuries on Carbone himself. He wouldn't have gone down easily.

So he went out there with someone he knew and trusted. I pictured him at ease, maybe chatting, maybe smiling like he had done in the bar in town. Maybe leading the way somewhere, his back to his attacker, suspecting nothing. Then I

131

pictured a tyre iron or a crowbar being fumbled out from under a coat, swinging, hitting with a crunching impact. Then again. And again. It had taken three hard blows to put him down. Three surprise blows. And a guy like Carbone doesn't get surprised very often.

My phone rang. I picked it up. It was Colonel Willard, the asshole in Garber's office, up in Rock Creek.

'Where are you?' he asked.

'In my office,' I said. 'How else would I be answering my phone?'

'Stay there,' he said. 'Don't go anywhere, don't do anything, don't call anyone. Those are my direct orders. Just sit there quietly and wait.'

'For what?'

'I'm on my way down.'

He clicked off. I put the phone back in its cradle.

I stayed there. I didn't go anywhere, I didn't do anything, I didn't call anyone. My sergeant brought me a cup of coffee. I accepted it. Willard hadn't told me to die of thirst.

After an hour I heard a voice in the outer office and then the young Delta sergeant came back in, alone. The one with the beard and the tan. I told him to take a seat and pondered my orders. *Don't go anywhere, don't do anything, don't call anyone.* I guessed talking with the guy would amount to doing something, which would contravene the *don't do anything* part of the command. But then, breathing was doing something, technically. So was metabolizing. My hair was growing, my beard was growing, all twenty of my nails were growing, I was losing weight. It was impossible not to do *anything.* So I decided that component of the order was purely rhetorical.

'Help you, sergeant?' I said.

'I think Carbone was gay,' the sergeant said.

'You *think* he was?'

'OK, he was.'

'Who else knew?'

'All of us.'

'And?'

'And nothing. I thought you should know, is all.'

132

'You think it has a bearing?'

He shook his head. 'We were comfortable with it. And whoever killed him wasn't one of us. It wasn't anyone in the unit. That's not possible. We don't do stuff like that. Outside the unit, nobody knew. Therefore it wasn't a factor.'

'So why tell me?'

'Because you're bound to find out. I wanted you to be ready for it. I didn't want it to be a surprise.'

'Because?'

'Then maybe you can keep it quiet. Since it's not a factor.'

I said nothing.

'It would trash his memory,' the sergeant said. 'And that's wrong. He was a nice guy and a good soldier. Being gay shouldn't be a crime.'

'I agree,' I said.

'The army needs to change.'

'The army hates change.'

'They say it damages unit cohesion,' he said. 'They should have come and seen our squadron working. With Carbone right there in it.'

'I can't keep it quiet,' I said. 'Maybe I would if I could. But the way the crime scene looked, everyone's going to get the message.'

'What? It was like a sex crime? You didn't say that before.'

'I was trying to keep it quiet,' I said.

'But nobody knew. Not outside the unit.'

'Someone must have,' I said. 'Or else the perp is in your unit.'

'That's not possible. No way, no how.'

'One thing or the other has got to be possible,' I said. 'Was he seeing anyone on the outside?'

'No, never.'

'So he was celibate for sixteen years?'

The guy paused a beat.

'I guess I don't really know,' he said.

'Someone knew,' I said. 'But actually I don't think it was a factor. I think someone just tried to make it look like it was. Maybe we can make that clear, at least.'

The sergeant shook his head. 'It'll be the only thing anyone remembers about him.'

133

'I'm sorry,' I said.

'I'm not gay,' he said.

'I don't really care either way.'

'I've got a wife and a kid.'

He left me with that information and I went back to obeying Willard's orders.

I spent the time thinking. There had been no weapon recovered at the scene. No significant forensics. No threads of clothing snagged on a bush, no footprints in the earth, none of his attacker's skin under Carbone's fingernails. All of that was easily explicable. The weapon had been taken away by the attacker, who had probably been wearing BDUs, which the Department of the Army specifies very carefully just so that they won't fall apart and leave threads all over the place. Textile mills across the nation have stringent quality targets to meet, in terms of wear and tear standards for military twill and poplin. The earth was frozen hard, so footprints were impossible. North Carolina probably had a reliable frost window of about a month, and we were smack in the middle of it. And it had been a surprise attack. Carbone had been given no time to turn around and claw and kick at his assailant.

So there was no material information. But we had some advantages. We had a fixed pool of possible suspects. It was a closed base, and the army is pretty good at recording who was where, at all times. We could start with yards of print-out paper and go through each name, on a simple binary basis, possible or not possible. Then we could collate all the possibles and go to work with the holy trinity of detectives everywhere: means, motive, opportunity. Means and opportunity wouldn't signify much. By definition nobody would be on the possibles list unless they had been proved to have opportunity. And everybody in the army was physically capable of swinging a tyre iron or a crowbar against the back of an unsuspecting victim's head. It was probably a rough equivalent of the most basic entry requirement.

So it would end up with motive, which is where it had started for me. What was the reason?

*   *   *

134

I sat for another hour. Didn't go anywhere, didn't do anything, didn't call anyone. My sergeant brought me more coffee. I mentioned that she might call Lieutenant Summer for me and suggest she stop by.

Summer showed up within five minutes. I had a whole raft of things to tell her, but she had anticipated every one of them. She had ordered a list of all base personnel, plus a copy of the gate log so we could add and subtract names as appropriate. She had arranged for Carbone's quarters to be sealed, pending a search. She had arranged an interview with his CO to develop a better picture of his personal and professional life.

'Excellent,' I said.

'What's this thing with Willard?' she asked.

'A pissing contest, probably,' I said. 'Important case like this, he wants to come down and direct things personally. To remind me I'm under a cloud.'

But I was wrong.

Willard finally showed after a total of exactly four hours. I heard his voice in the outer office. I was pretty sure my sergeant wasn't offering him coffee. She had better instincts than that. My door opened and he came in. He didn't look at me. Just closed the door behind him and turned around and sat down in my visitor's chair. Immediately started up with the shuffling thing. He was going at it hard and plucking at the knees of his pants like they were burning his skin.

'Yesterday,' he said. 'I want a complete record of your movements. I want to hear it from your own lips.'

'You're down here to ask *me* questions?'

'Yes,' he said.

I shrugged.

'I was on a plane until two,' I said. 'I was with you until five.'

'And then?'

'I got back here at eleven.'

'Six hours? I did it in four.'

'You drove, presumably. I took two buses and hitched a ride.'

'After that?'

'I spoke to my brother on the phone,' I said.

'I remember your brother,' Willard said. 'I worked with him.'

135

I nodded. 'He mentioned that.'

'And then what?'

'I spoke to Lieutenant Summer,' I said. 'Socially.'

'And then?'

'Carbone's body was discovered about midnight.'

He nodded and twitched and shuffled and looked uncomfortable.

'Did you keep your bus tickets?' he said.

'I doubt it,' I said.

He smiled. 'Remember who gave you a ride to the post?'

'I doubt it. Why?'

'Because I might need to know. To prove I didn't make a mistake.'

I said nothing.

'*You* made mistakes,' he said.

'Did I?'

He nodded. 'I can't decide whether you're an idiot or whether you're doing this on purpose.'

'Doing what?'

'Are you *trying* to embarrass the army?'

'What?'

'What's the big picture here, major?' he said.

'You tell me, colonel.'

'The Cold War is ending. Therefore there are big changes coming. The status quo will not be an option. Therefore we've got every part of the military trying to stand tall and make the cut. And you know what?'

'What?'

'The army is always at the bottom of the pile. The air force has got all those glamorous airplanes. The navy has got submarines and carriers. The Marines are always untouchable. And we're stuck down there in the mud, literally. The bottom of the pile. The army is *boring*, Reacher. That's the view in Washington.'

'So?'

'This Carbone guy was a shirtlifter. He was a damn *fudgepacker*, for Christ's sake. An elite unit has got *perverts* in it? You think the army needs for people to know that? At a time like this? You should have written him up as a training accident.'

136

'That wouldn't have been true.'

'Who cares?'

'He wasn't killed because of his orientation.'

'Of course he was.'

'I do this stuff for a living,' I said. 'And I say he wasn't.'

He glared at me. Went quiet for a moment.

'OK,' he said. 'We'll come back to that. Who else but you saw the body?'

'My guys,' I said. 'Plus a Psy-Ops light colonel I wanted an opinion from. Plus the pathologist.'

He nodded. 'You deal with your guys. I'll tell Psy-Ops and the doctor.'

'Tell them what?'

'That we're writing it up as a training accident. They'll understand. No harm, no foul. No investigation.'

'You're kidding.'

'You think the army wants this to get around? Now? That Delta had an illegal soldier for four years? Are you nuts?'

'The sergeants want an investigation.'

'I'm pretty sure their CO won't. Believe me. You can take that as gospel.'

'You'll have to give me a direct order,' I said. 'Words of one syllable.'

'Watch my lips,' he said. 'Do not investigate the fag. Write a situation report indicating that he died in a training accident. A night manoeuvre, a run, an exercise, anything. He tripped and fell and hit his head. Case closed. That is a direct order.'

'I'll need it in writing,' I said.

'Grow up,' he said.

We sat quiet for a moment or two, just glaring at each other across the desk. I sat still, and Willard rocked and plucked. I clenched my fist, out of his sight. I imagined smashing a straight right to the centre of his chest. I figured I could stop his lousy heart with a single blow. I could write it up as a training accident. I could say he had been practising getting in and out of his chair, and he had slipped and caught his sternum on the corner of the desk.

'What was the time of death?' he asked.

'Nine or ten last night,' I said.

'And you were off post until eleven?'

'Asked and answered,' I said.

'Can you prove that?'

I thought of the gate guards in their booth. They had logged me in.

'Do I have to?' I said.

He went quiet again. Leaned to his left in the chair.

'Next item,' he said. 'You claim the butt-bandit wasn't killed because he was a butt-bandit. What's your evidence?'

'The crime scene was overdone,' I said.

'To obscure the real motive?'

I nodded. 'That's my judgement.'

'What was the real motive?'

'I don't know. That would have required an investigation.'

'Let's speculate,' Willard said. 'Let's assume the hypothetical perpetrator would have benefited from the homicide. Tell me how.'

'The usual way,' I said. 'By preventing some future action on Sergeant Carbone's part. Or to cover up a crime that Sergeant Carbone was a party to or had knowledge of.'

'To silence him, in other words.'

'To dead-end something,' I said. 'That would be my guess.'

'And you do this stuff for a living.'

'Yes,' I said. 'I do.'

'How would you have located this person?'

'By conducting an investigation.'

Willard nodded. 'And when you found this person, hypothetically, assuming you were able to, what would you have done?'

'I would have taken him into custody,' I said. *Protective custody*, I thought. I pictured Carbone's squadron buddies in my mind, pacing anxiously, ready to lock and load.

'And your suspect pool would have been whoever was on post at the time?'

I nodded. Lieutenant Summer was probably struggling with reams of print-out paper even as we spoke.

'Verified via strength lists and gate logs,' I said.

'Facts,' Willard said. 'I would have thought that facts would be very important to someone who does this stuff for a living. This

138

post covers nearly a hundred thousand acres. It was last strung with perimeter wire in 1943. Those are facts. I discovered them with very little trouble, and you should have too. Doesn't it occur to you that not everyone on the post has to come through the main gate? Doesn't it occur to you that someone recorded as *not* being here could have slipped in through the wire?'

'Unlikely,' I said. 'It would have given him a walk of well over two miles, in pitch dark, and we run random motor patrols all night.'

'The patrols might have missed a trained man.'

'Unlikely,' I said again. 'And how would he have rendez-voused with Sergeant Carbone?'

'Prearranged location.'

'It wasn't a location,' I said. 'It was just a spot near the track.'

'Map reference, then.'

'Unlikely,' I said, for the third time.

'But possible?'

'Anything's possible.'

'So a man could have met with the shirtlifter, then killed him, then gotten back out through the wire, and then walked around to the main gate, and then signed in?'

'Anything's possible,' I said again.

'What kind of timescale are we looking at? Between killing him and signing in?'

'I don't know. I would have to work out the distance he walked.'

'Maybe he ran.'

'Maybe he did.'

'In which case he would have been out of breath when he passed the gate.'

I said nothing.

'Best guess,' Willard said. 'How much time?'

'An hour or two.'

He nodded. 'So if the fairy was offed at nine or ten, the killer could have been logging in at eleven?'

'Possible,' I said.

'And the motive would have been to dead-end something.'

I nodded. Said nothing.

'And you took six hours to complete a four-hour journey,

thereby leaving a potential two-hour gap, which you explain with the vague claim that you took a slow route.'

I said nothing.

'And you just agreed that a two-hour window is generous in terms of getting the deed done. In particular the two hours between nine and eleven, which by chance are the same two hours that you can't account for.'

I said nothing. He smiled.

'And you arrived at the gate out of breath,' he said. 'I checked.'

I didn't reply.

'But what would have been your motive?' he said. 'I assume you didn't know Carbone well. I assume you don't move in the same social circles that he did. At least I sincerely hope you don't.'

'You're wasting your time,' I said. 'And you're making a big mistake. Because you really don't want to make an enemy out of me.'

'Don't I?'

'No,' I said. 'You really don't.'

'What do you need dead-ended?' he asked me.

I said nothing.

'Here's an interesting fact,' Willard said. 'Sergeant First Class Christopher Carbone was the soldier who lodged the complaint against you.'

He proved it to me by unfolding a copy of the complaint from his pocket. He smoothed it out and passed it across my desk. There was a reference number at the top and then a date and a place and a time. The date was January 2nd, the place was Fort Bird's Provost Marshal's office, and the time was 0845. Then came two paragraphs of sworn affidavit. I glanced through some of the stiff, formal sentences. *I personally observed a serving Military Police major named Reacher strike the first civilian with a kicking action against the right knee. Immediately subsequent to that Major Reacher struck the second civilian in the face with his forehead. To the best of my knowledge both attacks were unprovoked. I saw no element of self-defence.* Then came a signature with Carbone's name and number typed below it. I

140

recognized the number from Carbone's file. I looked up at the slow silent clock on the wall and pictured Carbone in my mind, slipping out of the lounge bar door into the parking lot, looking at me for a second, and then merging with the knot of men leaning on cars and drinking beer from bottles. Then I looked down again and opened a drawer and slipped the sheet of paper inside.

'Delta Force looks after its own,' Willard said. 'We all know that. I guess it's part of their mystique. So what are they going to do now? One of their own is beaten to death after lodging a complaint against a smart-ass MP major, and the smart-ass MP major in question needs to save his career, and he can't exactly account for his time on the night it went down?'

I said nothing.

'The Delta CO's office gets its own copy,' Willard said. 'Standard procedure with disciplinary complaints. Multiple copies all over the place. So the news will leak very soon. Then they'll be asking questions. So what shall I tell them? I could tell them you're definitely not a suspect. Or I could suggest you definitely *are* a suspect, but there's some type of technicality in the way that means I can't touch you. I could see how their sense of right and wrong deals with that kind of injustice.'

I said nothing.

'It's the only complaint Carbone ever made,' he said. 'In a sixteen-year career. I checked that, too. And it stands to reason. A guy like that has to keep his head down. But Delta as a whole will see some significance in it. Carbone comes up over the parapet for the first time in his life, they're going to think you boys had some previous history. They'll think it was a grudge match. Won't make them like you any better.'

I said nothing.

'So what should I do?' Willard said. 'Should I go over there and drop some hints about awkward legal technicalities? Or shall we trade? I keep Delta off your back, and you start toeing the line?'

I said nothing.

'I don't really think you killed him,' he said. 'Not even you would go that far. But I wouldn't have minded if you had. Fags in the army deserve to be killed. They're here under

141

false pretences. You would have chosen the wrong reason, is all.'

'It's an empty threat,' I said. 'You never told me he lodged the complaint. You didn't show it to me yesterday. You never gave me a name.'

'Their sergeants' mess won't buy that for a second. You're a special unit investigator. You do this stuff for a living. Easy enough for you to weasel a name out of all the paperwork they think we do.'

I said nothing.

'Wake up, major,' Willard said. 'Get with the programme. Garber's gone. We're going to do things my way now.'

'You're making a mistake,' I said. 'Making an enemy out of me.'

He shook his head. 'I don't agree. I'm not making a mistake. And I'm not making an enemy out of you. I'm bringing this unit into line, is all. You'll thank me, later. All of you. The world is changing. I can see the big picture.'

I said nothing.

'Help the army,' he said. 'And help yourself at the same time.'

I said nothing.

'Do we have a deal?' he said.

I didn't reply. He winked at me.

'I think we have a deal,' he said. 'You're not that dumb.'

He got up and walked out of the office and closed the door behind him. I sat there and watched the stiff vinyl cushion on my visitor's chair regain its shape. It happened slowly, with quiet hissing sounds as air leaked back into it.

TEN

THE WORLD IS CHANGING. I HAD ALWAYS BEEN A LONER, BUT AT that point I started to feel lonely. And I had always been a cynic, but at that point I began to feel hopelessly naive. Both of my families were disappearing out from under me, one because of simple relentless chronology, and the other because its reliable old values seemed suddenly to be evaporating. I felt like a man who wakes alone on a deserted island to find that the rest of the world has stolen away in boats in the night. I felt like I was standing on a shore, watching small receding shapes on the horizon. I felt like I had been speaking English, and now I realized everyone else had been speaking a different language entirely. The world was changing. And I didn't want it to.

Summer came back three minutes later. I guessed she had been hiding around a corner, waiting for Willard to leave. She had folds of printer paper under her arm, and big news in her eyes.

'Vassell and Coomer were here again last night,' she said. 'They're listed on the gate log.'

'Sit down,' I said.

She paused, surprised, and then she sat where Willard had.

143

'I'm toxic,' I said. 'You should walk away from me right now.'

'What do you mean?'

'We were right,' I said. 'Fort Bird is a very embarrassing place. First Kramer, then Carbone. Willard is closing both cases down, to spare the army's blushes.'

'He can't close *Carbone* down.'

'Training accident,' I said. 'He tripped and fell and hit his head.'

'What?'

'He's using it as a test for me. Am I with the programme or not?'

'Are you?'

I didn't answer.

'They're illegal orders,' Summer said. 'They have to be.'

'Are you prepared to challenge them?'

She didn't reply. The only practical way to challenge illegal orders was to disobey them and then take your chances with the resulting general court martial, which would inevitably become a *mano a mano* struggle with a guy way higher on the food chain, in front of a presiding judge who was well aware of the army's preference that orders should never be questioned.

'So nothing ever happened,' I said. 'Bring all your paperwork here and forget you ever heard of me or Kramer or Carbone.'

She said nothing.

'And speak to the guys who were there last night. Tell them to forget what they saw.'

She looked down at the floor.

'Then go back to the O Club and wait for your next assignment.'

She looked up at me.

'Are you serious?' she said.

'Totally,' I said. 'I'm giving you a direct order.'

She stared at me. 'You're not the man I thought you were.'

I nodded.

'I agree,' I said. 'I'm not.'

She walked out and I gave her a minute to get clear and then I picked up the folded paper she had left behind. There was a lot of it. I found the page I wanted, and I stared at it.

144

Because I don't like coincidences.

Vassell and Coomer had entered Bird by the main gate at six forty-five in the evening of the night Carbone had died. They had left again at ten o'clock. Three and a quarter hours, right across Carbone's time of death.

Or, right across dinner time.

I picked up the phone and called the O Club dining room. A mess sergeant told me the NCO in charge would call me back. Then I called my own sergeant and asked her to find out who was my opposite number at Fort Irwin, and to get him on the line. She came in four minutes later with a mug of coffee for me.

'He's all tied up,' she said. 'Could be half an hour. His name is Franz.'

'Can't be,' I said. 'Franz is in Panama. I talked to him there face to face.'

'Major Calvin Franz,' she said. 'That's what they told me.'

'Call them back,' I said. 'Double check.'

She left my coffee on my desk and went back out to her phone. Came in again after another four minutes and confirmed that her information had been correct.

'Major Calvin Franz,' she said again. 'He's been there since December twenty-ninth.'

I looked down at my calendar. *January 5th.*

'And you've been *here* since December twenty-ninth,' she said.

I looked straight at her.

'Call some more posts,' I said. 'The big ones only. Start with Fort Benning, and work through the alphabet. Get me the names of their MP XOs, and find out how long they've been there.'

She nodded and went back out. The NCO from the dining room called me back. I asked him about Vassell and Coomer. He confirmed they had eaten dinner in the O Club. Vassell had gone with the halibut, and Coomer had opted for the steak.

'Did they eat on their own?' I asked.

'No, sir, they were with an assortment of senior officers,' the guy said.

'Was it a date?'

'No, sir, we had the impression it was impromptu. It was an

145

odd collection of people. I think they all hooked up in the bar, over aperitifs. Certainly we had no reservation for the group.'

'How long were they there?'

'They were seated before seven thirty, and they got up just before ten o'clock.'

'Nobody left and came back?'

'No, sir, they were under our eye throughout.'

'All the time?'

'We paid close attention to them, sir. It was a question of the general's rank, really.'

I hung up. Then I called the main gate. Asked who had actually eyeballed Vassell and Coomer in and out. They gave me a sergeant's name. I told them to find the guy and have him call me back.

I waited.

The guy from the gate was the first to get back to me. He confirmed he had been on duty all through the previous evening, and he confirmed he had personally witnessed Vassell and Coomer arrive at six forty-five and leave again at ten.

'Car?' I asked.

'Big black sedan, sir,' he said. 'A Pentagon staff car.'

'Grand Marquis?' I asked.

'I'm pretty sure, sir.'

'Was there a driver?'

'The colonel was driving,' the guy said. 'Colonel Coomer, that is. General Vassell was in the front passenger seat.'

'Just the two of them in the car?'

'Affirmative, sir.'

'Are you sure?'

'That's definite, sir. No question about it. At night we use flashlights. Black sedan, DoD plates, two officers in the front, proper IDs displayed, rear seat vacant.'

'OK, thanks,' I said, and hung up. The phone rang again immediately. It was Calvin Franz, in California.

'Reacher?' he said. 'What the hell are you doing there?'

'I could ask you the exact same question.'

The phone went quiet for a beat.

'No idea what the hell I'm doing here,' he said. 'Irwin's all quiet. It usually is, they tell me. Weather's nice, though.'

'Did you check your orders?'

'Sure,' he said. 'Didn't you? Most fun I've had since Grenada, and now I'm staring at the sands of the Mojave? Seems to have been Garber's personal brainwave. I thought I must have upset him. Now I'm not so sure what's going on. Unlikely that we both upset him.'

'What exactly were your orders?' I said.

'Temporary XO for the Provost Marshal.'

'Is he there right now?'

'No, actually. He got a temporary detachment the same day I got in.'

'So you're acting CO?'

'Looks that way,' he said.

'Me too.'

'What's going on?'

'No idea,' I said. 'If I ever find out, I'll tell you. But first I need to ask you a question. I came across a bird colonel and a one-star over here, supposed to be heading out to you for an Armored conference on New Year's Day. Vassell and Coomer. Did they ever show?'

'That conference was cancelled,' Franz said. 'We heard their two-star bought the farm somewhere. Guy called Kramer. They seemed to think there was no point going ahead without him. Either that, or they can't think at all without him. Or they're all too busy fighting over who's going to get his command.'

'So Vassell and Coomer never came to California?'

'They never came to Irwin,' Franz said. 'That's for sure. Can't speak for California. It's a big state.'

'Who else was supposed to attend?'

'Armored's inner circle. Some are based here. Some showed and went away again. Some never showed at all.'

'Did you hear anything about the agenda?'

'I wouldn't expect to. Was it important?'

'I don't know. Vassell and Coomer said there wasn't one.'

'There's always an agenda.'

'That's what I figured.'

'I'll keep my ears open.'

'Happy New Year,' I said. Then I put the phone down and sat

147

quiet. Thought hard. Calvin Franz was one of the good guys. Actually, he was one of the *best* guys. Tough, fair, as competent as the day was long. Nothing ever knocked him off his stride. I had been happy enough to leave Panama, knowing that he was still there. But he wasn't still there. I wasn't there, and he wasn't there. So who the hell was?

I finished my coffee and carried my mug outside and put it back next to the machine. My sergeant was on the phone. She had a page of scribbled notes in front of her. She held up a finger like she had big news. Then she went back to writing. I went back to my desk. She came in five minutes later with her scribbled page. Thirteen lines, three columns. The third column was made up of numbers. Dates, probably.

'I got as far as Fort Rucker,' she said. 'Then I stopped. Because there's a very obvious pattern developing.'

'Tell me,' I said.

She reeled off thirteen posts, alphabetically. Then she reeled off the names of their MP executive officers. I knew all thirteen names, including Franz's and my own. Then she reeled off the dates they had been transferred in. Every date was exactly the same. Every date was December 29th. Eight days ago.

'Say the names again,' I told her.

She read them again. I nodded. Inside the arcane little world of military law enforcement, if you wanted to pick an all-star squad, and if you thought long and hard about it all through the night, those thirteen names were what you would have come up with. No doubt about it. They made up a major league, heavy-duty baker's dozen. There would have been about ten other obvious guys in the mix, but I had no doubt at all that a couple of them would be right there on posts farther along in the alphabet, and the other eight or so in significant places around the globe. And I had no doubt at all that all of them had been there just eight days. Our heavy hitters. I wouldn't have wanted to say how high or how low I ranked among them individually, but collectively, down there at the field level, we were the army's top cops, no question about it.

'Weird,' I said. And it was weird. To shuffle that many specific individuals around on the same day took some kind of will and planning, and to do it during Just Cause took some kind of

148

an urgent motive. The room seemed to go quiet, like I was straining to hear the other shoe fall.

'I'm going over to the Delta station,' I said.

I drove myself in a Humvee because I didn't want to walk. I didn't know if the asshole Willard was off the post yet, and I didn't want to cross his path again. The sentry let me into the old prison and I went straight to the adjutant's office. He was still at his desk, looking a little more tired than when I had seen him in the early morning.

'It was a training accident,' I said.

He nodded. 'So I heard.'

'What kind of training was he doing?' I asked.

'Night manoeuvres,' the guy said.

'Alone?'

'Escape and evasion, then.'

'On post?'

'OK, he was jogging. Burning off the holiday calories. Whatever.'

'I need this to sound kosher,' I said. 'My name's going to be on the report.'

The captain nodded. 'Then forget the jogging. I don't think Carbone was a runner. He was more of a gym rat. A lot of them are.'

'A lot of who are?'

He looked straight at me.

'Delta guys,' he said.

'Did he have a specialization?'

'They're all generalists. They're all good at everything.'

'Not radio, not medic?'

'They all do radio. And they're all medics. It's a safeguard. If they're captured individually, they can claim to be the company medic. Might save them from a bullet. And they can demonstrate the expertise, if they're tested.'

'Any medical training take place at night?'

The captain shook his head. 'Not specifically.'

'Could he have been out testing comms gear?'

'He could have been out road testing a vehicle,' the captain said. 'He was good with mechanical things. I guess as much as

149

anyone he looked after the unit's trucks. That was probably as close as he got to a specialization.'

'OK,' I said. 'Maybe he blew a tyre, and his truck fell off the jack and crushed his head?'

'Works for me,' the captain said.

'Uneven terrain, maybe a soft spot under the jack, the whole thing would be unstable.'

'Works for me,' the captain said again.

'I'll say my guys towed the truck back.'

'OK.'

'What kind of truck was it?'

'Any kind you like.'

'Your CO around?' I said.

'He's away. For the holidays.'

'Who is he?'

'You won't know him.'

'Try me.'

'Colonel Brubaker,' the captain said.

'David Brubaker?' I said. 'I know him.' Which was partially true. I knew him by reputation. He was a real hairy-assed Special Forces evangelist. According to him the rest of us could fold our tents and go home and the whole world could hide behind his hand-picked units. Maybe some helicopter battalions could stay in harness, to ferry his people around. Maybe a single Pentagon office could stay open, to procure the weapons he wanted.

'When will he be back?' I said.

'Sometime tomorrow.'

'Did you call him?'

The captain shook his head. 'He won't want to be involved. And he won't want to talk to you. But I'll get him to reissue some operational safety procedures, as soon as we find out what kind of an accident it was.'

'Crushed by a truck,' I said. 'That's what it was. That should make him happy. Vehicular safety is a shorter section than weapons safety.'

'In what?'

'In the field manual.'

The captain smiled.

150

'Brubaker doesn't use the field manual,' he said.

'I want to see Carbone's quarters,' I said.

'Why?'

'Because I need to sanitize them. If I'm going to sign off on a truck accident, I don't want any loose ends around.'

Carbone had bunked the same way as his unit as a whole, on his own in one of the old cells. It was a six-by-eight space made of painted concrete and it had its own sink and toilet. It had a standard army cot and a footlocker and a shelf on the wall as long as the bed. All in all, it was pretty good accommodations for a sergeant. There were plenty around the world who would have traded in the blink of an eye.

Summer had had police tape stuck across the doorway. I pulled it down and balled it up and put it in my pocket. Stepped inside the room.

Special Forces Detachment D is very different from the rest of the army in its approach to discipline and uniformity. Relationships between the ranks are very casual. Nobody even remembers how to salute. Tidiness is not prized. Uniform is not compulsory. If a guy feels comfortable in a previous-issue fatigue jacket that he's had for years, he wears it. If he likes New Balance running shoes better than GI combat boots, he wears them. If the army buys four hundred thousand Beretta sidearms, but the Delta guy likes SIGs better, he uses a SIG.

So Carbone had no closet full of clean and pressed uniforms. There were no serried ranks of undershirts, crisp and laundered, folded ready for use. There were no gleaming boots under his bed. His clothing was all piled on the first three-quarters of the long shelf above his cot. There wasn't much of it. It was all basically olive green, but apart from that it wasn't stuff that a current quartermaster would recognize. There were some old pieces of the army's original extended cold-weather clothing system. There were some faded pieces of standard BDUs. Nothing was marked with unit or regimental insignia. There was a green bandanna. There were some old green T-shirts, washed so many times they were nearly transparent. There was a neatly rolled ALICE harness next to the T-shirts.

ALICE stands for All-Purpose Lightweight Carrying Equipment, which is what the army calls a nylon belt that you hang things from.

The final quarter of the shelf's length held a collection of books, and a small colour photograph in a brass frame. The photograph was of an older woman that looked a little like Carbone himself. His mother, without a doubt. I remembered his tattoo, sliced across by the K-bar. An eagle, holding a scroll with *Mother* on it. I remembered my mother, shooing us away into the tiny elevator after we had hugged her goodbye.

I moved on to Carbone's books.

There were five paperbacks and one tall thin hardcover. I ran my finger along the paperbacks. I didn't recognize any of the titles or any of the authors. They all had cracked concave spines and yellow-edged pages. They all seemed to be adventure stories involving prototype airplanes or lost submarines. The lone hardcover was a souvenir publication from a Rolling Stones concert tour. Judging by the style of the print on the spine it was about ten years old.

I lifted his mattress up off the cot springs and checked under it. Nothing there. I checked the toilet tank and under the sink. Nothing doing. I moved on to the footlocker. First thing I saw after opening it was a brown leather jacket folded across the top. Underneath the jacket were two white button-down shirts and two pairs of blue jeans. The cotton items were worn and soft and the jacket was neither cheap nor expensive. Together they made up a soldier's typical Saturday-night outfit. Shit, shave and shower, throw on the civilian duds, pile into someone's car, hit a couple of bars, have some fun.

Underneath the jeans was a wallet. It was small, and made out of brown leather that almost matched the jacket. Like the clothes above it, it was set up for a typical Saturday night's requirements. There were forty-three dollars in cash in it, sufficient for enough rounds of beers to get the fun started. There was a military ID card and a North Carolina driver's licence in it, in case the fun concluded inside an MP jeep or a civilian black-and-white. There was an unopened condom, in case the fun got serious.

There was a photograph of a girl, behind a plastic window.

152

Maybe a sister, maybe a cousin, maybe a friend. Maybe nobody. Camouflage, for sure.

Underneath the wallet was a shoe box half full of six-by-four prints. They were all amateur snapshots of groups of soldiers. Carbone himself was in some of them. Small groups of men were standing and posing, like chorus lines, arms around each other's shoulders. Some shots were under a blazing sun and the men were shirtless, wearing beanie hats, squinting and smiling. Some were in jungles. Some were in wrecked and snowy streets. All showed the same tight camaraderie. Comrades in arms, off duty, still alive, and happy about it.

There was nothing else in Carbone's six-by-eight cell. Nothing significant, nothing out of the ordinary, nothing explanatory. Nothing that revealed his history, his nature, his passions, or his interests. He had lived his life in secret, buttoned down, like his Saturday-night shirts.

I walked back to my Humvee. Turned a corner and came face to face with the young sergeant with the beard and the tan. He was in my way, and he wasn't about to move.

'You made a fool out of me,' he said.

'Did I?'

'About Carbone. Letting me talk the way I did. Company clerk just showed us some interesting paperwork.'

'So?'

'So we're thinking now.'

'Don't tire yourselves out,' I said.

'Think this is funny? You won't think it's funny if we find out it was you.'

'It wasn't.'

'Says you.'

I nodded. 'Says me. Now get out of my way.'

'Or?'

'Or I'll kick your ass.'

He stepped up close. 'Think you could kick my ass?'

I didn't move. 'You're wondering whether I kicked Carbone's ass. And he was probably twice the soldier you are.'

'You won't even see it coming,' he said.

I said nothing.

153

'Believe me,' he said.

I looked away. I believed him. If Delta put a hit on me, I wouldn't see it coming. That was for sure. Weeks from now or months from now or years from now I would walk into a dark alley somewhere and a shadow would step out and a K-bar would slip between my ribs or my neck would snap with a loud *crack* that would echo off the bricks around me, and that would be the end of it.

'You've got a week,' the guy said.

'To do what?'

'To show us it wasn't you.'

I said nothing.

'Your choice,' the guy said. 'Show us, or make those seven days count. Make sure you cover all your lifetime ambitions. Don't start a long book.'

ELEVEN

I DROVE THE HUMVEE BACK TO MY OFFICE. LEFT IT PARKED RIGHT outside my door. The sergeant with the baby son had gone. The small dark corporal who I thought was from Louisiana was there in her place. The coffee pot was cold and empty. There were two message slips on my desk. The first was: *Major Franz called. Please call him back.* The second said: *Detective Clark returned your call.* I dialled Franz in California first.

'Reacher?' he said. 'I asked about the Armored agenda.'

'And?'

'There wasn't one. That's their story, and they're sticking to it.'

'But?'

'We both know that's bullshit. There's always an agenda.'

'So did you get anywhere?'

'Not really,' he said. 'But I can prove an incoming secure fax from Germany late on December thirtieth, and I can prove significant Xeroxing activity on the thirty-first, in the afternoon. And then there was some shredding and burning on New Year's Day, after the Kramer news broke. I spoke to the incinerator guy. One burn bag, full of paper shreds, maybe enough for about sixty sheets.'

155

'How secure is their secure fax line?'

'How secure do you want it to be?'

'Extremely secure. Because the only way I can make sense out of this is if the agenda was really secret. I mean, *really* secret. And if it was really secret, would they have put it on paper in the first place?'

'They're XII Corps, Reacher. They've been living on the front line for forty years. All they've got is secrets.'

'How many people were scheduled to attend the conference?'

'I spoke to the mess. There were fifteen bag lunches booked.'

'Sixty pages, fifteen people, that's a four-page agenda, then.'

'Looks that way. But they went up in smoke.'

'Not the original that was faxed from Germany,' I said.

'They'll have burned that one over there.'

'No, my guess is Kramer was hand-carrying it when he died.'

'So where is it now?'

'Nobody knows. It got away.'

'Is it worth chasing?'

'Nobody knows,' I said again. 'Except the guy who wrote it, and he's dead. And Vassell and Coomer. They must have seen it. They probably helped with it.'

'Vassell and Coomer went back to Germany. This morning. First flight out of Dulles. The staffers here were talking about it.'

'You ever met this new guy Willard?' I asked him.

'No.'

'Try not to. He's an asshole.'

'Thanks for the warning. What did we do to deserve him?'

'I have no idea,' I said. We hung up and I dialled the Virginia number and asked for Detective Clark. I got put on hold. Then I heard a click and a second's worth of squad room sounds and a voice came on the line.

'Clark,' it said.

'Reacher,' I said. 'U.S. Army, down at Fort Bird. Did you want me?'

'You wanted me, as I recall,' Clark said. 'You wanted a progress report. But there isn't any progress. We're looking at a brick wall here. We're looking for help, actually.'

'Nothing I can do. It's your case.'

156

'I wish it wasn't,' he said.

'What have you got?'

'Lots of nothing. The perp was in and out without maybe touching a thing. Gloves, obviously. There was a light frost on the ground. We've got some residual grit from the driveway and the path, but we're not even close to a footprint.'

'Neighbours see anything?'

'Most of them were out, or drunk. It was New Year's Eve. I've had people up and down the street canvassing, but nothing's jumping out at me. There were some cars around, but there would be anyway, on New Year's Eve, with folks heading back and forth to parties.'

'Any tyre tracks on the driveway?'

'None that mean anything.'

I said nothing.

'The victim was killed with a crowbar,' Clark said. 'Probably the same tool as was used on the door.'

'I figured that,' I said.

'After the attack the perp wiped it on the rug and then washed it clean in the kitchen sink. We found stuff in the pipe. No prints on the faucet. Gloves, again.'

I said nothing.

'Something else we haven't got,' Clark said. 'There's nothing much to say your general ever really lived there.'

'Why?'

'We gave it the full-court press, forensically. We printed the whole place, we took hair and fibre from everywhere including the sink and shower traps, like I said. Everything belonged to the victim except a couple of stray prints. Bingo, we thought, but the database brought them back as the husband's. And the ratio of hers to his suggests he was hardly there over the last five years or so. Is that usual?'

'He'll have stayed on post a lot,' I said. 'But he should have been home for the holidays every year. The story here is that the marriage wasn't so great.'

'People like that should just go ahead and get divorced,' Clark said. 'I mean, that's not a dealbreaker even for a general, right?'

'Not that I've heard,' I said. 'Not any more.'

157

Then he went quiet for a minute. He was thinking.

'How bad was the marriage?' he asked. 'Bad enough that we should be looking at the husband for the doer?'

'The timing doesn't work,' I said. 'He was dead when it happened.'

'Was there money involved?'

'Nice house,' I said. 'Probably hers.'

'So what about a paid hit, maybe set up way ahead of time?'

Now he was really clutching at straws.

'He'd have arranged it for when he was away in Germany.'

Clark said nothing to that.

'Who called you for this progress report?' I asked him.

'You did,' he said. 'An hour ago.'

'I don't recall doing that.'

'Not you personally,' he said. 'Your people. It was the little black chick I met at the scene. Your lieutenant. I was too busy to talk. She gave me a number, but I left it somewhere. So I called back on the number you gave me originally. Did I do wrong?'

'No,' I said. 'You did fine. Sorry we can't help you.'

We hung up. I sat quiet for a moment and then I buzzed my corporal.

'Ask Lieutenant Summer to come see me,' I said.

Summer showed up inside ten minutes. She was in BDUs and between her face and her body language I could see she was feeling a little nervous of me and a little contemptuous of me all at the same time. I let her sit down and then I launched right into it.

'Detective Clark called back,' I said.

She said nothing.

'You disobeyed my direct order,' I said.

She said nothing.

'Why?' I asked.

'Why did you give me the order?'

'Why do you think?'

'Because you're toeing Willard's line.'

'He's the CO,' I said. 'It's a good line to toe.'

'I don't agree.'

158

'You're in the army now, Summer. You don't obey orders just because you agree with them.'

'We don't cover things up just because we're told to, either.'

'We do,' I said. 'We do that all the time. We always have.'

'Well, we shouldn't.'

'Who made you Chief of Staff?'

'It's unfair to Carbone and Mrs Kramer,' she said. 'They're innocent victims.'

I paused. 'Why did you start with Mrs Kramer? You see her as more important than Carbone?'

Summer shook her head. 'I didn't start with Mrs Kramer. I got to her second. I had already started on Carbone. I went through the personnel lists and the gate log and marked who was here at the time and who wasn't.'

'You gave me that paperwork.'

'I copied it first.'

'You're an idiot,' I said.

'Why? Because I'm not chicken?'

'How old are you?'

'Twenty-five.'

'OK,' I said. 'So next year you'll be twenty-six. You'll be a twenty-six-year-old black woman with a dishonourable discharge from the only career you've ever had. Meanwhile the civilian job market will be flooded because of force reduction and you'll be competing with people with chests full of medals and pockets full of testimonials. So what are you going to do? Starve? Go work up at the strip club with Sin?'

She said nothing.

'You should have left it to me,' I said.

'You weren't doing anything.'

'I'm glad you thought so,' I said. 'That was the plan.'

'What?'

'I'm going to take Willard on,' I said. 'It's going to be him or me.'

She said nothing.

'I work for the army,' I said. 'Not for Willard. I believe in the army. I don't believe in Willard. I'm not going to let him trash everything.'

She said nothing.

159

'I told him not to make an enemy out of me. But he didn't listen.'

'Big step,' she said.

'One that you already took,' I said.

'Why did you cut me out?'

'Because if I blow it I don't want to take anyone down with me.'

'You were protecting me.'

I nodded.

'Well don't,' she said. 'I can think for myself.'

I said nothing.

'How old are *you*?' she asked.

'Twenty-nine,' I said.

'So next year you'll be thirty. You'll be a thirty-year-old white man with a dishonourable discharge from the only job you've ever had. And whereas I'm young enough to start over, you're not. You're institutionalized, you've got no social skills, you've never been in the civilian world, and you're good for nothing. So maybe it should be *you* lying in the weeds, not me.'

I said nothing.

'You should have talked it over,' she said.

'It's a personal choice,' I said.

'I already made my personal choice,' she said. 'Seems like you know that now. Seems like Detective Clark accidentally ratted me out.'

'That's exactly what I mean,' I said. 'One stray phone call and you could be out on the street. This is a high-stakes game.'

'And I'm right here in it with you, Reacher. So bring me up to speed.'

Five minutes later she knew what I knew. All questions, no answers.

'Garber's signature was a forgery,' she said.

I nodded.

'So what about Carbone's, on the complaint? Is that forged too?'

'Maybe,' I said. I took the copy that Willard had given me out of my desk drawer. Smoothed it out on the blotter and passed it across to her. She folded it neatly and put it in her inside pocket.

'I'll get the writing checked,' she said. 'Easier for me than you, now.'

'Nothing's easy for either of us now,' I said. 'You need to be very clear about that. So you need to be very clear about what you're doing.'

'I'm clear,' she said. 'Bring it on.'

I sat quiet for a minute. Just looked at her. She had a small smile on her face. She was plenty tough. But then, she had grown up poor in an Alabama shack with churches burning and exploding all around her. I guessed watching her back against Willard and a bunch of Delta vigilantes might represent progress, of a sort, in her life.

'Thank you,' I said. 'For being on my side.'

'I'm not on your side,' she said. 'You're on mine.'

My phone rang. I picked it up. It was the Louisiana corporal, calling from his desk outside my door.

'North Carolina State Police on the line,' he said. 'They want a duty officer. You want to take it?'

'Not really,' I said. 'But I guess I better.'

There was a click and some dead air and another click. Then a dispatcher came on the line and told me a trooper in an I-95 patrol car had found an abandoned green canvas briefcase on the highway shoulder. He told me it had a wallet inside that identified the owner as a General Kenneth R. Kramer, U.S. Army. He told me he was calling Fort Bird because he figured it was the closest military installation to where the briefcase had been found. And he was calling to tell me where the briefcase was currently being held, in case I was interested in having someone sent out to pick it up.

TWELVE

SUMMER DROVE. WE TOOK THE HUMVEE I HAD LEFT ON THE KERB. We didn't want to take time to sign out a sedan. It cramped her style a little. Humvees are big slow trucks that are good for a lot of things, but covering paved roads fast isn't one of them. She looked tiny behind the wheel. The vehicle was full of noise. The engine was thrashing and the tyres were whining loud. It was four o'clock on a dull day and it was starting to go dark.

We drove north to Kramer's motel and turned east through the cloverleaf and then north on I-95 itself. We covered fifteen miles and passed a rest area and started looking for the right State Police building. We found it twelve miles farther on. It was a long low one-storey brick structure with a forest of tall radio masts bolted to its roof. It was maybe forty years old. The brick was dull tan. It was impossible to say whether it had started out yellow and then faded in the sun or whether it had started out white and gotten dirty from the traffic fumes. There were stainless steel letters in an art deco style spelling out *North Carolina State Police* all along its length.

We pulled in and parked in front of a pair of glass doors. Summer shut the Humvee down and we sat for a second and then slid out. Crossed a narrow sidewalk and pulled the doors and stepped inside the facility. It was a typical police place, built for function and floored with linoleum which was shined every night whether it needed it or not. The walls had many layers of slick paint directly over concrete blocks. The air was hot and smelled faintly of sweat and stewed coffee.

There was a desk guy behind a reception counter. We were in battledress uniform and our Humvee was visible behind us through the doors, so he made the connection fast enough. He didn't ask for ID or enquire why we were there. He didn't speculate as to why General Kramer hadn't shown up himself. He just glanced at me and spent a little longer looking at Summer and then leaned down under his counter and came back up with the briefcase. It was in a clear plastic bag. Not an evidence bag. Just some kind of a shopping bag. It had a store's name printed across it in red.

The briefcase itself matched Kramer's suit carrier in every way. Same colour, same design, same age, same level of wear and tear, no monogram. I opened it and looked inside. There was a wallet. There were plane tickets. There was a passport. There was a paperclipped itinerary three sheets thick. There was a hardcover book.

There was no conference agenda.

I closed the case up again and laid it down on the counter. Butted it square with the edge. I was disappointed, but not surprised.

'Was it in the plastic bag when the trooper found it?' I asked.

The desk guy shook his head. He was looking at Summer, not me.

'I put it in the bag myself,' he said. 'I wanted to keep it clean. I wasn't sure how soon someone would get here.'

'Where exactly was it found?' I asked him.

He paused a beat and looked away from Summer and ran a thick fingertip down a desk ledger and across a line to a mile marker code. Then he turned around and used the same finger-tip on a map. The map was a large-scale plan of North Carolina's portion of I-95 and was long and narrow, like a ribbon five inches wide. It showed every mile of the highway from where it entered from South Carolina and exited again into Virginia.

The guy's finger hovered for a second and then came down, decisively.

'Here,' he said. 'Northbound shoulder, a mile past the rest area, about eleven miles south of where we are right now.'

'Any way of knowing how long it had been there?'

'Not really,' he said. 'We're not out there specifically looking for trash on the shoulders. Stuff can be there a month.'

'So how was it found?'

'Routine traffic stop. The trooper just saw it there, walking from his car to the car he had stopped.'

'When was this exactly?'

'Today,' the guy said. 'Start of the second watch. Not long after noon.'

'It wasn't there a month,' I said.

'When did he lose it?'

'New Year's Eve,' I said.

'Where?'

'It was stolen from where he was staying.'

'Where was he staying?'

'A motel about thirty miles south of here.'

'So the bad guys were coming back north.'

'I guess,' I said.

The guy looked at me like he was asking permission and then picked the case up with both hands and looked at it like he was a connoisseur and it was a rare piece. He turned it in the light and stared at it from every angle.

'January,' he said. 'We've got a little night dew right now. And it's cold enough that we're worried about ice. So we've got salt down. Things age fast, this time of year on the highway shoulder. And this looks old and worn, but not very deteriorated. It's got some grit on it, in the weave of the canvas. But not very much. It hasn't been out there since New Year's Eve, that much is for damn sure. Less than twenty-four hours, I'd say. One night, not more.'

'Can you be certain?' Summer asked.

He shook his head. Put the case back on the counter.

'Just a guess,' he said.

'OK,' I said. 'Thanks.'

'You'll have to sign for it.'

164

I nodded. He reversed the desk ledger and pushed it towards me. I had *Reacher* in a subdued-pattern stencil above my right breast pocket, but I figured he hadn't paid much attention to it. He had spent most of his time looking at Summer's pockets. So I scrawled *K. Kramer* on the appropriate line in the book and picked up the briefcase and turned away.

'Funny sort of burglary,' the desk guy said. 'There's an Amex card and money still in the wallet. We inventoried the contents.'

I didn't reply. Just went out through the doors, back to the Humvee.

Summer waited for a gap in the traffic and then drove across all three lanes and bounced straight onto the soft grass median. She went down a slope and through a drainage ditch and straight up the other side. Paused and waited and turned left back onto the blacktop and headed south. That was the kind of thing a Humvee was good for.

'Try this,' she said. 'Last night Vassell and Coomer leave Bird at ten o'clock with the briefcase. They head north for Dulles or D.C. They extract the agenda and throw the case out the car window.'

'They were in the bar and the dining room their whole time at Bird.'

'So one of their dinner companions passed it on. We should check who they ate with. Maybe one of the women on the Humvee list was there.'

'They were all alibied.'

'Only superficially. New Year's Eve parties are pretty chaotic.'

I looked out the window. Afternoon was fading fast. Evening was coming on. The world looked dark and cold.

'Sixty miles,' I said. 'The case was found sixty miles north of Bird. That's an hour. They would have grabbed the agenda and ditched the case faster than that.'

Summer said nothing.

'And they would have stopped at the rest area to do it. They would have put the case in a garbage can. That would have been safer. Throwing a briefcase out of a car window is pretty conspicuous.'

'Maybe there really wasn't an agenda.'

'It would be the first time in military history.'

'Then maybe it really wasn't important.'

'They ordered bag lunches at Irwin. Two-stars, one-stars, and colonels were planning to work through their lunch hour. That might be the first time in military history too. That was an important conference, Summer, believe me.'

She said nothing.

'Do that U-turn thing again,' I said. 'Across the median. Then go back north a little. I want to look at the rest area.'

The rest area was the same as on most American interstates I had seen. The northbound highway and the southbound highway eased apart to put a long fat bulge into the median. The buildings were shared by both sets of travellers. Therefore they had two fronts and no backs. They were built of brick and had dormant flower beds and leafless trees all around them. There were gas pumps. There were angled parking slots. Right then the place seemed to be halfway between quiet and busy. It was the end of the holidays. Families were struggling home, ready for school, ready for work. The parking slots were maybe one-third filled with cars. Their distribution was interesting. People had grabbed the first parking spot they saw rather than chancing something farther on, even though that might have put them ultimately a little closer to the food and the bathrooms. Maybe it was human nature. Some kind of insecurity.

There was a small semicircular plaza at the facility's main entrance. I could see bright neon signs inside at the food stations. Outside, there were six trash cans all fairly close to the doors. There were plenty of people around, looking in, looking out.

'Too public,' Summer said. 'This is going nowhere.'

I nodded again. 'I'd forget it in a heartbeat if it wasn't for Mrs Kramer.'

'Carbone is more important. We should prioritize.'

'That feels like we're giving up.'

We went north out of the rest area and Summer did her off-roading thing across the median again and turned south. I got as comfortable as it was possible to get in a military vehicle and

166

settled in for the ride back. Darkness unspooled on my left. There was a vague sunset in the west, to my right. The road looked damp. Summer didn't seem very worried about the possibility of ice.

I did nothing for the first twenty minutes. Then I switched the dome light on and searched Kramer's briefcase, thoroughly. I didn't expect to find anything, and I wasn't proved wrong. His passport was a standard item, seven years old. He looked a little better in the picture than he had dead in the motel, but not much. He had plenty of stamps in and out of Germany and Belgium. The future battlefield and NATO HQ, respectively. He hadn't been anywhere else. He was a true specialist. For at least seven years he had concentrated exclusively on the world's last great tank arena and its command structure.

The plane tickets were exactly what Garber had said they should be. Frankfurt to Dulles, and Washington National to Los Angeles, both round trip. They were all coach class and government rate, booked three days before the first departure date.

The itinerary matched the details on the plane tickets exactly. There were seat assignments. It seemed like Kramer preferred the aisle. Maybe his age was affecting his bladder. There was a reservation for a single room in Fort Irwin's Visiting Officers' Quarters, which he had never reached.

His wallet contained thirty-seven American dollars and sixty-seven German marks, all in mixed small bills. The Amex card was the basic green item, due to expire in a year and a half. He had carried one since 1964, according to the *Member Since* rubric. I figured that was pretty early for an army officer. Back then most got by with cash and military scrip. Kramer must have been a sophisticated guy, financially.

There was a Virginia driver's licence. He had been using Green Valley as his permanent address, even though he avoided spending time there. There was a standard military ID card. There was a photograph of Mrs Kramer, behind a plastic window. It showed a much younger version of the woman I had seen dead on her hallway floor. It was at least twenty years old. She had been pretty back then. She had long auburn hair that

167

showed up a little orange from the way the photograph had faded with age.

There was nothing else in the wallet. No receipts, no restaurant checks, no Amex carbons, no phone numbers, no scraps of paper. I wasn't surprised. Generals are often neat, organized people. They need fighting talent, but they need bureaucratic talent too. I guessed Kramer's office and desk and quarters would be the same as his wallet. They would contain everything he needed and nothing he didn't.

The hardcover book was an academic monograph from a Midwestern university about the Battle of Kursk. Kursk happened in July of 1943. It was Nazi Germany's last grand offensive of World War Two and its first major defeat on an open battlefield. It turned into the greatest tank battle the world has ever seen, and ever will see, unless people like Kramer himself are eventually turned loose. I wasn't surprised by his choice of reading material. Some small part of him must have feared the closest he would ever get to truly cataclysmic action was reading about the hundreds of Tigers and Panthers and T-34s whirling and roaring through the choking summer dust all those years ago.

There was nothing else in the briefcase. Just a few furred paper shreds trapped in the seams. It looked like Kramer was the sort of guy who emptied his case and turned it upside down and shook it every time he packed for a trip. I put everything back inside and buckled the little straps and laid the case on the floor by my feet.

'Speak to the dining-room guy,' I said. 'When we get back. Find out who was at the table with Vassell and Coomer.'

'OK,' Summer said. She drove on.

We got back to Bird in time for dinner. We ate in the O Club bar with a bunch of fellow MPs. If Willard had spies among them, they would have seen nothing except a couple of tired people doing not very much of anything. But Summer slipped away between courses and came back with news in her eyes. I ate my dessert and drank my coffee slowly enough that nobody could think I had urgent business anywhere. Then I stood up and wandered out. Waited in the cold on the sidewalk. Summer came out five minutes later. I smiled. It felt like we were conducting a clandestine affair.

'Only one woman ate with Vassell and Coomer,' she said.

'Who?' I asked.

'Lieutenant Colonel Andrea Norton.'

'The Psy-Ops person?'

'The very same.'

'She was at a party on New Year's Eve.'

Summer made a face. 'You know what those parties are like. A bar in town, hundreds of people, in and out all the time, noise, confusion, drinks, people disappearing two by two. She could have slipped away.'

'Where was the bar?'

'Thirty minutes from the motel.'

'Then she would have been gone an hour, absolute minimum.'

'That's possible.'

'Was she in the bar at midnight? Holding hands and singing "Auld Lang Syne"? Whoever was standing next to her should be able to say for sure.'

'People say she was there. But she could have made it back by then anyway. The kid said the Humvee left at eleven twenty-five. She'd have been back with five minutes to spare. It could have looked natural. You know, everybody comes out of the woodwork, ready for the ball to drop. The party kind of starts over.'

I said nothing.

'She would have taken the case to sanitize it. Maybe her phone number was in there, or her name or her picture. Or a diary. She didn't want the scandal. But once she was through with it, she didn't need the rest of the stuff any more. She'd have been happy to hand it back when asked.'

'How would Vassell and Coomer know who to ask?'

'Hard to hide a long-standing affair in this fishbowl.'

'Not logical,' I said. 'If people knew about Kramer and Norton, why would someone go to the house in Virginia?'

'OK, maybe they didn't *know*. Maybe it was just there on the list of possibilities. Maybe way down the list. Maybe it was something that people thought was over.'

I nodded. 'What can we get from her?'

'We can get confirmation that Vassell and Coomer arranged to take possession of the briefcase last night. That would prove they were looking for it, which puts them in the frame for Mrs Kramer.'

'They made no calls from the hotel, and they didn't have time to get down there themselves. So I don't see how we can put them in the frame. What else can we get?'

'We can be certain about what happened to the agenda. We can know that Vassell and Coomer got it back. Then at least the army can relax because we'll know for sure it isn't going to wind up on some public trash pile for a journalist to find.'

I nodded. Said nothing.

'And maybe Norton saw it,' Summer said. 'Maybe she read it. Maybe she could tell us what all this fuss is about.'

'That's tempting.'

'It sure is.'

'Can we just walk in and ask her?'

'You're from the 110th. You can ask anyone anything.'

'I have to stay under Willard's radar.'

'She doesn't know he warned you off.'

'She does. He spoke to her after the Carbone thing.'

'I think we have to talk to her.'

'Difficult kind of a talk to have,' I said. 'She's likely to get offended.'

'Only if we do it wrong.'

'What are the chances of doing it right?'

'We might be able to manipulate the situation. There'll be an embarrassment factor. She won't want it broadcast.'

'We can't push her to the point where she calls Willard.'

'You scared of him?'

'I'm scared of what he can do to us bureaucratically. Doesn't help anyone if we both get transferred to Alaska.'

'Your call.'

I was quiet for a long moment. Thought back to Kramer's hardcover book. This was like July 13th, 1943, the pivotal day of the Battle of Kursk. We were like Alexander Vasilevsky, the Soviet general. If we attacked now, this minute, we had to keep on and on attacking until the enemy was run off his feet and the war was won. If we bogged down or paused for breath even for a second, we would be overrun again.

'OK,' I said. 'Let's do it.'

We found Andrea Norton in the O Club lounge and I asked her if she would spare us a minute in her office. I could see she was puzzled as to why. I told her it was a confidential matter. She stayed puzzled. Willard had told her that Carbone was a closed case, and she couldn't see what else we would have to talk to her about. But she agreed. She told us she would meet us there in thirty minutes.

Summer and I spent the thirty minutes in my office with her list of who was on post and who wasn't at Carbone's time of death. She had yards of computer paper neatly folded into a large concertina about an inch thick. There was a name, rank and number printed on each line with pale dot-matrix ink. Almost every name had a check mark next to it.

'What are the marks?' I asked her. 'Here or not here?'

'Here,' she said.

I nodded. I was afraid of that. I riffed through the concertina with my thumb.

'How many?' I asked.

'Nearly twelve hundred.'

I nodded again. There was nothing intrinsically difficult about boiling down twelve hundred names and finding one sole perpetrator. Police files everywhere are full of larger suspect pools. There had been cases in Korea where the entire U.S. military strength had been the suspect pool. But cases like that require unlimited manpower, big staffs, and endless resources. And they require everybody's total co-operation. They can't be handled behind a CO's back, in secret, by two people acting alone.

'Impossible,' I said.

'Nothing's impossible,' Summer said.

'We have to go at it a different way.'

'How?'

'What did he take to the scene?'

'Nothing.'

171

'Wrong,' I said. 'He took himself.'

Summer shrugged. Dragged her fingers up the folded edges of her paper. The stack thickened and then thinned back down as the air sighed out from between the pages.

'Pick a name,' she said.

'He took a K-bar,' I said.

'Twelve hundred names, twelve hundred K-bars.'

'He took a tyre iron or a crowbar.'

She nodded.

'And he took yogurt,' I said.

She said nothing.

'Four things,' I said. 'Himself, a K-bar, a blunt instrument, and yogurt. Where did the yogurt come from?'

'His refrigerator in his quarters,' Summer said. 'Or one of the mess kitchens, or one of the mess buffets, or the commissary, or a supermarket or a deli or a grocery store somewhere off post.'

I pictured a man, breathing hard, walking fast, maybe sweating, a bloodstained knife and a crowbar clutched together in his right hand, an empty yogurt pot in his left, stumbling in the dark, nearing a destination, looking down, seeing the pot, hurling it into the undergrowth, putting the knife in his pocket, slipping the crowbar under his coat.

'We should look for the container,' I said.

Summer said nothing.

'He'll have ditched it,' I said. 'Not close to the scene, but not far from it either.'

'Will it help us?'

'It'll have some kind of a product code on it. Maybe a *best before* date. Stuff like that. It might lead us to where it was bought.'

Then I paused.

'And it might have prints on it,' I said.

'He'll have worn gloves.'

I shook my head. 'I've seen people opening yogurt containers. But I've never seen anyone do it with gloves on. There's a foil closure. With a tiny little tab to pull.'

'We're on a hundred thousand acres here.'

I nodded. *Square one.* Normally a couple of phone calls would

172

get me all the grunts on the post lined up a yard apart on their knees, crawling slowly across the terrain like a giant human comb, staring down at the ground and parting every blade of grass by hand. And then doing it again the next day, and the next, until one of them found what we were looking for. With manpower like the army has, you can find a needle in a haystack. You can find both halves of a broken needle. You can find the tiny chip of chrome that flaked off the break.

Summer looked at the clock on the wall.

'Our thirty minutes are up,' she said.

We used the Humvee to get over to Psy-Ops and parked in a slot that was probably reserved for someone else. It was nine o'clock. Summer killed the motor and we opened the doors and slipped out into the cold.

I took Kramer's briefcase with me.

We walked through the old tiled corridors and came to Norton's door. Her light was on. I knocked and we went in. Norton was behind her desk. All her textbooks were back on her shelves. There were no legal pads on view. No pens or pencils. Her desktop was clear. The pool of light from her lamp was a perfect circle on the empty wood.

She had three visitor chairs. She waved us towards them. Summer sat on the right. I sat on the left. I propped Kramer's briefcase on the centre chair, facing Norton, like a ghost at the feast. She didn't look at it.

'How can I help you?' she said.

I made a point of adjusting the briefcase's position so that it was completely upright on the chair.

'Tell us about the dinner party last night,' I said.

'What dinner party?'

'You ate with some Armored staffers who were visiting.'

She nodded.

'Vassell and Coomer,' she said. 'So?'

'They worked for General Kramer.'

She nodded again. 'So I believe.'

'Tell us about the meal.'

'The food?'

'The atmosphere,' I said. 'The conversation. The mood.'

173

'It was just dinner in the O Club,' she said.

'Someone gave Vassell and Coomer a briefcase.'

'Did they? What, like a present?'

I said nothing.

'I don't remember that,' Norton said. 'When?'

'During dinner,' I said. 'Or as they were leaving.'

Nobody spoke.

'A briefcase?' Norton said.

'Was it you?' Summer asked.

Norton looked at her, blankly. She was either genuinely puzzled, or she was a superb actress. 'Was it me what?'

'Who gave them the briefcase.'

'Why would I give them a briefcase? I hardly knew them.'

'How well did you know them?'

'I met them once or twice, years ago.'

'At Irwin?'

'I believe so.'

'Why did you eat with them?'

'I was in the bar. They asked me. It would have been rude to decline.'

'Did you know they were coming?' I asked.

'No,' she said. 'I had no idea. I was surprised they weren't in Germany.'

'So you knew them well enough to know where they're based.'

'Kramer was an Armored Branch commander in Europe. They were his staffers. I wouldn't expect to find them based in Hawaii.'

Nobody spoke. I watched Norton's eyes. She hadn't looked at Kramer's briefcase longer than about half a second. Just long enough to figure I was some guy who carried a briefcase, and then to forget all about it.

'What's going on here?' she said.

I didn't answer.

'Tell me.'

I pointed to the briefcase. 'This is General Kramer's. He lost it on New Year's Eve and it showed up again today. We're trying to figure out where it's been.'

'Where did he lose it?'

Summer moved in her chair.

'In a motel,' she said. 'During a sexual assignation with a woman from this post. The woman was driving a Humvee. Therefore we're looking for women who knew Kramer, and who have permanent access to Humvees, and who were off post on New Year's Eve, and who were at dinner last night.'

'I was the only woman at dinner last night.'

Silence.

Summer nodded. 'We know that. And we promise we can keep the whole thing quiet, but first we need you to confirm who you gave the briefcase to.'

The room stayed quiet. Norton looked at Summer like she had told a joke with a punch line she didn't quite understand.

'You think I was sleeping with General Kramer?' she said.

Summer said nothing.

'Well, I wasn't,' Norton said. 'God forbid.'

Nobody spoke.

'I don't know whether to laugh or cry,' she said. 'I'm seriously conflicted. That's a completely absurd accusation. I'm astonished you made it.'

Nobody spoke for a long time. Norton smiled, like the main component of her reaction was amusement. Not anger. She closed her eyes and opened them a moment later, like she was erasing the conversation from her memory.

'Is there something missing from the briefcase?' she asked me.

I didn't answer.

'Help me out here,' she said. 'Please. I'm trying to see the point of this extraordinary visit. Is there something missing from the briefcase?'

'Vassell and Coomer say not.'

'But?'

'I don't believe them.'

'You probably should. They're senior officers.'

I said nothing.

'What does your new CO say?'

'He doesn't want it pursued. He's worried about embarrassment.'

'You should be guided by him.'

'I'm an investigator. I have to ask questions.'

'The army is a family,' she said. 'We're all on the same side.'

'Did Vassell or Coomer leave with this briefcase last night?' I said.

Norton closed her eyes again. At first I thought she was just exasperated, but then I realized she was picturing last night's scene, at the O Club coat check.

'No,' she said. 'Neither one of them left with that briefcase.'

'Are you absolutely sure?'

'I'm totally certain.'

'What was their mood during dinner?'

She opened her eyes.

'They were relaxed,' she said. 'Like they were passing an empty evening.'

'Did they say why they were at Bird again?'

'General Kramer's funeral was yesterday, at noon.'

'I didn't know that.'

'I believe Walter Reed released the body and the Pentagon handled the details.'

'Where was the funeral?'

'Arlington Cemetery,' she said. 'Where else?'

'That's three hundred miles away.'

'Approximately. As the crow flies.'

'So why did they come down here for dinner?'

'They didn't tell me,' she said.

I said nothing.

'Anything else?' she asked.

I shook my head.

'A motel?' she said. 'Do I look like the kind of woman who would agree to meet a man in a motel?'

I didn't answer.

'Dismissed,' she said.

I stood up. Summer did the same. I took Kramer's briefcase from the centre chair and walked out of the room. Summer followed behind me.

'Did you believe her?' Summer asked me.

We were sitting in the Humvee outside the Psy-Ops building.

176

The engine was idling and the heater was blowing hot stale air that smelled of diesel.

'Totally,' I said. 'As soon as she didn't look at the briefcase. She'd have gotten very flustered if she'd ever seen it before. And I certainly believed her about the motel. It would cost you a suite at the Ritz to get in her pants.'

'So what did we learn?'

'Nothing,' I said. 'Nothing at all.'

'No, we learned that Bird is a very attractive place, apparently. Vassell and Coomer keep coming all the way down here, for no very obvious reason.'

'Tell me about it,' I said.

'And that Norton thinks we're a family.'

'Officers,' I said. 'What do you expect?'

'You're an officer. I'm an officer.'

I nodded.

'I was at West Point for four years,' I said. 'I should know better. I should have changed my name and come back in as a private. Three promotions, I'd be an E-4 specialist by now. Maybe even an E-5 sergeant. I wish I was.'

'What now?'

I checked my watch. It was close to ten o'clock.

'Sleep,' I said. 'First light, we go out looking for a yogurt container.'

THIRTEEN

I HAD NEVER EATEN YOGURT MYSELF BUT I HAD SEEN SOME AND MY impression was that individual portions came in small pots about two inches wide, which meant you could fit about three hundred of them in a square yard. Which meant you could fit nearly a million and a half of them in an acre. Which meant you could hide 150 billion of them inside Fort Bird's perimeter wire. Which meant that looking for one would be like looking for a single anthrax spore in Yankee Stadium. I did the calculation while I showered and dressed in the pre-dawn darkness.

Then I sat on my bed and waited for some light in the sky. No point in going out there and missing the one-in-150-billion chance because it was too dark to see properly. But as I sat I started to figure we could narrow the odds by being intelligent about where exactly we looked. The guy with the yogurt obviously made it back from A to B. We knew where A was. A was where Carbone had been killed. And there was a limited choice of places for B. B was either a random hole in the perimeter wire or somewhere among the main post buildings. So if we were smart, we could cut the billions to millions, and find the thing in a hundred years instead of a thousand.

Unless it was already licked clean inside some starving raccoon's den.

I met Summer in the MP motor pool. She was bright and full of energy but we didn't talk. There was nothing to say, except that the task we had set for ourselves was impossible. And I guessed neither of us wanted to confirm that out loud. So we didn't speak. We just picked a Humvee at random and headed out. I drove, for a change, the same three-minute journey I had driven thirty-some hours before.

According to the Humvee's trip meter we travelled exactly a mile and a half and according to its compass we travelled south and west, and then we arrived at the crime scene. There were still tatters of MP tape on some of the trees. We parked ten yards off the track and got out. I climbed up on the hood and sat on the roof above the windshield. Gazed west and north, and then turned around and gazed east and south. The air was cold. There was a breeze. The landscape was brown and dead and immense. The dawn sun was weak and pale.

'Which way did he go?' I called.

'North and east,' Summer called back.

She sounded pretty sure about it.

'Why?' I called.

She climbed up on the hood and sat next to me.

'He had a vehicle,' she said.

'Why?'

'Because we didn't find one left out here, and I doubt if they walked.'

'Why?'

'Because if they'd walked, it would have happened closer to where they started. This is at least a thirty-minute walk from anywhere. I don't see the bad guy concealing a tyre iron or a crowbar for thirty solid minutes, not walking side by side. Under a coat, it would make him move like a robot. Carbone would have twigged. So they drove. In the bad guy's vehicle. He had the weapon under a jacket or something on the back seat. Maybe the knife and the yogurt too.'

'Where did they start?'

'Doesn't matter. Only thing that matters to us now is where the bad guy went afterwards. And if he was in a vehicle, he

179

didn't drive outward towards the wire. We can assume there are no vehicle-size holes in it. Man-size maybe, or deer-size, but nothing big enough to drive a truck or a car through.'

'OK,' I said.

'So he headed back to the post. He can't have gone anywhere else. Can't just drive a vehicle into the middle of nowhere. He drove back along the track and parked his vehicle and went about his business.'

I nodded. Looked at the western horizon ahead of me. Turned and looked north and east, back along the track. Back towards the post. *A mile and a half of track.* I pictured the aerodynamics of an empty yogurt container. Lightweight plastic, cup-shaped, a torn foil closure flapping like an air brake. I pictured throwing one, hard. It would sail and stall in the air. It would travel ten feet, tops. A mile and a half of track, ten feet of shoulder, on the left, on the driver's side. I felt millions shrink to thousands. Then I felt them expand all the way back up to billions.

'Good news and bad news,' I said. 'I think you're right, so you've cut the search area down by about ninety-nine per cent. Maybe more. Which is good.'

'But?'

'If he was in a vehicle, did he throw it out at all?'

Summer was silent.

'He could have just dropped it on the floor,' I said. 'Or chucked it in the back.'

'Not if it was a pool vehicle.'

'So maybe he put it in a sidewalk trash can later, after he parked. Or maybe he took it home with him.'

'Maybe. It's a fifty-fifty situation.'

'Seventy-thirty at best,' I said.

'We should look anyway.'

I nodded. Braced the palms of my hands on the windshield's header rail and vaulted down to the ground.

It was January, and the conditions were pretty good. February would have been better. In a temperate northern hemisphere climate, vegetation dies right back in February. It gets as thin and sparse as it ever will. But January was OK. The under-growth was low and the ground was flat and brown. It was the colour of dead bracken and leaf litter. There was no snow. The landscape was even and neutral and organic. It was a good background. I figured a container for a dairy product would be bright white. Or cream. Or maybe pink, for a strawberry or a raspberry flavour. Whatever, it would be a helpful colour. It wouldn't be black, for instance. Nobody puts a dairy product in a black container. So if it was there and we came close to it, we would find it.

We checked a ten-foot belt all around the perimeter of the crime scene. Found nothing. So we went back to the track and set off north and east along it. Summer walked five feet from the track's right-hand edge. I walked five feet to her right. If we both scanned both ways we would cover a fifteen-foot strip, with two pairs of eyes on the crucial five-foot lane between us, which is exactly where the container should have landed, according to my aerodynamic theory.

We walked slow, maybe half-speed. I used short paces and settled into a rhythm of moving my head from one side to the other with every step. I felt pretty stupid doing it. I must have looked like a penguin. But it was an efficient method. I lapsed into a kind of autopilot mode and the ground blurred beneath me. I wasn't seeing individual leaves and twigs and blades of grass. I was tuning out what should be there. I felt like something that shouldn't be there would leap right out at me.

We walked for ten minutes and found nothing.

'Swap?' Summer said.

We changed places and moved on. We saw a million tons of forest debris, and nothing else. Army posts are kept scrupulously clean. The weekly litter patrol is a religion. Outside the wire we would have been tripping over all kinds of stuff. Inside, there was nothing. Nothing at all. We did another ten minutes, another three hundred yards, and then we paused and swapped positions again. Moving slow in the cold air was chilling me. I stared at the earth like a maniac. I felt we were close to our best chance. A mile and a half is 2,640 yards. I figured the first few hundred and the last few hundred were poor hunting grounds. At first the guy would have been feeling the pure urge to escape. Then close to the post buildings he knew he had to be ready and done and composed. So the middle stretch was where he would have sanitized. Anyone with any sense would have coasted to a stop, breathed in, breathed out, and thought things through. He would have buzzed his window down and felt the night air on his face. I slowed down and looked harder, left and right, left and right. Saw nothing.

'Did he have blood on him?' I said.

'A little, maybe,' Summer said, on my right.

I didn't look at her. I kept my eyes on the ground.

'On his gloves,' she said. 'Maybe on his shoes.'

'Less than he might have expected,' I said. 'Unless he was a doctor he would have expected some pretty bad bleeding.'

'So?'

'So he didn't use a pool car. He expected blood and didn't want to risk leaving it all over a vehicle that someone else was going to drive the next day.'

'So like you said, with his own car, he'll have thrown it in the back. So we aren't going to find anything out here.'

I nodded. Said nothing. Walked on.

We covered the whole of the middle section and found nothing. Two thousand yards of dormant organic material and not one single man-made item. Not a cigarette butt, not a scrap of paper, no rusted cans, no empty bottles. It was a real tribute to the post commander's enthusiasm. But it was disappointing. We stopped with the main post buildings clearly visible, three hundred yards in front of us.

'I want to backtrack,' I said. 'I want to do the middle part again.'

'OK,' she said. 'About face.'

She turned and we switched positions. We decided we would cover each three-hundred-yard section the opposite way around from the first pass. Where I had walked inboard, I would walk outboard, and vice versa. No real reason, except our perspectives were different and we felt we should alternate. I was more than a foot taller than she was, and therefore simple trigonometry meant I could see more than a foot farther in either direction. She was closer to the ground and she claimed her eyes were good for detail.

We walked back, slow and steady.

Nothing in the first section. We swapped positions. I took up station ten feet from the track. Scanned left and right. The wind was in our faces, and my eyes started watering from the cold. I put my hands in my pockets.

Nothing in the second section. We changed positions again. I walked five feet from the track, parallel to its edge. Nothing in the third section. We changed yet again. I did math in my head as we walked. So far we had swept a fifteen-foot swath along a 2,340-yard length. That made 11,700 square yards, which was a hair better than 2.4 acres. Nearly two and a half acres, out of a hundred thousand. Odds of 40,000 to one, approximately. Better than driving to town and spending a dollar on a lottery ticket. But not much better.

We walked on. The wind got stronger and we got colder. We saw nothing.

Then I saw something.

It was far to my right. Maybe twenty feet from me. Not a yogurt container. Something else. I almost ignored it because it was well outside the zone of possibility. No lightweight plastic unaerodynamic item could have gone that far after being thrown from a car on the track. So my eyes spotted it and my brain processed it and rejected it instantly, on a purely pre-programmed basis.

And then it hung up on it. Out of pure animal instinct.

Because it looked like a snake. The lizard part of my brain whispered *snake* and I got that little primeval jolt of fright that had kept my ancestors alive and well way back in evolution. It was all over in a split second. It was smothered immediately. The modern educated part of my mind stepped in and said *no snakes here in January, bud. Way too cold.* I breathed out and moved on a step and then paused to look back, purely out of curiosity.

There was a curved black shape in the dead grass. Belt? Garden hose? But it was settled deeper down among the stiff brown stalks than something made of leather or fabric or rubber could have fallen. It was right down there among the roots. Therefore it was heavy. And it had to be heavy to have travelled so far from the track. Therefore it was metal. Solid, not tubular. Therefore it was unfamiliar. Very little military equipment is curved.

I walked over. Got close. Knelt down.

It was a crowbar.

A black-painted crowbar, all matted on one end with blood and hair.

I stayed with it and sent Summer to get the truck. She must have jogged all the way back for it because she returned sooner than I expected and out of breath.

'Do we have an evidence bag?' I asked.

'It's not evidence,' she said. 'Training accidents don't need evidence.'

'I'm not planning on taking it to court,' I said. 'I just don't want to touch it, is all. Don't want my prints on it. That might give Willard ideas.'

She checked the back of the truck.

'No evidence bags,' she said.

I paused. Normally you take exquisite care not to contaminate evidence with foreign prints and hairs and fibres, so as not to confuse the investigation. If you screw up, you can get your ass chewed by the prosecutors. But this time the motivation had to be different, with Willard in the mix. If I screwed up, I could get my ass sent to jail. Means, motive, opportunity, my prints on the weapon. Too good to be true. If the training accident story came back to bite him, he would jump all over anything he could get.

'We could bring a specialist out here,' Summer said. She was standing right behind me. I could sense her there.

'Can't involve anyone else,' I said. 'I didn't even want to involve you.'

She came around beside me and crouched low. Smoothed stalks of grass out of the way with her hands, for a closer look.

'Don't touch it,' I said.

'Wasn't planning to,' she said.

We looked at it together, close up. It was a hand-held wrecking bar forged from octagonal-section steel. It looked like a high-quality tool. It looked brand new. It was painted gloss black with the kind of paint people use on boats or cars. It was shaped a little like an alto saxophone. The main shaft was about three feet long, slightly S-shaped, and it had a shallow curve on one end and a full curve on the other, the shape of a capital letter *J*. Both tips were flattened and notched into claws, ready for levering nails out of planks of wood. Its design was stream-lined and evolved, and simple, and brutal.

'Hardly used,' Summer said.

'Never used,' I said. 'Not for construction, anyway.'

I stood up.

'We don't need to print it,' I said. 'We can assume the guy was wearing gloves when he swung it.'

Summer stood up next to me.

'We don't need to type the blood either,' she said. 'We can assume it's Carbone's.'

I said nothing.

'We could just leave it here,' Summer said.

'No,' I said. 'We can't do that.'

I bent down and untied my right boot. Pulled the lace all the way out and used a reef knot to tie the ends together. That gave me a closed loop about fifteen inches in diameter. I draped it over my right palm and dragged the free end across the dead stubble until I snagged it under the crowbar's tip. Then I closed my fist and lifted the heavy steel weight carefully out of the grass. I held it up, like a proud angler with a fish.

'Let's go,' I said.

I limped around to the front passenger seat with the crowbar swinging gently in midair and my boot half off. I sat close to the transmission tunnel and steadied the crowbar against the floor just enough to stop it touching my legs as the vehicle moved.

'Where to?' Summer asked.

'The mortuary,' I said.

I was hoping the pathologist and his staff would be out eating breakfast, but they weren't. They were all in the building, working. The pathologist himself caught us in the lobby. He was on his way somewhere with a file in his hand. He looked at us and then he looked at the trophy dangling from my boot lace. Took him half of a second to understand what it was, and the other half to realize it put us all in a very awkward situation.

185

'We could come back later,' I said. *When you're not here.*

'No,' he said. 'We'll go to my office.'

He led the way. I watched him walk. He was a small dark man with short legs, brisk, competent, a little older than me. He seemed nice enough. And I guessed he wasn't stupid. Very few medics are. They have all kinds of complicated stuff to learn, before they get to be where they want to be. And I guessed he wasn't unethical. Very few medics were that either, in my experience. They're scientists at heart, and scientists generally retain a good-faith interest in facts and the truth. Or at least they retain some kind of innate curiosity. All of which was good, because this guy's attitude was going to be crucial. He could stay out of our way, or he could sell us out with a single phone call.

His office was a plain square room full of original-issue grey steel desks and file cabinets. It was crowded. There were framed diplomas on the walls. There were shelves full of books and manuals. No specimen jars. No weird stuff pickled in formaldehyde. It could have been an army lawyer's office, except the diplomas were from medical schools, not law schools.

He sat down in his rolling chair. Placed his file on his desk. Summer closed his door and leaned on it. I stood in the middle of the floor, with the crowbar hanging in space. We all looked at each other. Waited to see who would make the opening bid.

'Carbone was a training accident,' the doctor said, like he was moving his first pawn two squares forward.

I nodded.

'No question,' I said, like I was moving my own pawn.

'I'm glad we've got *that* straight,' he said.

But he said it in a voice that meant: *can you believe this shit?*

I heard Summer breathe out, because we had an ally. But we had an ally who wanted distance. We had an ally who wanted to hide behind an elaborate charade. And I didn't altogether blame him. He owed years of service in exchange for his medical school tuition. Therefore he was cautious. Therefore he was an ally whose wishes we had to respect.

'Carbone fell and hit his head,' I said. 'It's a closed case. Pure accident, very unfortunate for all concerned.'

186

'But?'

I held the crowbar a little higher.

'I think this is what he hit his head on,' I said.

'Three times?'

'Maybe he bounced. Maybe there were dead twigs under the leaves, made the ground a little springy, like a trampoline.'

The doctor nodded. 'Terrain can be like that, this time of year.'

'Lethal,' I said.

I lowered the crowbar again. Waited.

'Why did you bring it here?' the doctor asked.

'There might be an issue of contributory negligence,' I said. 'Whoever left it lying around for Carbone to fall on might need a reprimand.'

The doctor nodded again. 'Littering is a grave offence.'

'In this man's army,' I said.

'What do you want me to do?'

'Nothing,' I said. 'We're here to help you out, is all. With it being a closed case, we figured you wouldn't want to clutter your place up with those plaster casts you made. Of the wound site. We figured we could haul them to the trash for you.'

The doctor nodded for a third time.

'You could do that,' he said. 'It would save me a trip.'

He paused for a long moment. Then he cleared the file away from in front of him and opened some drawers and laid sheets of clean white paper on the desktop and arranged half a dozen glass microscope slides on the paper.

'That thing looks heavy,' he said to me.

'It is,' I said.

'Maybe you should put it down. Take the weight off your shoulder.'

'Is that medical advice?'

'You don't want ligament damage.'

'Where should I put it down?'

'Any flat surface you can find.'

I stepped forward and laid the crowbar gently on his desk, on top of the paper and the glass slides. Unhooked my boot lace and picked the knot out of it. Squatted down and threaded it back through all the eyelets. Tightened it up and tied it off. I looked up in time to see the doctor move a microscope slide. He picked it up and scraped it against the end of the crowbar where it was matted with blood and hair.

'Damn,' he said. 'I got this slide all dirty. Very careless of me.'

He made the exact same error with five more slides.

'Are we interested in fingerprints?' he said.

I shook my head. 'We're assuming gloves.'

'We should check, I think. Contributory negligence is a serious matter.'

He opened another drawer and peeled a latex glove out of a box and snapped it on his hand. It made a tiny cloud of talcum dust. Then he picked the crowbar up and carried it out of the room.

He came back less than ten minutes later. He still had his glove on. The crowbar was washed clean. The black paint gleamed. It looked indistinguishable from new.

'No prints,' he said.

He put the crowbar down on his chair and pulled a file drawer and came out with a plain brown cardboard box. Opened it up and took out two chalk-white plaster casts. Both were about six inches long and both had *Carbone* handwritten in black ink on the underside. One was a positive, formed by pressing wet plaster into the wound. The other was a negative, formed by moulding more plaster over the positive. The negative showed the shape of the wound the weapon had made, and therefore the positive showed the shape of the weapon itself.

The doctor put the positive on the chair next to the crowbar. Lined them up, parallel. The cast was about six inches long. It was white and a little pitted from the moulding process but was otherwise identical to the smooth black iron. Absolutely identical. Same section, same thickness, same contours.

Then the doctor put the negative on the desk. It was a little bigger than the positive, and a little messier. It was an exact replica of the back of Carbone's shattered head. The doctor picked up the crowbar. Hefted it in his hand. Lined it up, speculatively. Brought it down, very slowly, *one*, for the first

188

blow, then *two* for the second. Then *three* for the last. He touched it to the plaster. The third and final wound was the best defined. It was a clear three-quarter-inch trench in the plaster, and the crowbar fitted it perfectly.

'I'll check the blood and the hair,' the doctor said. 'Not that we don't already know what the results will be.'

He lifted the crowbar out the plaster and tried it again. It went in again, precisely, and deep. He lifted it out and balanced it across his open palms, like he was weighing it. Then he grasped it by the straighter end and swung it, like a batter going after a high fastball. He swung it again, harder, a compact, violent stroke. It looked big in his hands. Big, and a little heavy for him. A little out of control.

'Very strong man,' he said. 'Vicious swing. Big tall guy, right-handed, physically very fit. But that describes a lot of people on this post, I guess.'

'There was no guy,' I said. 'Carbone fell and hit his head.'

The doctor smiled briefly and balanced the bar across his palms again.

'It's handsome, in its way,' he said. 'Does that sound strange?'

I knew what he meant. It was a nice piece of steel, and it was everything it needed to be and nothing it didn't. Like a Colt Detective Special, or a K-bar, or a cockroach.

He slid it inside a long steel drawer. The metals scraped one on the other and then boomed faintly when he let it go and dropped it the final inch.

'I'll keep it here,' he said. 'If you like. Safer that way.'

'OK,' I said.

He closed the drawer.

'Are you right-handed?' he asked me.

'Yes,' I said. 'I am.'

'Colonel Willard told me you did it,' he said. 'But I didn't believe him.'

'Why not?'

'You were very surprised when you saw who it was. When I put his face back on. You had a definite physical reaction. People can't fake that sort of thing.'

'Did you tell Willard that?'

The doctor nodded. 'He found it inconvenient. But it didn't

really deflect him. And I'm sure he's already developed a theory to explain it away.'

'I'll watch my back,' I said.

'Some Delta sergeants came to see me too. There are rumours starting. I think you should watch your back very carefully.'

'I plan to,' I said.

'*Very* carefully,' the doctor said.

Summer and I got back in the Humvee. She fired it up and put it in gear and sat with her foot on the brake.

'Quartermaster,' I said.

'It wasn't military issue,' she said.

'It looked expensive,' I said. 'Expensive enough for the Pentagon, maybe.'

'It would have been green.'

I nodded. 'Probably. But we should still check. Sooner or later we're going to need all our ducks in a row.'

She took her foot off the brake and headed for the quartermaster building. She had been at Bird much longer than me and she knew where everything was. She parked again in front of the usual type of warehouse. I knew there would be a long counter inside with massive off-limits storage areas behind it. There would be huge bales of clothing, tyres, blankets, mess kits, entrenching tools, equipment of every kind.

We went in and found a young guy in new BDUs behind the counter. He was a cheerful corn-fed country boy. He looked like he was working in his dad's hardware store, and he looked like it was his life's ambition. He was enthusiastic. I told him we were interested in construction equipment. He opened a manual the size of eight phone books. Found the correct section. I asked him to find listings for crowbars. He licked his forefinger and turned pages and found two entries. *Prybar, general issue, long, claw on one end* and then *crowbar, general issue, short, claw on both ends*. I asked him to show us an example of the latter.

He went away and disappeared among the tall stacks. We waited. Breathed in the unique quartermaster smell of old dust and new rubber and damp cotton twill. He came back after five long minutes with a GI crowbar. Laid it down on the counter in front of us. It landed with a heavy thump. Summer had been right. It was painted olive green. And it was a completely different item from the one we had just left in the pathologist's office. Different section, six inches shorter, slightly thinner, slightly different curves. It looked carefully designed. It was probably a perfect example of the way the army does things. Years ago it had probably been the ninety-ninth item on some-one's re-equipment agenda. A subcommittee would have been formed, with expert input from survivors of the old construction battalions. A specification would have been drawn up concerning length and weight and durability. Metal fatigue would have been investigated. Arenas of likely use would have been considered. Brittleness in the frozen winters of northern Europe would have been evaluated. Malleability in the severe heat of the equator would have been taken into account. Detailed drawings would have been made. Then tenders would have gone out. Mills all over Pennsylvania and Alabama would have priced the job. Prototypes would have been forged. They would have been tested, exhaustively. One and only one winner would have been approved. Paint would have been supplied, and the thickness and uniformity of its application would have been specified and carefully monitored. Then the whole business would have been completely forgotten. But the product of all those long months of deliberation was still coming through, thousands of units a year, needed or not.

'Thanks, soldier,' I said.

'You need to take it?' the kid asked.

'Just needed to see it,' I said.

We went back to my office. It was mid-morning, a dull day, and I felt aimless. So far, the new decade wasn't doing much for me. I wasn't a huge fan of the 1990s yet, at that point, six days in.

'Are you going to write the accident report?' Summer asked.

'For Willard? Not yet.'

'He'll expect it today.'

I nodded. 'I know. But I'm going to make him ask, one more time.'

191

'Why?'

'I guess because it's a fascinating experience. Like watching maggots writhing around in something that died.'

'What died?'

'My enthusiasm for getting out of bed in the morning.'

'One bad apple,' she said. 'Doesn't mean much.'

'Maybe,' I said. 'If it is just one.'

She said nothing.

'Crowbars,' I said. 'We've got two separate cases with crowbars, and I don't like coincidences. But I can't see how they can be connected. There's no way to join them up. Carbone was a million miles from Mrs Kramer, in every way imaginable. They were in completely different worlds.'

'Vassell and Coomer join them up,' she said. 'They had an interest in something that could have been in Mrs Kramer's house, and they were here at Bird the night Carbone was killed.'

I nodded. 'That's what's driving me crazy. It's a perfect connection, except it isn't. They took one call in D.C., they were too far from Green Valley to do anything to Mrs Kramer themselves, and they didn't call anyone from the hotel. Then they were here the night Carbone died, but they were in the O Club with a dozen witnesses the whole time, eating steak and fish.'

'First time they were here, they had a driver. Major Marshall, remember? But the second time, they were on their own. That feels a little clandestine to me. Like they were here for a secret reason.'

'Nothing very secret about hanging around in the O Club bar and then eating in the O Club dining room. They weren't out of sight for a minute, all night long.'

'But why didn't they have their driver? Why come on their own? I assume Marshall was at the funeral with them. But they chose to drive more than three hundred miles by themselves? And more than three hundred back?'

'Maybe Marshall was unavailable,' I said.

'He's their blue-eyed boy,' she said. 'He's available when they say so.'

'Why did they come here at all? It's a very long way for a very average dinner.'

'They came for the briefcase, Reacher. Norton's wrong. She must be. Someone gave it to them. They left with it.'

'I don't think Norton's wrong. She convinced me.'

'Then maybe they picked it up in the parking lot. Norton wouldn't have seen that. I assume she didn't go out there in the cold and wave them off. But they left with it, for sure. Why else would they be happy to fly back to Germany?'

'Maybe they just gave up on it. They were due back in Germany anyway. They couldn't stay here for ever. They've got Kramer's command to fight over.'

Summer said nothing.

'Whatever,' I said. 'There's no possible connection.'

'It's a random universe.'

I nodded. 'So they stay on the back burner. Carbone stays on the front.'

'Are we going back out to look for the yogurt pot?'

I shook my head. 'It's in the guy's car, or in his trash.'

'Could have been useful.'

'We'll work with the crowbar instead. It's brand new. It was probably bought just as recently as the yogurt was.'

'We have no resources.'

'Detective Clark up in Green Valley will do it for us. He's already looking for *his* crowbar, presumably. He'll be canvassing hardware stores. We'll ask him to widen his radius and stretch his time frame.'

'That's a lot of extra work for him.'

I nodded. 'We'll have to offer him something. We'll have to string him along. We'll tell him we're working on something that might help him.'

'Like what?'

I smiled. 'We could fake it. We could give him Andrea Norton's name. We could show her exactly what kind of a family we are.'

I called Detective Clark. I didn't give him Andrea Norton's name. I told him a few lies instead. I told him I recalled the damage to Mrs Kramer's door, and the damage to her head, and that I figured a crowbar was involved, and I told him that as it happened we had a rash of break-ins at military

193

installations all up and down the Eastern seaboard that also seemed to involve crowbars, and I asked him if we could piggy-back on the legwork he was undoubtedly already doing in terms of tracing the Green Valley weapon. He paused at that point, and I filled the silence by telling him that military quartermasters currently had no crowbars on general issue and therefore I was convinced our bad guys had used a civilian source of supply. I gave him some guff about not wanting to duplicate his efforts because we had a more promising line of inquiry to spend our time on. He paused again at that point, like cops everywhere, waiting to hear the proffered quid pro quo. I told him that as soon as we had a name or a profile or a description he would have it too, just as fast as stuff can travel down a fax line. He perked up then. He was a desperate man, staring at a brick wall. He asked what exactly I wanted. I told him it would be helpful to us if he could expand his canvass to a three-hundred-mile radius around Green Valley, and check hardware store purchases during a window that started late on New Year's Eve and extended through, say, January 4th.

'What's your promising line of inquiry?' he asked.

'There might be a military connection with Mrs Kramer. We might be able to give you the guy on a plate all tied up with a bow.'

'I'd really like that.'

'Co-operation,' I said. 'Makes the world go around.'

'Sure does,' he said.

He sounded happy. He bought the whole bill of goods. He promised to expand his search and copy me in. I hung up the phone and it rang again immediately. I picked it up and heard a woman's voice. It sounded warm and intimate and southern. It asked me to 10-33 a 10-16 from the MP XO at Fort Jackson, which meant *please stand by to take a secure landline call from your opposite number in South Carolina*. I waited with the phone by my ear and heard empty electronic hiss for a moment. Then there was a loud click and my oppo in South Carolina came on and told me I should know that Colonel David C. Brubaker, Fort Bird's Special Forces CO, had been found that morning with two bullets in his head in an alley in a crummy district of

Columbia, which was South Carolina's capital city, and which was all of two hundred miles from the North Carolina golf course hotel where he had been spending his holiday furlough with his wife. And according to the local paramedics he had been dead for a day or two.

FOURTEEN

MY OPPO AT JACKSON WAS A GUY CALLED SANCHEZ. I KNEW him fairly well, and I liked him better. He was smart, and he was good. I put the call on the speaker to include Summer and we talked briefly about jurisdiction, but without much enthusiasm. Jurisdiction was always a grey area, and we all knew we were beaten from the get-go. Brubaker had been on vacation, he had been in civilian clothes, he had been in a city alley, and therefore the Columbia PD was claiming him. There was nothing we could do about it. And the Columbia PD had notified the FBI, because Brubaker's last known whereabouts were the North Carolina golf hotel, which added a possible interstate dimension to the situation, and interstate homicide was the Bureau's bag. And also because an army officer is technically a federal employee, and killing federal employees is a separate offence, which would give them another charge to throw at the perp if by any miracle they ever found him. Neither Sanchez nor I nor Summer cared a whole hell of a lot about the difference between state courts and federal courts, but we all knew if the FBI was involved the case was well beyond our grasp. We agreed the very best we could hope for was that we might eventually see some of the relevant

196

documentation, strictly for informational purposes only, and strictly as a courtesy. Summer made a face and turned away. I took the phone off the speaker and picked it up and spoke to Sanchez one on one again.

'Got a feeling?' I asked him.

'Someone he knew,' Sanchez said. 'Not easy to surprise a Delta soldier as good as Brubaker was, in an alley.'

'Weapon?'

'Paramedics figured it for a nine-millimetre handgun. And they should know. They see plenty of GSWs. Apparently they do a lot of cleaning up every Friday and Saturday night, in that part of town.'

'Why was he there?'

'No idea. Rendezvous, presumably. With someone he knew.'

'Got a feeling about when?'

'The body's stone cold, the skin is a little green, and rigor is all gone. They're saying twenty-four or forty-eight hours. Safe bet would be to split the difference. Let's call it the middle of the night before last. Maybe three or four a.m. City garbage truck found him at ten this morning. Weekly trash collection.'

'Where were you on December twenty-eighth?'

'Korea. You?'

'Panama.'

'Why did they move us?'

'I keep thinking we're about to find out,' I said.

'Something weird is going on,' Sanchez said. 'I checked, because I was curious, and there are more than twenty of us in the same boat, worldwide. And Garber's signature is on all the orders, but I don't think it's legit.'

'I'm certain it isn't legit,' I said. 'Anything happening down there before this Brubaker situation?'

'Not a thing. Quietest week I ever spent.'

We hung up. I sat still for a long moment. Seemed to me that Columbia in South Carolina was about two hundred miles from Fort Bird. Drive southwest on the highway, cross the state line, find I-20 heading west, drive some more, and you were there. About two hundred miles. The night before last was the night we found Carbone's body. I had left Andrea Norton's office just before two o'clock in the morning. She could alibi me up until that point. Then I had been in the mortuary at seven o'clock, for the post-mortem. The pathologist could confirm that. So I had two unconnected alibi bookends. But 0200 until 0700 still gave me a possible five-hour window, with Brubaker's likely time of death right there in the middle of it. Could I have driven two hundred miles there and two hundred miles back in five hours?

'What?' Summer said.

'The Delta guys have already got me in the frame for Carbone. Now I'm wondering whether they're going to be coming at me for Brubaker, too. How does four hundred miles in five hours sound to you?'

'I could probably do it,' she said. 'Average of eighty miles an hour all the way. Depends on what car I was using, of course, and road construction, and traffic, and weather, and cops. It's definitely possible.'

'Terrific.'

'But it's marginal.'

'It better be marginal. Killing Brubaker will be like killing God, to them.'

'You going over there to break the news?'

I nodded. 'I think I have to. It's a question of respect. But you inform the post commander for me, OK?'

The Special Forces adjutant was an asshole, but he was human, too. He got very still and went very pale when I told him about Brubaker and there was clearly more to it than an anticipation of mere bureaucratic hassle. From what I had heard Brubaker was stern and distant and authoritarian, but he was a real father figure, to his men individually and to his unit as a whole. And to his unit as a concept. Special Forces generally and Delta in particular hadn't always been popular inside the Pentagon and on Capitol Hill. The army hates change and it takes a long time to get used to things. The idea of a ragtag bunch of hunter-killers had been a hard sell at the outset, and Brubaker had been one of the guys doing the selling, and he had never let up since. His death was going to hit Special Forces the way the death of a president would hit the nation as a whole.

'Carbone was bad enough,' the adjutant said. 'But this is unbelievable. Is there a connection?'

I looked at him.

'Why would there be a connection?' I said. 'Carbone was a training accident.'

He said nothing.

'Why was Brubaker at a hotel?'

'Because he likes to play golf. He's got a house near Bragg from way back, but he doesn't like the golf there.'

'Where was the hotel?'

'Outside of Raleigh.'

'Did he go there a lot?'

'Every chance he got.'

'Does his wife play golf?'

The adjutant nodded. 'They play together.'

Then he paused.

'Played,' he said, and then he went quiet and looked away from me. I pictured Brubaker in my mind. I had never met him, but I knew guys just like him. One day they're talking about how to angle a claymore mine so the little ball bearings explode outward at exactly the right angle to rip the enemy's spines out of their backs with maximum efficiency. Next day they're wearing pastel shirts with small crocodiles on the breast, playing golf with their wives, maybe holding hands and smiling as they ride together along the fairways in their little electric carts. I knew plenty of guys like that. My own father had been one. Not that he had ever played golf. He watched birds. He had been in most countries in the world, and he had seen a lot of birds.

I stood up.

'Call me if you need me,' I said. 'You know, if there's anything I can do.'

The adjutant nodded.

'Thanks for the visit,' he said. 'Better than a phone call.'

I went back to my office. Summer wasn't there. I wasted more than an hour with her personnel lists. I made a short-cut decision and took the pathologist out of the mix. I took Summer out. I took Andrea Norton out. Then I took all the women out. The medical evidence was pretty clear about the attacker's height and strength. I took the O Club dining-room staff out.

199

Their NCO had said they were all hard at work, fussing over their guests. I took the cooks out, and the bar staff, and the MP gate guards. I took out anyone listed as hospitalized and non-ambulatory. I took myself out. I took Carbone out, because it wasn't suicide.

Then I counted the remaining check marks, and wrote the number 973 on a slip of paper. That was our suspect pool. I stared into space. My phone rang. I picked it up. It was Sanchez again, down at Fort Jackson.

'Columbia PD just called me,' he said. 'They're sharing their initial findings.'

'And?'

'Their medical examiner doesn't entirely agree with me. Time of death wasn't three or four in the morning. It was one twenty-three a.m., the night before last.'

'That's very precise.'

'Bullet caught his wristwatch.'

'A broken watch? Can't necessarily rely on that.'

'No, it's firm enough. They did a lot of other tests. Wrong season for measurable insect activity, which would have helped, but the stomach contents were exactly right for five or six hours after he ate a heavy dinner.'

'What does his wife say?'

'He disappeared at eight that night, after a heavy dinner. Got up from the table and never came back.'

'What did she do about it?'

'Nothing,' Sanchez said. 'He was Special Forces. Their whole marriage, he'll have been disappearing with no warning, the middle of dinner, the middle of the night, days or weeks at a time, never able to say where or why afterwards. She was used to it.'

'Did he get a phone call or something?'

'She assumes he did, at some point. She's not really sure. She was in the spa before dinner. They'd just played twenty-seven holes.'

'Can you call her yourself? She'll talk to you faster than civilian cops.'

'I could try, I suppose.'

'Anything else?' I said.

200

'The GSWs were nine millimetre,' he said. 'Two rounds fired, both of them through and through, neat entry wounds, bad exit wounds.'

'Full metal jackets,' I said.

'Contact shots,' he said. 'There were powder burns. And soot.'

I paused. I couldn't picture it. *Two rounds fired? Contact shots?* So one of the bullets goes in, comes out, loops all the way around, comes back and drops down and smashes his wrist-watch?

'Did he have his hands on his head?'

'He was shot from behind, Reacher. A double tap, to the back of the skull. *Bang bang*, thank you and goodnight. The second round must have gone through his head and caught his watch. Downward trajectory. Tall shooter.'

I said nothing.

'Right,' Sanchez said. 'How likely *is* all that? Did you know him?'

'Never met him,' I said.

'He was way above average. He was a real pro. And he was a thinker. Any angle, any advantage, any wrinkle, he knew it and he was ready to use it.'

'But he got himself shot in the back of the head?'

'He knew the guy, definitely. Had to. Why else would he turn his back, in the middle of the night, in an alley?'

'You looking at people from Jackson?'

'That's a lot of people.'

'Tell me about it.'

'Did he have enemies at Bird?'

'Not that I've heard,' I said. 'He had enemies up the chain of command.'

'Those pussies don't meet people in alleys in the middle of the night.'

'Where was the alley?'

'Not in a quiet part of town.'

'So did anyone hear anything?'

'Nobody,' Sanchez said. 'Columbia PD ran a canvass and came up empty.'

'That's weird.'

201

'They're civilians. What else would they be?'

He went quiet.

'You met Willard yet?' I asked him.

'He's on his way here right now. Seems to be a real hands-on type of asshole.'

'What was the alley like?'

'Whores and crack dealers. Nothing that the Columbia city fathers are likely to put in their tourism brochures.'

'Willard hates embarrassment,' I said. 'He's going to be nervous about image.'

'Columbia's image? What does he care?'

'The army's image,' I said. 'He won't want Brubaker put next to whores and crack dealers. Not an elite colonel. He figures this Soviet stuff is going to shake things up. He figures we need good PR right now. He figures he can see the big picture.'

'The big picture is I can't get near this case anyway. So what kind of pull does he have with the Columbia PD and the FBI? Because that's what it's going to take.'

'Just be ready for trouble,' I said.

'Are we in for seven lean years?'

'Not that long.'

'Why not?'

'Just a feeling,' I said.

'You happy with me handling liaison down here? Or should I get them to call you direct? Brubaker is your dead guy, technically.'

'You do it,' I said. 'I've got other things to do.'

We hung up and I went back to Summer's lists. *Nine hundred seventy-three*. Nine hundred seventy-two innocent, one guilty. But which one?

Summer came back inside another hour. She walked in and gave me a sheet of paper. It was a photocopy of a weapons requisition that Sergeant First Class Christopher Carbone had made four months ago. It was for a Heckler & Koch P7 hand-gun. Maybe he had liked the H&K sub-machine guns Delta was using, and therefore he wanted the P7 for his personal side-arm. He had asked for it to be chambered for the standard nine-millimetre Parabellum cartridge. He had asked for the

13-round magazine, and three spares. It was a perfectly standard requisition form, and a perfectly reasonable request. I was sure it had been granted. There would have been no political sensitivities. H&K was a German outfit and Germany was a NATO country, last time I checked. There would have been no compatibility issues, either. Nine-millimetre Parabellums were standard NATO loads. The U.S. Army had no shortage of them. We had warehouses crammed full of them. We could have filled 13-round magazines with them a million times over, every day for the rest of history.

'So?' I said.

'Look at the signature on it,' Summer said. She took my copy of Carbone's complaint out of her inside pocket and handed it over. I spread it out on my desk, side by side with the requisition form. Looked from one to the other.

The two signatures were identical.

'We're not handwriting experts,' I said.

'We don't need to be. They're the same, Reacher. Believe it.'

I nodded. Both signatures read *C. Carbone*, and the four capital letter *C*s were very distinctive. They were fast, elongated, curling flourishes. The lower-case *e* on the end of each sample was distinctive too. It made a small round shape, and then the tail of the letter whipped way out to the right of the page, well beyond the name itself, horizontally, and exuberantly. The *a-r-b-o-n* in the middle was fast and fluid and linear. As a whole it was a bold, proud, legible, self-confident signature, developed no doubt by long years of signing checks and bar bills and leases and car papers. No signature was impossible to forge, of course, but I figured this one would have been a real challenge. A challenge that I guessed would have been impossible to meet, between midnight and 0845 on a North Carolina army post.

'OK,' I said. 'The complaint is genuine.'

I left it on the desk. Summer reversed it and read it through, although she must have read it plenty of times already.

'It's cold,' she said. 'It's like a knife in the back.'

'It's weird,' I said. 'That's what it is. I never met this guy before. I'm absolutely sure of that. And he was Delta. Not

203

too many gentle pacifist souls over there. Why would he be offended? It wasn't *his* leg I broke.'

'Maybe it was personal. Maybe the fat guy was his friend.'

I shook my head. 'He'd have stepped in. He'd have stopped the fight.'

'It's the only complaint he ever made in a sixteen-year career.'

'You been talking to people?'

'All kinds of people. Right here, and by phone far and wide.'

'Were you careful?'

'Very. And it's the only complaint you ever had made against you.'

'You checked that too?'

She nodded. 'All the way back to when God's dog was a puppy.'

'You wanted to know what kind of a guy you're dealing with here?'

'No, I wanted to be able to show the Delta guys you don't have a history. With Carbone or with anyone else.'

'You're protecting *me* now?'

'Someone's going to have to. I was just over there, and they're plenty mad.'

I nodded. *Brubaker.*

'I'm sure they are,' I said. I pictured their lonely prison barracks, first designed to keep people in, then used to keep strangers out, now serving to keep their unity boiling like a pressure cooker. I pictured Brubaker's office, wherever it was, quiet and deserted. I pictured Carbone's cell, standing empty.

'So where was Carbone's new P7?' I said. 'I didn't find it in his quarters.'

'In their armoury,' Summer said. 'Cleaned, oiled, and loaded. They check their personal weapons in and out. They've got a cage inside their hangar. You should see that place. It's like Santa's grotto. Special armoured Humvees wall to wall, trucks, explosives, grenade launchers, claymores, night vision stuff. They could equip a Central African dictatorship all by themselves.'

'That's very reassuring,' I said.

'Sorry,' she said.

'Why did he file the complaint?'

'I don't know,' she said.

I pictured Carbone in the strip club, New Year's night. I had walked in and I had seen a group of four men I took to be sergeants. The swirl of the crowd had turned three of them away from me and one of them towards me in a completely random dynamic. I hadn't known who was going to be there, they hadn't known I was going to show up. I had never met any of them before. The encounter was as close to pure chance as it was possible to get. Yet Carbone had tagged me for the kind of tame mayhem he must have seen a thousand times before. The kind of tame mayhem he must have *joined in with* a hundred times before. Show me an enlisted man who claims never to have fought a civilian in a bar, and I'll show you a liar.

'Are you Catholic?' I asked.

'No, why?' Summer said.

'I wondered if you knew any Latin.'

'It's not just Catholics who know Latin. I went to school.'

'OK, *cui bono*?' I said.

'Who benefits? What, from the complaint?'

'It's always a good guide to motive,' I said. 'You can explain most things with it. History, politics, everything.'

'Like, follow the money?'

'Approximately,' I said. 'Except I don't think there's money involved here. But there must have been some benefit for Carbone. Otherwise why would he do it?'

'Could have been a moral thing. Maybe he was driven to do it.'

'Not if it was his first complaint in sixteen years. He must have seen far worse. I only broke one leg and one nose. It was no kind of a big deal. This is the army, Summer. I assume he hadn't been confusing it with a gardening club all these years.'

'I don't know,' she said again.

I slid her the slip of paper with *973* written on it.

'That's our suspect pool,' I said.

'He was in the bar until eight o'clock,' she said. 'I checked that, too. He left alone. Nobody saw him again after that.'

'Anyone say anything about his mood?'

'Delta guys don't have moods. Too much danger of appearing human.'

'Had he been drinking?'

'One beer.'

'So he just walked out of the mess at eight, no nerves, no worries?'

'Apparently so.'

'He knew the guy he was meeting,' I said.

Summer said nothing.

'Sanchez called again while you were out,' I said. 'Colonel Brubaker was shot in the back of the head. A double-tap, close in, from behind.'

'So he knew the guy he was meeting, too.'

'Very likely,' I said. 'One twenty-three in the morning. Bullet caught his watch. Between three and a half and four and a half hours after Carbone.'

'That puts you in the clear with Delta. You were still here at one twenty-three.'

'Yes,' I said. 'I was. With Norton.'

'I'll spread the word.'

'They won't believe you.'

'Do you think there's a connection between Carbone and Brubaker?'

'Common sense says there has to be. But I don't see how. And I don't see why. I mean, sure, they were both Delta soldiers. But Carbone was here and Brubaker was there, and Brubaker was a high-profile mover and shaker, and Carbone was a nobody who kept himself to himself. Maybe because he thought he had to.'

'You think we'll ever have gays in the military?'

'We've already got gays in the military. We always have had. World War Two, the western allies had fourteen million men in uniform. Any kind of reasonable probability says at least a million of them were gay. And we won that war, as I recall, last time I checked with the history books. We won it big time.'

'It's a hell of a step,' she said.

'They took the same step when they let black soldiers in. And women. Everyone pissed and moaned about that, too. Bad for morale, bad for unit cohesion. It was crap then and it's crap now. Right? You're here and you're doing OK.'

'Are you a Catholic?'

I shook my head. 'My mother taught us the Latin. She cared about our education. She taught us things, me and my brother Joe.'

'You should call her.'

'Why?'

'To see how her leg is.'

'Maybe later,' I said.

I went back to the personnel lists and Summer went out and came back in with a map of the eastern United States. She taped it flat to the wall below the clock and marked our location at Fort Bird with a red push pin. Then she marked Columbia, South Carolina, where Brubaker had been found. Then she marked Raleigh, North Carolina, where he had been playing golf with his wife. I gave her a clear plastic ruler from my desk drawer and she checked the map's scale and started calculating times and distances.

'Bear in mind most of us don't drive as fast as you do,' I said.

'None of you drive as fast as I do,' she said.

She measured four and a half inches between Raleigh and Columbia and called it five to allow for the way U.S.1 snaked slightly. She held the ruler against the scale in the legend box.

'Two hundred miles,' she said. 'So if Brubaker left Raleigh after dinner, he could have been in Columbia by midnight, easily. An hour or so before he died.'

Then she checked the distance between Fort Bird and Columbia. She came up with a hundred and fifty miles, less than I had originally guessed.

'Three hours,' she said. 'To be comfortable.'

Then she looked at me.

'It could have been the same guy,' she said. 'If Carbone was killed at nine or ten, the same guy could have been in Columbia at midnight or one, ready for Brubaker.'

She put her little finger on the Fort Bird pin.

'Carbone,' she said.

Then she spanned her hand and put her index finger on the Columbia pin.

'Brubaker,' she said. 'It's a definite sequence.'

'It's a definite guess,' I said.

She didn't reply.

'Do we know that Brubaker drove down from Raleigh?' I said.

'We can assume he did.'

'We should check with Sanchez,' I said. 'See if they found his car anywhere. See if his wife says he took it with him in the first place.'

'OK,' she said. She went out to my sergeant's desk to make the call. Left me with the interminable personnel lists. She came back in ten minutes later.

'He took his car,' she said. 'His wife told Sanchez they had two cars up at the hotel. His and hers. They always did it that way because he was always rushing off somewhere and she was always concerned about getting stuck.'

'What kind of car?' I said. I figured she would have asked.

'Chevy Impala SS.'

'Nice car.'

'He left after dinner and his wife's assumption was that he was driving back here to Bird. That would have been normal. But the car hasn't turned up anyplace yet. At least not according to the Columbia PD and the FBI.'

'OK,' I said.

'Sanchez thinks they're holding out on him, like they know something we don't.'

'That would be normal, too.'

'He's pressing them. But it's difficult.'

'It always is.'

'He'll call us,' she said. 'As soon as he gets anywhere.'

We got a call thirty minutes later. But not from Sanchez. Not about Brubaker or Carbone. The call was from Detective Clark, in Green Valley, Virginia. It was about Mrs Kramer's case.

'Got something,' he said.

He sounded very pleased with himself. He launched into a blow-by-blow account of the moves he had made. They sounded reasonably intelligent. He had used a map to figure out all the likely approaches to Green Valley from as much as three hundred miles away. Then he had used phone books to compile a list of hardware sources that lay along those approaches. He had started his guys calling them all, one by one, beginning right in the centre of the spiderweb. He had figured that crow-bar sales would be slow in winter. Major remodelling happens from springtime onward. Nobody wants their walls torn down for kitchen extensions when the weather is cold. So he had expected to get very few positive reports. After three hours he had gotten none at all. People had spent the post-Christmas period buying power drills and electric screwdrivers. Some had bought chainsaws, to keep their woodburning stoves going. Those with pioneer fantasies had bought axes. But nobody had been interested in inert and prosaic things like crowbars.

So he made a lateral jump and fired up his crime databases. Originally he planned to look for reports of other crimes that involved doors and crowbars. He thought that might narrow down a location. He didn't find anything that matched his parameters. But instead, right there on his NCIC computer, he found a burglary at a small hardware store in Sperryville, Virginia. The store was a lonely place on a dead-end street. According to the owner the front window had been kicked in sometime in the early hours of New Year's Day. Because it was a holiday, there had been no money left in the register. As far as the store owner could tell, the only thing that had been stolen was a single crowbar.

Summer stepped back to the map on the wall and put a push pin through the centre of Sperryville, Virginia. Sperryville was a small place and the plastic barrel of the pin obscured it completely. Then she put another pin through Green Valley. The two pins finished up about a quarter-inch apart. They were almost touching. They represented about ten miles of separation.

'Look at this,' Summer said.

I got up and stepped over. Looked at the map. Sperryville was on the elbow of a crooked road that ran southwest to Green Valley and beyond. In the other direction it didn't really go anywhere at all except Washington D.C. So Summer put a pin in Washington D.C. She put the tip of her little finger on it. Put her middle finger on Sperryville and her index finger on Green Valley.

'Vassell and Coomer,' she said. 'They left D.C., they stole the crowbar in Sperryville, they broke into Mrs Kramer's house in Green Valley.'

'Except they didn't,' I said. 'They were just in from the airport. They didn't have a car. And they didn't call for one. You checked the phone records yourself.'

She said nothing.

'Plus they're lard-ass staff officers,' I said. 'They wouldn't know how to burgle a hardware store if their lives depended on it.'

She took her hand off the map. I stepped back to my desk and sat down again and butted the personnel lists into a neat pile.

'We need to concentrate on Carbone,' I said.

'Then we need a new plan,' she said. 'Detective Clark is going to stop looking for crowbars now. He's found the one he's interested in.'

I nodded. 'Back to traditional time-honoured methods of investigation.'

'Which are?'

'I don't really know. I went to West Point. I didn't go to MP school.'

My phone rang. I picked it up. The same warm southern voice I had heard before went through the same *10-33, 10-16 from Jackson* routine I had heard before. I acknowledged and hit the speaker button and leaned all the way back in my chair and waited. The room filled with electronic hum. Then there was a click.

'Reacher?' Sanchez said.

'And Lieutenant Summer,' I said. 'We're on the speaker.'

'Anyone else in the room?'

'No,' I said.

'Door closed?'

'Yes. What's up?'

'Columbia PD came through again, is what. They're feeding me stuff bit by bit. And they're having themselves a real good time doing it. They're gloating like crazy.'

'Why?'

'Because Brubaker had heroin in his pocket, that's why. Three dime bags of brown. And a big wad of cash money. They're saying it was a drug deal that went bad.'

FIFTEEN

I WAS BORN IN 1960, WHICH MADE ME SEVEN DURING THE
Summer of Love, and thirteen at the end of our effective
involvement in Vietnam, and fifteen at the end of our official
involvement there. Which meant I missed most of the American
military's collision with narcotics. The heavy-duty Purple
Haze years passed me by. I had caught the later, stable phase.
Like many soldiers I had smoked a little weed from time
to time, maybe just enough to develop a preference among
different strains and sources, but nowhere near enough to put
me high on the list of U.S. users in terms of lifetime volume
consumed. I was a part-timer. I was one of those guys who
bought, not sold.

But as an MP, I had seen plenty sold. I had seen drug deals. I
had seen them succeed, and I had seen them fail. I knew the
drill. And one thing I knew for sure was that if a bad deal ends
up with a dead guy on the floor, there's nothing in the dead
guy's pocket. No cash, no product. No way. Why would there
be? If the dead guy was the buyer, the seller runs away with his
dope intact *and* the buyer's cash. If the dead guy was the seller,
then the buyer gets the whole stash for free. The deal money
walks right back home with him. Either way someone takes a

211

nice big profit in exchange for a couple of bullets and a little rummaging around.

'It's bullshit, Sanchez,' I said. 'It's faked.'

'Of course it is. I know that.'

'Did you make that point?'

'Did I need to? They're civilians, but they ain't stupid.'

'So why are they gloating?'

'Because it gives them a free pass. If they can't close the case, they can just write it off. Brubaker ends up looking bad, not them.'

'They found any witnesses yet?'

'Not a one.'

'Shots were fired,' I said. 'Someone must have heard something.'

'Not according to the cops.'

'Willard is going to freak,' I said.

'That's the least of our problems.'

'Are you alibied?'

'Me? Do I need to be?'

'Willard's going to be looking for leverage. He's going to use anything he can invent to get you to toe the line.'

Sanchez didn't answer right away. Some kind of electronic circuitry in the phone line brought the background hiss up loud to cover the silence. Then he spoke over it.

'I think I'm fireproof here,' he said. 'It's the Columbia PD making the accusations, not me.'

'Just take care,' I said.

'Bet on it,' he said.

I clicked the phone off. Summer was thinking. Her face was tense and her lower lids were moving.

'What?' I said.

'You sure it was faked?' she said.

'Had to be,' I said.

'OK,' she said. 'Good.' She was still standing next to the map. She put her hand back on it. Little finger on the Fort Bird pin, index finger on the Columbia pin. 'We agree that it was faked. We're sure of it. So there's a pattern now. The drugs and the money in Brubaker's pocket are the exact same thing as the branch up Carbone's ass and the yogurt on his back. Elaborate misdirection. Concealment of the true motive. It's a definite MO. It's not just a guess any more. The same guy did both. He killed Carbone here and then jumped in his car and drove down to Columbia and killed Brubaker there. It's a clear sequence. Everything fits. Times, distances, the way the guy thinks.'

I looked at her standing there. Her small brown hand was stretched like a starfish. She had clear polish on her nails. Her eyes were bright.

'Why would he ditch the crowbar?' I said. 'After Carbone but before Brubaker?'

'Because he preferred a handgun,' she said. 'Like anyone normal would. But he knew he couldn't use one here. Too noisy. A mile from the main post, late in the evening, we'd have all come running. But in a bad part of a big city, nobody was going to think twice. Which is how it turned out, apparently.'

'Could he have been sure of that?'

'No,' she said. 'Not entirely sure. He set up the rendezvous, so he knew where he was going. But he couldn't be exactly certain about what he would find when he got there. So I guess he would have liked to keep a back-up weapon. But the crowbar was all covered with Carbone's blood and hair by then. There was no opportunity to clean it. He was in a hurry. The ground was frozen. No patch of soft grass to wipe it on. So he couldn't see having it in the car with him. Maybe he was worried about a traffic stop on the way south. So he ditched it.'

I nodded. Ultimately, the crowbar was disposable. A handgun was a more reliable weapon against a fit and wary opponent. Especially in the tight confines of a city alley, as opposed to the kind of dark and wide-open spaces where he had taken Carbone down. I yawned. Closed my eyes. *The wide-open spaces where he had taken Carbone down*. I opened my eyes again.

'He killed Carbone here,' I repeated. 'And then he jumped in his car and drove to Columbia and killed Brubaker there.'

'Yes,' Summer said.

'But you figured he was *already* in a car,' I said.

'Yes,' she said again. 'I did.'

'You figured he drove out on the track with Carbone, hit him in the head, arranged the scene, and then drove back here to the post. Your reasoning was pretty good. And where we found the crowbar kind of confirmed it.'

'Thank you,' she said.

'And then we figured he parked his car and went about his business.'

'Correct,' she said.

'But he can't have parked his car and gone about his business. Because now we're saying he drove straight to Columbia, South Carolina, instead. To meet with Brubaker. Three-hour drive. He was in a hurry. Not much time to waste.'

'Correct,' she said again.

'So he didn't park his car,' I said. 'He didn't even touch the brake. He drove straight out the main gate instead. There's no other way off the post. He drove straight out the main gate, Summer, immediately after he killed Carbone, somewhere around nine or ten o'clock.'

'Check the gate log,' she said. 'There's a copy right there on the desk.'

We checked the gate log together. Operation Just Cause in Panama had moved all domestic installations up one level on the DefCon scale and therefore all closed posts were recording entrances and exits in detail in bound ledgers that had pre-printed page numbers in the top right-hand corner. We had a good clear Xerox of the page for January 4th. I was confident it was genuine. I was confident it was complete. And I was confident it was accurate. The Military Police has numerous failings, but snafus with basic paperwork aren't any of them.

Summer took the page from me and taped it to the wall next to the map. We stood side by side and looked at it. It was ruled into six columns. There were spaces for date, time in, time out, plate number, occupants, and reason.

'Traffic was light,' Summer said.

I said nothing. I was in no position to know whether nineteen entries represented light traffic or not. I wasn't used to Bird and it had been a long time since I had pulled gate duty anywhere else. But certainly it seemed quiet compared to the multiple pages I had seen for New Year's Eve.

'Mostly people reporting back for duty,' Summer said.

I nodded. Fourteen lines had entries in the *time in* column but no corresponding entries in the *time out* column. That meant fourteen people had come in and stayed in. Back to work, after time away from the post for the holidays. Or after time away from the post for other reasons. I was right there among them: 1-4-90, 2302, Reacher, J., Mjr, RTB. *January 4th 1990, two minutes past eleven in the evening, Major J. Reacher, returning to base.* From Paris, via Garber's old office in Rock Creek. My vehicle plate number was listed as: *Pedestrian.* My sergeant was there, coming in from her off-post address to work the night shift. She had arrived at nine thirty, driving something with North Carolina plates.

Fourteen in, to stay in.

Only five exits.

Three of them were routine food deliveries. Big trucks, probably. An army post gets through a lot of food. Lots of hungry mouths to feed. Three trucks in a day seemed about right to me. Each of them was timed inward at some point during the early afternoon and then timed outward again a plausible hour or so later. The last time out was just before three o'clock.

Then there was a seven-hour gap.

The last-but-one recorded exit was Vassell and Coomer themselves, on their way out after their O Club dinner. They had passed through the gate at 2201. They had previously been timed in at 1845. At that point their Department of Defense plate number had been written down and their names and ranks had been entered. Their reason had been stated as *courtesy visit.*

Five exits. Four down.

One to go.

The only other person to have left Fort Bird on the fourth of January was logged as: *1-4-90, 2211, Trifonov, S., Sgt.* There was a North Carolina passenger vehicle plate number written in the relevant space. There was no time in recorded. There was nothing in the reason column. Therefore a sergeant called Trifonov had been on post all day or all week and then he had left at eleven minutes past ten in the evening. No reason had been recorded because there was no directive to enquire as to why a soldier was leaving. The assumption was that he was going out for a drink or a meal or for some other form of entertainment. *Reason* was a question the gate guards asked of people trying to get in, not trying to get out.

We checked again, just to be absolutely sure. We came up with the same result. Apart from General Vassell and Colonel Coomer in their self-driven Mercury Grand Marquis, and then a sergeant called Trifonov in some other kind of car, nobody had passed through the gate in an outward direction in a vehicle or on foot at any time on the fourth of January, apart from three food trucks in the early part of the afternoon.

'OK,' Summer said. 'Sergeant Trifonov. Whoever he is. He's the one.'

'Has to be,' I said.

I called the main gate. Got the same guy I had spoken to before, when I was checking on Vassell and Coomer earlier. I recognized his voice. I asked him to search forward through his log, starting from the page number immediately following the one we were looking at. Asked him to check exactly when a sergeant named Trifonov had returned to Bird. Told him it could be any time after about four thirty in the morning on January 5th. There was a moment's delay. I could hear the guy turning the stiff parchment pages in the ledger. He was doing it slowly, paying close attention.

'Sir, five o'clock in the morning precisely,' the guy said. 'January fifth, 0500, Sergeant Trifonov, returning to base.' I heard another page turn. 'He left at 2211 the previous evening.'

'Remember anything about him?'

'He left about ten minutes after those Armored staffers you were asking me about before. He was in a hurry, as I recall. Didn't wait for the barrier to go all the way up. He squeezed right underneath it.'

'What kind of car?'

'A Corvette, I think. Not a new one. But it looked pretty good.'

'Were you still on duty when he got back?'

'Yes, sir, I was.'

'Remember anything about that?'

'Nothing that stands out. I spoke to him, obviously. He has a foreign accent.'

216

'What was he wearing?'

'Civilian stuff. A leather jacket, I think. I assumed he had been off duty.'

'Is he on the post now?'

I heard pages turning again. I imagined a finger, tracing slowly down all the lines written after 0500 on the morning of the fifth.

'We haven't logged him out again, sir,' the guy said. 'Not as of right now. So he must be on post somewhere.'

'OK,' I said. 'Thanks, soldier.'

I hung up. Summer looked at me.

'He got back at 0500,' I said. 'Three and a half hours after Brubaker's watch stopped.'

'Three-hour drive,' she said.

'And he's here now.'

'Who is he?'

I called post headquarters. Asked the question. They told me who he was. I put the phone down and looked straight at Summer.

'He's Delta,' I said. 'He was a defector from Bulgaria. They brought him in as an instructor. He knows stuff our guys don't.'

I got up from my desk and stepped over to the map on the wall. Put my own fingers on the push pins. Little finger on Fort Bird, index finger on Columbia. It was like I was validating a theory by touch alone. A hundred and fifty miles. Three hours and twelve minutes to get there, three hours and thirty-seven minutes to get back. I did the math in my head. An average speed of forty-seven miles an hour going, and forty-one coming back. At night, on empty roads, in a Chevrolet Corvette. He could have done it with the parking brake on.

'Should we have him picked up?' Summer said.

I shook my head.

'No,' I said. 'I'll do it myself. I'll go over there.'

'Is that smart?'

'Probably not. But I don't want those guys to think they got to me.'

She paused.

217

'I'll come with you,' she said.

'OK,' I said.

It was five o'clock in the afternoon, exactly thirty-six hours to the minute since Trifonov arrived back on post. The weather was dull and cold. We took sidearms and handcuffs and evidence bags. We walked to the MP motor pool and found a Humvee that had a cage partition bolted behind the front seats and no inside handles on the back doors. Summer drove. She parked at Delta's prison gate. The sentry let us through on foot. We walked around the outside of the main block until I found the entrance to their NCO Club. I stopped, and Summer stopped beside me.

'You going in there?' she said.

'Just for a minute.'

'Alone?'

I nodded. 'Then we're going to their armoury.'

'Not smart,' she said. 'I should come in with you.'

'Why?'

She hesitated. 'As a witness, I guess.'

'To what?'

'To whatever they do to you.'

I smiled, briefly.

'Terrific,' I said.

I pushed in through the door. The place was pretty crowded. The light was dim and the air was full of smoke. There was a lot of noise. Then people saw me and went quiet. I moved onward. People stood where they were. Stock still. Then they turned to face me. I pushed past them, one by one. Through the crowd. Nobody moved out of my way. They bumped me with their shoulders, left and right. I bumped back, in the silence. I stand six feet five inches tall and I weigh two hundred thirty pounds. I can hold my own in a shoving competition.

I made it through the lobby and moved into the bar. Same thing happened. The noise died fast. People turned towards me. Stared at me. I pushed and shoved and bumped my way through the room. There was nothing to hear except tense breathing and the scrape of feet on the floor and the soft thump of shoulder on shoulder. I kept my eyes on the far wall. The

218

young guy with the beard and the tan stepped out into my path. He had a glass of beer in his hand. I kept going straight and he leaned to his right and we collided and his glass slopped half its contents on the linoleum tile.

'You spilled my drink,' he said.

I stopped. Looked down at the floor. Then I looked into his eyes.

'Lick it up,' I said.

We stood face to face for a second. Then I moved on past him. I felt an itch in my back. I knew he was staring at me. But I wasn't about to turn around. No way. Not unless I heard a bottle shatter against a table behind me.

I didn't hear a bottle. I made it all the way to the far wall. Touched it like a swimmer at the end of a lap. Turned around and started back. The return journey was no different. The room was silent. I picked up the pace a little. Drove faster through the crowd. Bumped harder. Momentum has its advantages. By the time I was ten paces from the lobby people were starting to move out of my way. They were backing off a little.

I figured we had communicated effectively. So in the lobby I started to deviate slightly from a purely straight path. Other people returned the compliment. I made it back to the entrance like any other civilized person in a crowded situation. I stopped at the door. Turned around. Scanned the faces in the room, slowly, one group at a time, *one thousand, two thousand, three thousand, four thousand.* Then I turned my back on them all and stepped out into the cold fresh air.

Summer wasn't there.

I looked around and a second later saw her slip out of a service entrance ten feet away. It had gotten her in behind the bar. I figured she had been watching my back.

She looked at me.

'Now you know,' she said.

'Know what?'

'How the first black soldier felt. And the first woman.'

She showed me the way to the old airplane hangar where their armoury was. We walked across twenty feet of swept concrete and went in through a personnel door set in the side. She hadn't been kidding about equipping an African dictatorship. There were arc lights blazing high in the roof of the hangar and they showed a small fleet of specialist vehicles and vast stacks of every kind of man-portable weapon you could imagine. I guessed David Brubaker had done a very effective lobbying job, up at the Pentagon.

'Over here,' Summer said.

She led me to a wire pen. It was about fifteen feet square. It had three walls and a roof made out of some kind of hurricane fencing. Like a dog run. There was a wire door standing open with an open padlock hung on the chain-link by its tongue. Behind the door was a stand-up writing table. Behind the writing table was a man in BDUs. He didn't salute. Didn't come to attention. But he didn't turn away, either. He just stood there and looked at me neutrally, which was as close to proper etiquette as Delta ever got.

'Help you?' he said, like he was a clerk in a store and I was a customer. Behind him on racks were well-used sidearms of every description. I saw five different sub-machine gun models. There were some M-16s, A1s and A2s. There were handguns. Some were new and fresh, some were old and worn. They were stored neatly and precisely, but without ceremony. They were tools of a trade, nothing less, nothing more.

In front of the guy on the desk was a log book.

'You check them in and check them out?' I asked.

'Like valet parking,' the guy said. 'Post regulations won't allow personal weapons in the accommodations areas.' He was looking at Summer. I guessed he had been through the same question-and-answer with her, when she was looking for Carbone's new P7.

'What does Sergeant Trifonov use for a handgun?' I asked.

'Trifonov? He favours the Steyr GB.'

'Show me.'

He turned away to the pistol rack and came back with a black Steyr GB. He was holding it by the barrel. It looked oiled and well maintained. I had an evidence bag out and ready and he dropped it straight in. I zipped the bag shut and looked at the gun through the plastic.

220

'Nine millimetre,' Summer said.

I nodded. It was a fine gun, but an unlucky one. Steyr-Daimler-Puch built it with the prospect of big orders from the Austrian Army dancing in its eyes, but a rival outfit named Glock came along and stole the prize. Which left the GB an unhappy orphan, like Cinderella. And like Cinderella it had many excellent qualities. It packed eighteen rounds, which was a lot, but it weighed less than two and a half pounds unloaded, which wasn't. You could take it apart and put it back together in twelve seconds, which was fast. Best of all, it had a very smart gas management system. All automatic weapons work by using the explosion of gas in the chamber to cycle the action, to get the spent case out and the next cartridge in. But in the real world some cartridges are old or weak or badly assembled. They don't all explode with the same force. Put an out-of-spec weak load in some guns, and the action just wheezes and won't cycle at all. Put a too-heavy load in, and the gun can blow up in your hand. But the Steyr was designed to deal with anything that came its way. If I was a Special Forces soldier taking dubious-quality ammunition from whatever ragtag bunch of partisans I was hanging with, I'd use a Steyr. I would want to be sure that whatever I was depending on would fire, ten times out of ten.

Through the plastic I pressed the magazine catch behind the trigger and shook the bag until the magazine fell out of the butt. It was an eighteen-round magazine, and there were sixteen cartridges in it. I gripped the slide and ejected one round from the chamber. So he had gone out with nineteen shells. Eighteen in the magazine, and one in the chamber. He had come back with seventeen shells. Sixteen in the magazine, and one in the chamber. Therefore he had fired two.

'Got a phone?' I said.

The clerk nodded at a booth in the corner of the hangar, twenty feet from his station. I walked over there and called my sergeant's desk. The Louisiana guy answered. The corporal. The night-shift woman was probably still at home in her trailer, putting her baby to bed, showering, getting ready for the trek to work.

'Get me Sanchez at Jackson,' I said.

221

I held the phone by my ear and waited. One minute. Two.

'What?' Sanchez said.

'Did they find the shell cases?' I said.

'No,' he said. 'The guy must have cleaned up at the scene.'

'Pity. We could have matched them for a slam dunk.'

'You *found* the guy?'

'I'm holding his gun right now. Steyr GB, fully loaded, less two fired.'

'Who is he?'

'I'll tell you later. Let the civilians sweat for a spell.'

'One of ours?'

'Sad, but true.'

Sanchez said nothing.

'Did they find the bullets?' I said.

'No,' he said.

'Why not? It was an alley, right? How far could they go? They'll be buried in the brick somewhere.'

'Then they won't do us any good. They'll be flattened beyond recognition.'

'They were jacketed,' I said. 'They won't have broken up. We could weigh them, at least.'

'They haven't found them.'

'Are they looking?'

'I don't know.'

'They dug up any witnesses yet?'

'No.'

'Did they find Brubaker's car?'

'No.'

'It's got to be right there, Sanchez. He drove down and arrived at midnight or one o'clock. In a distinctive car. Aren't they looking for it?'

'There's something they're not sharing. I can feel it.'

'Did Willard get there yet?'

'I expect him any minute.'

'Tell him Brubaker is all wrapped up,' I said. 'And tell him you heard the other thing wasn't a training accident after all. That should make his day.'

Then I hung up. Walked back to the wire cage. Summer had stepped inside and she was shoulder-to-shoulder with the

222

armoury clerk behind the stand-up desk. They were leafing through his log book together.

'Look at this,' she said.

She used both forefingers to show me two separate entries. Trifonov had signed out his personal Steyr GB nine-millimetre pistol at seven thirty in the evening of January 4th. He had signed it back in at a quarter past five on the morning of the fifth. His signature was big and awkward. He was Bulgarian. I guessed he had grown up with the Cyrillic alphabet and was new to writing with Roman letters.

'Why did he take it?' I said.

'We don't ask for a reason,' the clerk said. 'We just do the paperwork.'

We came out of the hangar and walked towards the accommodation block. Passed the end of an open parking lot. There were forty or fifty cars in it. Typical soldiers' rides. Not many imports. There were some battered plain-vanilla sedans, but mostly there were pick-up trucks and big Detroit coupés, some of them painted with flames and stripes, some of them with hiked back ends and chrome wheels and fat raised-letter tyres. There was only one Corvette. It was red, parked all by itself on the end of a row, three spaces from anything else.

We detoured to take a look at it.

It was about ten years old. It looked immaculately clean, inside and out. It had been washed and waxed, thoroughly, within the last day or two. The wheel arches were clean. The tyres were black and shiny. There was a coiled hose on the hangar wall, thirty feet away. We bent down and peered in through the windows. The interior looked like it had been soaked with detailing fluid and wiped and vacuumed. It was a two-place car, but there was a parcel shelf behind the seats. It was a small space. Small, but probably big enough for a crowbar hidden under a coat. Summer knelt down and ran her fingers under the sills. Came up with clean hands.

'No grit from the track,' she said. 'No blood on the seats.'

'No yogurt pot on the floor,' I said.

'He cleaned up after himself.'

We walked away. We went out through their main gate and

locked Trifonov's gun in the front of our Humvee. Then we turned around and headed back inside.

I didn't want to involve the adjutant. I just wanted to get Trifonov out of there before anyone knew what was going down. So we went in through the mess kitchen door and I found a steward and told him to find Trifonov and bring him out through the kitchen on some kind of a pretext. Then we stepped back into the cold and waited. The steward came out alone five minutes later and told us Trifonov wasn't anywhere in the mess.

So we headed for the cells. Found a soldier coming out of the showers and he told us where to look. We walked past Carbone's empty room. It was quiet and undisturbed. Trifonov bunked three doors further down. We got there. His door was standing open. The guy was right there in his room, sitting on the narrow cot, reading a book.

I had no idea what to expect. As far as I knew Bulgaria had no Special Forces. Truly elite units were not common inside the Warsaw Pact. Czechoslovakia had a pretty good airborne brigade, and Poland had airborne and amphibious divisions. The Soviet Union itself had a few *Vysotniki* tough guys. Apart from that, sheer weight of numbers was the name of the game, in the eastern part of Europe. Throw enough bodies into the fray, and eventually you win, as long as you regard two-thirds of them as expendable. And they did.

So who was this guy?

NATO Special Forces put a lot of emphasis on endurance in selection and training. They have guys running fifty miles carrying everything including the kitchen sink. They keep them awake and hiking over appalling terrain for a week at a time. Therefore NATO elite troops tended to be small whippy guys, built like marathon runners. But this Bulgarian was huge. He was at least as big as me. Maybe even bigger. Maybe six-six, maybe two-fifty. He had a shaved head. He had a big square face that would be somewhere between brutally plain and reasonably good-looking depending on the light. At that point the fluorescent tube on the ceiling of his cell wasn't doing him any favours. He looked tired. He had piercing eyes set deep and close together in hooded sockets. He was a few years older than me, somewhere in his early thirties. He had huge hands. He was wearing brand new woodland BDUs, no name, no rank, no unit.

'On your feet, soldier,' I said.

He put his book down on the bed next to him, carefully, face down and open, like he was saving his place.

We put handcuffs on him and got him into the Humvee without any trouble. He was big, but he was quiet. He seemed resigned to his fate. Like he knew it had been only a matter of time before all the various log books in his life betrayed him.

We drove him back and got him to my office without incident. We sat him down and unlocked the handcuffs and redid them so that his right wrist was cuffed to the chair leg. Then we took a second pair of cuffs and did the same thing with his left. He had big wrists. They were as thick as most men's ankles.

Summer stood next to the map, staring at the push pins, like she was leading his gaze towards them and saying: *We know.*

I sat at my desk.

'What's your name?' I said. 'For the record?'

'Trifonov,' he said. His accent was heavy and abrupt, all in his throat.

'First name?'

'Slavi.'

'Slavi Trifonov,' I said. 'Rank?'

'I was a colonel at home. Now I'm a sergeant.'

'Where's home?'

'Sofia,' he said. 'In Bulgaria.'

'You're very young to have been a colonel.'

'I was very good at what I did.'

'And what did you do?'

He didn't answer.

'You have a nice car,' I said.

'Thank you,' he said. 'A car like that was always a dream to me.'

'Where did you take it on the night of the fourth?'

225

He didn't answer.

'There are no Special Forces in Bulgaria,' I said.

'No,' he said. 'There are not.'

'So what did you do there?'

'I was in the regular army.'

'Doing what?'

'Three-way liaison between the Bulgarian army, the Bulgarian secret police, and our friends in the Soviet *Vysotniki*.'

'Qualifications?'

'I had five years' training with the GRU.'

'Which is what?'

He smiled. 'I think you know what it is.'

I nodded. The Soviet GRU was a kind of a cross between a military police corps and Delta Force. They were plenty tough, and they were just as ready to turn their fury inwards as outwards.

'Why are you here?' I asked.

'In America?' he said. 'I'm waiting.'

'For what?'

'For the end of the communist occupation of my country. It will happen soon, I think. Then I'm going back. I'm proud of my country. It's a beautiful place full of beautiful people. I'm a nationalist.'

'What are you teaching Delta?'

'Things that are out of date now. How to fight against the things I was trained to do. But that battle is already over, I think. You won.'

'You need to tell us where you were on the night of the fourth.'

He said nothing.

'Why did you defect?'

'Because I was a patriot,' he said.

'Recent conversion?'

'I was always a patriot. But I came close to being discovered.'

'How did you get out?'

'Through Turkey. I went to the American base there.'

'Tell me about the night of the fourth.'

He said nothing.

'We've got your gun,' I said. 'You signed it out. You left the post at eleven minutes past ten and got back at five in the morning.'

He said nothing.

'You fired two rounds.'

He said nothing.

'Why did you wash your car?'

'Because it's a beautiful car. I wash it twice a week. Always. A car like that was a dream to me.'

'You ever been to Kansas?'

'No.'

'Well, that's where you're headed. You're not going home to Sofia. You're going to Fort Leavenworth instead.'

'Why?'

'You know why,' I said.

Trifonov didn't move. He sat absolutely still. He was hunched way forward, with his wrists fastened to the chair down near his knees. I sat still, too. I wasn't sure what to do. Our own Delta guys were trained to resist interrogation. I knew that. They were trained to counter drugs and beatings and sensory deprivation and anything else anyone could think of. Their instructors were encouraged to employ hands-on training methods. So I couldn't even imagine what Trifonov had been through, in five years with the GRU. There was nothing much I could do to him. I wasn't above smacking people around. But I figured this guy wouldn't say a word even if I disassembled him limb by limb.

So I moved on to traditional policing techniques. Lies, and bribery.

'Some people figure Carbone was an embarrassment,' I said. 'You know, to the army. So we wouldn't necessarily want to pursue it too far. You spill the beans now, we could send you back to Turkey. You could wait there until it was time to go home and be a patriot.'

'It was you who killed Carbone,' he said. 'People are talking about it.'

'People are wrong,' I said. 'I wasn't here. And I didn't kill Brubaker. Because I wasn't there, either.'

'Neither was I,' he said. 'Either.'

He was very still. Then something dawned on him. His eyes

227

started moving. He looked left, and then right. He looked up at Summer's map. Looked at the pins. Looked at her. Looked at me. His lips moved. I saw him say *Carbone* to himself. Then *Brubaker*. He made no sound, but I could lip-read his awkward accent.

'Wait,' he said.

'For what?'

'No,' he said.

'No what?'

'No, sir,' he said.

'Tell me, Trifonov,' I said.

'You think I had something to do with Carbone and *Brubaker*?'

'You think you didn't?'

He went quiet again. Looked down.

'Tell me, Trifonov,' I said.

He looked up.

'It wasn't me,' he said.

I just sat there. Watched his face. I had been handling investigations of various kinds for six long years, and Trifonov was at least the thousandth guy to look me in the eye and say *it wasn't me*. Problem was, a percentage of those thousand guys had been telling the truth. And I was starting to think maybe Trifonov was, too. There was something about him. I was starting to get a very bad feeling.

'You're going to have to prove it,' I said.

'I can't.'

'You're going to have to. Or they'll throw away the key. They might let Carbone slide, but they sure as hell aren't going to let Brubaker slide.'

He said nothing.

'Start over,' I said. 'The night of January fourth, where were you?'

He just shook his head.

'You were somewhere,' I said. 'That's for damn sure. Because you weren't here. You logged in and out. You and your gun.'

He said nothing. Just looked at me. I stared back at him and didn't speak. He went into the kind of desperate conflicted silence I had seen many times before. He was moving in the

228

chair. Almost imperceptibly. Tiny violent movements, from side to side. Like he was fighting two alternating opponents, one on his left, one on his right. Like he knew he had to tell me where he had been, but like he knew he couldn't. He was jumping around like the absolute flesh-and-blood definition of a rock and a hard place.

'The night of January fourth,' I said. 'Did you commit a crime?'

His deep-set eyes came up to meet mine. Locked on.

'OK,' I said. 'Time to choose up sides. Was it a worse crime than shooting Brubaker in the head?'

He said nothing.

'Did you go up to Washington D.C. and rape the president's ten-year-old granddaughters, one after the other?'

'No,' he said.

'I'll give you a clue,' I said. 'Where you're sitting, that would be about the only worse crime than shooting Brubaker in the head.'

He said nothing.

'Tell me.'

'It was a private thing,' he said.

'What kind of a private thing?'

He didn't answer. Summer sighed and moved away from her map. She was starting to figure that wherever Trifonov had been, chances were it wasn't Columbia, South Carolina. She looked at me, eyebrows raised. Trifonov moved in his chair. His handcuffs clinked against the metal of the legs.

'What's going to happen to me?' he asked.

'That depends on what you did,' I said.

'I got a letter,' he said.

'Getting mail isn't a crime.'

'From a friend of a friend.'

'Tell me about the letter.'

'There's a man in Sofia,' he said.

He sat there, hunched forward, his wrists cuffed to the chair legs, and he told us the story of the letter. The way he framed it, he made it sound like he thought there was something uniquely Bulgarian about it. But there wasn't, really. It was a story that could have been told by any of us.

229

There was a man in Sofia. He had a sister. The sister had been a minor gymnast and had defected on a college tour of Canada and had eventually settled in the United States. She had gotten married to an American. She had become a citizen. Her husband had turned out bad. The sister wrote about it to the brother back home. Long, unhappy letters. There were beatings, and abuse, and cruelty, and isolation. The sister's life was hell. The communist censors had passed the letters, because anything that made America look bad was OK with them. The brother in Sofia had a friend in town who knew his way around the city's dissident network. The friend had an address for Trifonov, at Fort Bird in North Carolina. Trifonov had been in touch with the dissident network before he skipped to Turkey. The friend had packaged up a letter from the man in Sofia and given it to a guy who bought machine parts in Austria. The machine parts guy had gone to Austria and mailed the letter. The letter made its way to Fort Bird. Trifonov received it on January 2nd, early in the morning, at mail call. It had his name on it in big Cyrillic letters and it was all covered in foreign stamps and *Luftpost* stickers.

He had read the letter alone in his room. He knew what was expected of him. Time and distance and relationships compressed under the pressure of nationalist loyalty, so that it was like his own sister who was getting smacked around. The woman lived near a place called Cape Fear, which Trifonov thought was an appropriate name, given her situation. He had gone to the company office and checked a map, to find out where it was.

His next available free time was the evening of January 4th. He made a plan and rehearsed a speech, which centred around the inadvisability of abusing Bulgarian women who had friends within driving distance.

'Still got the letter?' I asked.

He nodded. 'But you won't be able to read it, because it's written in Bulgarian.'

'What were you wearing that night?'

'Plain clothes. I'm not stupid.'

'What kind of plain clothes?'

230

'Leather jacket. Blue jeans. Shirt. American. They're all the plain clothes I've got.'

'What did you do to the guy?'

He shook his head. Wouldn't answer.

'OK,' I said. 'Let's all go to Cape Fear.'

We kept Trifonov cuffed and put him in the back of the MP Humvee. Summer drove. Cape Fear was on the Atlantic coast, south and east, maybe a hundred miles. It was a tedious ride, in a Humvee. It would have been different in a Corvette. Although I couldn't remember ever being in a Corvette. I had never known anyone who owned one.

And I had never been to Cape Fear. It was one of the many places in America I had never visited. I had seen the movie, though. Couldn't remember where, exactly. In a tent, somewhere hot, maybe. Black and white, with Gregory Peck having some kind of a major problem with Robert Mitchum. It was good enough entertainment, as I recalled, but fundamentally annoying. There was a lot of jeering from the audience. Robert Mitchum should have gone down early in the first reel. Watching civilians dither around just to spin out a story for ninety minutes had no real appeal for soldiers.

It was full dark before we got anywhere near where we were going. We passed a sign near the outer part of Wilmington that billed the town as an historic and picturesque old port city but we ignored it because Trifonov called through from the rear and told us to make a left through some kind of a swamp. We drove out through the darkness into the middle of nowhere and made another left towards a place called Southport.

'Cape Fear is off of Southport,' Summer said. 'It's an island in the ocean. I think there's a bridge.'

But we stopped well short of the coast. We didn't even get to Southport itself. Trifonov called through again as we passed a trailer park on our right. It was a large flat rectangular area of reclaimed land. It looked like someone had dredged part of the swamp to make a lake and then spread the fill over an area the size of a couple of football fields. The land was bordered by drainage ditches. There were power lines coming in on poles and maybe a hundred trailers studded all over the rectangle.

231

Our headlights showed that some of them were fancy double-wide affairs with add-ons and planted gardens and picket fences. Some of them were plain and battered. A couple had fallen off their blocks and were abandoned. We were maybe ten miles inland, but the ocean storms had a long reach.

'Here,' Trifonov said. 'Make a right.'

There was a wide centre track with narrower tracks branching left and right. Trifonov directed us through the maze and we stopped outside a sagging lime-green trailer that had seen better days. Its paint was peeling and the tar paper roof was curling. It had a smoking chimney and the blue light of a television behind its windows.

'Her name is Elena,' Trifonov said.

We left him locked in the Humvee. Knocked on Elena's door. The woman who opened it could have stepped straight into the encyclopedia under *B* for *Battered Woman*. She was a mess. She had old yellow bruises all around her eyes and along her jaw and her nose was broken. She was holding herself in a way that suggested old aches and pains and maybe even newly broken ribs. She was wearing a thin house dress and men's shoes. But she was clean and bathed and her hair was tied back neatly. There was a spark of something in her eyes. Some kind of pride, maybe, or satisfaction at having survived. She peered out at us nervously, from behind the triple oppressions of poverty and suffering and foreign status.

'Yes?' she said. 'Can I help you?' Her accent was like Trifonov's, but much higher pitched. It was quite appealing.

'We need to talk to you,' Summer said, gently.

'What about?'

'About what Slavi Trifonov did for you,' I said.

'He didn't do anything,' she said.

'But you know the name.'

She paused.

'Please come in,' she said.

I guessed I was expecting some kind of mayhem inside. Maybe empty bottles strewn about, full ashtrays, dirt and confusion. But the trailer was neat and clean. There was nothing out of place. It was cold, but it was OK. And there was nobody else in it.

232

'Your husband not here?' I said.

She shook her head.

'Where is he?'

She didn't answer.

'My guess is he's in the hospital,' Summer said. 'Am I right?'

Elena just looked at her.

'Mr Trifonov helped you,' I said. 'Now you need to help him.'

She said nothing.

'If he wasn't here doing something good, he was somewhere else doing something bad. That's the situation. So I need to know which it was.'

She said nothing.

'This is very, very important,' I said.

'What if both things were bad?' she asked.

'The two things don't compare,' I said. 'Believe me. Not even close. So just tell me exactly what happened, OK?'

She didn't answer right away. I moved a little deeper into the trailer. The television was tuned to PBS. The volume was low. I could smell cleaning products. Her husband had gone, and she had started a new phase in her life with a mop and a pail, and education on the tube.

'I don't know exactly what happened,' she said. 'Mr Trifonov just came here and took my husband away.'

'When?'

'The night before last, at midnight. He said he had gotten a letter from my brother in Sofia.'

I nodded. *At midnight. He left Bird at 2211, he was here an hour and forty-nine minutes later. One hundred miles, an average of dead-on fifty-five miles an hour, in a Corvette.* I glanced at Summer. She nodded. *Easy.*

'How long was he here?'

'Just a few minutes. He was quite formal. He introduced himself, and he told me what he was doing, and why.'

'And that was it?'

She nodded.

'What was he wearing?'

'A leather jacket. Jeans.'

'What kind of car was he in?'

233

'I don't know what it's called. Red, and low. A sports car. It made a loud noise with its exhaust pipes.'

'OK,' I said. I nodded to Summer and we moved towards the door.

'Will my husband come back?' Elena said.

I pictured Trifonov as I had first seen him. Six-six, two-fifty, shaved head. The thick wrists, the big hands, the blazing eyes, and the five years with GRU.

'I seriously doubt it,' I said.

We climbed back into the Humvee. Summer started the engine. I turned around and spoke to Trifonov through the wire cage.

'Where did you leave the guy?' I asked him.

'On the road to Wilmington,' he said.

'When?'

'Three o'clock in the morning. I stopped at a pay phone and called nine one one. I didn't give my name.'

'You spent three hours on him?'

He nodded, slowly. 'I wanted to be sure he understood the message.'

Summer threaded her way out of the trailer park and turned west and then north towards Wilmington. We passed the tourist sign on the outskirts and went looking for the hospital. We found it a quarter-mile in. It looked like a reasonable place. It was mostly two-storey and had an ambulance entrance with a broad canopy. Summer parked in a slot reserved for a doctor with an Indian name and we got out. I unlocked the rear door and let Trifonov out to join us. I took the cuffs off him. Put them in my pocket.

'What was the guy's name?' I asked him.

'Pickles,' he said.

The three of us walked in together and I showed my special unit badge to the orderly behind the triage desk. Truth is it confers no rights or privileges on me out in the civilian world, but the guy reacted like it gave me unlimited powers, which is what most civilians do when they see it.

'Early morning of January fifth,' I said. 'Sometime after three o'clock, there was an admission here.'

234

The guy riffed through a stack of aluminum clipboards in a stand to his right. Pulled two of them partway out.

'Male or female?' he said.

'Male.'

He dropped one of the clipboards back in its slot. Pulled the other all the way out.

'John Doe,' he said. 'Indigent male, no ID, no insurance, claims his name is Pickles. Cops found him on the road.'

'That's our guy,' I said.

'Your guy?' he said, looking at my uniform.

'We might be able to take care of his bill,' I said.

He paid attention to that. Glanced at his stack of clipboards, like he was thinking *one down, two hundred to go.*

'He's in post-op,' he said. He pointed towards the elevator. 'Second floor.'

He stayed behind his counter. We rode up, the three of us together. Got out and followed the signs to the post-op ward. A nurse at a station outside the door stopped us. I showed her my badge.

'Pickles,' I said.

She pointed us to a private room with a closed door, across the hallway.

'Five minutes only,' she said. 'He's very sick.'

Trifonov smiled. We walked across the corridor and opened the private room's door. The light was dim. There was a guy in the bed. He was asleep. Impossible to tell whether he was big or small. I couldn't see much of him. He was mostly covered in plaster casts. His legs were in traction and he had big GSW bandage packs around both knees. Opposite his bed was a long lightbox at eye level that was pretty much covered with X-ray exposures. I clicked the light and took a look. Every film had a date and the name *Pickles* scrawled in the margin. There were films of his arms and his ribs and his chest and his legs. The human body has more than two hundred ten bones in it, and it seemed like this guy Pickles had most of them broken. He had put a big dent in the hospital's radiography budget all by himself.

I clicked the light off and kicked the leg of the bed, twice. The guy in it stirred. Woke up. Focused in the dim light and the look on his face when he saw Trifonov was all the alibi Trifonov was ever going to need. It was a look of stark, abject terror.

'You two wait outside,' I said.

Summer led Trifonov out the door and I moved up to the head of the bed.

'How are you, asshole?' I said.

The guy called Pickles was all white in the face. Sweating, and trembling inside his casts.

'That was the man,' he said. 'Right there. He did this to me.'

'Did what to you?'

'He shot me in the legs.'

I nodded. Looked at the GSW packs. Pickles had been knee-capped. Two knees, two bullets. Two rounds fired.

'Front or side?' I said.

'Side,' he said.

'Front is worse,' I said. 'You were lucky. Not that you deserved to be lucky.'

'I didn't do anything.'

'Didn't you? I just met your wife.'

'Foreign bitch.'

'Don't say that.'

'It's her own fault. She won't do what I tell her. A man needs to be obeyed. Like it says in the Bible.'

'Shut up,' I said.

'Aren't you going to do something?'

'Yes,' I said. 'I am. Watch.'

I swung my hand like I was brushing a fly off his sheets. Caught him with a soft backhander on the side of his right knee. He screamed and I walked away and stepped out the door. Found the nurse looking over in my direction.

'He's very sick,' I said.

We rode down in the elevator and avoided the guy at the triage desk by using the main entrance. We walked around to the Humvee in silence. I opened the rear door for Trifonov but stopped him on the way in. I shook his hand.

'I apologize,' I said.

'Am I in trouble?' he said.

'Not with me,' I said. 'You're my kind of guy. But you're very

236

lucky. You could have hit a femoral artery. You could have killed him. Then it might have been different.'

He smiled, briefly. He was calm.

'I trained five years with GRU,' he said. 'I know how to kill people. And I know how not to.'

SIXTEEN

W E GAVE TRIFONOV HIS STEYR BACK AND LET HIM OUT AT THE Delta gate. He probably signed the gun back in and then legged it to his room and picked up his book. Probably carried on reading right where he left off. We drove on and parked the Humvee in the MP motor pool. Walked back to my office. Summer went straight to the copy of the gate log. It was still taped to the wall, next to the map.

'Vassell and Coomer,' she said. 'They were the only other people who left the post that night.'

'They went north,' I said. 'If you want to say they threw the briefcase out of the car, then you have to agree they went north. They didn't go south to Columbia.'

'OK,' she said. 'So the same guy didn't do Carbone and Brubaker. There's no connection. We just wasted a lot of time.'

'Welcome to the real world,' I said.

The real world got a whole lot worse when my phone rang twenty minutes later. It was my sergeant. The woman with the baby son. She had Sanchez on the line, calling from Fort Jackson. She put him through.

'Willard has been and gone,' he said. 'Unbelievable.'

'Told you so.'

'He pitched all kinds of hissy fits.'

'But you're fireproof.'

'Thank God.'

I paused. 'Did you tell him about my guy?'

He paused. 'You told me to. Shouldn't I have?'

'It was a dry hole. Looked good at first, but it wasn't in the end.'

'Well, he's on his way up to see you about it. He left here two hours ago. He's going to be very disappointed.'

'Terrific,' I said.

'What are you going to do?' Summer asked.

'What is Willard?' I said. 'Fundamentally?'

'A careerist,' she said.

'Correct,' I said.

Technically the army has a total of twenty-six separate ranks. A grunt comes in as an E-1 private, and as long as he doesn't do anything stupid he is automatically promoted to an E-2 private after a year, and to an E-3 private first class after another year, or even a little earlier if he's any good. Then the ladder stretches all the way up to a five-star General of the Army, although I wasn't aware of anyone except George Washington and Dwight David Eisenhower who ever made it that far. If you count the E-9 sergeant major grade as three separate steps to acknowledge the Command Sergeant Majors and the Sergeant Major of the Army, and if you count all four warrant officer grades, then a major like me has seven steps above him and eighteen steps below him. Which gives a major like me considerable experience of insubordination, going both ways, up and down, giving and taking. With a million people on twenty-six separate rungs on the ladder, insubordination was a true art form. And the canvas was one-on-one privacy.

So I sent Summer away and waited for Willard on my own. She argued about it. In the end I got her to agree that one of us should stay under the radar. She went to get a late dinner. My sergeant brought me a sandwich. Roast beef and Swiss cheese, white bread, a little mayo, a little mustard. The beef was pink. It was a good sandwich. Then she brought me coffee. I was halfway through my second cup when Willard arrived.

He came straight in. He left the door open. I didn't get up. Didn't salute. Didn't stop sipping my coffee. He tolerated it, like I knew he would. He was being very tactical. As far as he knew I had a suspect that could take Brubaker's case away from the Columbia PD and break the link between an elite colonel and drug dealers in a crack alley. So he was prepared to start out warm and friendly. Or maybe he was looking for a bonding experience with one of his staff. He sat down and started plucking at his trouser legs. He put a man-to-man expression on his face, like we had just been through some kind of a shared experience together.

'Wonderful drive from Jackson,' he said. 'Great roads.'

I said nothing.

'Just bought a vintage Pontiac GTO,' he said. 'Fine car. I put polished headers on it, big bore pipes. Goes like shit off a shiny shovel.'

I said nothing.

'You like muscle cars?'

'No,' I said. 'I like to take the bus.'

'That's not much fun.'

'OK, let me put it another way. I'm happy with the size of my penis. I don't need compensation.'

He went white. Then he went red. The same shade as Trifonov's Corvette. He glared at me like he was a real tough guy.

'Tell me about the progress on Brubaker,' he said.

'Brubaker's not my case.'

'Sanchez told me you found the guy.'

'False alarm,' I said.

'Are you sure?'

'Totally.'

'Who were you looking at?'

'Your ex-wife.'

'What?'

'Someone told me she slept with half the colonels in the army. Always had, like a hobby. So I figured that might include Brubaker. I mean, it was a fifty-fifty chance.'

240

He stared at me.

'Only kidding,' I said. 'It was nobody. Just a dry hole.'

He looked away, furious. I got up and closed my office door. Stepped back to my desk. Sat down again. Faced him.

'Your insolence is incredible,' he said.

'So make a complaint, Willard. Go up the chain of command and tell someone I hurt your feelings. See if anyone believes you. Or see if anyone believes you can't fix a thing like that all by yourself. Watch *that* note go in your file. See what kind of an impression it makes at your one-star promotion board.'

He squirmed in his chair. Hitched his body from side to side and stared around the room. Fixed his gaze on Summer's map.

'What's that?' he said.

'It's a map,' I said.

'Of what?'

'Of the eastern United States.'

'What are the pins for?'

I didn't answer. He got up and stepped over to the wall. Touched the pins with his fingertips, one at a time. D.C., Sperryville, and Green Valley. Then Raleigh, Fort Bird, Cape Fear, and Columbia.

'What is all this?' he said.

'They're just pins,' I said.

He pulled the pin out of Green Valley, Virginia.

'Mrs Kramer,' he said. 'I told you to leave that alone.'

He pulled all the other pins out. Threw them down on the floor. Then he saw the gate log. Scanned down it and stopped when he got to Vassell and Coomer.

'I told you to leave them alone as well,' he said.

He tore the list off the wall. The tape took scabs of paint with it. Then he tore the map down. More paint came with it. The pins had left tiny holes in the sheet rock. They looked like a map all by themselves. Or a constellation.

'You made holes in the wall,' he said. 'I won't have army property abused in this way. It's unprofessional. What would visitors to this room think?'

'They'd have thought there was a map on the wall,' I said. 'It was you that pulled it down and made the mess.'

He dropped the crumpled paper on the floor.

'You want me to walk over to the Delta station?' he said.

'Want me to break your back?'

He went very quiet.

'You should think about *your* next promotion board,' he said. 'You think you're going to make lieutenant colonel while I'm still here?'

'No,' I said. 'I really don't. But then, I don't expect you'll be here very long.'

'Think again. This is a nice niche. The army will always need cops.'

'But it won't always need clueless assholes like you.'

'You're speaking to a senior officer.'

I looked around the room. 'But what am I saying? I don't see any witnesses.'

He said nothing.

'You've got an authority problem,' I said. 'It's going to be fun watching you try to solve it. Maybe we could solve it man to man, in the gym. You want to try that?'

'Have you got a secure fax machine?' he said.

'Obviously,' I said. 'It's in the outer office. You passed it on your way in. What are you? Blind as well as stupid?'

'Be standing next to it at exactly nine hundred hours tomorrow. I'll be sending you a set of written orders.'

He glared at me one last time. Then he stepped outside and slammed the door so hard that the whole wall shook and the air current lifted the map and the gate log an inch off the floor.

I stayed at my desk. Dialled my brother in Washington, but he didn't answer. I thought about calling my mother. But then I figured there was nothing to say. Whatever I talked about she would know I had called to ask: *Are you still alive?* She would know that was what was on my mind.

So I got out of my chair and picked up the map and smoothed it out. Taped it back on the wall. I picked up all seven pins and put them back in place. Taped the gate log alongside the map. Then I pulled it down again. It was useless. I balled it up and threw it in the trash. Left the map there all on its own. My sergeant came in with more coffee. I wondered briefly about her baby's father. Where was he? Had he been an abusive husband? If so, he was probably buried in a swamp somewhere. Or several swamps, in several pieces. My phone rang and she answered it for me. Passed me the receiver.

'Detective Clark,' she said. 'Up in Virginia.'

I trailed the phone cord around the desk and sat down again.

'We're making progress now,' he said. 'The Sperryville crowbar is our weapon, for sure. We got an identical sample from the hardware store and our medical examiner matched it up.'

'Good work,' I said.

'So I'm calling to tell you I can't keep on looking. We found ours, so we can't be looking for yours any more. I can't justify the overtime budget.'

'Sure,' I said. 'We anticipated that.'

'So you're on your own with it now, bud. And I'm real sorry about that.'

I said nothing.

'Anything at your end? You got a name for me yet?'

I smiled. *You can forget about a name*, I thought. *Bud*. No *quo*, no *quid*. Not that there ever was a name in the first place.

'I'll let you know,' I said.

Summer came back after thirty more minutes and I told her to take the rest of the night off. Told her to meet me for breakfast in the O Club. At nine o'clock exactly, when Willard's orders were due. I figured we could have a long leisurely meal, plenty of eggs, plenty of coffee, and we could stroll back over about ten fifteen.

'You moved the map,' she said.

'Willard tore it down. I put it back up.'

'He's dangerous.'

'Maybe,' I said. 'Maybe not. Time will tell.'

She went back to her quarters and I went back to mine. I was in a room in the Bachelor Officers' row. It was pretty much like a motel. There was a street named after some long-dead Medal of Honor winner and a path branching off from the sidewalk that led to my door. There were posts every twenty yards with street lights on them. The one nearest my door was out. It was out because it had been busted with a stone. I could see glass on the path. And three guys in the shadows. I walked past the first one. He was the Delta sergeant with the beard and the tan. He tapped the face of his watch with his forefinger. The second guy did the same thing. The third guy just smiled. I got inside and closed my door. Didn't hear them walk away. I didn't sleep well.

They were gone by morning. I made it to the O Club OK. At nine o'clock the dining room was pretty much empty, which was an advantage. The disadvantage was that whatever food remained had been stewing on the buffet for a while. But on balance I thought it was a good situation. I was more of a loner than a gourmet. Summer and I sat across from each other at a small table in the centre of the room. Between us we ate almost everything that was left. Summer consumed about a pound of grits and two pounds of biscuits. She was small, but she could eat. That was for damn sure. We took our time with our coffee and walked over to my office at ten twenty. There was mayhem inside. Every phone was ringing. The Louisiana corporal looked harassed.

'Don't answer your phone,' he said. 'It's Colonel Willard. He wanted immediate confirmation that you'd gotten your orders. He's mad as hell.'

'What are the orders?'

He ducked back to his desk and offered me a sheet of fax paper. The phones kept on ringing. I didn't take the sheet of paper. I just stood there and read it over my corporal's shoulder. There were two closely spaced paragraphs. Willard was ordering me to examine the quartermaster's inward delivery note file and his outward distribution log. I was to use them to work out on paper exactly what ought to be there in the on-post warehouse. Then I was to verify my conclusion by means of a practical search. Then I was to compile a list of all missing items and propose a course of action in writing to track down their current whereabouts. I was to execute the order in a prompt and timely fashion. I was to call him to confirm receipt of the order immediately it was in my hand.

It was a classic make-work punishment. In the bad old days they ordered you to paint coal white or fill sandbags with teaspoons or scrub floors with toothbrushes. This was the modern-day MP equivalent. It was a mindless task that would take two weeks to complete. I smiled.

The phones were still ringing.

'The order was never in my hand,' I said. 'I'm not here.'

'Where are you?'

'Tell him someone dropped a gum wrapper in the flower bed outside the post commander's office. Tell him I won't have army real estate abused in that way. Tell him I've been on the trail since well before dawn.'

I led Summer back out onto the sidewalk, away from the ringing phones.

'Asshole,' I said.

'You should lie low,' she said. 'He'll be calling all over.'

I stood still. Looked around. Cold weather. Grey buildings, grey sky.

'Let's take the day off,' I said. 'Let's go somewhere.'

'We've got things to do.'

I nodded. *Carbone. Kramer. Brubaker.*

'Can't stay here,' I said. 'So we can't do much about Carbone.'

'Want to go down to Columbia?'

'Not our case,' I said. 'Nothing we can do that Sanchez isn't doing.'

'Too cold for the beach,' Summer said.

I nodded again. Suddenly wished it wasn't too cold for the beach. I would have liked to see Summer on the beach. In a bikini. A very small one, for preference.

'We have to work,' she said.

I looked south and west, beyond the post buildings. I could see the trees, cold and dead against the horizon. I could see a tall pine, dull and dormant, a little nearer. I figured it was close to where we had found Carbone.

Carbone.

'Let's go to Green Valley,' I said. 'Let's visit with Detective Clark. We could ask him for his crowbar notes. He made a start for us. So maybe we could finish up. A four-hour drive might be a good investment at this point.'

'And four hours back.'

'We could have lunch. Maybe dinner. We could go AWOL.'

'They'd find us.'

I shook my head.

'Nobody would find me,' I said. 'Not ever.'

I stayed there on the sidewalk and Summer went away and came back five minutes later in the green Chevy we had used before. She pulled in tight to the kerb and buzzed her window down before I could move.

'Is this smart?' she said.

'It's all we've got,' I said.

'No, I mean you're going to be on the gate log. Time out, ten thirty. Willard could check it.'

I said nothing. She smiled.

'You could hide in the trunk,' she said. 'You could get out again when we're through the gate.'

I shook my head. 'I'm not going to hide. Not because of an asshole like Willard. If he checks the log I'll tell him the hunt for the gum-wrapper guy suddenly went interstate. Or global, even. We could go to Tahiti.'

I got in beside her and racked the seat all the way back and started thinking about bikinis again. She took her foot off the brake and accelerated down the main drag. Slowed and stopped at the gate. An MP private came out with a clipboard. He noted our plate number and we showed him ID. He wrote our names down. Glanced into the car, checked the empty rear seat. Then he nodded to his partner in the guard shack and the barrier went up in front of us, very slowly. It was a thick pole with a counterweight, red and white stripes. Summer waited until it was exactly vertical and then she dropped the hammer and we took off in a cloud of blue government-funded smoke from the Chevy's rear tyres.

The weather got better as we drove north. We slid out from under a shelf of low grey cloud into bright winter sunshine. It was an army car so there was no radio in it. Just a blank panel where the civilian model would have had AM and FM and a cassette slot. So we talked from time to time and whiled the rest away riding in aimless silence. It was a curious feeling, to be free. I had spent just about my whole life being where the military told me to be, every minute of every day. Now I felt like

246

a truant. There was a world out there. It was going about its business, chaotic and untidy and undisciplined, and I was a part of it, just briefly. I lay back in the seat and watched it spool by, bright and stroboscopic, random images flashing past like sunlight on a running river.

'Do you wear a bikini or a one-piece?' I asked.

'Why?'

'Just checking,' I said. 'I was thinking about the beach.'

'Too cold.'

'Won't be in August.'

'Think you'll be here in August?'

'No,' I said.

'Pity,' she said. 'You'll never know what I wear.'

'You could mail me a picture.'

'Where to?'

'Fort Leavenworth, probably,' I said. 'The maximum security wing.'

'No, where will you be? Seriously?'

'I have no idea,' I said. 'August is eight months away.'

'Where's the best place you ever served?'

I smiled. Gave her the same answer I give anyone who asks that question.

'Right here,' I said. 'Right now.'

'Even with Willard on your back?'

'Willard's nothing. He'll be gone before I am.'

'Why is he here at all?'

I moved in my seat. 'My brother figures they're copying what corporations do. Know-nothings aren't invested in the status quo.'

'So a guy trained to write fuel consumption algorithms winds up with two dead soldiers in his first week. And he doesn't want to investigate either one of them.'

'Because that would be old-fashioned thinking. We have to move on. We have to see the big picture.'

She smiled and drove on. Took the Green Valley ramp, going way too fast.

The Green Valley Police Department had a building north of town. It was a bigger place than I had expected, because Green

Valley itself was bigger than I had expected. It encompassed the pretty centre we had already seen, but then it bulged north through some country that was mostly strip malls and light industrial units, almost all the way up to Sperryville. The police station looked big enough for twenty or thirty cops. It was built the way most places are where land is cheap. It was long and low and sprawling, with a one-storey centre core and two wings. The wings were built at right-angles, so the place was U-shaped. The façades were concrete, moulded to look like stone. There was a brown lawn in front and parking lots at both sides. There was a flagpole dead centre on the lawn. Old Glory was up there, weather-beaten and limp in the windless air. The whole place looked a little grand, and a little bleached in the pale sunlight.

We parked in the right-hand lot in an empty slot between two white police cruisers. We got out into the brightness. Walked over to the front doors and went in and asked the desk guy for Detective Clark. The desk guy made an internal call and then pointed us towards the left-hand wing. We walked through an untidy corridor and ended up in a room the size of a basketball court. Pretty much the whole thing was a detectives' bullpen. There was a wooden fence that enclosed a line of four visitor chairs and then there was a gate with a receptionist's desk next to it. Beyond the gate was a lieutenant's office way off in one corner and then nothing else except three pairs of back-to-back desks covered with phones and paper. There were file cabinets against the walls. The windows were grimy and most of them had skewed and broken blinds.

There was no receptionist at the desk. There were two detectives in the room, both of them wearing tweed sport coats, both of them sitting with their backs to us. Clark was one of them. He was talking on the phone. I rattled the gate latch. Both guys turned around. Clark paused for a second, surprised, and then he waved us in. We pulled chairs around and sat at the ends of his desk, one on each side. He kept on talking into the phone. We waited. I spent the time looking around the room. The lieutenant's office had glass walls from waist-height upward. There was a big desk in there. Nobody behind it. But on it I could see two plaster casts, just like the ones our own

248

pathologist had made. I didn't get up and go look at them. Didn't seem polite.

Clark finished his call. Hung up the phone and made a note on a yellow pad. Then he breathed out and pushed his chair way back so he could see both of us at the same time. He didn't say anything. He knew we weren't making a social call. But equally he didn't want to come right out and ask if we had a name for him. Because he didn't want to look foolish if we didn't.

'Just passing through,' I said.

'OK,' he said.

'Looking for a little help,' I said.

'What kind of help?'

'Thought you might give us your crowbar notes. Now that you don't need them any more. Now that you've found yours.'

'Notes?'

'You listed all kinds of hardware stores. I figured it could save us some time if we picked up where you left off.'

'I could have faxed them,' he said.

'There's probably a lot of them. We didn't want to cause you the trouble.'

'I might not have been here.'

'We were passing by anyway.'

'OK,' he said again. 'Crowbar notes.' He swivelled his chair and got up out of it and walked over to a file cabinet. Came back with a green folder about a half-inch thick. He dropped it on his desk. It made a decent thump.

'Good luck,' he said.

He sat down again and I nodded to Summer and she picked up the folder. Opened it. It was full of paper. She leafed through. Made a face. Passed it across to me. It was a long, long list of places that stretched from New Jersey to North Carolina. There were names and addresses and phone numbers. The first ninety or so had check marks against them. Then there were about four hundred that didn't.

'You have to be careful,' Clark said. 'Some places call them crowbars and some call them wrecking bars. You have to be sure they know what you're talking about.'

'Do they have different sizes?'

'Lots of different sizes. Ours is pretty big.'

'Can I see it? Or is it in your evidence room?'

'It's not evidence,' Clark said. 'It's not the actual weapon. It's just an identical sample on loan from the Sperryville store. We can't take it to court.'

'But it fits your plaster casts.'

'Like a glove,' he said. He got up again and walked into his lieutenant's office and took the casts off the desk. Carried them back one in each hand and put them down on his own desk. They were very similar to ours. There was a positive and a negative, just like we had. Mrs Kramer's head had been a lot smaller than Carbone's, in terms of diameter. Therefore the crowbar had caught less of its circumference. Therefore the impression of the fatal wound was a little shorter in length than ours. But it was just as deep and ugly. Clark picked it up and ran his fingertip through the trench.

'Very violent blow,' he said. 'We're looking for a tall guy, strong, right-handed. You seen anyone like that?'

'Every time I look in the mirror,' I said.

The cast of the weapon itself was a little shorter than ours, too. But other than that, it looked very much the same. Same chalky section, pitted here and there with microscopic imperfections in the plaster, but basically straight and smooth and brutal.

'Can I see the actual crowbar?' I said.

'Sure,' Clark said. He leaned down and opened a drawer in his desk. Left it open like a display and moved his chair to get out of my way. I leaned forward and looked down and saw the same curved black thing I had seen the previous morning. Same shape, same contours, same colour, same size, same claws, same octagonal section. Same gloss, same precision. It was exactly identical in every way to the one we had left behind in Fort Bird's mortuary office.

We drove ten miles to Sperryville. I looked through Clark's list to find the hardware store's address. It was right there on the fifth line, because it was close to Green Valley. But there was no check mark against its phone number. There was a pencilled note instead: *No answer.* I guessed the owner had been busy with a glazier and an insurance company. I guessed Clark's guys would have gotten around to making a second call eventually, but they had been overtaken by the NCIC search.

Sperryville wasn't a big place, so we just cruised around looking for the address. We found a bunch of stores on a short strip and after driving it three times we found the right street name on a green sign. It pointed us down what was basically a narrow dead-end alley. We passed between the sides of two clapboard structures and then the alley widened into a small yard and we saw the hardware store facing us at the far end. It was like a small one-storey barn, painted up to look more urban than rural. It was a real mom-and-pop place. It had a family name painted on an old sign. No indication that it was part of a franchise. It was just an American small business, standing alone, weathering the booms and busts from one generation to the next.

But it was an excellent place for a dead-of-night burglary. Quiet, isolated, invisible to passers-by on the main street, no living accommodation on the second floor. In the front wall it had a display window on the left set next to an entrance door on the right, separated only by the width of the door frame. There was a moon-shaped hole in the window glass, temporarily backed by a sheet of unfinished plywood. The plywood had been neatly trimmed to the right size. I figured the hole had been punched through by the sole of a shoe. It was close to the door. I figured a tall guy could put his left arm through the hole up to the shoulder and get his hand around to the door latch easily enough. But he would have had to reach all the way in first and then bend his elbow slowly and deliberately, to avoid snagging his clothes. I pictured him with his left cheek against the cold glass, in the dark, breathing hard, groping blindly.

We parked right in front of the store. Got out and spent a minute looking in the window. It was full of items on display. But whoever had put them there wasn't about to move on to Saks Fifth Avenue anytime soon. Not for their famous holiday windows. Because there was no art involved. No design. No temptation. Everything was just lined up neatly on hand-built shelves. Everything had a price tag. The window was saying:

This is what we've got. If you want it, come in and get it. But it all looked like quality stuff. There were some strange items. I had no idea what some of them were for. I didn't know much about tools. I had never really used any, except knives. But it was clear to me that this store chose what it carried pretty carefully.

We went in. There was a mechanical bell on the door that rang as we entered. The plain neatness and organization we had seen in the window was maintained inside. There were tidy racks and shelves and bins. A wide-plank wooden floor. There was a faint smell of machine oil. The place was quiet. No customers. There was a guy behind the counter, maybe sixty years old, maybe seventy. He was looking at us, alerted by the bell. He was medium height and slender and a little stooped. He wore round eyeglasses and a grey cardigan sweater. They made him look intelligent, but they also made him look like he wasn't accustomed to handling anything bigger than a small screwdriver. They made him look like selling tools was a definite second best to being at a university, teaching a course about their design and their history and their development.

'May I help you?' he asked.

'We're here about the stolen wrecking bar,' I said. 'Or the stolen crowbar, if that's what you prefer to call it.'

He nodded.

'Crowbar,' he said. 'Wrecking bar is a little uncouth, in my opinion.'

'OK, we're here about the stolen crowbar,' I said.

He smiled, briefly. 'You're the army. Has martial law been declared?'

'We have a parallel inquiry,' Summer said.

'Are you military police?'

'Yes,' Summer said. She told him our names and ranks. He reciprocated with his own name, which matched the sign above his door.

'We need some background,' I said. 'About the crowbar market.'

He made a face like he was interested, but not very excited. It was like asking a forensics guy about fingerprinting instead of DNA. I got the impression that crowbar development had slowed to a halt a long time ago.

252

'Where can I start?' he said.

'How many different sorts are there?'

'Dozens,' he said. 'There are at least six manufacturers that I would consider dealing with myself. And plenty of others I wouldn't.'

I looked around the store. 'Because you only carry quality stuff.'

'Exactly,' he said. 'I can't compete with the big chains on price alone. So I have to offer absolutely top quality and service.'

'Niche marketing,' I said.

He nodded again.

'Low-end crowbars would come from China,' he said. 'Mass produced, cast iron, wrought iron, low-grade forged steel. I wouldn't be interested.'

'So what do you carry?'

'I import a few titanium crowbars from Europe,' he said. 'Very expensive, but very strong. More importantly, very light. They were designed for police and firefighters. Or for underwater work, where corrosion would otherwise be an issue. Or for anyone else that needs something small and durable and easily portable.'

'But it wasn't one of those that was stolen.'

The old guy shook his head. 'No, the titanium bars are specialist items. The others I offer are slightly more main-stream.'

'And what are those?'

'This is a small store,' he said. 'I have to choose what I carry very carefully. Which in some ways is a burden, but which is also a delight, because choice is very liberating. These decisions are mine, and mine alone. So obviously, for a crow-bar, I would choose high carbon chromium steel. Then the question is, should it be single-tempered or double-tempered? My honest preference would always be double-tempered, for strength. And I would want the claws to be very slim, for utility, and therefore case-hardened, for safety. That could be a life-saver, in some situations. Imagine a man on a high roof beam, whose claw shattered. He'd fall off.'

'I guess he would,' I said. 'So, the right steel, double-tempered, with the hard claws. What did you pick?'

'Well, actually I compromised with one of the items I carry. My preferred manufacturer won't make anything shorter than eighteen inches. But I needed a twelve-inch, obviously.'

I must have looked blank.

'For studs and joists,' the old guy said. 'If you're working inside sixteen-inch centres, you can't use an eighteen-inch bar, can you?'

'I guess not,' I said.

'So I take a twelve-inch with a half-inch section from one source, even though it's only single-tempered. I think it's satisfactory, though. In terms of strength. With only twelve inches of leverage, the force a person generates isn't going to overwhelm it.'

'OK,' I said.

'Apart from that particular item and the titanium specialties, I order exclusively from a very old Pittsburgh company called Fortis. They make two models for me. An eighteen-inch, and a three-footer. Both of them are three-quarter-inch section. High carbon double-tempered chromium steel, case-hardened claws, very fine quality paint.'

'And it was the three-footer that was stolen,' I said.

He looked at me like I was clairvoyant.

'Detective Clark showed us the sample you lent him,' I said.

'I see,' he said.

'So, is the thirty-six-inch three-quarter-section Fortis a rare item?'

He made a face, like he was a little disappointed.

'I sell one a year,' he said. 'Two, if I'm very lucky. They're expensive. And appreciation for quality is declining shamefully. Pearls before swine, I say.'

'Is that the same everywhere?'

'Everywhere?' he repeated.

'In other stores. Regionally. With the Fortis crowbars.'

'I'm sorry,' he said. 'Perhaps I didn't make myself quite clear. They're made for me. To my own design. To my own exact specification. They're custom items.'

I stared at him. 'They're exclusive to this store?'

He nodded. 'The privilege of independence.'

'Literally exclusive?'

He nodded again. 'Unique in all the world.'

'When did you last sell one?'

'About nine months ago.'

'Does the paint wear off?'

'I know what you're asking,' he said. 'And the answer is yes, of course. If you find one that looks new, it's the one that was stolen on New Year's Eve.'

We borrowed an identical sample from him for comparative purposes, the same way Detective Clark had. It was dewed with machine oil and had tissue paper wrapped around the centre shaft. We laid it like a trophy across the Chevy's back seat. Then we ate in the car. Burgers, from a drive-through a hundred yards north of the tool store.

'Tell me three new facts,' I said.

'One, Mrs Kramer and Carbone were killed by the same individual weapon. Two, we're going to drive ourselves nuts trying to find a connection between them.'

'And three?'

'I don't know.'

'Three, the bad guy knew Sperryville pretty well. Could you have found that store in the dark, in a hurry, unless you knew the town?'

We looked ahead through the windshield. The mouth of the alley was just about visible. But then, we knew it was there. And it was full daylight.

Summer closed her eyes.

'Focus on the weapon,' she said. 'Forget everything else. Visualize it. The custom crowbar. Unique in all the world. It was carried out of that alley, right there. Then it was in Green Valley at two a.m. on January first. And then it was inside Fort Bird at nine p.m. on the fourth. It went on a journey. We know where it started, and we know where it finished. We don't know for sure where it went in between, but we do know for certain it passed one particular point along the way. It passed Fort Bird's main gate. We don't know when, but we know for sure that it *did*.'

She opened her eyes.

'We have to get back there,' she said. 'We have to look at the logs again. The earliest it could have passed the gate is six a.m.

255

on January first, because Bird is four hours from Green Valley. The latest it could have passed the gate is, say, eight p.m. on January fourth. That's an eighty-six-hour window. We need to check the gate logs for everybody who entered during that time. Because we know for sure that the crowbar came in, and we know for sure that it didn't walk in by itself.'

I said nothing.

'I'm sorry,' she said. 'There'll be a lot of names.'

The truant feeling was completely gone. We got back on the road and headed east, looking for I-95. We found it and we turned south, towards Bird. Towards Willard on the phone. Towards the angry Delta station. We slid back under the shelf of grey cloud just before the North Carolina state line. The sky went dark. Summer put the headlights on. We passed the State Police building on the opposite shoulder. Passed the spot where Kramer's briefcase had been found. Passed the rest area a mile later. We merged with the east-west highway spur and came off at the cloverleaf next to Kramer's motel. We left it behind us and drove the thirty miles down to Fort Bird's gate. The guard shack MPs signed us in at 1930 hours exactly. I told them to copy their logs starting at 0600 hours January 1st and ending at 2000 hours January 4th. I told them to have a Xerox record of that eighty-six-hour slice of life delivered to my office immediately.

My office was very quiet. The morning mayhem was long gone. The sergeant with the baby son was back on duty. She looked tired. I realized she didn't sleep much. She worked all night and probably played with her kid all day. Tough life. She had coffee going. I figured she was just as interested in it as I was. Maybe more.

'Delta guys are restless,' she said. 'They know you arrested the Bulgarian guy.'

'I didn't arrest him. I just asked him some questions.'

'That's a distinction they don't seem willing to make. People have been in and out of here looking for you.'

'Were they armed?'

'They don't need to be armed. Not those guys. You should

have them confined to quarters. You could do that. You're acting MP CO here.'

I shook my head. 'Anything else?'

'You need to call Colonel Willard before midnight, or he's going to write you up as AWOL. He said that's a promise.'

I nodded. It was Willard's obvious next move. An AWOL charge wouldn't reflect badly on a CO. Wouldn't make him look like he had lost his grip. An AWOL charge was always on the man who ran, fair and square.

'Anything else?' I said again.

'Sanchez wants a ten-sixteen,' she said. 'Down at Fort Jackson. And your brother called again.'

'Any message?' I said.

'No message.'

'OK,' I said.

I went inside to my desk. Picked up my phone. Summer stepped over to the map. Traced her fingers across the pins, D.C. to Sperryville, Sperryville to Green Valley, Green Valley to Fort Bird. I dialled Joe's number. He answered, second ring.

'I called Mom,' he said. 'She's still hanging in there.'

'She said soon, Joe. Doesn't mean we have to mount a daily vigil.'

'Bound to be sooner than we think. And than we want.'

'How was she?'

'She sounded shaky.'

'You OK?'

'Not bad,' he said. 'You?'

'Not a great year so far.'

'You should call her next,' he said.

'I will,' I said. 'In a few days.'

'Do it tomorrow,' he said.

He hung up and I sat for a minute. Then I dabbed the cradle to clear the line and asked my sergeant to get Sanchez for me. Down at Jackson. I held the phone by my ear and waited. Summer was looking right at me.

'A daily vigil?' she said.

'She's waiting for the plaster to come off,' I said. 'She doesn't like it.'

Summer looked at me a little more and then turned back to

257

the map. I put the phone on speaker and laid the handset down on the desk. There was a click on the line and we heard Sanchez's voice.

'I've been hassling the Columbia PD about Brubaker's car,' he said.

'Didn't they find it yet?' I said.

'No,' he said. 'And they weren't putting any effort into finding it. Which was inconceivable to me. So I kept on hassling them.'

'And?'

'They dropped the other shoe.'

'Which is?'

'Brubaker wasn't killed in Columbia,' he said. 'He was dumped there, is all.'

SEVENTEEN

S ANCHEZ TOLD US THE COLUMBIA MEDICAL EXAMINERS HAD FOUND confused lividity patterns on Brubaker's body that in their opinion meant he had been dead about three hours before being tossed in the alley. Lividity is what happens to a person's blood after death. The heart stops, blood pressure collapses, liquid blood drains and sinks and settles into the lowest parts of the body under the simple force of gravity. It rests there and over a period of time it stains the skin liverish purple. Somewhere between three and six hours later the colour fixes permanently, like a developed photograph. A guy who falls down dead on his back will have a pale chest and a purple back. Vice versa for a guy who falls down dead on his front. But Brubaker's lividity was all over the place. The Columbia medical examiners figured he had been killed, then kept on his back for about three hours, then dumped in the alley on his front. They were pretty confident about their estimate of the three-hour duration, because three hours was the point where the stains would first start to fix. They said he had signs of early fixed lividity on his back and major fixed lividity on his front. They also said he had a broad stripe across the middle of his back where the dead flesh had been partially cooked.

259

'He was in the trunk of a car,' I said.

'Right over the muffler,' Sanchez said. 'Three-hour journey, plenty of temperature.'

'This changes a lot of things.'

'It explains why they never found his Chevy in Columbia.'

'Or any witnesses,' I said. 'Or the shell cases or the bullets.'

'So what are we looking at?'

'Three hours in a car?' I said. 'At night, with empty roads? Anything up to a two-hundred-mile radius.'

'That's a pretty big circle,' Sanchez said.

'A hundred and twenty-five thousand square miles,' I said. 'Approximately. Pi times the radius squared. What's the Columbia PD doing about it?'

'Dropping it like a hot potato. It's an FBI case now.'

'What does the Bureau think about the dope thing?'

'They're a little sceptical. They figure heroin isn't our bag. They figure we're more into marijuana and amphetamines.'

'I wish,' I said. 'I could use a little of both right now.'

'On the other hand they know Delta guys go all over. Pakistan, South America. Which is where heroin comes from. So they'll keep it in their back pocket, in case they don't get anywhere, just like the Columbia PD was going to.'

'They're wasting their time. Heroin? A guy like Brubaker would die first.'

'They're thinking, maybe he did.'

His end of the line clicked off. I killed the speaker and put the handset back.

'It happened to the north, probably,' Summer said. 'Brubaker started out in Raleigh. We should be looking for his car somewhere up there.'

'Not our case,' I said.

'OK, the FBI should be looking.'

'I'm sure they already are.'

There was a knock at the door. It opened up and an MP corporal came in with sheets of paper under his arm. He saluted smartly and stepped a pace forward and placed the sheets of paper on my desk. Stepped the same pace back and saluted again.

'Copies of the gate log, sir,' he said. 'First through fourth of this month, times as requested.'

He turned around and walked back out of the room. Closed the door. I looked at the pile of paper. There were about seven sheets in it. *Not too bad.*

'Let's go to work,' I said.

Operation Just Cause helped us again. The raised DefCon level meant a lot of leave had been cancelled. No real reason, because the Panama thing was no kind of a big deal, but that was how the military worked. No point in having DefCon levels if they couldn't be raised up and dropped down, no point in moving them at all if there weren't any associated consequences. No point in staging little foreign dramas unless the whole establishment felt a remote and vicarious thrill.

No point in cancelling leave without giving people something to fill their time, either. So there were extra training sessions and daily readiness exercises. Most of them were arduous and started early. Therefore the big bonus for us was that almost everyone who had gone out to celebrate New Year's Eve was back on post and in the rack relatively early. They must have straggled back around three or four or five in the morning, because there was very little gate activity recorded after six.

Incoming personnel during the eighteen hours we were looking at on New Year's Day totalled nineteen. Summer and I were two of them, returning from Green Valley and D.C. after the widow trip and the visit to Walter Reed. We crossed ourselves off the list.

Incoming personnel other than ourselves on January 2nd totalled sixteen. Twelve, on January 3rd. Seventeen, before 2000 hours on January 4th. Sixty-two names in total, during the eighty-six-hour window. Nine of them were civilian delivery drivers. We crossed them off. Eleven of them were repeats. They had come in, gone out, come in again. Like commuters. My night-duty sergeant was one of them. We crossed her off, because she was a woman. And short. Elsewhere we deleted the second and any subsequent entries in each case.

We ended up with forty-one individuals, listed by name, rank and initial. No way of telling which were men and which were

261

women. No way of telling which of the men were tall and strong and right-handed.

'I'll work on the genders,' Summer said. 'I've still got the basic strength lists. They have full names on them.'

I nodded. Left her to it. Got on the phone and scared up the pathologist and asked him to meet me in the mortuary, right away.

I drove our Chevy between my office and his because I didn't want to be seen walking around with a crowbar. I parked outside the mortuary entrance and waited. The guy showed up inside five minutes, walking, from the direction of the O Club. I probably interrupted his dessert. Or maybe even his main course. I slid out to meet him and leaned back in and took the crowbar out of the back seat. He glanced at it. Led me inside. He seemed to understand what I wanted to do. He unlocked his office and hit the lights and unlocked his drawer. Opened it and lifted out the crowbar that had killed Carbone. Laid it on his desk. I laid the borrowed specimen next to it. Pulled the tissue paper off it. Lined it up at the same angle. It was exactly identical.

'Are there wide variations?' the pathologist asked. 'With crowbars?'

'More than you would think,' I said. 'I just had a big crowbar lesson.'

'These two look the same.'

'They are the same. They're peas in a pod. Count on it. They're custom made. They're unique in all the world.'

'Did you ever meet Carbone?'

'Very briefly,' I said.

'What was his posture like?'

'In what way?'

'Did he stoop?'

I thought back to the dim interior of the lounge bar. To the hard light in the parking lot. Shook my head.

'He wasn't tall enough to stoop,' I said. 'He was a wiry guy, solid, stood up pretty straight. Kind of on the balls of his feet. He looked athletic.'

'OK.'

262

'Why?'

'It was a downward blow. Not a downward chop, but a horizontal swing that dipped as it hit. Maybe it was just below horizontal. Carbone was seventy inches tall. The wound was sixty-five inches off the ground, assuming he wasn't stooping. But it was delivered from above. So his attacker was tall.'

'You told us that already,' I said.

'No, I mean *tall*,' he said. 'I've been working on it. Mapping it out. The guy had to be six-four or six-five.'

'Like me,' I said.

'And as heavy as you, too. Not easy to break a skull as badly as that.'

I thought back to the crime scene. It had been pocked with small hummocks of dead grass and there were wrist-thick branches here and there on the ground, but it was basically a flat area. No way one guy could have been standing higher than the other. No way of assuming a relative height difference when there really wasn't one.

'Six-four or six-five,' I said. 'Are you prepared to go to bat on that?'

'In court?'

'It was a training accident,' I said. 'We're not going to court. This is just between you and me. Am I wasting my time looking at people less than six feet four inches tall?'

The doctor breathed in, breathed out.

'Six-three,' he said. 'To be on the safe side. To allow a margin for experimental error. I'd go to bat on six-three. Count on it.'

'OK,' I said.

He shooed me out the door and hit the lights and locked up again.

Summer was sitting behind my desk when I got back, doing nothing. She was through with the gender analysis. It hadn't taken her long. The strength lists were comprehensive and accurate and alphabetical, like most army paperwork.

'Thirty-three men,' she said. 'Twenty-three enlisted, ten officers.'

'Who are they?'

'A little bit of everything. Delta and Ranger leave was

completely cancelled, but they had evening passes. Carbone himself was in and out on the first, obviously.'

'We can cross him off.'

'OK, thirty-two men,' she said. 'The pathologist is one of them.'

'We can take him out, too.'

'Thirty-one, then,' she said. 'And Vassell and Coomer are still in there. In and out on the first and in again on the fourth at seven o'clock.'

'Take them out,' I said. 'They were eating dinner. Fish, and steak.'

'Twenty-nine,' she said. 'Twenty-two enlisted, seven officers.'

'OK,' I said. 'Now go to Post HQ and pull their medical records.'

'Why?'

'To find out how tall they are.'

'Can't do that for the driver Vassell and Coomer had on New Year's Day. Major Marshall. He was a visitor. His records won't be here.'

'He wasn't here the night Carbone died,' I said. 'So you can take him out too.'

'Twenty-eight,' she said.

'So go pull twenty-eight sets of records,' I said.

She slid me a slip of white paper. I picked it up. It was the one I had written *973* on. Our original suspect pool.

'We're making progress,' she said.

I nodded. She smiled and stood up. Walked out the door. I took her place behind the desk. The chair was warm from her body. I savoured the feeling, until it went away. Then I picked up the phone. Asked my sergeant to get the post quartermaster on the line. It took her a few minutes to find him. I figured she had to drag him out of the mess hall. I figured I had just ruined his dinner, too, as well as the pathologist's. But then, I hadn't eaten anything yet myself.

'Yes, sir?' the guy said. He sounded a little annoyed.

'I've got a question, chief,' I said. 'Something only you will know.'

'Like what?'

'Average height and weight for a male U.S. Army soldier.'

The guy said nothing, but I felt his annoyance fade away. The Quartermaster Corps buys millions of uniforms a year, and twice as many boots, all on a budget, so you can bet it knows the tale of the tape to the nearest half-inch and the nearest half-ounce. It can't afford not to, literally. And it loves to show off its specialized knowledge.

'No problem,' the guy said. 'Male adult population aged twenty to fifty as a whole in America goes five-nine and a half, and one-seventy-eight. We're over-represented with Hispanics by comparison with the nation as a whole which brings our median height down one whole inch to five-eight and a half. We train pretty hard which brings our median weight up three pounds to one-eighty-one, muscle being generally heavier than fat.'

'Those are this year's figures?'

'Last year's,' he said. 'This year is only a few days old.'

'What's the spread in height?'

'What are you looking for?'

'How many guys have we got six-three or better?'

'One in ten,' he said. 'In the army as a whole, maybe ninety thousand. Call it a Superbowl crowd. On a post this size, maybe a hundred and twenty. Call it a half-empty airplane.'

'OK, chief,' I said. 'Thanks.'

I hung up. *One in ten.* Summer was going to come back with twenty-eight medical charts. Nine out of ten of them were going to be for guys too small to worry about. So out of twenty-eight, if we were lucky, only two of them would need looking at. Three, if we were unlucky. Two or three, down from nine hundred seventy-three. *Making progress.* I looked at the clock. Eight thirty. I smiled to myself. *Shit happens, Willard,* I thought.

Shit happened, for sure, but it happened to us, not Willard. Averages and medians played their little arithmetic tricks and Summer came back with twenty-eight charts and all twenty-eight of them were for short guys. Tallest among them was a marginal six-foot-one, and he was a reed-thin one hundred sixty pounds, and he was a padre.

Once when I was a kid we lived for a month in an off-post

bungalow somewhere. It had no dining table. My mother called people and had one delivered. It came packed flat in a carton. I tried to help her put it together. All the parts were there. There was a laminated tabletop, and four chrome legs, and four big steel bolts. We laid them out on the floor in the dining nook. The top, four legs, four bolts. But there was no way to fit them together. No way at all. It was some kind of an inexplicable design. Nothing would join up. We knelt side by side and worked on it. We sat cross-legged on the floor, with the dust bunnies and the cockroaches. The smooth chrome was cold in my hands. The edges were rough, where the laminate was shaped on the corners. We couldn't put it together. Joe came in, and tried, and failed. My dad tried, and failed. We ate in the kitchen for a month. We were still trying to put that table together when we moved out. Now I felt like I was wrestling with it all over again. Nothing went together. Everything looked good at first, and then everything stalled and died.

'The crowbar didn't walk in by itself,' Summer said. 'One of those twenty-eight names brought it in. Obviously. It can't have gotten here any other way.'

I said nothing.

'Want dinner?' she said.

'I think better when I'm hungry,' I said.

'We've run out of things to think about.'

I nodded. Gathered the twenty-eight medical charts together and piled them neatly. Put Summer's original list of thirty-three names on top. Thirty-three, minus Carbone, because he didn't bring the crowbar in himself and commit suicide with it. Minus the pathologist, because he wasn't a convincing suspect, and because he was short, and because his practice swings with the crowbar had been weak. Minus Vassell and Coomer and their driver, Marshall, because their alibis were too good. Vassell and Coomer had been stuffing their faces, and Marshall hadn't even come at all.

'Why wasn't Marshall here?' I said.

Summer nodded. 'That's always bothered me. It's like Vassell and Coomer had something to hide from him.'

'All they did was eat dinner.'

'But Marshall must have been right there at Kramer's funeral with them. So they must have specifically told him *not* to drive them here. Like a positive order to get out of the car and stay home.'

I nodded. Pictured the long line of black government sedans at Arlington National Cemetery, under a leaden January sky. Pictured the ceremony, the folding of the flag, the salute from the riflemen. The shuffling procession back to the cars, bareheaded men with their chins ducked into their collars against the cold, maybe snow in the air. I pictured Marshall holding the Mercury's rear doors, for Vassell first, then for Coomer. He must have driven them back to the Pentagon lot and then gotten out and watched Coomer move up into the driver's seat.

'We should talk to him,' I said. 'Find out exactly what they told him. What kind of reason they gave him. It must have been a slightly awkward moment. A blue-eyed boy like that must have felt a little excluded.'

I picked up the phone and spoke to my sergeant. Asked her to get a number for Major Marshall. Told her he was a XII Corps staffer based at the Pentagon. She said she would get back to me. Summer and I sat quiet and waited. I gazed at the map on the wall. I figured we should take the pin out of Columbia. It distorted the picture. Brubaker hadn't been killed there. He had been killed somewhere else. North, south, east, or west.

'Are you going to call Willard?' Summer asked me.

'Probably,' I said. 'Tomorrow, maybe.'

'Not before midnight?'

'I don't want to give him the satisfaction.'

'That's a risk.'

'I'm protected,' I said.

'Might not last for ever.'

'Doesn't matter. I'll have Delta Force coming after me soon. That'll make everything else seem kind of academic.'

'Call Willard tonight,' she said. 'That would be my advice.'

I looked at her.

'As a friend,' she said. 'AWOL is a big deal. No point making things worse.'

'OK,' I said.

'Do it now,' she said. 'Why not?'

267

'OK,' I said again. I reached out for the phone but before I could get my hand on it my sergeant put her head in the door. She told us Major Marshall was no longer based in the United States. His temporary detached duty had been prematurely terminated. He had been recalled to Germany. He had been flown out of Andrews Air Force Base late in the morning of the fifth of January.

'Whose orders?' I asked her.

'General Vassell's,' she said.

'OK,' I said.

She closed the door.

'The fifth of January,' Summer said.

'The morning after Carbone and Brubaker died,' I said.

'He knows something.'

'He wasn't even here.'

'Why else would they hide him away afterwards?'

'It's a coincidence.'

'You don't like coincidences.'

I nodded.

'OK,' I said. 'Let's go to Germany.'

EIGHTEEN

N O WAY WAS WILLARD ABOUT TO AUTHORIZE ANY FOREIGN expeditions so I walked over to the Provost Marshal's office and took a stack of travel vouchers out of the company clerk's desk. I carried them back to my own office and signed them all with my name on the *CO* lines and respectable forgeries of Leon Garber's signature on the *authorized by* lines.

'We're breaking the law,' Summer said.

'This is the Battle of Kursk,' I said. 'We can't stop now.'

She hesitated.

'Your choice,' I said. 'In or out, no pressure from me.'

She said nothing.

'These vouchers won't come back for a month or two,' I said. 'By then either Willard will be gone, or we will. We've got nothing to lose.'

'OK,' she said.

'Go pack,' I said. 'Three days.'

She left and I asked my sergeant to figure out who was next in line for acting CO. She came back with a name I recognized as the female captain I had seen in the O Club dining room. The one with the busted arm. I wrote her a note explaining I would be out for three days. I told her she was in charge. Then I picked up the phone and called Joe.

'I'm going to Germany,' I said.

'OK,' he said. 'Enjoy. Have a safe trip.'

'I can't go to Germany without stopping by Paris on the way back. You know, in the circumstances.'

He paused.

'No,' he said. 'I guess you can't.'

'Wouldn't be right not to,' I said. 'But she shouldn't think I care more than you do. That wouldn't be right either. So you should come over too.'

'When?'

'Take the overnight flight two days from now. I'll meet you at Roissy-Charles de Gaulle. Then we'll go see her together.'

Summer met me on the sidewalk outside my quarters and we carried our bags to the Chevy. We were both in BDUs because we figured our best shot was a night transport out of Andrews Air Force Base. We were too late for a civilian red-eye and we didn't want to wait all night for the breakfast flights. We got in the car and logged out at the gate. Summer was driving, of course. She accelerated hard and then dropped into a smooth rhythm that was about ten miles an hour faster than the other cars heading our way.

I sat back and watched the road. Watched the shoulders, and the strip malls, and the traffic. We drove north thirty miles and passed by Kramer's motel. Hit the cloverleaf and jogged east to I-95. Headed north. We passed the rest area. Passed the spot a mile later where the briefcase had been found. I closed my eyes.

I slept all the way to Andrews. We got there well after midnight. We parked in a restricted lot and swapped two of our travel vouchers for two places on a Transportation Corps C-130 that was leaving for Frankfurt at three in the morning. We waited in a lounge that had fluorescent lighting and vinyl benches and was filled with the usual ragtag bunch of transients. The military is always on the move. There are always people going somewhere, any time of the night or day. Nobody talked.

Nobody ever did. We all just sat there, stiff and tired and uncomfortable.

The loadmaster came to get us thirty minutes before takeoff. We filed out onto the tarmac and walked up the ramp into the belly of the plane. There was a long line of cargo pallets in the centre bay. We sat on webbing jump seats with our backs to the fuselage wall. On the whole I figured I preferred the first-class section on Air France. The Transportation Corps doesn't have stewardesses and it doesn't brew in-flight coffee.

We took off a little late, heading west into the wind. Then we turned a slow one-eighty over D.C. and struck out east. I felt the movement. There were no windows, but I knew we were above the city. Joe was down there somewhere, sleeping.

The fuselage wall was very cold at altitude so we all leaned forward with our elbows on our knees. It was too noisy to talk. I stared at a pallet of tank ammunition until my vision blurred and I fell back to sleep. It wasn't comfortable, but one thing you learn in the army is how to sleep anywhere. I woke up maybe ten times and spent most of the trip in a state of suspended animation. The roar of the engines and the rush of the slip-stream helped induce it. It was relatively restful. It was about sixty per cent as good as being in bed.

We were in the air nearly eight hours before we started our initial descent. There was no intercom. No cheery message from the pilot. Just a change in the engine note and a downward lurching movement and a sharp sensation in the ears. All around me people were standing up and stretching. Summer had her back flat against an ammunition crate, rubbing like a cat. She looked pretty good. Her hair was too short to get messy and her eyes were bright. She looked determined, like she knew she was heading for doom or glory and was resigned to not knowing which.

We all sat down again and held tight to the webbing for the landing. The wheels touched down and the reverse thrust howled and the brakes jammed on tight. The pallets jerked forward against their straps. Then the engines cut back and we taxied a long way and stopped. The ramp came down and a dim dusk sky showed through the hole. It was five o'clock in the afternoon in Germany, six hours ahead of the east coast, one hour ahead of Zulu time. I was starving. I had eaten nothing since the burger in Sperryville the previous day. Summer and I stood up and grabbed our bags and got in line. Shuffled down the ramp with the others and out onto the tarmac. The weather was cold. It felt pretty much the same as North Carolina.

We were way out in the restricted military corner of the Frankfurt airport. We took a personnel bus to the public terminal. After that we were on our own. Some of the other guys had transport waiting, but we didn't. We joined a bunch of civilians in the taxi line. Shuffled up, one by one. When our turn came we gave the driver a travel voucher and told him to drive us east to XII Corps. He was happy enough to comply. He could swap the voucher for hard currency at any U.S. post and I was certain he would pick up a couple of XII Corps guys going out into Frankfurt for a night on the town. No deadheading. No empty running. He was making a living off of the U.S. Army, just like plenty of Germans had for four and a half decades. He was driving a Mercedes-Benz.

The trip took thirty minutes. We drove east through suburbs. They looked like a lot of West German places. There were vast tracts of pale honey buildings built back in the fifties. The new neighbourhoods ran west to east in random curving shapes, following the routes the bombers had followed. No nation ever lost a war the way Germany lost. Like everyone I had seen the pictures taken in 1945. *Defeat* was not a big enough word. *Armageddon* would be better. The whole country had been smashed to powdered rubble by a juggernaut. The evidence would be there for all time, written in the architecture. And under the architecture. Every time the phone company dug a trench for a cable, they found skulls and bones and tea cups and shells and rusted-out *panzerfausts*. Every time ground was broken for a new foundation, a priest was standing by before the steam shovels took their first bite. I was born in Berlin, surrounded by Americans, surrounded by whole square miles of patched-up devastation. *They started it*, we used to say.

The suburban streets were neat and clean. There were discreet stores with apartments above them. The store windows were full of shiny items. Street signs were black-on-white, written in an archaic script that made them hard to read. There were small U.S. Army road signs here and there, too. You couldn't go very far without seeing one. We followed the XII Corps arrows, getting closer all the time. We left the built-up area and drove through a couple of kilometres of farmland. It felt like a moat. Like insulation. The eastern sky ahead of us was dark.

XII Corps was based in a typical glory-days installation. Some Nazi industrialist had built a thousand-acre factory site out in the fields, back in the 1930s. It had featured an impressive home office building and ranks of low metal sheds stretching hundreds of metres behind it. The sheds had been bombed to twisted shards, over and over again. The home office building had been only partially damaged. Some weary U.S. Army armoured division had set up camp in it in 1945. Thin Frankfurt women in headscarves and faded print dresses had been brought in to pile the rubble, in exchange for food. They worked with wheelbarrows and shovels. Then the Army Corps of Engineers had fixed up the office building and bulldozed the piles of rubble away. Successive huge waves of Pentagon spending had rolled in. By 1953 the place was a flagship installation. There was cleaned brick and shining white paint and a strong perimeter fence. There were flagpoles and sentry boxes and guard shacks. There were mess halls and a medical clinic and a PX. There were barracks and workshops and warehouses. Above all there was a thousand acres of flat land and by 1953 it was covered with American tanks. They were all lined up, facing east, ready to roll out and fight for the Fulda Gap.

When we got there thirty-seven years later it was too dark to see much. But I knew that nothing fundamental would have changed. The tanks would be different, but that would be all. The M4 Shermans that had won World War 2 were long gone, except for two fine examples standing preserved outside the main gate, one on each side, like symbols. They were placed halfway up landscaped concrete ramps, noses high, tails low, like they were still in motion, breasting a rise. They were lit up theatrically. They were beautifully painted, glossy green, with bright white stars on their sides. They looked much better than they had originally. Behind them was a long driveway with white-painted kerbs and the floodlit front of the office building, which was now the post headquarters. Behind that would be the tank lagers, with M1A1 Abrams main battle tanks lined up shoulder-to-shoulder, hundreds of them, at nearly four million bucks a piece.

We got out of the taxi and crossed the sidewalk and headed for the main gate guard shack. My special unit badge got us past it. It would get us past any U.S. Army checkpoint anywhere except the inner ring of the Pentagon. We carried our bags down the driveway.

'Been here before?' Summer asked me.

I shook my head as I walked.

'I've been in Heidelberg with the infantry,' I said. 'Many times.'

'Is that near?'

'Not far,' I said.

There were broad stone steps leading up to the doors. The whole place looked like a capitol building in some small state back home. It was immaculately maintained. We went up the steps and inside. There was a soldier at a desk just behind the doors. Not an MP. Just a XII Corps office grunt. We showed him our IDs.

'Your VOQ got space for us?' I asked.

'Sir, no problem,' he said.

'Two rooms,' I said. 'One night.'

'I'll call ahead,' he said. 'Just follow the signs.'

He pointed to the back of the hallway. There were more doors there that would lead out into the complex. I checked my watch. It said noon exactly. It was still set to East Coast time. Six in the evening, in West Germany. Already dark.

'I need to see your MP XO,' I said. 'Is he still in his office?'

The guy used his phone and got an answer. Pointed us up a broad staircase to the second floor.

'On your right,' he said.

We went up the stairs and turned right. There was a long corridor with offices on both sides. They had hardwood doors with reeded glass windows. We found the one we wanted and went in. It was an outer chamber with a sergeant in it. It was pretty much identical to the one back at Bird. Same paint, same

274

floor, same furniture, same temperature, same smell. Same coffee, in the same standard-issue machine. The sergeant was like plenty I had seen before, too. Calm, efficient, stoic, ready to believe he ran the place all by himself, which he probably did. He was behind his desk and he looked up at us as we came in. Spent half a second deciding who we were and what we wanted.

'I guess you need the major,' he said.

I nodded. He picked up his phone and buzzed through to the inner office.

'Go straight through,' he said.

We went in through the inner door and I saw a desk with a guy called Swan behind it. I knew Swan pretty well. Last time I had seen him was in the Philippines, three months earlier, when he was starting a tour of duty that was scheduled to last a year.

'Don't tell me,' I said. 'You got here December twenty-ninth.'

'Froze my ass off,' he said. 'All I had was Pacific gear. Took XII Corps three days to find me a winter uniform.'

I wasn't surprised. Swan was short, and wide. Almost cubic. He probably owned a percentile all his own, on the quartermasters' charts.

'Your Provost Marshal here?' I said.

He shook his head. 'Temporarily reassigned.'

'Garber signed your orders?'

'Allegedly.'

'Figured it out yet?'

'Not even close.'

'Me either,' I said.

He shrugged, like he was saying, *hey, the army, what can you do?*

'This is Lieutenant Summer,' I said.

'Special unit?' Swan said.

Summer shook her head.

'But she's cool,' I said.

Swan stretched a short arm over his desk and they shook hands.

'I need to see a guy called Marshall,' I said. 'A major. Some kind of a XII Corps staffer.'

'Is he in trouble?'

275

'Someone is. I'm hoping Marshall will help me figure out who. You know him?'

'Never heard of him,' Swan said. 'I only just got here.'

'I know,' I said. 'December twenty-ninth.'

He smiled and gave me the *what can you do* shrug again and picked up his phone. I heard him ask his sergeant to find Marshall and tell him I wanted to see him at his convenience. I looked around while we waited for the response. Swan's office looked borrowed and temporary, just like mine did back in North Carolina. It had the same kind of clock on the wall. Electric, no second hand. No tick. It said ten minutes past six.

'Anything happening here?' I said.

'Not much,' Swan said. 'Some helicopter guy went shopping in Heidelberg and got run over. And Kramer died, of course. That's shaken things up some.'

'Who's next in line?'

'Vassell, I guess.'

'I met him,' I said. 'Wasn't impressed.'

'It's a poisoned chalice. Things are changing. You should hear these guys talk. They're real gloomy.'

'The status quo is not an option,' I said. 'That's what I'm hearing.'

His phone rang. He listened for a minute and put it down.

'Marshall's not on post,' he said. 'He's out on a night exercise in the countryside. Back in the morning.'

Summer glanced at me. I shrugged.

'Have dinner with me,' Swan said. 'I'm lonely here with all these cavalry types. The O Club in an hour?'

We carried our bags over to the Visiting Officers' Quarters and found our rooms. Mine looked pretty much the same as the one Kramer had died in, except it was cleaner. It was a standard American motel layout. Presumably some hotel chain had bid for the government contract, way back when. Then they had air-freighted all the fixtures and fittings, right down to the sinks and the towel rails and the toilet bowls.

I shaved and took a shower and dressed in clean BDUs. Knocked on Summer's door fifty-five minutes into Swan's hour. She opened up. She looked clean and fresh. Behind her the

276

room looked the same as mine, except it already smelled like a woman's. There was some kind of nice eau de toilette in the air.

We found the O Club without any trouble. It occupied half of one of the ground-floor wings of the main building. It was a grand space, with high ceilings and intricate plaster mouldings. There was a lounge, and a bar, and a dining room. We found Swan in the bar. He was with a lieutenant colonel who was wearing Class As with a combat infantryman's badge on the coat. It was an odd thing to see, on an Armored post. His name plate said: *Simon*. He introduced himself to us. I got the feeling he was going to join us for dinner. He told us he was a liaison officer, working on behalf of the infantry. He told us there was an Armored guy down in Heidelberg, doing the same job in reverse.

'Been here long?' I asked him.

'Two years,' he said, which I was glad about. I needed some background, and Swan didn't have it any more than I knew anything about Fort Bird. Then I realized it was no accident that Simon was joining the party. Swan must have figured out what I wanted and set about providing it without being asked. Swan was that kind of a guy.

'Pleased to meet you, colonel,' I said, and then I nodded to Swan, like I was saying thanks. We drank cold American beers from tall frosted glasses and then we went through to the dining room. Swan had made a reservation. The steward put us at a table in the corner. I sat where I could watch the whole room at once. I didn't see anyone I knew. Vassell wasn't around. Nor was Coomer.

The menu was absolutely standard. We could have been in any O Club in the world. O Clubs aren't there to introduce you to local cuisine. They're there to make you feel at home, somewhere deep inside the army's own interpretation of America. There was a choice of fish or steak. The fish was probably European, but the steak would have been flown in across the Atlantic. Some politician in one of the ranch states would have leveraged a sweet deal with the Pentagon.

We small-talked for a spell. We bitched about pay and benefits. Talked about people we knew. We mentioned Just Cause in Panama. Lieutenant Colonel Simon told us he had been to Berlin two days previously and had gotten himself a chip of concrete from the Wall. Told us he planned to have it encased in a plastic cube. Planned to hand it on down the generations, like an heirloom.

'Do you know Major Marshall?' I asked him.

'Fairly well,' he said.

'Who is he exactly?' I asked.

'Is this official?'

'Not really,' I said.

'He's a planner. A strategist, basically. Long-term kind of guy. General Kramer seemed to like him. Always kept him close by, made him his intelligence officer.'

'Does he have an intelligence background?'

'Not formally. But he'll have done rotations, I'm sure.'

'So is he a part of the inner team? I heard Kramer and Vassell and Coomer mentioned all in the same breath, but not Marshall.'

'He's on the team,' Simon said. 'That's for sure. But you know what flag officers are like. They need a guy, but they aren't about to admit it. So they abuse him a little. He fetches and carries and drives them around, but when push comes to shove they ask his opinion.'

'Is he going to move up now Kramer's gone? Maybe into Coomer's slot?'

Simon made a face. 'He should. He's an Armor fanatic to the core, like the rest of them. But nobody really knows what the hell is going to happen. Kramer dying couldn't have come at a worse time for them.'

'The world is changing,' I said.

'And what a world it was,' Simon said. 'Kramer's world, basically, beginning to end. He graduated the Point in 'fifty-two, and places like this one were all buttoned up by 'fifty-three, and they've been the centre of the universe for almost forty years. These places are so dug in, you wouldn't believe it. You know who has done the most in this country?'

'Who?'

'Not Armored. Not the infantry. This theatre is all about the Army Corps of Engineers. Sherman tanks way back weighed thirty-eight tons and were nine feet wide. Now we're all the way

278

up to the M1A1 Abrams, which weighs seventy tons and is eleven feet wide. Every step of the way for forty years the Corps of Engineers has had work to do. They've widened roads, hundreds of miles of them, all over West Germany. They've strengthened bridges. Hell, they've *built* roads and bridges. Dozens of them. You want a stream of seventy-ton tanks rolling east to battle, you better make damn sure the roads and bridges can take it.'

'OK,' I said.

'Billions of dollars,' Simon said. 'And of course, they knew which roads and bridges to look at. They knew where we were starting, and they knew where we were going. They talked to the war gamers, they looked at the maps, and they got busy with the concrete and the rebar. Then they built way stations everywhere we needed them. Permanent hardened fuel stores, ammunition dumps, repair shops, hundreds of them, all along strictly predetermined routes. So we're embedded here, literally. We're dug in, literally. The Cold War battlefields are literally set in stone, Reacher.'

'People are going to say we invested and we won.'

Simon nodded. 'And they'd be correct. But what comes next?'

'More investment,' I said.

'Exactly,' he said. 'Like in the navy, when the big battleships were superseded by aircraft carriers. The end of one era, the beginning of the next. The Abrams tanks are like battleships. They're magnificent, but they're out of date. About the only way we can use them is down custom-built roads in directions we've already planned to go.'

'They're mobile,' Summer said. 'Like any tank.'

'Not very mobile,' Simon said. 'Where is the next fight going to be?'

I shrugged. I wished Joe was there. He was good at all the geopolitical stuff.

'The Middle East?' I said. 'Iran or Iraq, maybe. They've both gotten their breath back, they'll be looking for the next thing to do.'

'Or the Balkans,' Swan said. 'When the Soviets finally collapse, there's a forty-five-year-old pressure cooker waiting for the lid to come off.'

'OK,' Simon said. 'Look at the Balkans, for instance. Yugoslavia, maybe. That'll be the first place anything happens, for sure. Right now they're just waiting for the starting gun. What do we do?'

'Send in the airborne,' Swan said.

'OK,' Simon said again. 'We send in the 82nd and the 101st. Lightly armed, we might get three battalions there inside a week. But what do we do after we get there? We're speed bumps, that's all, nothing more. We have to wait for the heavy units. And that's the first problem. An Abrams tank weighs seventy tons. Can't airlift it. Got to put it on a train, and then put it on a ship. And that's the good news. Because you don't just ship the tank. For every ton of tank, you have to ship four tons of fuel and other equipment. These suckers get a half-mile to the gallon. And you need spare engines, ammunition, huge maintenance crews. The logistics tail is a mile long. Like moving an iron mountain. To ship enough tank brigades to make a worthwhile difference, you're looking at a six-month build-up, minimum, and that's working right around the clock.'

'During which time the airborne troops are deep in the shit,' I said.

'Tell me about it,' Simon said. 'And those are my boys, and I worry about them. Lightly armed paratroops against any kind of foreign armour, we'd get slaughtered. It would be a very, very anxious six months. And it gets worse. Because what happens when the heavy brigades eventually get there? What happens is they roll off the ships and they get bogged down two blocks later. Roads aren't wide enough, bridges aren't strong enough, they never make it out of the port area. They sit there stuck in the mud and watch the infantry getting killed far away in the distance.'

Nobody spoke.

'Or take the Middle East,' Simon said. 'We all know Iraq wants Kuwait back. Suppose they go there? Long term, it's an easy win for us, because the open desert is pretty much the same for tanks as the steppes in Europe, except it's a little hotter and dustier. The war plans we've got will work out just fine. But do we even get that far? We've got the infantry sitting there like tiny little speed bumps for six whole months. Who says the Iraqis won't roll right over them in the first two weeks?'

'Air power,' Summer said. 'Attack helicopters.'

'I wish,' Simon said. 'Planes and whirlybirds are sexy as hell, but they don't win anything on their own. Never have, never will. Boots on the ground is what wins things.'

I smiled. Part of that was a combat infantryman's standard-issue pride. But part of it was true, too.

'So what's going to happen?' I asked.

'Same thing as happened with the navy in 1941,' Simon said. 'Overnight, battleships were history and carriers were the new thing. So for us, now, we need to integrate. We need to understand that our light units are too vulnerable and our heavy units are too slow. We need to ditch the whole light-heavy split. We need integrated rapid-response brigades with armoured vehicles lighter than twenty tons and small enough to fit in the belly of a C-130. We need to get places faster and fight smarter. No more planning for set-piece battles between herds of dinosaurs.'

Then he smiled.

'Basically we'll have to put the infantry in charge,' he said.

'You ever talk to people like Marshall about this kind of stuff?'

'*Their* planners? No way.'

'What do they think about the future?'

'I have no idea. And I don't care. The future belongs to the infantry.'

Dessert was apple pie, and then we had coffee. It was the usual excellent brew. We slid back from the future into present-day small talk. The stewards moved around, silently. Just another evening, in an Officers' Club four thousand miles from the last one.

'Marshall will be back at dawn,' Swan told me. 'Look for a scout car at the rear of the first incoming column.'

I nodded. Figured dawn in January in Frankfurt would be about 0700 hours. I set my mental alarm for six. Lieutenant Colonel Simon said goodnight and wandered off. Summer pushed her chair back and sprawled in it, as much as a tiny

281

person can sprawl. Swan sat forward with his elbows on the table.

'You think they get much dope on this post?' I asked him.

'You want some?' he said.

'Brown heroin,' I said. 'Not for my personal use.'

Swan nodded. 'Guys here say there are Turkish guest workers in Germany who could get you some. One of the speed dealers could supply it, I'm sure.'

'You ever met a guy called Willard?' I asked him.

'The new boss?' he said. 'I got the memo. Never met him. But some of the guys here know him. He was an intelligence wonk, something to do with Armor.'

'He wrote algorithms,' I said.

'For what?'

'Soviet T-80 fuel consumption, I think. Told us what kind of training they were doing.'

'And now he's running the 110th?'

I nodded.

'I know,' I said. 'Bizarre.'

'How did he do that?'

'Obviously someone liked him.'

'We should find out who. Start sending hate mail.'

I nodded again. Nearly a million men in the army, hundreds of billions of dollars, and it all came down to who liked who. *Hey, what can you do?*

'I'm going to bed,' I said.

My VOQ room was so generic I lost track of where I was within a minute of closing my door. I hung my uniform in the closet and washed up and crawled between the sheets. They smelled of the same detergent the army uses everywhere. I thought of my mother in Paris and Joe in D.C. My mother was already in bed, probably. Joe would still be working, at whatever it was he did. I said *six a.m.* to myself and closed my eyes.

Dawn broke at 0650 by which time I was standing next to Summer at XII Corps' east road gate. We had mugs of coffee in our hands. The ground was frozen and there was mist in the air. The sky was grey and the landscape was a shade of pastel

282

green. It was low and undulating and unexciting, like a lot of Europe. There were stands of small neat trees here and there. Dormant winter earth, giving off cold organic smells. It was very quiet.

The road ran through the gate and then turned and headed east and a little north, into the fog, towards Russia. It was wide and straight, made from reinforced concrete. The kerb stones were nicked here and there by tank tracks. Big wedge-shaped chunks had been knocked out of them. A tank is a difficult thing to steer.

We waited. Still quiet.

Then we heard them.

What is the twentieth century's signature sound? You could have a debate about it. Some might say the slow drone of an aero engine. Maybe from a lone fighter crawling across an azure 1940s sky. Or the scream of a fast jet passing low overhead, shaking the ground. Or the *whup whup whup* of a helicopter. Or the roar of a laden 747 lifting off. Or the crump of bombs falling on a city. All of those would qualify. They're all uniquely twentieth-century noises. They were never heard before. Never, in all of history. Some crazy optimists might lobby for a Beatles' song. A *yeah, yeah, yeah* chorus fading under the screams of their audience. I would have sympathy for that choice. But a song and screaming could never qualify. Music and desire have been around since the dawn of time. They weren't invented after 1900.

No, the twentieth century's signature sound is the squeal and clatter of tank tracks on a paved street. That sound was heard in Warsaw, and Rotterdam, and Stalingrad, and Berlin. Then it was heard again in Budapest and Prague, and Seoul and Saigon. It's a brutal sound. It's the sound of fear. It speaks of a massive overwhelming advantage in power. And it speaks of remote, impersonal indifference. Tank treads squeal and clatter and the very noise they make tells you they can't be stopped. It tells you you're weak and powerless against the machine. Then one track stops and the other keeps on going and the tank wheels around and lurches straight towards you, roaring and squealing. That's the real twentieth-century sound.

We heard the XII Corps Abrams column a long time before

we saw it. The noise came at us through the fog. We heard the tracks, and the whine of the turbines. We heard the grind of the drive gear and felt fast pattering bass shudders through the soles of our feet as each new tread plate came off the cogs and thumped down into position. We heard grit and stone crushed under their weight.

Then we saw them. The lead tank loomed at us through the mist. It was moving fast, pitching a little, staying flat, its engine roaring. Behind it was another, and another. They were all in line, single file, like an armada from hell. It was a magnificent sight. The M1A1 Abrams is like a shark, evolved to a point of absolute perfection. It is the undisputed king of the jungle. No other tank on earth can even begin to damage it. It is wrapped in armour made out of a depleted uranium core sandwiched between rolled steel plate. The armour is dense and impregnable. Battlefield shells and rockets and kinetic devices bounce right off it. But its main trick is to stand off so far that no battlefield shell or rocket or kinetic device can even reach it. It sits there and watches enemy rounds fall short in the dirt. Then it traverses its mighty gun and fires and a second later and a mile and a half in the distance its assailant blows up and burns. It is the ultimate unfair advantage.

The lead tank rolled past us. Eleven feet wide, twenty-six feet long, nine and a half feet tall. Seventy tons. Its engine bellowed and its weight shook the ground. Its tracks squealed and clattered and slid on the concrete. Then the second tank rolled by. And the third, and the fourth, and the fifth. The noise was deafening. The huge bulk of exotic metal buffeted the air. The gun barrels dipped and swayed and bounced. Exhaust fumes swirled all around.

There were altogether twenty tanks in the formation. They drove in through the gate and their noise and vibration faded behind us and then there was a short gap and a scout car came out of the mist straight towards us. It was a shoot-and-scoot Humvee armed with a TOW-2 anti-tank missile launcher. Two guys in it. I stepped into its path and raised my hand. Paused. I didn't know Marshall and I had only ever seen him once, in the dark interior of the Grand Marquis outside Fort Bird's post headquarters. But even so I was pretty sure that neither of the guys in the Humvee was him. I remembered Marshall as large and dark and these guys were small, which is much more usual for Armored people. One thing there isn't a lot of inside an Abrams is room.

The Humvee came to a stop right in front of me and I tracked around to the driver's window. Summer took up station on the passenger side, standing easy. The driver rolled his glass down. Stared out at me.

'I'm looking for Major Marshall,' I said.

The driver was a captain and his passenger was a captain, too. They were both dressed in Nomex tank suits, with balaclavas and Kevlar helmets with built-in headphones. The passenger had sleeve pockets full of pens. He had clipboards strapped to both thighs. They were all covered with notes. Some kind of score sheets.

'Marshall's not here,' the driver said.

'So where is he?'

'Who's asking?'

'You can read,' I said. I was wearing last night's BDUs. They had oak leaves on the collar and *Reacher* on the stencil.

'Unit?' the guy said.

'You don't want to know.'

'Marshall went to California,' he said. 'Emergency deployment to Fort Irwin.'

'When?'

'I'm not sure.'

'Try to be.'

'Last night sometime.'

'That's not very specific.'

'I'm honestly not sure.'

'What kind of an emergency have they got at Irwin?'

'I'm not sure about that, either.'

I nodded. Stepped back.

'Drive on,' I said.

Their Humvee moved out from the space between us and Summer joined me in the middle of the road. The air smelled of diesel and gas turbine exhaust and the concrete was scored fresh white by the passage of the tank tracks.

'Wasted trip,' Summer said.

285

'Maybe not,' I said. 'Depends exactly when Marshall left. If it was after Swan's phone call, that tells us something.'

We were shunted between three different offices, trying to find out exactly what time Marshall left XII Corps. We ended up in a second-storey suite that housed General Vassell's operation. Vassell himself wasn't there. We spoke to yet another captain. He seemed to be in charge of an administrative company.

'Major Marshall took a civilian flight at 2300,' he said. 'Frankfurt to Dulles. Seven-hour layover and on to LAX from National. I issued the vouchers myself.'

'When?'

'As he was leaving.'

'Which was when?'

'He left here three hours before his flight.'

'Eight o'clock?'

The captain nodded. 'On the dot.'

'I was told he was scheduled for night manoeuvres.'

'He was. That plan changed.'

'Why?'

'I'm not sure.'

I'm not sure seemed to be XII Corps' standard-issue answer for everything.

'What's the panic at Irwin?' I said.

'I'm not sure.'

I smiled, briefly. 'When were Marshall's orders issued?'

'At seven o'clock.'

'Written?'

'Verbal.'

'By?'

'General Vassell.'

'Did Vassell countersign the travel vouchers himself?'

The captain nodded.

'Yes,' he said. 'He did.'

'I need to speak to him,' I said.

'He went to London.'

'London?' I said.

'For a short-notice meeting with the British Ministry of Defence.'

286

'When did he leave?'

'He travelled to the airport with Major Marshall.'

'Where's Colonel Coomer?'

'Berlin,' the guy said. 'Souvenir hunting.'

'Don't tell me,' I said. 'He went to the airport with Vassell and Marshall.'

'No,' the captain said. 'He took the train.'

'Terrific,' I said.

Summer and I went to the O Club for breakfast. We got the same corner table we had used the night before. We sat side by side, backs to the wall, watching the room.

'OK,' I said. 'Swan's office called for Marshall's whereabouts at 1810 and fifty minutes later he had orders for Irwin. An hour after that he was off the post.'

'And Vassell lit out for London,' Summer said. 'And Coomer jumped on a train for Berlin.'

'A night train,' I said. 'Who goes on a night train just for the fun of it?'

'Everybody's got something to hide,' she said.

'Except me and my monkey.'

'What?'

'The Beatles,' I said. 'One of the sounds of the century.'

She just looked at me.

'What are they hiding?' she said.

'You tell me.'

She put her hands on the table, palms down. Took a breath.

'I can see part of it,' she said.

'Me too.'

'The agenda,' she said. 'It was the other side of the coin from what Colonel Simon was talking about last night. Simon was salivating about the infantry taking Armored down a peg or two. Kramer must have seen all of that coming. Two-star generals aren't stupid. So the Irwin conference on New Year's Day was about fighting the opposite corner. It was about resistance, I guess. They don't want to give up what they've got.'

'Hell of a thing to give up,' I said.

'Believe it,' she said. 'Like battleship captains, way back.'

'So what was in the agenda?'

287

'Part defence, part offence,' she said. 'That's the obvious way to do it. Arguments against integrated units, ridicule of light-weight armoured vehicles, advocacy for their own specialized expertise.'

'I agree,' I said. 'But it's not enough. The Pentagon is going to be neck-deep in position papers full of shit like that, starting any day now. For, against, if, but and however, we're going to be bored to death with it. But there was something else in that agenda that made them totally desperate to get Kramer's copy back. What was it?'

'I don't know.'

'Me either,' I said.

'And why did they run last night?' Summer said. 'By now they must have destroyed Kramer's copy and every other copy. So they could have lied through their teeth about what was in it, to put your mind at rest. They could even have given you a phony document. They could have said, here you go, this was it, check it out.'

'They ran because of Mrs Kramer,' I said.

She nodded. 'I still think Vassell and Coomer killed her. Kramer croaks, the ball is in their court, in the circumstances they know it's their responsibility to go out and round up all the loose paperwork. Mrs Kramer goes down as collateral damage.'

'That would make perfect sense,' I said. 'Except that neither one of them looked particularly tall and strong to me.'

'They're both a lot taller and stronger than Mrs Kramer was. Plus, you know, heat of the moment, pumped up with panic, we could be seeing ambiguous forensic results. And we don't know how good the Green Valley people are anyway. Could be some family doctor doing a two-year term as coroner, and what the hell would he know?'

'Maybe,' I said. 'But I still don't see how it can have happened. Take out the drive time from D.C., take out ten minutes to find that store and steal the crowbar, they had ten minutes to react. And they didn't have a car, and they didn't call for one.'

'They could have taken a taxi. Or a town car. Direct from the hotel lobby. And we'd never trace it. New Year's Eve, it was the busiest night of the year.'

'It would have been a long ride,' I said. 'Big fare. It might stand out in some driver's memory.'

'New Year's Eve,' she said again. 'D.C. taxis and town cars are all over three states. All kinds of weird destinations. It's a possibility.'

'I don't think so,' I said. 'You don't take a taxi on a trip where you break into a hardware store and a house.'

'No reason for the driver to have seen anything. Vassell or Coomer or both could have walked into that alley in Sperryville on foot. Come back five minutes later with the crowbar under their coat. Same thing with Mrs Kramer's house. The cab could have stopped on the driveway. All the action was around the back.'

'Too big of a risk. A D.C. cab driver reads the papers same as anyone else. Maybe more than anyone else, with all that traffic. He sees the story from Green Valley, he remembers his two passengers.'

'They didn't see it as a risk. They weren't anticipating a story. Because they thought Mrs Kramer wasn't going to be home. They thought she would be at the hospital. And they figured no way would a couple of trivial burglaries in Sperryville and Green Valley make it into the D.C. papers.'

I nodded. Thought back to something Detective Clark had said, days ago. *I had people up and down the street, canvassing. There were some cars around.*

'Maybe,' I said. 'Maybe we should check taxis.'

'Worst night of the year,' Summer said. 'Like for alibis.'

'It would be a hell of a thing,' I said. 'Wouldn't it? Taking a cab to do a thing like that?'

'Nerves of steel.'

'If they've got nerves of steel, why did they run away last night?'

She was quiet for a moment.

'That really doesn't make any sense,' she said. 'Because they can't run for ever. They must know that. They must know that sooner or later they're going to have to turn around and bite back.'

'I agree. And they should have done it right here. Right now. This is their turf. I don't understand why they didn't.'

'It will be a hell of a bite. Their whole professional lives are on the line. You should be very careful.'

'You too,' I said. 'Not just me.'

'Offence is the best defence.'

'Agreed,' I said.

'So are we going after them?'

'You bet your ass.'

'Which one first?'

'Marshall,' I said. 'He's the one I want.'

'Why?'

'Rule of thumb,' I said. 'Chase the one they sent furthest away, because they see him as the weakest link.'

'Now?' she said.

I shook my head.

'We're going to Paris next,' I said. 'I have to see my mom.'

NINETEEN

WE REPACKED OUR BAGS AND MOVED OUT OF OUR VOQ rooms and paid a final courtesy visit to Swan in his office. He had some news for us.

'I'm supposed to arrest you both,' he said.

'Why?' I said.

'You're AWOL. Willard put a hit out on you.'

'What, worldwide?'

Swan shook his head. 'This post only. They found your car at Andrews and Willard talked to Transportation Corps. So he knew you were headed here.'

'When did you get the telex?'

'An hour ago.'

'When did we leave here?'

'An hour before that.'

'Where did we go?'

'No idea. You didn't say. I assumed you were returning to base.'

'Thanks,' I said.

'Better not tell me where you're really going.'

'Paris,' I said. 'Personal time.'

'What's going on?'

'I wish I knew.'

'You want me to call you a cab?'

'That would be great.'

Ten minutes later we were in another Mercedes-Benz, heading back the way we had come.

We had a choice of Lufthansa or Air France from Frankfurt-am-Main to Paris. I chose Air France. I figured their coffee would be better, and I figured if Willard got around to checking civilian carriers he would hit on Lufthansa first. I figured he was that kind of a simpleton.

We swapped two more of the forged travel vouchers for two seats in coach on the ten o'clock flight. Waited in the gate lounge. We were in BDUs, but we didn't really stand out. There were American military uniforms all over the airport. I saw some XII Corps MPs, prowling in pairs. But I wasn't worried. I figured they were on routine co-operation with the civilian cops. They weren't looking for us. I had the feeling that Willard's telex was going to stay on Swan's desk for an hour or two.

We boarded on time and stuffed our bags in the overhead. Buckled up and settled in. There were a dozen military on the plane with us. Paris always was a popular R&R destination for people stationed in Germany. The weather was still misty. But it wasn't bad enough to delay us any. We took off on time and climbed over the grey city and struck out south and west across pastel fields and huge tracts of forest. Then we climbed through the cloud into the sun and we couldn't see the ground any more.

It was a short flight. We started our descent during my second cup of coffee. Summer was drinking juice. She looked nervous. Part excited, and part worried. I figured she had never been to Paris before. And I figured she had never been AWOL before, either. I could see it was weighing on her. Truth is it was weighing on me a little, too. It was a complicating factor. I could have done without it. But I wasn't surprised to be hit with it. It had always been the obvious next step for Willard to take. Now I figured we were going to be chased around the world by

BOLO messages. *Be on the lookout for.* Or else we were going to have a generalized all-points bulletin dumped on us.

We landed at Roissy-Charles de Gaulle and were off the plane and in the jetway by eleven thirty in the morning. The airport was crowded. The taxi line was a zoo, just like it had been when Joe and I arrived the last time. So we gave up on it and walked to the *navette* station. Waited in line and climbed into the little bus. It was packed and uncomfortable. But Paris was warmer than Frankfurt had been. There was a watery sun out and I knew the city was going to look spectacular.

'Been here before?' I said.

'Never,' Summer said.

'Don't look at the first twenty klicks,' I said. 'Wait until we're inside the Périphérique.'

'What's that?'

'Like a ring road. Like the Beltway. That's where the good part starts.'

'Your mom live inside it?'

I nodded. 'On one of the nicest avenues in town. Where all the embassies are. Near the Eiffel Tower.'

'Are we going straight there?'

'Tomorrow,' I said. 'We're going to be tourists first.'

'Why?'

'I have to wait until my brother gets in. I can't go on my own. We have to go together.'

She said nothing to that. Just glanced at me. The bus started up and pulled away from the kerb. She watched out the window the whole way. I could see by the reflection of her face in the glass that she agreed with me. Inside the Périphérique was better.

We got out at the Place de l'Opéra and stood on the sidewalk and let the rest of the passengers swarm ahead of us. I figured we should choose a hotel and dump our bags before we did anything else.

We walked south on the Rue de la Paix, through the Place Vendôme, down to the Tuileries. Then we turned right and walked straight up the Champs Élysées. There might have been better places to walk with a pretty woman on a lazy day under a

293

watery winter sun, but right then I couldn't readily recall any. We made a left onto the Rue Marbeuf and came out on the Avenue George V just about opposite the George V hotel.

'OK for you?' I said.

'Will they let us in?' Summer asked.

'Only one way to find out.'

We crossed the street and a guy in a top hat opened the door for us. The girl at the desk had a bunch of little flags on her lapel, one for each language she spoke. I used French, which pleased her. I gave her two vouchers and asked for two rooms. She didn't hesitate. She went right ahead and gave us keys just like I had paid with gold bullion, or a credit card. The George V was one of those places. There was nothing they hadn't seen before. Or if there was, they weren't about to admit it to anyone.

The rooms the multilingual girl gave us both faced south and both had a partial view of the Eiffel Tower. One was decorated in shades of pale blue and had a sitting area and a bathroom the size of a tennis court. The other was three doors down the hall. It was done in parchment yellow and it had an iron Juliet balcony.

'Your choice,' I said.

'I'll take the one with the balcony,' she said.

We dumped our bags and washed up and met in the lobby fifteen minutes later. I was ready for lunch, but Summer had other ideas.

'I want to buy clothes,' she said. 'Tourists don't wear BDUs.'

'This one does,' I said.

'So break out,' she said. 'Live a little. Where should we go?'

I shrugged. You couldn't walk twenty yards in Paris without falling over at least three clothes stores. But most of them wanted a month's pay for a single garment.

'We could try Bon Marché,' I said.

'What's that?'

'Department store,' I said. 'It means cheap, literally.'

'A department store called Cheap?'

'My kind of place,' I said.

'Anywhere else?'

'Samaritaine,' I said. 'On the river, at the Pont Neuf. There's a terrace at the top with a view.'

'Let's go there.'

It was a long walk along the river, all the way to the tip of the Île de la Cité. It took us an hour, because we kept stopping to look at things. We passed the Louvre. We browsed the little green stalls set up on the river wall.

'What does Pont Neuf mean?' Summer asked me.

'New Bridge,' I said.

She looked ahead at the ancient stone structure.

'It's the oldest bridge in Paris,' I said.

'So why do they call it new?'

'Because it was new once.'

We stepped into the warmth of the store. Like all such places the cosmetics came first and filled the air with scent. Summer led me up one floor to the women's clothes. I sat in a comfortable chair and let her look around. She was gone for a good half hour. She came back wearing a complete new outfit. Black shoes, a black pencil skirt, a grey-and-white Breton sweater, a grey wool jacket. And a beret. She looked like a million dollars. Her BDUs and her boots were in a Samaritaine bag in her hand.

'You next,' she said. She took me up to the men's department. The only pants they had with 95-centimetre inseams were Algerian knock-offs of American blue jeans, so that set the tone. I bought a light blue sweatshirt and a black cotton bomber jacket. I kept my army boots on. They looked OK with the jeans and they matched the jacket.

'Buy a beret,' Summer said, so I bought a beret. It was black with a leather binding. I paid for the whole lot with American dollars at a pretty good rate of exchange. I dressed in the changing cubicle. Put my camouflage gear in the carrier bag. Checked the mirror and adjusted the beret to a rakish angle and stepped out.

Summer said nothing.

'Lunch now,' I said.

We went up to the ninth-floor café. It was too cold to sit out on the terrace, but we sat at a window and got pretty much the same view. We could see the Notre-Dame cathedral to the east and the Montparnasse tower all the way to the south. The sun was still out. It was a great city.

'How did Willard find our car?' Summer said. 'How would he even know where to look? The United States is a big country.'

'He didn't find it,' I said. 'Not until someone told him where it was.'

'Who?'

'Vassell,' I said. 'Or Coomer. Swan's sergeant used my name on the phone, back at XII Corps. So at the same time as they were getting Marshall off the post they were calling Willard back in Rock Creek, telling him I was over there in Germany and hassling them again. They were asking him why the hell he had let me travel. And they were telling him to recall me.'

'They can't dictate where a special unit investigator goes.'

'They can now, because of Willard. They're old buddies. I just figured it out. Swan as good as told us, but it didn't click right away. Willard has ties to Armored from his time in Intelligence. Who did he talk to all those years? About that Soviet fuel crap? Armored, that's who. There's a relationship there. That's why he was so hot about Kramer. He wasn't worried about embarrassment for the army in general. He was worried about embarrassment for Armored Branch in particular.'

'Because they're his people.'

'Correct. And that's why Vassell and Coomer ran last night. They didn't *run*, as such. They're just giving Willard time and space to deal with us.'

'Willard knows he didn't sign our travel vouchers.'

I nodded. 'That's for sure.'

'So we're in serious trouble now. We're AWOL and we're travelling on stolen vouchers.'

'We'll be OK.'

'How exactly?'

'When we get a result.'

'Are we going to?'

I didn't answer.

After lunch we crossed the river and walked a long roundabout route back to the hotel. We looked just like tourists, in our casual clothes, carrying our Samaritaine bags. All we needed was a camera. We window shopped in the Boulevard Saint Germain and looked at the Luxembourg gardens. We saw

Les Invalides and the École Militaire. Then we walked up the Avenue Bosquet, which took me within fifty yards of the back of my mother's apartment house. I didn't tell Summer that. She would have made me go in and see her. We crossed the Seine again at the Pont de l'Alma and got coffee in a bistro on the Avenue New-York. Then we strolled up the hill to the hotel.

'Siesta time,' Summer said. 'Then dinner.'

I was happy enough to go for a nap. I was pretty tired. I lay down on the bed in the pale blue room and fell asleep within minutes.

Summer woke me up two hours later by calling me on the phone from her room. She wanted to know if I knew any restaurants. Paris is full of restaurants, but I was dressed like an idiot and I had less than thirty bucks in my pocket. So I picked a place I knew on the Rue Vernet. I figured I could go there in jeans and a sweatshirt without getting stared at and without paying a fortune. And it was close enough to walk. No cab fare.

We met in the lobby. Summer still looked great. Her skirt and jacket looked as good for the evening as they had for the afternoon. She had abandoned her beret. I had kept mine on. We walked up the hill toward the Champs Élysées. Halfway there, Summer did a strange thing. She took my hand in hers. It was going dark and we were surrounded by strolling couples and I guessed it felt natural to her. It felt natural to me, too. It took me a minute to realize she had done it. Or, it took me a minute to realize there was anything wrong with it. It took her the same minute. At the end of it she got flustered and looked up at me and let go again.

'Sorry,' she said.

'Don't be,' I said. 'It felt good.'

'It just happened,' she said.

We walked on and turned into the Rue Vernet. Found the restaurant. It was early in the evening in January and the owner found us a table right away. It was in a corner. There were flowers and a lit candle on it. We ordered water and a *pichet* of red wine to drink while we thought about the food.

297

'You're at home here,' Summer said to me.

'Not really,' I said. 'I'm not at home anywhere.'

'You speak pretty good French.'

'I speak pretty good English too. Doesn't mean I feel at home in North Carolina, for instance.'

'But you like some places better than others.'

I nodded. 'This one is OK.'

'Done any long-term thinking?'

'You sound like my brother. He wants me to make a plan.'

'Everything is going to change.'

'They'll always need cops,' I said.

'Cops who go AWOL?'

'All we need is a result,' I said. 'Mrs Kramer, or Carbone. Or Brubaker, maybe. We've got three bites of the cherry. Three chances.'

She said nothing.

'Relax,' I said. 'We're out of the world for forty-eight hours. Let's enjoy ourselves. Worrying isn't going to get us anywhere. We're in Paris.'

She nodded. I watched her face. Watched her try to get past it. Her eyes were expressive in the candlelight. It was like she had troubles in front of her, maybe piled high into stacks, like cartons. I saw her shoulder her way around them, to the quiet place in the back of the closet.

'Drink your wine,' I said. 'Have fun.'

My hand was resting on the table. She reached out and squeezed it and picked up her glass.

'We'll always have North Carolina,' she said.

We ordered three courses each off the fixed-price page of the menu. Then we took three hours to eat them. We kept the conversation away from work. We talked about personal things instead. She asked me about my family. I told her a little about Joe, and not much about my mother. She told me about her folks, and her brothers and sisters, and enough cousins that I lost track about who was who. Mostly I watched her face in the candlelight. Her skin had a copper tone mixed behind pure ebony black. Her eyes were like coal. Her jaw was delicate, like fine china. She looked impossibly small and gentle, for a

298

soldier. But then I remembered her sharpshooter badges. More than I had.

'Am I going to meet your mom?' she said.

'If you want to,' I said. 'But she's very sick.'

'Not just a broken leg?'

I shook my head.

'She has cancer,' I said.

'Is it bad?'

'As bad as it gets.'

Summer nodded. 'I figured it had to be something like that. You've been upset ever since you came over here the first time.'

'Have I?'

'It's bound to bother you.'

I nodded in turn. 'More than I thought it would.'

'Don't you like her?'

'I like her fine. But, you know, nobody lives for ever. Conceptually these things don't come as a surprise.'

'I should probably stay away. It wouldn't be appropriate if I came. You should go with Joe. Just the two of you.'

'She likes meeting new people.'

'She might not be feeling good.'

'We should wait and see. Maybe she'll want to go out for lunch.'

'How does she look?'

'Terrible,' I said.

'Then she won't want to meet new people.'

We sat in silence for a spell. Our waiter brought the check. We counted our cash and paid half each and left a decent tip. We held hands all the way back to the hotel. It felt like the obvious thing to do. We were alone together in a sea of troubles, some of them shared, some of them private. The guy with the top hat opened the door for us and wished us *bonne nuit. Good night.* We rode up in the elevator, side by side, not touching. When we got out on our floor Summer had to go left and I had to go right. It was an awkward moment. We didn't speak. I could see she wanted to come with me and I sure as hell wanted to go with her. I could see her room in my mind. The yellow walls, the smell of perfume. The bed. I imagined lifting her new sweater over her head. Unzipping her new skirt and hearing it fall to the floor. I figured it would have a silk lining. I figured it would make a rustling sound.

I knew it wouldn't be right. But we were already AWOL. We were already in all kinds of deep shit. It would be comfort and consolation, apart from whatever else it would be.

'What time in the morning?' she said.

'Early for me,' I said. 'I have to be at the airport at six.'

'I'll come with you. Keep you company.'

'Thanks.'

'My pleasure,' she said.

We stood there.

'We'll have to get up about four,' she said.

'I guess,' I said. 'About four.'

We stood there.

'Good night then, I guess,' she said.

'Sleep well,' I said.

I turned right. Didn't look back. I heard her door open and close a second after mine.

It was eleven o'clock. I went to bed but I didn't sleep. I just lay there and stared at the ceiling for an hour. There was city light coming in the window. It was cold and yellow and hazy. I could see the pulses from the Eiffel Tower's party lights. They flashed gold, on and off, somewhere between fast and slow and relentless. They changed the pattern on the plaster above my head, once a second. I heard the sound of brakes on a distant street, and the yap of a small dog, and lonely footsteps far below my window, and the beep of a faraway horn. Then the city went quiet and silence crowded in on me. It howled all around me, like a siren. I raised my wrist. Checked my watch. It was midnight. I dropped my wrist back down on the bed and was hit by a wave of loneliness so bad it left me breathless.

I put the light on and rolled over to the phone. There were instructions printed on a little plate below the dial buttons. *To call another guest's room, press three and enter the room number.* I pressed three and entered the room number. She answered, first ring.

'You awake?' I said.

'Yes,' she said.

300

'Want company?'

'Yes,' she said.

I pulled my jeans and sweatshirt on and walked barefoot down the corridor. Knocked at her door. She opened it and reached out her hand and pulled me inside. She was still fully dressed. Still in her skirt and sweater. She kissed me hard at the door and I kissed her back, harder. The door swung shut behind us. I heard the hiss of its closer and the click of its latch. We headed for the bed.

She wore dark red underwear. It was made of silk, or satin. I could smell her perfume everywhere. It was in the room and on her body. She was tiny and delicate and quick and strong. The same city light was coming in the window. Now it bathed me in warmth. Gave me energy. I could see the Eiffel Tower's lights on her ceiling. We matched our rhythm to their rhythm, slow, fast, relentless. Afterwards we turned away from them and lay like spoons, burned out and breathing hard, close but not speaking, like we weren't sure exactly what we had done.

I slept an hour and woke up in the same position. I had a strong sensation of something lost and something gained, but I couldn't explain either feeling. Summer stayed asleep. She was nestled solidly into the curve of my body. She smelled good. She felt warm. She felt lithe and strong and peaceful. She was breathing slow. My left arm was under her shoulders and my right arm was draped across her waist. Her hand was cupped in mine, half open, half curled.

I turned my head and watched the play of light on the ceiling. I heard the faint noise of a motorbike maybe a mile away, on the other side of the Arc de Triomphe. I heard a dog bark in the distance. Other than that the city was silent. Two million people were asleep. Joe was in the air, somewhere on the Great Circle route, maybe closing in on Iceland. I couldn't picture my mother. I closed my eyes. Tried to sleep again.

The alarm clock in my head went off at four. Summer was still asleep. I eased my arm out from under her and worked some kind of circulation back into my shoulder and slid out of bed and padded across the carpet to the bathroom. Then I put my pants on and shrugged into my sweatshirt and woke Summer with a kiss.

'Rise and shine, lieutenant,' I said.

She stretched her arms up high and arched her back. The sheet fell away to her waist.

'Good morning,' she said.

I kissed her again.

'I like Paris,' she said. 'I had fun here.'

'Me too.'

'Lots of fun.'

'Lobby in half an hour,' I said.

I went back to my own room and called room service for coffee. I was through shaving and showering before it arrived. I took the tray at the door wearing just a towel. Then I dressed in fresh BDUs and poured my first cup and checked my watch. It was four twenty in the morning in Paris, which made it ten twenty in the evening on the east coast, which made it well after the end of bankers' hours. And which made it seven twenty in the evening on the west coast, which was early enough that a hard-working guy might still be at his desk. I checked the plate on the phone again and hit nine for a line. Dialled the only number I had ever permanently memorized, which was the Rock Creek switchboard back in Virginia. An operator answered on the first ring.

'This is Reacher,' I said. 'I need a number for Fort Irwin's MP XO.'

'Sir, there's a standing order from Colonel Willard that you should return to base immediately.'

'I'll be right there, soon as I can. But I need that number first.'

'Sir, where are you now?'

'In a whorehouse in Sydney, Australia,' I said. 'Give me that Irwin number.'

He gave me the number. I repeated it to myself and hit nine again and dialled it. Calvin Franz's sergeant answered, second ring.

'I need Franz,' I said.

There was a click and then silence and I was settling in for a long wait when Franz came through.

'I need you to do something for me,' I said.

302

'Like what?'

'You've got a XII Corps guy called Marshall there. You know him?'

'No.'

'I need him to stay there until I can get there myself. It's very important.'

'I can't stop people leaving the post unless I arrest them.'

'Just tell him I called from Berlin. That should do it. As long as he thinks I'm in Germany, he'll stay in California.'

'Why?'

'Because that's what he's been told to do.'

'Does he know you?'

'Not personally.'

'Then that's an awkward conversation for me to have. Like, I can't just walk up to a guy I never met and say, hey, hot news, another guy *you* never met called Reacher wants you to know he's stuck in Berlin.'

'So be subtle,' I said. 'Tell him I asked you to ask him a question for me, because there's no way I can get there myself.'

'What question?'

'Ask him about the day of Kramer's funeral. Was he at Arlington? What did he do the rest of the day? Why didn't he drive his guys to North Carolina? What reason did they give him for wanting to drive themselves?'

'That's four questions.'

'Whatever, just make it sound like you're asking on my behalf because California isn't in my travel plans.'

'Where can I get back to you?'

I looked down at the phone and read out the George V's number.

'That's France,' he said. 'Not Germany.'

'Marshall doesn't need to know that,' I said. 'I'll be back here later.'

'When are you coming to California?'

'Within forty-eight hours, I hope.'

'OK,' he said. 'Anything else?'

'Yes,' I said. 'Call Fort Bird for me and ask my sergeant to get histories on General Vassell and Colonel Coomer. Specifically I want to know if either one of them has a connection with a town called Sperryville in Virginia. Born there, grew up there, family there, any kind of connection that would indicate they might know what kind of retail outlet was where. Tell her to sit on the answers until I get in touch.'

'OK,' he said again. 'Is that it?'

'No,' I said. 'Also tell her to call Detective Clark in Green Valley and have him fax his street canvasses relating to the night of New Year's Eve. She'll know what I'm talking about.'

'I'm glad someone will,' Franz said.

He paused. He was writing stuff down.

'So is *that* it?' he said.

'For now,' I said.

I hung up and made it down to the lobby about five minutes after Summer. She was waiting there. She had been much faster than me. But then, she didn't have to shave and I don't think she had made any calls or taken time for coffee. Like me, she was back in BDUs. Somehow she had cleaned her boots, or had gotten them cleaned. They were gleaming.

We didn't have money for a cab to the airport. So we walked back through the pre-dawn darkness to the Place de l'Opéra and caught the bus. It was less crowded than the last time but just as uncomfortable. We got brief glimpses of the sleeping city and then we crossed the Périphérique and ground slowly through the dismal outer suburbs.

We got to Roissy-Charles de Gaulle just before six. It was busy there. I guessed airports worked on floating time zones all their own. It was busier at six in the morning than it would be in the middle of the afternoon. There were crowds of people everywhere. Cars and buses were loading and unloading, red-eyed travellers were coming out and going in and struggling with bags. It looked like the whole world was on the move.

The arrivals screen showed that Joe's flight was already on the ground. We hiked around to the customs area's exit doors. Took our places among a big crowd of meeters and greeters. I figured Joe would be one of the first passengers through. He would have walked fast from the plane and he wouldn't have checked any luggage. No delays.

We saw a few stragglers coming out from the previous flight.

304

They were mostly families slowed by young children or individuals who had waited for odd-sized luggage. People in the crowd turned towards them expectantly and then turned away again when they realized they weren't who they were looking for. I watched them do it for a spell. It was an interesting physical dynamic. Just subtle adjustments of posture were enough to display interest, and then lack of interest. Welcome, and then dismissal. A half-turn inward, and then a half-turn away. Sometimes it was nothing more than a transfer of body weight from one foot to the other.

The last stragglers were mixed in with the first people off of Joe's flight. There were businessmen moving fast, humping briefcases and suit carriers. There were young women in high heels and dark glasses, expensively dressed. Models? Actresses? Call girls? There were government people, French and American. I could pick them out by the way they looked. Smart and serious, plenty of eyeglasses, but their shoes and suits and coats weren't the best quality. Low-level diplomats, probably. The flight was from D.C., after all.

Joe came out about twelfth in line. He was in the same overcoat I had seen before, but a different suit and a different tie. He looked good. He was walking fast and carrying a black leather overnight bag. He was a head taller than anyone else. He came out of the door and stopped dead and scanned around.

'He looks just like you,' Summer said.

'But I'm a nicer person,' I said.

He saw me right away, because I was also a head taller than anyone else. I pointed to a spot outside of the main traffic stream. He shuffled through the crowd and made his way towards it. We looped around and joined him there.

'Lieutenant Summer,' he said. 'I'm very pleased to meet you.'

I hadn't seen him look at the tapes on her jacket, where it said *Summer, U.S. Army.* Or at the lieutenant's bars on her collar. He must have remembered her name and her rank from when we had talked before.

'You OK?' I asked him.

'I'm tired,' he said.

'Want breakfast?'

'Let's get it in town.'

305

The taxi line was a mile long and moving slow. We ignored it. Headed straight for the *navette* again. We missed one and were first in line for the next. It came inside ten minutes. Joe spent the waiting time asking Summer about her visit to Paris. She gave him chapter and verse, but not about the events after midnight. I stood on the kerb with my back to the roadway, watching the eastern sky above the terminal roof. Dawn was breaking fast. It was going to be another sunny day. It was the tenth of January, and the weather was the best I had seen in the new decade so far.

We got in the bus and sat in three seats together that faced sideways opposite the luggage rack. Summer sat in the middle seat. Joe sat forward of her and I sat to the rear. They were small, uncomfortable seats. Hard plastic. No leg room. Joe's knees were up around his ears and his head was swaying from side to side with the motion. He looked pale. I guessed putting him on a bus was not much of a welcome, after an overnight flight across the Atlantic. I felt a little bad about it. But then, I was the same size. I had the same accommodation problem. And I hadn't gotten a whole lot of sleep either. And I was broke. And I guessed being on the move was better for him than standing in the taxi line for an hour.

He brightened up some after we crossed the Périphérique and entered Haussmann's urban splendour. The sun was well up by then and the city was bathed in gold and honey. The cafés were already busy and the sidewalks were already crowded with people moving at a measured pace and carrying baguettes and newspapers. Legislation limited Parisians to a 35-hour work week, and they spent a lot of the remaining 133 taking great pleasure in not doing very much of anything. It was relaxing just to watch them.

We got out at the familiar spot in the Place de l'Opéra. Walked south the same way we had walked the week before, crossing the river at the Pont de la Concorde, turning west on the Quai d'Orsay, turning south into the Avenue Rapp. We got as far as the Rue de l'Université where the Eiffel Tower was visible, and then Summer stopped.

'I'll go look at the tower,' she said. 'You guys go on ahead and see your mom.'

Joe looked at me. *Does she know?* I nodded. *She knows.*

'Thanks, lieutenant,' he said. 'We'll go see how she is. If she's up for it, maybe you could join us at lunch.'

'Call me at the hotel,' she said.

'You know where it is?' I said.

She turned and pointed north along the avenue. 'Across the bridge right there and up the hill, on the left side. Straight line.'

I smiled. She had a decent sense of geography. Joe looked a little puzzled. He had seen the direction she had pointed, and he knew what was up there.

'The George V?' he said.

'Why not?' I said.

'Is that on the army's dime?'

'More or less,' I said.

'Outstanding.'

Summer stretched up tall and kissed me on the cheek and shook Joe's hand. We stayed there with the weak sun on our shoulders and watched her walk away towards the base of the tower. There was already a thin stream of tourists heading the same way. We could see the souvenir sellers unpacking. We stood and watched them in the distance. Watched Summer get smaller and smaller as she got further away.

'She's very nice,' Joe said. 'Where did you find her?'

'She was at Fort Bird.'

'You figured out what's going on there yet?'

'I'm a little closer.'

'I would hope you are. You've been there nearly two weeks.'

'Remember that guy I asked you about? Willard? He would have spent time with Armored, right?'

Joe nodded. 'I'm sure he reported to them direct. Fed his stuff straight into their intelligence operation.'

'Do you remember any names?'

'In Armored Branch? Not really. I never paid much attention to Willard. His thing wasn't very mainstream. It was a side issue.'

'Ever heard of a guy called Marshall?'

'Don't remember him,' Joe said.

I said nothing. Joe turned and looked south down the avenue.

Wrapped his coat tighter around him and turned his face up to the sun.

'Let's go,' he said.

'When did you call her last?'

'The day before yesterday. It was your turn next.'

We moved off and walked down the avenue, side by side, matching our pace to the leisurely stroll of the people around us.

'Want breakfast first?' I said. 'We don't want to wake her.'

'The nurse will let us in.'

We passed the post office. There was a car abandoned half-way up on the sidewalk. It had been in some kind of an accident. It had a smashed fender and a flat tyre. We stepped out into the street to pass it by. Saw a large black vehicle double-parked on the road forty yards ahead.

We stared at it.

'*Un corbillard*,' Joe said.

A hearse.

We stared at it. Tried to figure which building it was waiting at. Tried to gauge the distance. The head-on perspective made it difficult. I glanced upward at the roof lines. First came a limestone Belle Époque façade, seven storeys high. Then a drop to my mother's plainer six-storey building. I traced my gaze vertically all the way down the frontage. To the street. To the hearse. It was parked right in front of my mother's door.

We ran.

There was a man in a black silk hat standing on the sidewalk. The street door to my mother's building was open. We glanced at the man in the hat and went in through the door to the courtyard. The concierge was standing in her doorway. She had a handkerchief in her hand and tears in her eyes. She paid us no attention. We headed for the elevator. Rode up to five. The elevator was agonizingly slow.

The door to the apartment was standing open. I could see men in black coats inside. Three of them. We went in. The men in the coats stood back. They said nothing. The girl with the luminous eyes came out of the kitchen. She looked pale. She stopped when she saw us. Then she turned and walked slowly across the room to meet us.

308

'What?' Joe said.

She didn't answer.

'When?' I said.

'Last night,' she said. 'It was very peaceful.'

The men in the coats realized who we must be and shuffled out into the hallway. They were very quiet. They made no noise at all. Joe took an unsteady step and sat down on the sofa. I stayed where I was. I stood still in the middle of the floor.

'When?' I said again.

'At midnight,' the girl said. 'In her sleep.'

I closed my eyes. Opened them again a minute later. The girl was still there. Her eyes were on mine.

'Were you with her?' I said.

She nodded.

'All the time,' she said.

'Was there a doctor here?'

'She sent him away.'

'What happened?'

'She said she felt well. She went to bed at eleven. She slept an hour, and then she just stopped breathing.'

I looked up at the ceiling. 'Was she in pain?'

'Not at the end.'

'But she said she felt well.'

'Her time had come. I've seen it before.'

I looked at her, and then I looked away.

'Would you like to see her?' the girl said.

'Joe?' I said. He shook his head. Stayed on the sofa. I stepped towards the bedroom. There was a mahogany coffin set up on velvet-padded trestles next to the bed. It was lined with white silk and it was empty. My mother's body was still in the bed. The sheets were made up around her. Her head was resting gently on the pillow and her arms were crossed over her chest outside the covers. Her eyes were closed. She was barely recognizable.

Summer had asked me: *Does it upset you to see dead people?*

No, I had said.

Why not? she had asked me.

I don't know, I had said.

I had never seen my father's body. I was away somewhere

when he died. It had been a heart thing. Some VA hospital had done its best, but it was hopeless from the start. I had flown in on the morning of the funeral and had left again the same night.

Funeral, I thought.

Joe will handle it.

I stayed by my mother's bed for five long minutes, eyes open, eyes dry. Then I turned around and stepped back into the living room. It was crowded again. The *croque-morts* were back. The pallbearers. And there was an old man on the sofa, next to Joe. He was sitting stiffly. There were two walking sticks propped next to him. He had thin grey hair and a heavy dark suit with a tiny ribbon in the buttonhole. Red, white and blue, maybe a Croix de Guerre ribbon, or the *Médaille de la Résistance*. He had a small cardboard box balanced on his bony knees. It was tied with a piece of faded red string.

'This is Monsieur Lamonnier,' Joe said. 'Family friend.'

The old guy grabbed his sticks and started to struggle up to shake my hand but I waved him back down and stepped over close. He was maybe seventy-five or eighty. He was lean and dried-out and relatively tall for a Frenchman.

'You're the one she called Reacher,' he said.

I nodded.

'That's me,' I said. 'I don't remember you.'

'We never met. But I knew your mother a long time.'

'Thanks for stopping by.'

'You too,' he said.

Touché, I thought.

'What's in the box?' I said.

'Things she refused to keep here,' the old guy said. 'But things I felt should be found here, at a time like this, by her sons.'

He handed me the box, like it was a sacred burden. I took it and put it under my arm. It felt about halfway between light and heavy. I guessed there was a book in there. Maybe an old leather-bound diary. Some other stuff, too.

'Joe,' I said. 'Let's go get breakfast.'

We walked fast and aimlessly. We turned into the Rue Saint Dominique and passed by two cafés at the top of the Rue de l'Exposition without stopping. We crossed the Avenue Bosquet against the light and then we made an arbitrary left into the Rue Jean Nicot. Joe stopped at a *tabac* and bought cigarettes. I would have smiled if I had been able to. The street was named after the guy who discovered nicotine.

We lit up together on the sidewalk and then ducked into the first café we saw. We were all done walking. We were ready for the talking.

'You shouldn't have waited for me,' Joe said. 'You could have seen her one last time.'

'I felt it happen,' I said. 'Midnight last night, something hit me.'

'You could have been with her.'

'Too late now.'

'It would have been OK with me.'

'It wouldn't have been OK with her.'

'We should have stayed a week ago.'

'She didn't want us to stay, Joe. That wasn't in her plan. She was an individual, entitled to her privacy. She was a mother, but that wasn't all she was.'

He went quiet. The waiter brought us coffee and a small straw basket full of croissants. He seemed to sense the mood. He put them down gently and backed away.

'Will you see to the funeral?' I said.

He nodded. 'I'll make it four days from now. Can you stay?'

'No,' I said. 'But I'll get back.'

'OK,' he said. 'I'll stay a week or so. I guess I'll need to find her will. We'll probably have to sell her place. Unless you want it?'

I shook my head. 'I don't want it. You?'

'I don't see how I could use it.'

'It wouldn't have been right for me to go on my own,' I said.

Joe said nothing.

'We saw her last week,' I said. 'We were all together. It was a good time.'

'You think?'

'We had fun. That's the way she wanted it. That's why she made the effort. That's why she asked to go to Polidor. It wasn't like she ate anything.'

He just shrugged. We drank our coffee in silence. I tried a croissant. It was OK, but I had no appetite. I put it back in the basket.

'Life,' Joe said. 'What a completely weird thing it is. A person lives sixty years, does all kinds of things, knows all kinds of things, *feels* all kinds of things, and then it's over. Like it never happened at all.'

'We'll always remember her.'

'No, we'll remember parts of her. The parts she chose to share. The tip of the iceberg. The rest, only she knew about. Therefore the rest already doesn't exist. As of now.'

We smoked another cigarette each and sat quiet. Then we walked back, slowly, side by side, a little burned out, at some kind of peace.

The coffin was in the *corbillard* when we got back to her building. They must have stood it upright in the elevator. The concierge was out on the sidewalk, standing next to the old man with the medal ribbon. He was leaning on his walking sticks. The nurse was there too, standing on her own. The pallbearers had their hands clasped in front of them. They were looking down at the ground.

'They're taking her to the *dépôt mortuaire*,' the nurse said.

The funeral parlour.

'OK,' Joe said.

I didn't stay. I said goodbye to the nurse and the concierge and shook hands with the old guy. Then I nodded to Joe and set off walking up the avenue. I didn't look back. I crossed the Seine at the Pont de l'Alma and walked up the Avenue George V to the hotel. I went up in the elevator and back to my room. I still had the old guy's box under my arm. I dropped it on the bed and stood still, completely unsure about what to do next.

I was still standing there twenty minutes later when the phone rang. It was Calvin Franz, calling from Fort Irwin in California. He had to say his name twice. The first time, I couldn't recall who he was.

'I spoke to Marshall,' he said.

'Who?'

312

'Your XII Corps guy.'

I said nothing.

'You OK?'

'Sorry,' I said. 'I'm fine. You spoke to Marshall.'

'He went to Kramer's funeral. He drove Vassell and Coomer there and back. Then he claims he didn't drive them the rest of the day because he had important Pentagon meetings all afternoon.'

'But?'

'I didn't believe him. He's a gofer. If Vassell and Coomer had wanted him to drive, he'd have been driving, meetings or no meetings.'

'And?'

'And knowing what kind of a hard time you would give me if I didn't check, I checked.'

'And?'

'Those meetings must have been with himself in the toilet stall, because nobody else saw him around.'

'So what was he doing instead?'

'No idea. But he was doing something, that's for sure. The way he answered me was just way too smooth. I mean, this all was six days ago. Who the hell remembers what meetings they had six days ago? But this guy claims to.'

'You tell him I was in Germany?'

'He seemed to know already.'

'You tell him I was staying there?'

'He seemed to take it for granted you weren't heading for California anytime soon.'

'These guys are old buddies with Willard,' I said. 'He's promised them he'll keep me away from them. He's running the 110th like it's Armored's private army.'

'I checked those histories myself, by the way. For Vassell and Coomer, because you got me curious. There's nothing there to suggest either one of them ever heard of any place called Sperryville, Virginia.'

'Are you sure?'

'Completely. Vassell is from Mississippi and Coomer is from Illinois. Neither of them has ever lived or served anywhere near Sperryville.'

I was quiet for a second.

'Are they married?' I said.

'Married?' Franz said. 'Yes, there were wives and kids in there. But they were local girls. No in-laws in Sperryville.'

'OK,' I said.

'So what are you going to do?'

'I'm coming to California.'

I put the phone down and walked along the corridor to Summer's door. I knocked and waited. She opened up. She was back from sightseeing.

'She died last night,' I said.

'I know,' Summer said. 'Your brother just called me from the apartment. He wanted me to make sure you were OK.'

'I'm OK,' I said.

'I'm very sorry.'

I shrugged. 'Conceptually these things don't come as a surprise.'

'When was it?'

'Midnight. She just gave up.'

'I feel bad. You should have gone to see her yesterday. You shouldn't have spent the day with me. We shouldn't have done all that ridiculous shopping.'

'I saw her last week. We had fun. Better that last week was the last time.'

'I would have wanted whatever extra time I could have gotten.'

'It was always going to be an arbitrary date,' I said. 'I could have gone yesterday, in the afternoon, maybe. Now I'd be wishing I had stayed for the evening. If I had stayed for the evening, I'd be wishing I had stayed until midnight.'

'You were in here with me at midnight. I feel bad about that, too.'

'Don't,' I said. 'I don't feel bad about it. My mother wouldn't, either. She was French, after all. If she'd known those were my options, she'd have insisted.'

'You're just saying that.'

'Well, I guess she wasn't very broadminded. But she always wanted whatever made us happy.'

314

'Did she give up because she was left alone?'

I shook my head. 'She wanted to be left alone so she could give up.'

Summer said nothing.

'We're leaving,' I said. 'We'll get a night flight back.'

'California?'

'East coast first,' I said. 'There are things I need to check.'

'What things?' she said.

I didn't tell her. She would have laughed, and right then I couldn't have handled laughter.

Summer packed her bag and came back to my room with me. I sat on the bed and played with the string on Monsieur Lamonnier's box.

'What's that?' she said.

'Something some old guy brought around. He said it's something that should be found with my mother's stuff.'

'What's in it?'

'I don't know.'

'So open it.'

I shoved it across the counterpane. 'You open it.'

I watched her small neat fingers work on the tight old knot. Her clear nail varnish flashed in the light. She got the string off and lifted the lid. It was a shallow box made out of the kind of thick sturdy cardboard you don't see much any more. Inside were three things. There was a smaller box, like a jewel case. It was made of cardboard faced with dark blue watermarked paper. There was a book. And there was a cheese cutter. It was a simple length of wire with a handle on each end. The handles were turned from dark old wood. You could see a similar thing in any *épicerie* in France. Except this one had been restrung. The wire was too thick for cheese. It looked like piano wire. It was curled and corroded, like it had been stored for a very long time.

'What is it?' Summer said.

'Looks like a garrotte,' I said.

'The book is in French,' she said. 'I can't read it.'

She passed it to me. It was a printed book with a thin paper dust jacket. Not a novel. Some kind of a non-fiction memoir.

315

The corners of the pages were foxed and stained with age. The whole thing smelled musty. The title was something to do with railroads. I opened it up and took a look. After the title page was a map of the French railroad system in the 1930s. The opening chapter seemed to be about how all the lines in the north squeezed down through Paris and then fanned out again to points south. You couldn't travel anywhere without transiting the capital. It made sense to me. France was a relatively small country with a very big city in it. Most nations did it the same way. The capital city was always the centre of the spiderweb.

I flipped to the end of the book. There was a photograph of the author on the back flap of the dust jacket. The photograph was of a forty-years-younger Monsieur Lamonnier. I recognized him with no difficulty. The blurb underneath the picture said he had lost both legs in the battles of May 1940. I recalled the stiff way he had sat on my mother's sofa. And his walking sticks. He must have been using prosthetics. Wooden legs. What I had assumed were bony knees must have been complicated mechanical joints. The blurb went on to say he had built *Le Chemin de Fer Humain*. The Human Railroad. He had been awarded the Resistance Medal by President Charles de Gaulle, and the George Cross by the British, and the Distinguished Service Medal by the Americans.

'What is it?' Summer said.

'Seems like I just met an old Resistance hero,' I said.

'What's it got to do with your mom?'

'Maybe she and this Lamonnier guy were sweethearts way back.'

'And he wants to tell you and Joe about it? About what a great guy he was? At a time like this? That's a little self-centred, isn't it?'

I read on a little more. Like most French books it used a weird construction called the past historic tense, which was reserved for written stuff only. It made it hard for a non-native to read. And the first part of the story was not very gripping. It made the point very laboriously that trains incoming from the north disgorged their passengers at the Gare du Nord terminal, and if those passengers wanted to carry on south they had to cross Paris on foot or by car or subway or taxi to another

316

terminal like the Gare d'Austerlitz or the Gare de Lyon before joining a southbound train.

'It's about something called the human railroad,' I said. 'Except there aren't many humans in it so far.'

I passed the book to Summer and she flipped through it again.

'It's signed,' she said.

She showed me the first blank page. There was an old faded inscription on it. Blue ink, neat penmanship. Someone had written: *À Béatrice de Pierre.* To Beatrice from Pierre.

'Was your mother called Beatrice?' Summer asked.

'No,' I said. 'Her name was Josephine. Josephine Moutier, and then Josephine Reacher.'

She passed the book back to me.

'I think I've heard of the human railroad,' she said. 'It was a World War Two thing. It was about rescuing bomber crews that were shot down over Belgium and Holland. Local Resistance cells scooped them up and passed them along a chain all the way down to the Spanish border. Then they could get back home and get back in action. It was important because trained crews were valuable. Plus it saved people from years in a POW camp.'

'That would explain Lamonnier's medals,' I said. 'One from each Allied government.'

I put the book down on the bed and thought about packing. I figured I would throw the Samaritaine jeans and sweatshirt and jacket away. I didn't need them. Didn't want them. Then I looked at the book again and saw that some of the pages had different edges from some of the others. I picked it up and opened it and found some half-tone photographs. Most of them were posed studio portraits, reproduced head-and-shoulders six to a page. The others were clandestine action shots. They showed Allied airmen hiding in cellars lit by candles placed on barrels, and small groups of furtive men dressed in borrowed peasant clothing on country tracks, and Pyrenean guides amid snowy mountainous terrain. One of the action shots showed two men with a young girl between them. The girl was not much more than a child. She was holding both men's hands, smiling gaily, leading them down a street in a city. Paris, almost

317

certainly. The caption underneath the picture said: *Béatrice de service à ses travaux*. Beatrice on duty, doing her work. Beatrice looked to be about thirteen years old.

I was pretty sure Beatrice was my mother.

I flipped back to the pages of studio portraits and found her. It was some kind of a school photograph. She looked to be about sixteen in it. The caption was *Béatrice en 1947*. Beatrice in 1947. I flipped back and forth through the text and pieced together Lamonnier's narrative thesis. There were two main tactical problems with the human railroad. Finding the downed airmen was not one of them. They fell out of the sky, literally, all over the Low Countries, dozens of them every moonless night. If the Resistance got to them first, they stood a chance. If the Wehrmacht got to them first, they didn't. It was a matter of pure luck. If they got lucky and the Resistance got to them ahead of the Germans, they would be hidden out, their uniforms would be exchanged for some kind of plausible disguises, forged papers would be issued, rail tickets would be bought, and a courier would escort them on a train to Paris, and they would be on their way home.

Maybe.

The first tactical problem was the possibility of a spot check on the train itself, sometime during the initial journey. These were blond corn-fed farm boys from America, or red-headed British boys from Scotland, or anything else that didn't look dark and pinched and wartime French. They stood out. They didn't speak the language. Lots of subterfuges were developed. They would pretend to be asleep, or sick, or mute, or deaf. The couriers would do all the talking.

The second tactical problem was transiting Paris itself. Paris was crawling with Germans. There were random check points everywhere. Clumsy lost foreigners stuck out like sore thumbs. Private cars had disappeared completely. Taxis were hard to find. There was no gasoline. Men walking in the company of other men became targets. So women were used as couriers. And then one of the dodges Lamonnier dreamed up was to use a kid he knew. She would meet airmen at the Gare du Nord and lead them through the streets to the Gare de Lyon. She would laugh and skip and hold their hands and pass them off as older brothers or visiting uncles. Her manner was unexpected and disarming. She got people through check points like ghosts. She was thirteen years old.

Everyone in the chain had code names. Hers was Béatrice. Lamonnier's was Pierre.

I took the blue cardboard jewel case out of the box. Opened it up. Inside was a medal. It was *La Médaille de la Résistance.* The Resistance Medal. It had a fancy red white and blue ribbon and the medal itself was gold. I turned it over. On the back it was neatly engraved: *Joséphine Moutier.* My mother.

'She never told you?' Summer said.

I shook my head. 'Not a word. Not one, ever.'

Then I looked back in the box. *What the hell was the garrotte about?*

'Call Joe,' I said. 'Tell him we're coming over. Tell him to get Lamonnier back there.'

We were at the apartment fifteen minutes later. Lamonnier was already there. Maybe he had never left. I gave the box to Joe and told him to check it out. He was faster than I had been, because he started with the medal. The name on the back gave him a clue. He glanced through the book and looked up at Lamonnier when he recognized him in the author photograph. Then he scanned through the text. Looked at the pictures. Looked at me.

'She ever mention any of this to you?' he said.

'Never. You?'

'Never,' he said.

I looked at Lamonnier. 'What was the garrotte for?'

Lamonnier said nothing.

'Tell us,' I said.

'She was found out,' he said. 'By a boy at her school. A boy of her own age. An unpleasant boy, the son of collaborators. He teased and tormented her about what he was going to do.'

'What did he do?'

'At first, nothing. That was extremely unsettling for your mother. Then he demanded certain indignities as the price of his continued silence. Naturally, your mother refused. He told her he would inform on her. So she pretended to relent. She

319

arranged to meet him under the Pont des Invalides, late one night. She had to slip out of her house. But first she took her mother's cheese cutter from the kitchen. She replaced the wire with a string from her father's piano. It was the G below middle C, I think. It was still missing, years later. She met the boy and she strangled him.'

'She *what*?' Joe said.

'She strangled him.'

'She was thirteen years old.'

Lamonnier nodded. 'At that age the physical differences between girls and boys are not a significant handicap.'

'She was thirteen years old and she *killed a guy*?'

'They were desperate times.'

'What exactly happened?' I said.

'She used the garrotte. As she had planned. It's not a difficult instrument to use. Nerve and determination were all she needed. Then she used the original cheese wire to attach a weight to his belt. She slipped him into the Seine. He was gone and she was safe. The human railroad was safe.'

Joe stared at him. 'You let her do that?'

Lamonnier shrugged. An expressive, Gallic shrug, just like my mother's.

'I didn't know about it,' he said. 'She didn't tell me until afterwards. I suppose at first my instinct would have been to forbid it. But I couldn't have taken care of it myself. I had no legs. I couldn't have climbed down under the bridge and I wouldn't have been steady enough for fighting. I had a man loosely employed as an assassin, but he was busy elsewhere. In Belgium, I think. I couldn't have afforded the risk of waiting for him to get back. So on balance I think I would have told her to go ahead. They were desperate times, and we were doing vital work.'

'Did this really happen?' Joe said.

'I know it did,' Lamonnier said. 'Fish ate through the boy's belt. He floated up some days later, a short distance downstream. We passed a nervous week. But nothing came of it.'

'How long did she work for you?' I asked.

'All through 1943,' he said. 'She was extremely good. But her face became well known. At first her face was her guardian. It was so young and so innocent. How could anyone suspect a face like that? Then it became a liability. She became familiar to *les boches*. And how many brothers and cousins and uncles could one girl have? So I had to stand her down.'

'Did you recruit her?'

'She volunteered. She pestered me until I let her help.'

'How many people did she save?'

'Eighty men,' Lamonnier said. 'She was my best Paris courier. She was a phenomenon. The consequences of discovery didn't bear thinking about. She lived with the worst kind of fear in her gut for a whole year, but never once did she let me down.'

We all sat quiet.

'How did *you* start?' I asked.

'I was a war cripple,' he said. 'One of many. We were too medically burdensome for them to want us as hostage prisoners. We were useless as forced labourers. So they left us in Paris. But I wanted to do something. I wasn't physically capable of fighting. But I could organize. Those are not physical skills. I knew that trained bomber crews were worth their weight in gold. So I decided to get them home.'

'Why would my mother go her whole life without mentioning this stuff?'

Lamonnier shrugged again. Weary, unsure, still mystified all those years later.

'Many reasons, I think,' he said. 'France was a conflicted country in 1945. Many had resisted, many had collaborated, many had done neither. Most preferred a clean slate. And she was ashamed of killing the boy, I think. It weighed on her conscience. I told her it hadn't been a choice. It wasn't a voluntary action. I told her it had been the right thing to do. But she preferred to forget the whole thing. I had to beg her to accept her medal.'

Joe and I and Summer said nothing. We all sat quiet.

'I wanted her sons to know,' Lamonnier said.

Summer and I walked back to the hotel. We didn't talk. I felt like a guy who suddenly finds out he was adopted. *You're not the man I thought you were.* All my life I had assumed I was what I was because of my father, the career Marine. Now I felt

321

different genes stirring. My father hadn't killed the enemy at the age of thirteen. But my mother had. She had lived through desperate times and she had stepped up and done what was necessary. At that moment I started to miss her more than I would have thought possible. At that moment I knew I would miss her for ever. I felt empty. I had lost something I never knew I had.

We carried our bags down to the lobby and checked out at the desk. We gave back our keys and the multilingual girl prepared a long and detailed account. I had to countersign it. I knew I was in trouble as soon as I saw it. It was outrageously expensive. I had figured the army might overlook the forged vouchers in exchange for a result. But now I wasn't so sure. I figured the George V tariff might change their view. It was like adding insult to injury. We had been there one night, but we were being charged for two because we were late checking out. My room service coffee cost as much as a meal in a bistro. My phone call to Rock Creek cost as much as a three-course lunch at the best restaurant in town. My phone call to Franz in California cost as much as a five-course dinner. Summer's call to Joe less than a mile away in my mother's apartment asking him to get hold of Lamonnier was billed at less than two minutes and cost as much as the room service coffee. And we had been charged fees for taking incoming calls. One was from Franz to me and the other was from Joe to Summer, when he asked her to check I was OK. That little piece of sibling consideration was going to cost the government five bucks. Altogether it was the worst hotel bill I had ever seen.

The multilingual girl printed two copies. I signed one for her and she folded the other into an embossed George V envelope and gave it to me. For my records, she said. *For my court martial*, I thought. I put it in my inside jacket pocket. Took it out again about six hours later, when I finally realized who had done what, and to who, and why, and how.

TWENTY

W E MADE THE FAMILIAR TREK TO THE PLACE DE L'OPÉRA AND caught the airport bus. It was my sixth time on that bus in about a week. The sixth time was no more comfortable than the previous five. It was the discomfort that started me thinking.

We got out at international departures and found the Air France ticket desk. Swapped two vouchers for two seats to Dulles on the eleven o'clock red-eye. That gave us a long wait. We humped our bags across the concourse and started out in a bar. Summer wasn't conversational. I guess she couldn't think of anything to say. But the truth was I was doing OK at that point. Life was unfolding the same way it always had for everyone. Sooner or later you ended up an orphan. There was no escaping it. It had happened that way for a thousand generations. No point in getting all upset about it.

We drank bottles of beer and looked for somewhere to eat. I had missed breakfast and lunch and I guessed Summer hadn't eaten either. We walked past all the little tax-exempt boutiques and found a place that was made up to look like a sidewalk bistro. We pooled our few remaining dollars and checked the menu and worked out that we could afford one course each, plus juice for her and coffee for me, and a tip for the waiter. We ordered *steak frites*, which turned out to be a decent slab of meat with shoestring fries and mayonnaise. You could get good food anywhere in France. Even an airport.

After an hour we moved down to the gate. We were still early and it was almost deserted. Just a few transit passengers, all shopped out, or broke like us. We sat far away from them and stared into space.

'Feels bad, going back,' Summer said. 'You can forget how much trouble you're in when you're away.'

'All we need is a result,' I said.

'We're not going to get one. It's been ten days and we're nowhere.'

I nodded. Ten days since Mrs Kramer died, six days since Carbone died. Five days since Delta had given me a week to clear my name.

'We've got nothing,' Summer said. 'Not even the easy stuff. We didn't even find the woman from Kramer's motel. That shouldn't have been difficult.'

I nodded again. She was right. That shouldn't have been difficult.

The gate filled with travellers and we boarded forty minutes before take-off. Summer and I had seats behind an old couple in an exit row. I wished we could change places with them. I would have been glad of the extra room. We took off on time and I spent the first hour getting more and more cramped and uncomfortable. The stewardess served a meal that I couldn't have eaten even if I had wanted to, because I didn't have enough room to move my elbows and operate the silverware.

One thought led to another.

I thought about Joe flying in the night before. He would have flown coach. That was clear. A civil servant on a personal trip doesn't fly any other way. He would have been cramped and uncomfortable all night long, a little more than me because he was an inch taller. So I felt bad all over again about putting him in the bus to town. I recalled the hard plastic seats and his cramped position and the way his head was jerked around by the motion. I should have sprung for a cab from the city and kept it waiting at the kerb. I should have found a way to scare up some cash.

One thought led to another.

I pictured Kramer and Vassell and Coomer flying in from Frankfurt on New Year's Eve. American Airlines. A Boeing jet. No more spacious than any other jet. An early start from XII Corps. A long flight to Dulles. I pictured them walking down the jetway, stiff, airless, dehydrated, uncomfortable.

One thought led to another.

I pulled the George V bill out of my pocket. Opened the envelope. Read it through. Read it through again. Examined every line and every item.

The hotel bill, the airplane, the bus to town.

The bus to town, the airplane, the hotel bill.

I closed my eyes.

I thought about things that Sanchez and the Delta adjutant and Detective Clark and Andrea Norton and Summer herself had said to me. I thought about the crowd of meeters and greeters we had seen in the Roissy-Charles de Gaulle arrivals hall. I thought about Sperryville, Virginia. I thought about Mrs Kramer's house in Green Valley.

In the end dominoes fell all over the place and landed in ways that made nobody look very good. Least of all me, because I had made many mistakes, including one big one that I knew for sure was going to come right back and bite me in the ass.

I kept myself so busy pondering my prior mistakes that I let my preoccupation lead me into making another one. I spent all my time thinking about the past and no time at all thinking about the future. About countermeasures. About what would be waiting for us at Dulles. We touched down at two in the morning and came out through the customs hall and landed straight in a trap set by Willard.

Standing in the same place they had stood six days earlier were the same three warrant officers from the Provost Marshal General's office. Two W3s and a W4. I saw them. They saw us. I spent a second wondering how the hell Willard had done it. Did he have guys standing by at every airport in the country all day and all night? Did he have a Europe-wide trace out on our travel vouchers? Could he do that himself? Or was the FBI involved? The Department of the Army? The State Department? Interpol? NATO? I had no idea. I made an absurd mental note that one day I should try to find out.

Then I spent another second deciding what to do about the situation.

Delay was not an option. Not now. Not in Willard's hands. I needed freedom of movement and freedom of action for twenty-four or forty-eight more hours. Then I would go see Willard. I would go see him happily. Because at that point I would be ready to slap him around and arrest him.

The W4 walked up to us with his W3s at his back.

'I have orders to place you both in handcuffs,' he said.

'Ignore your orders,' I said.

'I can't,' he said.

'Try.'

'I can't,' he said again.

I nodded.

'OK, we'll trade,' I said. 'You try it with the handcuffs, I'll break your arms. You walk us to the car, we'll go quietly.'

He thought about it. He was armed. So were his guys. We weren't. But nobody wants to shoot people in the middle of an airport. Not unarmed people from your own unit. That would lead to a bad conscience. And paperwork. And he didn't want a fistfight. Not three against two. I was too big and Summer was too small to make it fair.

'Deal?' he said.

'Deal,' I lied.

'So let's go.'

Last time he had walked ahead of me and his hot-dog W3s had stayed on my shoulders. I sincerely hoped he would repeat that pattern. I guessed the W3s figured themselves for real bad-ass sons of bitches and I guessed they were close to being correct, but it was the W4 I was most worried about. He looked like the genuine article. But he didn't have eyes in the back of his head. So I hoped he would walk in front.

He did. Summer and I stayed side by side with our bags in our hands and the W3s formed up wide and behind us in an arrowhead pattern. The W4 led the way. We went out through the doors into the cold. Turned towards the restricted lane where they had parked last time. It was past two in the morning and the airport approach roads were completely deserted. There were lonely pools of yellow light from fixtures up on posts. It had been raining. The ground was wet.

We crossed the public pick-up lane and crossed the median where the bus shelters were. We headed onward into the dark. I could see the bulk of a parking garage half-left and the green Chevy Caprice far away to the right. We turned towards it. Walked in the roadway. Most other times of the day we would have been mown down by traffic. But right then the whole place was still and silent. Past two o'clock in the morning.

I dropped my bag and used both hands and shoved Summer out of the way. Stopped dead and jerked my right elbow backward and smashed the right-hand W3 hard in the face. Kept my feet planted and twisted the other way like a violent calisthenic exercise and smacked the left-hand W3 with my left elbow. Then I stepped forward and met the W4 as he spun towards the noise and came in for me. I hit him with a straight left to the chest. His weight was moving and my weight was moving and the blow messed him up pretty good. I followed it with a right hook to his chin and put him on the ground. Turned back to the W3s to check how they were doing. They were both down on their backs. There was some blood on their faces. Broken noses, loosened teeth. A lot of shock and surprise. An excellent stun factor. I was pleased. They were good, and I was better. I checked the W4. He wasn't doing much. I squatted down next to the W3s and took their Berettas out of their holsters. Then I twisted away and took the W4's out of his. Threaded all three guns on my forefinger. Then I used my other hand to find the car keys. The right-hand W3 had them in his pocket. I took them out and tossed them to Summer. She was back on her feet. She was looking a little dismayed.

I gave her the three Berettas and I dragged the W4 by his collar to the nearest bus shelter. Then I went back for the W3s and dragged them over one in each hand. I got them all lined up face down on the floor. They were conscious, but they were groggy. Heavy blows to the head are a lot more consequential in real life than they are in the movies. And I was breathing hard myself. Almost panting. The adrenalin was kicking in. Some kind of a delayed reaction. Fighting has an effect on both parties to the deal.

I crouched down next to the W4.

'I apologize, chief,' I said. 'But you got in the way.'

He said nothing. Just stared up at me. Anger, shock, wounded pride, confusion.

'Now listen,' I said. 'Listen carefully. You never saw us. We weren't here. We never came. You waited for hours, but we didn't show. You came back out and some thief had boosted your car in the night. That's what happened, OK?'

He tried to say something, but the words wouldn't come out right.

'Yes, I know,' I said. 'It's pretty weak and it makes you look real stupid. But how good does it make you look that you let us escape? That you didn't handcuff us like you were ordered to?'

He said nothing.

'That's your story,' I said. 'We didn't show, and your car was stolen. Stick to it or I'll put it about that it was the lieutenant who took you down. A ninety-pound girl. One against three. People will love that. They'll go nuts for it. And you know how rumours can follow you around for ever.'

He said nothing.

'Your choice,' I said.

He shrugged. Said nothing.

'I apologize,' I said. 'Sincerely.'

We left them there and grabbed our bags and ran to their car. Summer unlocked it and we slid in and she fired it up. Put it in gear and moved away from the kerb.

'Go slow,' I said.

I waited until we were alongside the bus shelter and then wound the window down and tossed the Berettas out on the sidewalk. Their cover story wouldn't hold up if they lost their weapons as well as their car. The three guns landed near the three guys and they all got up on their hands and knees and started to crawl towards them.

'Now go,' I said.

Summer hit the gas hard and the tyres lit up and about a second later we were well outside handgun range. She kept her

328

foot down and we left the airport doing about ninety miles an hour.

'You OK?' I said.

'So far,' she said.

'I'm sorry I had to shove you.'

'We should have just run,' she said. 'We could have lost them in the terminal.'

'We needed a car,' I said. 'I'm sick of taking the bus.'

'But now we're *way* out of line.'

'That's for sure,' I said.

I checked my watch. It was close to three in the morning. We were heading south from Dulles. Going nowhere, fast. In the dark. We needed a destination.

'You know my phone number at Bird?' I said.

'Sure,' Summer said.

'OK, pull over at the next place with a phone.'

She spotted an all-night gas station about five miles later. It was all lit up on the horizon. We pulled in and checked it out. There was a miniature grocery store behind the pumps but it was closed. At night you had to pay for your gas through a bulletproof window. There was a pay phone outside next to the air hose. It was in an aluminum box mounted on the wall. The box had phone shapes drilled into the sides. Summer dialled my Fort Bird office number and handed me the receiver. I heard one cycle of ring tone and then my sergeant answered. The night-duty woman. The one with the baby son.

'This is Reacher,' I said.

'You're in deep shit,' she said.

'And that's the good news,' I said.

'What's the bad news?'

'You're going to join me right there in it. What kind of babysitting arrangements have you got?'

'My neighbour's girl stays. From the trailer next door.'

'Can she stay an hour longer?'

'Why?'

'I want you to meet me. I want you to bring me some stuff.'

'It'll cost you.'

'How much?'

'Two dollars an hour. For the babysitter.'

'I haven't got two dollars. That's something I want you to bring. Money.'

'You want me to give you money?'

'A loan,' I said. 'Couple of days.'

'How much?'

'Whatever you've got.'

'When and where?'

'When you get off. At six. At the diner near the strip club.'

'What do you need me to bring?'

'Phone records,' I said. 'All calls made out of Fort Bird starting from midnight on New Year's Eve until maybe the third of January. And an army phone book. I need to speak to Sanchez and Franz and all kinds of other people. And I need Major Marshall's personal file. The XII Corps guy. I need you to get a copy faxed in from somewhere.'

'Anything else?'

'I want to know where Vassell and Coomer parked their car when they came down for dinner on the fourth. I want you to see if anyone noticed.'

'OK,' she said. 'Is that it?'

'No,' I said. 'I want to know where Major Marshall was on the second and the third. Scare up some travel clerk somewhere and see if any vouchers were issued. And I want a phone number for the Jefferson Hotel in D.C.'

'That's an awful lot to do in three hours.'

'That's why I'm asking you instead of the day guy. You're better than he is.'

'Stick it,' she said. 'Flattery doesn't work on me.'

'Hope springs eternal,' I said.

We got back into the car and got back on the road. Headed east for I-95. I told Summer to go slow. If she didn't, then the way she was likely to drive on empty roads at night would get us to the diner well before my sergeant, and I didn't want that to happen. My sergeant would get there around six thirty. I wanted to get there after her, maybe six forty. I wanted to check she hadn't done her duty and dropped a dime on me and set up an ambush. It was unlikely, but not impossible. I wanted to be able to drive by and check. I didn't want to be already in a booth drinking coffee when Willard showed up.

'Why do you want all that stuff?' Summer asked.

'I know what happened to Mrs Kramer,' I said.

'How?'

'I figured it out,' I said. 'Like I should have at the beginning. But I didn't think. I didn't have enough imagination.'

'It's not enough to *imagine* things.'

'It is,' I said. 'Sometimes that's what it's all about. Sometimes that's all an investigator has got. You have to imagine what people must have done. The way they must have thought and acted. You have to think yourself into *being* them.'

'Being who?'

'Vassell and Coomer,' I said. 'We know who they are. We know what they're like. Therefore we can predict what they did.'

'What did they do?'

'They got an early start and flew all day from Frankfurt. On New Year's Eve. They wore Class As, trying to get an upgrade. Maybe they succeeded, with American Airlines out of Germany. Maybe they didn't. Either way, they couldn't have counted on it. They must have been prepared to spend eight hours in coach.'

'So?'

'Would guys like Vassell and Coomer be happy to wait in the Dulles taxi line? Or take a shuttle bus to the city? All cramped and uncomfortable?'

'No,' Summer said. 'They wouldn't do either thing.'

'Exactly,' I said. 'They wouldn't do either thing. They're way too important for that. They wouldn't dream of it. Not in a million years. Guys like that, they need to be met by a car and a driver.'

'Who?'

'Marshall,' I said. 'That's who. He's their blue-eyed gofer. He was already over here, at their service. He must have picked them up at the airport. Maybe Kramer, too. Did Kramer take the Hertz bus to the rental lot? I don't think so. I think Marshall drove him there. Then he drove Vassell and Coomer to the Jefferson Hotel.'

'And?'

331

'And *he stayed there with them*, Summer. I think he had a room booked. Maybe they wanted him on the spot to drive them to National the next morning. He was going with them, after all. He was going to Irwin too. Or maybe they just wanted to talk to him, urgently. Just the three of them, Vassell, Coomer, and Marshall. Maybe it was easier to talk without Kramer there. And Marshall had a lot of stuff to talk about. They started his temporary detached duty in November. You told me that yourself. November was when the Wall started coming down. November was when the danger signals started coming in. So they sent him over here in November to get his ear close to the ground in the Pentagon. That's my guess. But whatever, Marshall stayed the night with Vassell and Coomer at the Jefferson Hotel. I'm sure of it.'

'OK, so?'

'Marshall was at the hotel, and his car was in valet parking. And you know what? I checked our bill from Paris. They charged an arm and a leg for everything. Especially the phone calls. But not *all* the phone calls. The room-to-room calls we made didn't show up at all. You called me at six, about dinner. Then I called you at midnight, because I was lonely. Those calls didn't show up anywhere on the bill. Hit three for another room, and it's free. Dial nine for a line, and it triggers the computer. There were no calls on Vassell and Coomer's bill and therefore we thought they had *made* no calls. But they *had* made calls. It's obvious. They made internal calls. Room to room. Vassell took the message from XII Corps in Germany, and then he called Coomer's room to discuss what the hell to do about the situation. And then one or other of them picked up the phone and called Marshall's room. They called their blue-eyed gofer and told him to run downstairs and jump in his car.'

'*Marshall* did it?'

I nodded. 'They sent him out into the night to clean up their mess.'

'Can we prove it?'

'We can make a start,' I said. 'I'll bet you three things. First, we'll call the Jefferson Hotel and we'll find a booking in Marshall's name for New Year's Eve. Second, Marshall's file will tell us he once lived in Sperryville, Virginia. And third, his file will tell us he's tall and heavy and right-handed.'

She went quiet. Her eyelids started moving.

'Is it enough?' she said. 'Is Mrs Kramer enough of a result to get us off the hook?'

'There's more to come,' I said.

It was like being in a parallel universe, watching Summer driving slow. We drifted down the highway with the world going half-speed outside our windows. The big Chevy engine was loafing along a little above idle. The tyres were quiet. We passed all our familiar landmarks. The state police facility, the spot where Kramer's briefcase had been found, the rest area, the spur to the small highway. We crawled off at the cloverleaf and I scanned the gas station and the greasy spoon and the lounge parking and the motel. The whole place was full of yellow light and fog and black shadow but I could see well enough. There was no sign of a set-up. Summer turned into the lot and drove a long slow circuit. There were three eighteen-wheelers parked like beached whales and a couple of old sedans that were probably abandoned. They had the look. They had dull paint and soft tyres and they were low on their springs. There was an old Ford pick-up truck with a baby seat strapped to the bench. I guessed that was my sergeant's. There was nothing else. Six forty in the morning, and the world was dark and still and quiet.

We put the car out of sight behind the lounge bar and walked across the lot to the diner. Its windows were misted by the cooking steam. There was hot white light inside. It looked like a Hopper painting. My sergeant was alone at a booth in back. We walked in and sat down beside her. She hauled a grocery bag up off the floor. It was full of stuff.

'First things first,' she said.

She put her hand in the bag and came out with a bullet. She stood it upright on the table in front of me. It was a standard nine-millimetre Parabellum. Standard NATO load. Full metal jacket. For a sidearm or a sub-machine gun. The shiny brass casing had something scratched on it. I picked it up. Looked at it. There was a word engraved there. It was

333

rough and uneven. It had been done fast and by hand. It said:
Reacher.

'A bullet with my name on it,' I said.

'From Delta,' my sergeant said. 'Hand delivered, yesterday.'

'Who by?'

'The young one with the beard.'

'Charming,' I said. 'Remind me to kick his ass.'

'Don't joke about it. They're awful stirred up.'

'They're looking at the wrong guy.'

'Can you prove that?'

I paused. Knowing and proving were two different things. I dropped the bullet into my pocket and put my hands on the table.

'Maybe I can,' I said.

'You know who killed Carbone too?' Summer said.

'One thing at a time,' I said.

'Here's your money,' my sergeant said. 'It's all I could get.'

She went into her bag again and put forty-seven dollars on the table.

'Thanks,' I said. 'Call it I owe you fifty. Three bucks interest.'

'Fifty-two,' she said. 'Don't forget the babysitter.'

'What else have you got?'

She came out with a concertina of printer paper. It was the kind with faint blue rulings and holes in the sides. There were lines and lines of numbers on it.

'The phone records,' she said.

Then she gave me a sheet of army memo paper with a 202 number on it.

'The Jefferson Hotel,' she said.

Then she gave me a roll of curled fax paper.

'Major Marshall's personal file,' she said.

She followed that with an army phone book. It was thick and green and had numbers in it for all our posts and installations worldwide. Then she gave me more curled fax paper. It was Detective Clark's street canvass results, from New Year's Eve, up in Green Valley.

'Franz in California told me you wanted it,' she said.

'Great,' I said. 'Thanks. Thanks for everything.'

She nodded. 'You better believe I'm better than the day guy.

And someone better be prepared to say so when they start with the force reduction.'

'I'll tell them,' I said.

'Don't,' she said. 'Won't help a bit, coming from you. You'll either be dead or in prison.'

'You brought all this stuff,' I said. 'You haven't given up on me yet.'

She said nothing.

'Where did Vassell and Coomer park their car?' I asked.

'On the fourth?' she said. 'Nobody knows for sure. The first night patrol saw a staff car backed in all by itself at the far end of the lot. But you can't take that to the bank. He didn't get a plate number, so it's not a positive ID. And the second night patrol can't remember it at all. Therefore it's one guy's report against another.'

'What exactly did the first guy see?'

'He called it a staff car.'

'Was it a black Grand Marquis?'

'It was a black something,' she said. 'But all staff cars are black or green. Nothing unique about a black car.'

'But it was out of the way.'

She nodded. 'On its own, far end of the lot. But the second guy can't confirm it.'

'Where was Major Marshall on the second and the third?'

'That was easier,' she said. 'Two travel warrants. To Frank-furt on the second, back here on the third.'

'An overnight in Germany?'

She nodded again. 'There and back.'

We sat quiet. The counterman came over with a pad and a pencil. I looked at the menu and the forty-seven dollars on the table and ordered less than two bucks' worth of coffee and eggs. Summer took the hint and ordered juice and biscuits. That was about as cheap as we could get, consistent with staying vertical.

'Am I done here?' my sergeant asked.

I nodded. 'Thanks. I mean it.'

Summer slid out to let her get up.

'Kiss your baby for me,' I said.

My sergeant just stood there, all bone and sinew. Hard as woodpecker lips. Staring straight at me.

'My mom just died,' I said. 'One day your son will remember mornings like these.'

She nodded once and walked to the door. A minute later we saw her in her pick-up truck, a small figure all alone at the wheel. She drove off into the dawn mist. A rope of exhaust followed behind her and then drifted away.

I shuffled all the paper into a logical pile and started with Marshall's personal file. The quality of the fax transmission wasn't great, but it was legible. There was the usual mass of information. On the first page I found out that Marshall had been born in September of 1958. Therefore he was thirty-one years old. He had no wife and no children. No ex-wives, either. He was wedded to the military, I guessed. He was listed at six-four and two hundred twenty pounds. The army needed to know that to keep their quartermaster percentiles up to speed. He was listed as right-handed. The army needed to know *that* because bolt-action sniper rifles are made for right-handers. Left-handed soldiers don't usually get assigned as snipers. Pigeon-holing starts on day one, in the military.

I turned the page.

Marshall had been born in Sperryville, Virginia, and had gone all the way through kindergarten and grade school and high school there.

I smiled. Summer looked at me, questions in her eyes. I separated the pages and slid them across to her and stretched over and used my finger to point out the relevant lines. Then I slid her the memo paper with the Jefferson Hotel number on it.

'Go find a phone,' I said.

She found one just inside the door, on the wall, near the register. I saw her put two quarters in, and dial, and talk, and wait. I saw her give her name and rank and unit. I saw her listen. I saw her talk some more. I saw her wait some more. And listen some more. She put more quarters in. It was a long call. I guessed she was getting transferred all over the place. Then I saw her say thank you. I saw her hang up. I saw her come back to me, looking grim and satisfied.

'He had a room,' she said. 'In fact he made the booking

336

himself, the day before. Three rooms, for him, and Vassell, and Coomer. And there was a valet parking charge.'

'Did you speak to the valet station?'

She nodded. 'It was a black Mercury. In just after lunch, out again at twenty to one in the morning, back in again at twenty past three in the morning, out again finally after breakfast on New Year's Day.'

I riffed through the pile of paper and found the fax from Detective Clark in Green Valley. The results of his house-to-house canvass. There was a fair amount of vehicle activity listed. It had been New Year's Eve and lots of people were heading to and from parties. There had been what someone thought was a taxi on Mrs Kramer's road, just before two o'clock in the morning.

'A staff car could be mistaken for a taxi,' I said. 'You know, a plain black sedan, clean condition but a little tired, a lot of miles on it, the same shape as a Crown Victoria.'

'Plausible,' Summer said.

'Likely,' I said.

We paid the check and left a dollar tip and counted what was left of my sergeant's loan. Decided we were going to have to keep on eating cheap, because we were going to need gas money. And phone money. And some other expenses.

'Where to now?' Summer asked me.

'Across the street,' I said. 'To the motel. We're going to hole up all day. A little more work, and then we sleep.'

We left the Chevy hidden behind the lounge bar and crossed the street on foot. Woke the skinny guy in the motel office and asked him for a room.

'One room?' he said.

I nodded. Summer didn't object. She knew we couldn't afford two rooms. And we weren't new to sharing. Paris had worked out OK for us, as far as night-time arrangements were concerned.

'Fifteen bucks,' the skinny guy said.

I gave him the money and he smiled and gave me the key to the room Kramer had died in. I figured it was an attempt at humour. I didn't say anything. I didn't mind. I figured a room a guy had died in was better than the rooms that rented by the hour.

We walked together down the row and unlocked the door and stepped inside. The room was still dank and brown and miserable. The corpse had been hauled away, but other than that it was exactly the same as when I had first seen it.

'It ain't the George V,' Summer said.

'That's for damn sure,' I said.

We put our bags on the floor and I put my sergeant's paper-work on the bed. The counterpane felt slightly damp. I fiddled with the heater under the window until I got some warmth out of it.

'What next?' Summer asked.

'The phone records,' I said. 'I'm looking for a call to a nine one nine area code.'

'That'll be a local call. Fort Bird is nine one nine too.'

'Great,' I said. 'There'll be a million local calls.'

I spread the print-out on the bed and started looking. There weren't a million local calls. But there were certainly hundreds. I started at midnight on New Year's Eve and worked forward from there. I ignored the numbers that had been called more than once from more than one phone. I figured those would be cab companies or clubs or bars. I ignored the numbers that had the same exchange code as Fort Bird. Those would be off-post housing, mainly. Soldiers on duty would have been calling them in the hour after midnight, wishing their spouses and children a happy new year. I concentrated on numbers that stood out. Numbers in other North Carolina cities. In particular I was looking for a number in another city that had been called once only maybe thirty or forty minutes after midnight. That was my target. I went through the print-out, patiently, line by line, page by page, looking for it. I was in no hurry. I had all day.

I found it after the third concertina fold. It was listed at twelve thirty-two. Thirty-two minutes after 1989 became 1990. That was right about when I would have expected it. It was a call that lasted nearly fifteen minutes. That was about right too, in terms of duration. It was a solid prospect. I scanned ahead. Checked the next twenty or thirty minutes. There was nothing else there that looked half as good. I went back and put my finger under the number I liked. It was my best bet. Or my only hope.

'Got a pen?' I said.

Summer gave me one from her pocket.

'Got quarters?' I said.

She showed me fifty cents. I wrote the best-bet number on the army memo paper right underneath the D.C. number for the Jefferson Hotel. Passed it to her.

'Call it,' I said. 'Find out who answers. You'll have to go back across the street to the diner. The motel phone is busted.'

She was gone about eight minutes. I spent the time cleaning my teeth. I had a theory: if you can't get time to sleep, a shower is a good substitute. If you can't get time to shower, cleaning your teeth is the next best thing.

I left my toothbrush in a glass in the bathroom and Summer came through the door. She brought cold and misty air in with her.

'It was a golf resort outside of Raleigh,' she said.

'Good enough for me,' I said.

'Brubaker,' she said. 'That's where Brubaker was. On vacation.'

'Probably dancing,' I said. 'Don't you think? At half past midnight on New Year's Eve? The desk clerk probably had to drag him out of the ballroom to the phone. That's why the call lasted a quarter of an hour. Most of it was waiting time.'

'Who called him?'

There were codes on the print-out indicating the location of the originating phone. They meant nothing to me. They were just numbers and letters. But my sergeant had supplied a key for me. On the sheet after the last concertina fold was a list of the codes and the locations they stood for. She had been right. She was better than the day guy. But then, she was an E-5 sergeant and he was an E-4 corporal, and sergeants made the U.S. Army worth serving in.

I checked the code against the key.

'Someone on a pay phone in the Delta barracks,' I said.

'So a Delta guy called his CO,' Summer said. 'How does that help us?'

339

'The timing is suggestive,' I said. 'Must have been an urgent matter, right?'

'Who was it?'

'One step at a time,' I said.

'Don't shut me out.'

'I'm not.'

'You are. You're walling up.'

I said nothing.

'Your mom died, and you're hurting, and you're closing in on yourself. But you shouldn't. You can't do this alone, Reacher. You can't live your whole life alone.'

I shook my head.

'It's not that,' I said. 'It's that I'm only guessing here. I'm holding my breath all the time. One long shot after another. And I don't want to fall flat on my face. Not right in front of you. You wouldn't respect me any more.'

She said nothing.

'I know,' I said. 'You already don't respect me because you saw me naked.'

She paused. Then she smiled.

'But you need to get used to that,' I said. 'Because it's going to happen again. Right now, in fact. We're taking the rest of the day off.'

The bed was awful. The mattress dipped in the middle and the sheets were damp. Maybe worse than damp. A place like that, if the room hadn't been rented since Kramer died, I was pretty sure the bed wouldn't have been changed, either. Kramer had never actually gotten into it, but he had died right on top of it. He had probably leaked all kinds of bodily fluids. Summer didn't seem to mind. But she hadn't seen him there, all grey and white and inert.

But then I figured, *what do you want for fifteen bucks?* And Summer took my mind off the sheets. She distracted me big time. We were plenty tired, but not too tired. We did well, second time around. The second time is often the best. That's been my experience. You're looking forward to it, and you're not bored with it yet.

Afterwards, we slept like babies. The heater finally put some

340

temperature into the room. The sheets warmed up. The traffic sounds on the highway were soothing. Like white noise. We were safe. Nobody would think of looking for us there. Kramer had chosen well. It was a hideaway. We rolled down into the mattress dip together and held each other tight. I ended up thinking it was the best bed I had ever been in.

We woke up much later, very hungry. It was after six o'clock in the evening. Already dark outside the window. The January days were spooling by one after the other, and we weren't paying much attention to them. We showered and dressed and headed across the street to eat. I took the army phone directory with me.

We went for the most calories for the fewest dollars but still ended up blowing more than eight bucks between us. I got my own back with the coffee. The diner had a bottomless cup policy and I exploited it ruthlessly. Then I camped out near the register and used the phone on the wall. Checked the number in the army book and called Sanchez down at Jackson.

'I hear you're in the shit,' he said.

'Temporarily,' I said. 'You heard anything more about Brubaker?'

'Like what?'

'Like, did they find his car yet?'

'Yes, they did. And it was a long way from Columbia.'

'Let me guess,' I said. 'Somewhere more than an hour due north of Fort Bird, and maybe east and a little south of Raleigh. How about Smithfield, North Carolina?'

'How the hell did you know that?'

'Just a feeling,' I said. 'Had to be close to where I-95 meets U.S.70. Right on a main drag. Do they think that's where he was killed?'

'No question about it. Killed right there in his car. Someone shot him from the back seat. The windshield was blown out in front of the driver's position and what was left of the glass was all covered in blood and brains. And there were spatters on the steering wheel that hadn't been smudged. Therefore nobody drove the car after he died. Therefore that's where he was killed. Right there in his car. Smithfield, North Carolina.'

341

'Did they find shell cases?'

'No shell cases. No significant trace evidence either, apart from the kind of normal shit they would expect to find.'

'Have they got a narrative theory?'

'It was an industrial unit parking lot. Big place, like a local landmark, with a big lot, busy in the daytime but deserted at night. They think it was a two-car rendezvous. Brubaker gets there first, the second car pulls up alongside, at least two guys get out of it, they get into Brubaker's car, one in the front and one in the back, they sit a spell, maybe they talk a little, then the guy in the back pulls a gun and shoots. Which by the way is how they figure Brubaker's watch got busted. They figure he had his left wrist up on the top of the wheel, the way guys do when they're sitting in their cars. But whatever, he goes down and they drag him out and they put him in the trunk of the other car and they drive him down to Columbia and they leave him there.'

'With dope and money in his pocket.'

'They don't know where that came from yet.'

'Why didn't the bad guys move his car?' I said. 'Seems kind of dumb to take the body to South Carolina and leave the car where it was.'

'Nobody knows why. Maybe because it's conspicuous to drive a car full of blood with a blown windshield. Or maybe because bad guys *are* dumb sometimes.'

'You got notes about what Mrs Brubaker said about the phone calls he took?'

'After dinner on the fourth?'

'No, earlier,' I said. 'On New Year's Eve. About half an hour after they all held hands and sang "Auld Lang Syne".'

'Maybe. I took some pretty good notes. I could go look.'

'Be quick,' I said. 'I'm on a pay phone here.'

I heard the receiver go down on his desk. Heard faint scratchy movement far away in his office. I waited. Put another pair of quarters in the slot. We were already down two bucks on toll calls. Plus twelve for eating and fifteen for the room. We had eighteen dollars left. Out of which I knew for sure I was going to be spending another ten, hopefully pretty soon. I began to wish the army didn't buy Caprices with big V-8s in them. A little

342

four-cylinder thing like Kramer had rented would have gotten us further, on eight bucks' worth of gas.

I heard Sanchez pick up the phone again.

'OK, New Year's Eve,' he said. 'She told me he was dragged out of a dinner dance around twelve thirty in the morning. She told me she was a little bit aggrieved about it.'

'Did he tell her anything about the call?'

'No. But she said he danced better after it. Like he was all fired up. Like he was on the trail of something. He was all excited.'

'She could tell that from the way he danced?'

'They were married a long time, Reacher. You get to know a person.'

'OK,' I said. 'Thanks, Sanchez. I got to go.'

'Be careful.'

'Always am.'

I hung up and walked back to our table.

'Where now?' Summer said.

'Now we're going to go see girls take their clothes off,' I said.

It was a short walk across the lot from the greasy spoon to the lounge bar. There were a few cars around, but not many. It was still early. It would be another couple of hours before the crowds really built up. The locals were still home, eating dinner, watching the sports news. Guys from Fort Bird were finishing chow time in the mess, showering, getting changed, hooking up in twos and threes, finding car keys, picking out designated drivers. But I still kept my eye out. I didn't want to bump into a crowd of Delta people. Not outside in the dark. Time was too precious to waste.

We pulled the door and stepped inside. There was a new face behind the register. Maybe a friend or a relative of the fat guy. I didn't know him. He didn't know me. And we were in BDUs. No unit designations. No indication that we were MPs. So the new face was happy enough to see us. He figured us for a nice little upward tick in his first-hour cash flow. We walked right past him.

The place was less than one-tenth full. It felt very different that way. It felt cold and vast and empty. Like some kind of a factory. Without a press of bodies the music was louder and tinnier than ever. There were whole expanses of vacant floor. Whole acres. Hundreds of unoccupied chairs. There was only one girl performing. She was on the main stage. She was bathed in warm red light, but she looked cold and listless. I saw Summer watching her. Saw her shudder. I had said: *So what are you going to do? Go work up at the strip club with Sin?* Face to face, it wasn't a very appealing option.

'Why are we here?' she asked.

'For the key to everything,' I said. 'My biggest mistake.'

'Which was?'

'Watch,' I said.

I walked around to the dressing-room door. Knocked twice. A girl I didn't know opened up. She kept the door close to her body and stuck her head around. Maybe she was naked.

'I need to see Sin,' I said.

'She's not here.'

'She is,' I said. 'She's got Christmas to pay for.'

'She's busy.'

'Ten dollars,' I said. 'Ten dollars to talk. No touching.'

The girl disappeared and the door swung shut behind her. I stood out of the way, so the first person Sin would see would be Summer. We waited. And waited. Then the door opened up again and Sin stepped out. She was in a tight sheath dress. It was pink. It sparkled. She was tall on clear plastic heels. I stepped behind her. Got between her and the dressing-room door. She turned and saw me. *Trapped.*

'Couple of questions,' I said. 'That's all.'

She looked better than the last time I had seen her. The bruises on her face were ten days old and were more or less healed up. Her make-up was maybe a little thicker than before. But that was the only sign of her troubles. Her eyes looked vacant. I guessed she had just shot up. Right between her toes. *Whatever gets you through the night.*

'Ten dollars,' she said.

'Let's sit,' I said.

We found a table far from a speaker. It was relatively quiet there. I took a ten-spot out of my pocket and held it out. Didn't let go of it.

'You remember me?' I said.

She nodded.

'Remember that night?' I said.

She nodded again.

'OK, here's the thing. Who hit you?'

'That soldier,' she said. 'The one you were talking to just before.'

TWENTY-ONE

I KEPT TIGHT HOLD OF THE TEN-DOLLAR BILL AND TOOK HER THROUGH it, step by step. She told us that after I slid her off my knee she had gone around looking for girls to check with. She had managed whispered conversations with most of them. But none of them knew anything. None of them had any information at all, either first-hand or second-hand. There were no rumours going around. No stories about a co-worker having a problem in the motel. She had checked back in the private room and heard nothing there either. Then she had gone to the dressing room. There was nobody in there. Business was good. Everybody else was either up on the stage or across the street. She knew she should have kept on asking. But there was no gossip. She felt sure someone would have heard something, if anything bad had actually happened. So she figured she would just give up on it and blow me off. Then the soldier I had been talking to stepped into the dressing room. She gave us a pretty good description of Carbone. Like most hookers she had trained herself to remember faces. Repeat customers like to be recognized. It makes them feel special. Makes them tip better. She told us Carbone had warned her not to tell any MP anything. She put emphasis in her voice, echoing his own from ten days before.

346

Any MP *anything*. Then to make sure she took him seriously he had slapped her twice, hard, fast, forehand, backhand. She had been stunned by the blows. She hadn't seen them coming. She sounded impressed by them. It was like she was ranking them against other blows she had received. Like a connoisseur. And looking at her I figured she was reasonably familiar with getting hit.

'Tell me again,' I said. 'It was the soldier, not the owner.'

She looked at me like I was crazy.

'The *owner* never hits us,' she said. 'We're his meal ticket.'

I gave her the ten bucks and we left her there at the quiet table.

'What does it mean?' Summer said.

'Everything,' I said.

'How did you know?'

I shrugged. We were back in Kramer's motel room, folding stuff, packing our bags, getting ready to hit the road one last time.

'I saw it wrong,' I said. 'I guess I started to realize in Paris. When we were waiting for Joe at the airport. That crowd. They were watching people coming out and they were kind of half-prepared to greet them and half-prepared to ignore them, depending. That's how it was in the bar that night. I walked in, I'm a big guy, so people saw me coming. They were curious for a split second. But they didn't know me and they didn't like what I was, so they turned away again and shut me out. Very subtle, all in the body language. Except for Carbone. He didn't shut me out. He turned towards me. I thought it was just random, but it wasn't. I thought I was selecting him, but he was selecting me just as much.'

'It had to be random. He didn't know you.'

'He didn't know *me*, but he knew MP badges when he saw them. He had been in the army sixteen years. He knew what he was looking at.'

'So why turn towards you?'

'It was like a double-take. Like a stutter step. He was turning away, then he changed his mind and turned back. He *wanted* me to come to him.'

347

'Why?'

'Because he wanted to know why I was there.'

'Did you tell him?'

I nodded. 'Looking back, yes I did. Not in detail. I just wanted him to stop people from getting worried, so I told him it was nothing to do with anyone, just some lost property across the street, maybe one of the hookers had it. He was a very smart guy. Very subtle. He reeled me in like a fish and got it out of me.'

'Why would he care?'

'Something I once said to Willard. I said things happen in order to dead-end other things. Carbone wanted my inquiries dead-ended. That was his aim. So he thought fast. And smart. Delta doesn't hire dumb guys, that's for sure. He went in and smacked the girl, to shut her up in case she knew anything. And then he came out and let me think the owner had done it. He didn't even lie about it. He just let me assume. He wound me up like a clockwork toy and pointed me in the direction he wanted. And off I went. I smacked the owner on the ear and we fought it out in the lot. And there was Carbone, watching. He saw me work the guy over like he knew I would and then he put in the complaint. So he got it coming and going. He got both ends bottled up. The girl was silenced and he thought I would be taken out of the picture because of the disciplinary procedure. He was a very smart guy, Summer. I wish I had met him before.'

'Why did he want you dead-ended? What was his motive?'

'He didn't want me to find out who took the briefcase.'

'Why not?'

I sat down on the bed.

'Why did we never find the woman Kramer met in here?'

'I don't know.'

'Because there never was a woman,' I said. 'Kramer met Carbone in here.'

She just stared at me.

'Kramer was gay too,' I said. 'He and Carbone were getting it on.'

*　　*　　*

348

'Carbone took the briefcase,' I said. 'Right out of this room. Because he had to keep the relationship secret. Just like we thought about the phantom woman, maybe he was worried there was something personal to him in it. Or maybe Kramer had been bragging about the Irwin conference. Talking about how Armored was going to fight its corner. So maybe Carbone was curious. Or even concerned. He'd been an infantryman for sixteen years. And the type of guy who gets into Delta, he's got a lot of unit loyalty. Maybe more loyalty to his unit than to his lover.'

'I don't believe it,' Summer said.

'You should,' I said. 'It all fits. Andrea Norton more or less told us. I think she knew about Kramer. Either consciously or subconsciously, I'm not sure which. We accused her, and she wasn't annoyed, remember? She was amused instead. Or bewildered, maybe. She was a sexual psychologist, she'd met the guy, maybe she'd picked up a vibe, professionally. Or the absence of a vibe, personally. So in our minds we had her in bed with Kramer, and she just couldn't make it compute. So she didn't get mad. It just didn't connect. And we know Kramer's marriage was a sham. No kids. He hadn't lived at home for five years. Detective Clark in Green Valley wondered why he wasn't divorced. He once asked me, divorce isn't a dealbreaker for a general, is it? I said no, it isn't. But being gay is. That's for damn sure. Being gay is a big-time dealbreaker for a general. That's why he kept the marriage going. It was cover, for the army. Just like the girlfriend photo in Carbone's wallet.'

'We have no proof.'

'But we can get close. Carbone had a condom in his wallet, as well as the girlfriend photo. A buck gets ten it's from the same pack as the one Walter Reed took off Kramer's body. And another buck gets ten we can comb old assignment orders and find out where and when they met. Some joint exercise somewhere, like we thought all along. Plus Carbone was a vehicle guy for Delta. Their adjutant told me that. He had access to their whole stable of Humvees, any old time he wanted it. So another buck gets ten we'll find he was out in one, alone, on New Year's Eve.'

'Was he killed for the briefcase? In the end? Like Mrs Kramer?'

I shook my head. 'Neither one of them was killed simply for the briefcase.'

She just looked at me.

'Later,' I said. 'One step at a time.'

'But he had the briefcase. You said so. He ran off with it.'

I nodded. 'And he searched it as soon as he got back to Bird. He found the agenda. He read it. And something in it made him call his CO immediately.'

'*He* called Brubaker? How could he do that? He couldn't say, hey, I was just sleeping with a general and guess what I found?'

'He could have said he found it somewhere else. On the sidewalk, maybe. But actually I'm wondering if Brubaker knew about Carbone and Kramer all along. It's possible. Delta is a family and Brubaker was a very hands-on type of CO. It's possible he knew. And maybe he exploited the situation. For intelligence purposes. These guys are incredibly competitive. And Sanchez told me Brubaker never missed any angle or any advantage or any wrinkle. So maybe the price of Brubaker's tolerance was that Carbone had to pass stuff on, from the pillow talk.'

'That's awful.'

I nodded. 'Like being a whore. I told you there would be no winners here. Everyone's going to come out looking bad.'

'Except us. If we get the results.'

'You're going to be OK. I'm not.'

'Why?'

'Wait and see,' I said.

We carried our bags to the Chevy, which was still hidden behind the lounge bar. We put them in the trunk. The lot was fuller than it had been before. The night was heating up. I checked my watch. Almost eight o'clock on the east coast, almost five on the west coast. I stood still, trying to decide. *If we pause for breath even for a second, we'll be overrun again.*

'I need to make two more calls,' I said.

I took the army phone book with me and we walked back to the greasy spoon. I checked every pocket for loose change and came up with a small pile. Summer contributed a quarter and a nickel. The counterman changed the pennies for silver. I fed the phone and dialled Franz at Fort Irwin. Five o'clock in the afternoon, it was the middle of his work day.

'Am I going to get past your main gate?' I asked him.

'Why wouldn't you?'

'Willard's chasing me. He's liable to warn anyplace he thinks I'm going.'

'I haven't heard from him yet.'

'Maybe you could switch your telex off for a day or two.'

'What's your ETA?'

'Tomorrow sometime.'

'Your buddies are already here. They just got in.'

'I haven't got any buddies.'

'Vassell and Coomer. They're fresh in from Europe.'

'Why?'

'Exercises.'

'Is Marshall still there?'

'Sure. He drove out to LAX to pick them up. They all came back together. Like one big happy family.'

'I need you to do two things for me,' I said.

'Two more things, you mean.'

'I need a ride from LAX myself. Tomorrow, first morning arrival from D.C. I need you to send someone.'

'And?'

'And I need you to get someone to locate the staff car Vassell and Coomer used back here. It's a black Mercury Grand Marquis. Marshall signed it out on New Year's Eve. By now it's either back in the Pentagon garage or parked at Andrews. I need someone to find it and to do a full court press on it, forensically. And fast.'

'What would they be looking for?'

'Anything at all.'

'OK,' Franz said.

'I'll see you tomorrow,' I said.

I hung up and turned the pages in the army directory all the way from *F* for *Fort Irwin* to *P* for *Pentagon*. Slid my finger down the sub-section to *C* for *Chief of Staff's Office*. I left it there, briefly.

'Vassell and Coomer are at Irwin,' I said.

351

'Why?' Summer said.

'Hiding out,' I said. 'They think we're still in Europe. They know Willard is watching the airports. They're sitting ducks.'

'Do we want them?' Summer said. 'They didn't know about Mrs Kramer. That was clear. They were shocked when you told them, that night in your office. So I guess they authorized the burglary, but not the collateral damage.'

I nodded. She was right. They had been surprised, that night in my office. Coomer had gone pale and asked: *Was it a burglary?* It was a question that came straight from a guilty conscience. That meant Marshall hadn't told them at that point. He had kept the really bad news to himself. He had come back to the D.C. hotel at twenty past three in the morning, and he had told them the briefcase hadn't been there, but he hadn't told them what else had gone down. Vassell and Coomer must have been piecing it together on the fly, that night in my office, in the dark and after the event. It must have been an interesting ride home. Harsh words must have been exchanged.

'It's down to Marshall alone,' Summer said. 'He panicked, is all.'

'Technically it was a conspiracy,' I said. 'Legally they all share the blame.'

'Hard to prosecute.'

'That's JAG Corps' problem.'

'It's a weak case. Hard to prove.'

'They did other stuff,' I said. 'Believe me, Mrs Kramer getting hit on the head is the least of their worries.'

I fed the phone again and dialled the Chief of Staff's office, deep inside the Pentagon. A woman's voice answered. It was a perfect Washington voice. Not high, not low, cultured, elegant, nearly accentless. I guessed she was a senior administrator, working late. I guessed she was about fifty, blonde going grey, powder on her face.

'Write this down,' I said to her. 'I am a military police major called Reacher. I was recently transferred out of Panama and into Fort Bird, North Carolina. I will be standing at the E-ring check point inside your building at midnight tonight. It is entirely up to the Chief of Staff whether he meets me there.'

I paused.

'Is that it?' the woman said.

'Yes,' I said, and hung up. I scooped fifteen remaining cents back into my pocket. Closed the phone book and wedged it under my arm.

'Let's go,' I said. We drove through the gas station and topped off the tank with eight bucks' worth of gas. Then we headed north.

'It's entirely up to the Chief of Staff whether he meets you there?' Summer said. 'What the hell is *that* about?'

We were on I-95, still three hours south of D.C. Maybe two and a half hours, with Summer at the wheel. It was full dark and the traffic was heavy. The holiday hangover was gone. The whole world was back at work.

'There's something heavy-duty going on,' I said. 'Why else would Carbone call Brubaker during a party? Anything less than truly amazing could have waited, surely. So it's heavy-duty, with heavy-duty people involved. Has to be. Who else could have moved twenty special unit MPs around the world all on the same day?'

'You're a major,' she said. 'So are Franz and Sanchez and all the others. Any colonel could have moved you.'

'But all the Provost Marshals were moved too. They were taken out of the way. To give us room to move. And most Provost Marshals are colonels themselves.'

'OK then, any brigadier general could have done it.'

'With forged signatures on the orders?'

'Anyone can forge a signature.'

'And hope to get away with it afterwards? No, this whole thing was put together by someone who knew he could act with impunity. Someone untouchable.'

'The Chief of Staff?'

I shook my head. 'No, the Vice-Chief, actually, I think. Right now the Vice-Chief is a guy who came up through the infantry. And we can assume he's a reasonably smart guy. They don't put dummies in that job. I think he saw the signs. He saw the Berlin Wall coming down, and he thought about it, and he realized that pretty soon everything else would be coming down, too. The whole established order.'

'And?'

'And he started to worry about some kind of a move by Armored Branch. Something dramatic. Like we said, those guys have got everything to lose. I think the Vice-Chief predicted trouble, and so he moved us all around to get the right people in the right places so we could stop it before it started. And I think he was right to be worried. I think Armored saw the danger coming and they planned to get a jump on it. They don't want integrated units bossed by infantry officers. They want things the way they were. So I think that Irwin conference was about starting something dramatic. Something bad. That's why they were so worried about the agenda getting out.'

'But change happens. Ultimately it can't be resisted.'

'Nobody ever accepts that fact,' I said. 'Nobody ever has, and nobody ever will. Go down to the Navy Yards, and I guarantee you'll find a million tons of fifty-year-old paper all stored away somewhere saying that battleships can never be replaced and that aircraft carriers are useless pieces of new-fangled junk. There'll have been admirals writing hundred-page treatises, putting their whole heart and soul into it, swearing blind that their way is the only way.'

Summer said nothing.

I smiled. 'Go back in *our* records and you'll probably find Kramer's granddad saying that tanks can never replace horses.'

'What exactly were they planning?'

I shrugged. 'We didn't see the agenda. But we can make some pretty good guesses. Discrediting of key opponents, obviously. Maximum use of dirty laundry. Almost certainly collusion with defence industries. If they could get key manufacturers to say that lightweight armoured vehicles can't be made safe, that would help. They could use public propaganda. They could tell people their sons and daughters were going to be sent to war in tin cans that a peashooter could penetrate. They could try to scare Congress. They could tell them that a C-130 airlift fleet big enough to make a difference would cost hundreds of billions of dollars.'

'That's just standard-issue bitching.'

'So maybe there's more. We don't know yet. Kramer's heart attack made the whole thing misfire. For now.'

354

'You think they'll start it up again?'

'Wouldn't you? If you had everything to lose?'

She took one hand off the wheel. Rested it in her lap. Turned slightly and looked at me. Her eyelids were moving.

'So why do you want to see the Chief of Staff?' she said. 'If you're right, then it's the Vice-Chief who's on your side. He brought you here. He's the one who's been protecting you.'

'Game of chess,' I said. 'Tug of war. Good guy, bad guy. The good guy brought me here, the bad guy sent Garber away. Harder to move Garber than me, therefore the bad guy outranks the good guy. And the only person who outranks the Vice-Chief is the Chief himself. They always rotate, we know the Vice-Chief is infantry, therefore we know the Chief is Armored. Therefore we know he has a stake.'

'The Chief of Staff is the bad guy?'

I nodded.

'So why demand to see him?'

'Because we're in the army, Summer,' I said. 'We're supposed to confront our enemies, not our friends.'

We got quieter and quieter the closer we got to D.C. I knew my strengths and my weaknesses and I was young enough and bold enough and dumb enough to consider myself any man's equal. But getting in the Chief of Staff's face was a whole other ballgame. It was a superhuman rank. There was nothing above it. There had been three of them during my years of service and I had never met any of them. Never even seen any of them, as far as I could remember. Nor had I ever seen a Vice-Chief, or an Assistant Secretary, or any other of the smooth breed who moved in those exalted circles. They were a species apart. Something made them different from the rest of us.

But they started out the same. I could have been one of them, theoretically. I had been to West Point, just like they had. But for decades the Point had been little more than a spit-shined engineering school. To get on the Staff track, you had to get sent on somewhere else afterwards. Somewhere better. You had to go to George Washington University, or Stanford or Harvard or Yale or MIT or Princeton, or even somewhere overseas like Oxford or Cambridge in England. You had to get a Rhodes scholarship. You had to get a Master's or a Ph.D. in economics or politics or international relations. You had to be a White House Fellow. That's where my career path diverged. Right after West Point. I looked at myself in the mirror and saw a guy who was better at cracking heads than cracking books. Other people looked and saw the same thing. Pigeon-holing starts on day one, in the military. So they went their way and I went mine. They went to the E-ring and the West Wing, and I went to dark dim-lit alleys in Seoul and Manila. If they came to my turf, they'd be crawling on their bellies. How I was going to do on their turf remained to be seen.

'I'm going in by myself,' I said.

'You are not,' Summer said.

'I am,' I said. 'You can call it what you like. Advice from a friend, or a direct order from a superior officer. But you're staying in the car. That's for sure. I'll handcuff you to the steering wheel if I have to.'

'We're in this together.'

'But we're allowed to be intelligent. This isn't like going to see Andrea Norton. This is as risky as it gets. No reason for both of us to go down in flames.'

'Would you stay in the car? If you were me?'

'I'd hide underneath it,' I said.

She said nothing. Just drove, as fast as ever. We hit the Beltway. Started the long clockwise quarter-circle up towards Arlington.

Pentagon security was a little tighter than usual. Maybe someone was worried about Noriega's leftover forces staging a two-thousand-mile northward penetration. But we got into the parking lot with no trouble at all. It was almost deserted. Summer drove a long slow circuit and came to rest near the main entrance. She killed the motor and jammed the parking brake on. She did it a little harder than she really needed to. I guessed she was making a point. I checked my watch. It was five minutes before midnight.

'Are we going to argue?' I said.

She shrugged.

'Good luck,' she said. 'And give him hell.'

I slid out into the cold. Closed the door behind me and stood still for a second. The bulk of the building loomed up over me in the dark. People said it was the world's largest office complex and right then I believed them. I started walking. There was a long ramp up to the doors. Then there was a guarded lobby the size of a basketball court. My special unit badge got me through that. Then I headed for the heart of the complex. There were five concentric pentagon-shaped corridors, called rings. Each one of them was protected by a separate check point. My badge was good enough to get me through B, C, and D. Nothing on earth was going to get me into the E-ring. I stopped outside the final check point and nodded to the guard. He nodded back. He was used to people waiting there.

I leaned against the wall. It was smooth-painted concrete and it felt cold and slick. The building was silent. I could hear nothing except water in pipes and the faint rush of forced-air heating and the guard's steady breathing. The floors were shined linoleum tile and they reflected the ceiling fluorescents in a long double image that ran away to a distant vanishing point.

I waited. I could see a clock in the guard's booth. It rolled past midnight. Past five after midnight. Then ten after. I waited. I started to figure my challenge had been ignored. These guys were political. Maybe they played a smarter game than I could conceive. Maybe they had more gloss and sophistication and patience. Maybe I was more than a little bit out of my league.

Or maybe the woman with the voice had thrown my message in the trash.

I waited.

Then at fifteen minutes past midnight I heard faraway heels echoing on the linoleum. Dress shoes, a staccato little rhythm that was part urgent and part relaxed. Like a man who was busy but not panicked. I couldn't see him. The sound of his heels on the floor was billowing out at me around an angled corner. It ran ahead of him down the deserted corridor like an early warning signal.

I listened to the sound and watched the spot where it told me he would appear, which was right where the fluorescent tubes

357

on the ceiling met their reflections in the floor. The sound kept on coming. Then a man stepped around the corner and walked through the flare of light. He kept on walking straight towards me, the rhythm of his heels unbroken, not slowing, not speeding up, still busy, not panicked. He came closer. He was the Chief of Staff of the Army. He was in formal evening mess dress. He was wearing a short blue jacket nipped in at the waist. Blue pants with two gold stripes. A bow tie. Gold studs and cufflinks. Elaborate knots and swirls of gold braid all over his sleeves and his shoulders. He was covered with gold insignia and badges and sashes and miniature versions of his medals. He had a full head of grey hair. He was about five-nine and one-eighty. Exactly average size for the modern army.

He got within ten feet of me and I snapped to attention and saluted. It was a pure reflex action. Like a Catholic meeting the Pope. He didn't salute back. He just looked at me. Maybe there was a protocol that forbade saluting while wearing the evening mess uniform. Or while bareheaded in the Pentagon. Or maybe he was just rude.

He put his hand out to shake.

'Very sorry I'm late,' he said. 'Good of you to wait. I was at the White House. For a state dinner with some foreign friends.'

I shook his hand.

'Let's go to my office,' he said.

He led me past the E-ring guard and we turned left into the corridor and walked a little way. Then we stepped into a suite and I met the woman with the voice. She looked more or less like I had predicted. But she sounded even better in person than she had on the phone.

'Coffee, major?' she said.

She had a fresh pot brewed. I guessed she had clicked the switch at about eleven fifty-three, so it had finished perking at midnight exactly. I guessed the Chief of Staff's suite was that sort of place. She gave me a saucer and a cup made of transparent bone china. I was afraid of crushing it like an eggshell. She was wearing civilian clothes. A dark suit so severe it was more formal than a uniform.

'This way,' the Chief of Staff said.

He led me into his office. My cup rattled on its saucer. His office was surprisingly plain. It had the same painted concrete walls as the rest of the building. The same type of steel desk I had seen in the Fort Bird pathologist's office.

'Take a seat,' he said. 'If you don't mind, we'll make this quick. It's late.'

I said nothing. He watched me.

'I got your message,' he said. 'Received and understood.'

I said nothing. He tried an ice-breaker.

'Noriega's top guys are still out there,' he said. 'Why do you suppose that is?'

'Thirty thousand square miles,' I said. 'A lot of space for people to hide in.'

'Will we get them all?'

'No question,' I said. 'Someone will sell them out.'

'You're a cynic.'

'A realist,' I said.

'What have you got to tell me, major?'

I sipped my coffee. The lights were low. I was suddenly aware that I was deep inside one of the world's most secure buildings, late at night, face to face with the nation's most powerful soldier. And I was about to make a serious accusation. And only one other person knew I was there, and maybe she was already in a cell somewhere.

'I was in Panama two weeks ago,' I said. 'Then I was transferred out.'

'Why do you think that was?'

I took a breath. 'I think the Vice-Chief wanted particular individuals on the ground in particular locations because he was worried about trouble.'

'What kind of trouble?'

'An internal coup by your old buddies in Armored Branch.'

He paused for a long moment.

'Would that have been a realistic worry?' he asked.

I nodded. 'There was a conference at Irwin scheduled for New Year's Day. I believe the agenda was certainly controversial, probably illegal, maybe treasonous.'

The Chief of Staff said nothing.

'But it misfired,' I said. 'Because General Kramer died. But there were potential problems from the fallout. So you personally intervened by moving Colonel Garber out of the 110th and replacing him with an incompetent.'

'Why would I do that?'

'So that nature would take its course and the investigation would misfire too.'

He sat still for another long moment. Then he smiled.

'Good analysis,' he said. 'The collapse of Soviet communism was bound to lead to stresses inside the U.S. military. Those stresses were bound to manifest themselves with all kinds of internal plotting and planning. The internal plotting and planning was bound to be anticipated and steps were bound to be taken to nip potential trouble in the bud. And as you say, there were bound to be tensions at the very top that led to moves and countermoves.'

I said nothing.

'Like a game of chess,' he said. 'The Vice-Chief moves, and I countermove. An inevitable conclusion, I suppose, because you were looking for a pair of senior individuals in which one outranks the other.'

I looked straight at him.

'Am I wrong?' I said.

'Only in two particulars,' he said. 'Obviously you're right in that there are huge changes coming. CIA was a little slow to spot Ivan's imminent demise, so we've had less than a year to think things through. But believe me, we've thought them through. We're in a unique situation now. We're like a heavyweight boxer who's trained for years for a shot at the world title, and then we wake up one morning and find our intended opponent has dropped dead. It's a very bewildering sensation. But we've done our homework.'

He leaned down and opened a drawer and struggled out with an enormous loose-leaf file. It was at least three inches thick. It thumped down on his desktop. It had a green jacket with a long word stencilled on it in black. He reversed it so I could read it. It said: *Transformation*.

'Your first mistake is that your focus was too close,' he said. 'You need to stand back and look at it from our perspective. From above. It's not just Armored Branch that is going to change. Everyone is going to change. Obviously we're going to move towards highly mobile integrated units. But it's a bad mistake to see them as infantry units with a few bells and whistles tacked on. They're going to be a completely new concept. They'll be something that has never existed before. Maybe we'll integrate attack helicopters too, and give the command to the guys in the sky. Maybe we'll move into electronic warfare and give the command to the guys with the computers.'

I said nothing.

He laid his hand on the file, palm down. 'My point is that nobody is going to come out of this unscathed. Yes, Armored is going to be professionally devastated. No question about that. But so is the infantry and so is the artillery, and so is transport, and so is logistics support, and so is everyone else, equally, just as much. Maybe more, for some people. Including the military police, probably. Everything is going to change, major. There will be no stone unturned.'

I said nothing.

'This is not about Armored versus the infantry,' he said. 'You need to understand that. That's a vast oversimplification. It's actually about everyone versus everyone else. There will be no winners, I'm afraid. But equally therefore, there will be no losers. You could choose to think about it that way. Everyone is in the same boat.'

He took his hand off the file.

'What's my second mistake?' I said.

'I moved you out of Panama,' he said. 'Not the Vice-Chief. He knew nothing about it. I selected twenty men personally and put them where I thought I needed them. I spread them around, because in my judgement it was fifty-fifty as to who was going to blink first. The light units, or the heavy units? It was impossible to predict. Once their commanders started thinking, they would all realize they have everything to lose. I sent you to Fort Bird, for instance, because I was a little worried about David Brubaker. He was a very proactive type.'

'But it was Armored who blinked first,' I said.

He nodded.

'Apparently,' he said. 'If you say so. It was always going to be a fifty-fifty chance. And I guess I'm a little disappointed. Those

361

were my boys. But I'm not defensive about them. I moved onward and upward. I left them behind. I'm perfectly happy to let the chips fall where they may.'

'So why did you move Garber?'

'I didn't.'

'So who did?'

'Who outranks me?'

'Nobody,' I said.

'I wish,' he said.

I said nothing.

'What does an M-16 rifle cost?' he said.

'I don't know,' I said. 'Not a lot, I guess.'

'We get them for about four hundred dollars,' he said. 'What does an Abrams M1A1 main battle tank cost?'

'About four million.'

'So think about the big defence contractors,' he said. 'Whose side are *they* on? The light units, or the heavy units?'

I didn't answer. I figured the question was rhetorical.

'Who outranks me?' he asked again.

'The Secretary of Defence,' I said.

He nodded. 'A nasty little man. A politician. Political parties take campaign contributions. And defence contractors can see the future the same as anyone else.'

I said nothing.

'A lot for you to think about,' the Chief of Staff said. He hefted the big Transformation file back into his drawer. Replaced it on his desktop with a slimmer jacket. It was marked: *Argon*.

'You know what argon is?' he asked.

'It's an inert gas,' I said. 'They use it in fire extinguishers. It spreads a layer low down over a fire and prevents it from taking hold.'

'That's why I chose the name. Operation Argon was the plan that moved you people at the end of December.'

'Why did you use Garber's signature?'

'Like you suggested in another context, I wanted to let nature take its course. MP orders signed by the Chief of Staff would have raised a lot of eyebrows. Everyone would have switched to best behaviour. Or smelled a rat and gone deeper underground.

It would have made your job harder. It would have defeated my purpose.'

'Your purpose?'

'I wanted prevention, of course. That was the main priority. But I was also curious, major. I wanted to see who would blink first.'

He handed me the file.

'You're a special unit investigator,' he said. 'By statute the 110th has extraordinary powers. You are authorized to arrest any soldier anywhere, including me, here in my office, if you so choose. So read the Argon file. I think you'll find it clears me. If you agree, go about your business elsewhere.'

He got up from behind his desk. We shook hands again. Then he walked out of the room. Left me all alone in his office, in the heart of the Pentagon, in the middle of the night.

Thirty minutes later I got back in the car with Summer. She had kept the motor off to save gas and it was cold inside.

'Well?' she said.

'One crucial error,' I said. 'The tug of war wasn't the Vice-Chief and the Chief. It was the Chief himself and the Secretary of Defence.'

'Are you sure?'

I nodded. 'I saw the file. There were memos and orders going back nine months. Different papers, different typewriters, different pens, no way to fake all that in four hours. It was the Chief of Staff's initiative all along, and he was always kosher.'

'So how did he take it?'

'Pretty well,' I said. 'Considering. But I don't think he'll feel like helping me.'

'With what?'

'With the trouble I'm in.'

'Which is?'

'Wait and see.'

She just looked at me.

'Where now?' she said.

'California,' I said.

TWENTY-TWO

THE CHEVY WAS RUNNING ON FUMES BY THE TIME WE GOT TO THE National airport. We put it in the long term lot and hiked back to the terminal. It was about a mile. There were no shuttle buses running. It was the middle of the night and the place was practically deserted. Inside the terminal we had to roust a clerk out of a back office. I gave him the last of our stolen vouchers and he booked us on the first morning flight to LAX. We were looking at a long wait.

'What's the mission?' Summer said.

'Three arrests,' I said. 'Vassell, Coomer, and Marshall.'

'Charge?'

'Serial homicide,' I said. 'Mrs Kramer, Carbone, and Brubaker.'

She stared at me. 'Can you prove it?'

I shook my head. 'I know exactly what happened. I know when, and how, and where, and why. But I can't prove a damn thing. We're going to have to rely on confessions.'

'We won't get them.'

'I've gotten them before,' I said. 'There are ways.'

She flinched.

'This is the army, Summer,' I said. 'It ain't a quilting bee.'

'Tell me about Carbone and Brubaker.'

'I need to eat,' I said. 'I'm hungry.'

'We don't have any money,' Summer said.

Most places had metal grilles down over their doors anyway. Maybe they would feed us on the plane. We carried our bags over to a seating area next to a twenty-foot window that had nothing but black night outside. The seats were long vinyl benches with fixed armrests every two feet to stop people from lying down and sleeping.

'Tell me,' she said.

'It's still a series of crazy long shots, one after the other.'

'Try me.'

'OK, start over with Mrs Kramer. Why did Marshall go to Green Valley?'

'Because it was the obvious first place to try.'

'But it wasn't. It was almost the obvious last place to try. Kramer had hardly been there in five years. His staff must have known that. They'd travelled with him many times before. Yet they made a fast decision and Marshall went straight there. Why?'

'Because Kramer had told them that's where he was going?'

'Correct,' I said. 'He told them he was with his wife to conceal the fact he was actually with Carbone. But then, why would he have to tell them anything?'

'I don't know.'

'Because there's a category of person you *have* to tell something.'

'Who?'

'Suppose you're a rich guy travelling with your mistress. You spend one night apart, you *have* to tell her something. And if you tell her you're dropping in on your wife purely to keep up appearances, she has to buy it. Maybe she doesn't like it, but she has to buy it. Because it's expected, occasionally. It's all part of the deal.'

'Kramer didn't have a mistress. He was gay.'

'He had Marshall.'

'No,' she said. 'No way.'

I nodded. 'Kramer was two-timing Marshall. Marshall was his main squeeze. They were in a relationship. Marshall wasn't an

365

intelligence officer but Kramer appointed him one anyway to keep him close. They were an item. But Kramer had a wandering eye. He met Carbone somewhere and started seeing him on the side. So on New Year's Eve Kramer told Marshall he was going to see his wife and Marshall believed him. Like the rich guy's mistress would. That's why Marshall went to Green Valley. In his heart he knew for sure Kramer had gone there. He was the one person in the world who felt he *would* know for sure. It was him who told Vassell and Coomer where Kramer was. But Kramer was lying to him. Like people do, in relationships.'

Summer was quiet for a long moment. She just stared out at the night.

'Does this affect what happened there?' she said.

'I think it does, slightly,' I said. 'I think Mrs Kramer talked to Marshall. She must have recognized him from her time on post in Germany. She probably knew all about him and her husband. Generals' wives are usually pretty smart. Maybe she even knew there was a second guy in the picture. Maybe she was pissed off and taunted Marshall about it. Like, you can't keep your man either, right? Maybe Marshall got mad and lashed out. Maybe that's why he didn't tell Vassell and Coomer right away. Because the collateral damage wasn't just about the burglary itself. It was also about an argument. That's why I said Mrs Kramer wasn't killed just for the briefcase. I think partly she was killed because she taunted a jealous guy who lost his temper.'

'This is all just guesswork.'

'Mrs Kramer is dead. That isn't a guess.'

'The rest of it is.'

'Marshall is thirty-one, never been married.'

'That doesn't prove a thing.'

'I know,' I said. 'I know. There's no proof anywhere. Proof is a scarce commodity right now.'

Summer was quiet for a beat. 'Then what happened?'

'Then Vassell and Coomer and Marshall started the hunt for the briefcase in earnest. They had an advantage over us because they knew they were looking for a man, not a woman. Marshall flew back to Germany on the second and searched

366

Kramer's office and his quarters. He found something that led to Carbone. Maybe a diary, or a letter, or a photograph. Or a name or a number in an address book. Whatever. He flew back on the third and they made a plan and they called Carbone. They blackmailed him. They set up a swap for the next night. The briefcase for the letter or the photograph or whatever it was. Carbone accepted the deal. He was happy to because he didn't want exposure and anyway he had already called Brubaker with the details of the agenda. He had nothing to lose and everything to gain. Maybe he'd been through the process before. Maybe more than once. Poor guy had been gay in the army for sixteen years. But this time it didn't work out for him. Because Marshall killed him during the exchange.'

'Marshall? Marshall wasn't even there.'

'He was,' I said. 'You figured it out yourself. You told me about it when we were leaving the post to go see Detective Clark about the crowbar. Remember? When Willard was chasing me on the phone? You made a suggestion.'

'What suggestion?'

'Marshall was in the trunk of the car, Summer. Coomer was driving, Vassell was in the passenger seat, and Marshall was in the trunk. That's how they got past the gate. Then they backed in at the far end of the O Club lot. Backed in, because Coomer popped the trunk before he got out. Marshall held the lid down low, but they still needed concealment. Then Vassell and Coomer went inside and started to build their cast-iron alibis. Meanwhile Marshall waits almost two hours in the trunk, holding the lid, until it's all quiet. Then he climbs out and he drives off. That's why the first night patrol remembers the car and the second patrol doesn't. The car was there, and then it wasn't. So Marshall picks Carbone up at some prearranged spot and they drive out to the woods together. Carbone is holding the briefcase. Marshall opens the trunk and gives Carbone an envelope or something. Carbone turns away into the moonlight to check it's what he's been promised. Even a guy as cautious as a Delta soldier would do that. His whole career is on the line. Behind him Marshall comes out with the crowbar and hits him. Not just because of the briefcase. He's going to get the briefcase anyway. The exchange is working. And Carbone can't afford to talk afterwards. Marshall hits him partly because he's mad at him. He's jealous of his time with Kramer. That's part of why he kills him. Then he retrieves the envelope and grabs the briefcase. Throws them both in the trunk. We know the rest. He's known all along what he was going to do and he's come equipped for the misdirection. Then he drives back to the post buildings and ditches the crowbar on the way. He parks the car in the original slot and gets back in the trunk. Vassell and Coomer come out of the O Club and they drive away.'

'And then what?'

'They drive, and they drive. They're excited and uptight. But they know by then what their blue-eyed boy did to Mrs Kramer. So they're also nervous and worried. They can't find anyplace they can stop where they can let a man who may or may not be bloodstained out of the trunk. First really safe place they find is the rest area an hour north. They park far away from other cars again and let Marshall out. Marshall hands over the briefcase. They resume their journey. They spend sixty seconds searching the briefcase and then they sling it out the window a mile further on.'

Summer sat quiet. She was thinking. Her lower lids were jacking upward a fraction at a time.

'It's just a theory,' she said.

'Can you explain what we know any other way?'

She thought about it. Then she shook her head.

'What about Brubaker?' she said.

A voice came out of speakers in the ceiling and told us our flight was ready to board. We picked up our bags and shuffled into line. It was still full dark outside. I counted the other passengers. Hoped there would be some spare seats, so there would be some spare breakfasts. I was very hungry. But it didn't look good. It was going to be a pretty full flight. I guessed LA's pull was pretty strong, in January, when you lived in D.C. I guessed people didn't need much of an excuse to schedule meetings out there.

'What about Brubaker?' Summer said again.

We shuffled down the aisle and found our seats. We had a window and a middle. The aisle was already occupied by a nun. She was old. I hoped her hearing was shot. I didn't want her eavesdropping. She moved and let us in. I made Summer sit next to her. I sat by the window. Buckled my belt. Kept quiet for a moment. Watched the airport scene outside. Busy guys were doing things under floodlights. Then we pushed back from the gate and started taxiing. There was no take-off queue. We were in the air within two minutes.

'I'm not sure about Brubaker,' I said. 'How did he get in the picture? Did they call him or did he call them? He knew about the agenda thirty minutes into New Year's Day. A proactive guy like that, maybe he tried a little pressure of his own. Or maybe Vassell and Coomer were just assuming a worst-case scenario. They might have figured a senior NCO like Carbone would have called his boss. So I'm not sure who called who first. Maybe they all called each other at the same time. Maybe there were mutual threats or maybe Vassell and Coomer suggested they could all work together to find a way where everybody benefits.'

'Would that be likely?'

'Who knows?' I said. 'These integrated units are going to be weird. Brubaker was certainly going to be popular, because he's already into weird warfare. So maybe Vassell and Coomer conned him into thinking they were looking for a strategic alliance. Whatever, they all set up a rendezvous for late on the fourth. Brubaker must have specified the location. He must have driven past that spot plenty of times, back and forth from Bird to his golf place. And he must have been feeling confident. He wouldn't have let Marshall sit behind him if he was worried.'

'How do you know it was Marshall behind him?'

'Protocol,' I said. 'He's a colonel talking to a general and another colonel. He'll have put Vassell in the front seat and Coomer in the back seat on the passenger's side so he could turn and see them both. Marshall could be out of sight and out of mind. He was only a major. Who needs him?'

'Did they intend to kill him? Or did it just happen?'

'They intended to, for sure. They had a plan ready. A faraway place to dump the body, heroin that Marshall picked up on his overnight in Germany, a loaded gun. So we were right, after all, but purely by accident. The same people that killed Carbone

369

drove straight out the main gate and killed Brubaker. Hardly touched the brakes.'

'Double misdirection,' Summer said. 'The heroin thing, and dumping him to the south, not the north.'

'Amateur hour,' I said. 'The Columbia medics must have spotted the lividity thing and the muffler burns immediately. Pure dumb luck for Vassell and Coomer that the medics didn't *tell* us immediately. Plus, they left Brubaker's car up north. That was serious brain fade.'

'They must have been tired. Stress, tension, all that driving. They came down from Arlington Cemetery, went back up to Smithfield, came back down to Columbia, went back up to Dulles. Maybe eighteen hours straight. No wonder they made an occasional mistake. But they'd have gotten away with it if you hadn't ignored Willard.'

I nodded. Said nothing.

'It's a very weak case,' Summer said. 'In fact it's incredibly weak. It isn't even circumstantial. It's just pure speculation.'

'Tell me about it. That's why we need confessions.'

'You need to think very carefully before you confront anyone. A case as weak as this, it could be you that goes to jail. For harassment.'

I heard activity behind me and the stewardess came into view with the breakfasts. She handed one to the nun, and one to Summer, and one to me. It was a pitiful meal. There was cold juice and a hot ham and cheese sandwich. That was all. Coffee later, I assumed. I hoped. I finished everything in about thirty seconds. Summer took about thirty-one. But the nun didn't touch her tray. She just left it right there in front of her. I nudged Summer in the ribs.

'Ask her if she's going to eat that,' I said.

'I can't,' she said.

'She's got a charitable obligation,' I said. 'It's what being a nun is all about.'

'I can't,' she said again.

'You can.'

She sighed. 'OK, in a minute.'

But she blew it. She waited too long. The nun opened the foil and started to eat the sandwich.

370

'Damn,' I said.

'Sorry,' Summer said.

I looked at her. 'What did you say?'

'I said I'm sorry.'

'No, before that. The last thing you said.'

'I said I can't just ask her.'

I shook my head. 'No, before the breakfasts came.'

'I said it's a very weak case.'

'Before that.'

I saw her rewind the tape in her head. 'I said Vassell and Coomer would have gotten away with it if you hadn't ignored Willard.'

I nodded. Thought about that fact for a minute. Then I closed my eyes.

I opened them again in Los Angeles. The plane touched down and the thump and screech of tyres on tarmac woke me up. Then the reverse thrust screamed and the brakes jerked me forward against my belt. It was first light outside. The dawn looked brown, like it often did there. A voice on the PA told us it was seven o'clock in the morning in California. We had been heading west for two solid days and each twenty-four-hour period was averaging more like twenty-eight. I had slept for a while and I didn't feel tired. But I still felt hungry.

We shuffled off the plane and walked down to the baggage claim. That was where drivers met people. I scanned around. Saw that Calvin Franz hadn't sent anyone. He had come himself instead. I was happy about that. He was a welcome sight. I felt like we were going to be in good hands.

'I've got news for you,' he said.

I introduced him to Summer. He shook her hand and took her bag and carried it. I guessed it was partly a courtly gesture and partly his way of hustling us out to his Humvee a little bit faster. It was parked there in the no-waiting zone. But the cops were staying well away from it. Camouflaged black-and-green Humvees tend to have that effect. We all piled in. I let Summer ride in front. Partly a courtly gesture of my own, and partly because I wanted to sprawl in the back. I was cramped from the plane.

'They found the Grand Marquis,' Franz said.

He gunned the big turbo-diesel and moved off the kerb. Irwin was just north of Barstow, which was about thirty miles away across the breadth of the city. I figured it would take him about an hour to get us there through the morning traffic. I saw Summer watching how he drove. Professional appraisal in her eyes. It would probably have taken her about thirty-five minutes.

'It was at Andrews,' Franz said. 'Dumped there on the fifth.'

'When Marshall was recalled to Germany,' I said.

Franz nodded at the wheel. 'That's what their gate log says. Parked by Marshall with a Transportation Corps reference on the docket. Our guys trailered it to the FBI. Faster that way. They had to call in a few favours. The Bureau worked on it all night. Reluctantly at first, but then they got interested in a big hurry. It seems to be tied in with a case they're working.'

'Brubaker,' I said.

He nodded again. 'The trunk mat had parts of Brubaker on it. Blood and brain matter, to be specific. It had been scrubbed with a paper towel, but not well enough.'

'Anything else?' I said.

'Lots of things. There was blood from a different source, just trace evidence of a transfer smear, maybe from a jacket sleeve or a knife blade.'

'Carbone's,' I said. 'From when Marshall was riding in the trunk afterwards. Did they find a knife?'

'No,' Franz said. 'But Marshall's prints are all over the inside of the trunk.'

'They would be,' I said. 'He spent several hours in there.'

'There was a single dog tag under the mat,' Franz said. 'Like the chain had been broken and one of them had slipped off and gotten away.'

'Carbone's?' I said.

'None other.'

'Amateur hour,' I said. 'Anything else?'

'Mostly normal stuff. It was an untidy car. Lots of hair and fibre, fast-food wrappers, soda cans, stuff like that.'

'Any yogurt pots?'

'One,' Franz said. 'In the trunk.'

372

'Strawberry or raspberry?'

'Strawberry. Marshall's prints on the foil tab. Seems like he had a snack.'

'He opened it,' I said. 'But he didn't eat it.'

'There was an empty envelope,' Franz said. 'Addressed to Kramer at XII Corps in Germany. Airmail, postmarked a year ago. No return address. Like a photo mailer, but it didn't have anything in it.'

I said nothing. He was looking at me in the mirror.

'Is any of this good news?' he said.

I smiled. 'It just moved us up from speculative to circumstantial.'

'A giant leap for mankind,' he said.

Then I stopped smiling and looked away. I started thinking about Carbone, and Brubaker, and Mrs Kramer. And Mrs Reacher. All over the world people were dying, in the early part of January 1990.

In the end it took us more than an hour to get to Irwin. I guessed it was true what people said about LA highways. The post looked the same as it usually did. As busy as always. It occupied a huge acreage of the Mojave desert. One or other of the armoured cavalry regiments lived there on a rotating basis and acted as the home team when other units came in to exercise. There was a real spring training atmosphere. The weather was always good, people always had fun in the sunshine playing with the big expensive toys.

'You want to take care of business right away?' Franz asked.

'Are you keeping an eye on them?'

He nodded. 'Discreetly.'

'So let's have breakfast first.'

A U.S. Army O Club was the perfect destination for people half-starved on airline food. The buffet was a mile long. Same menu as in Germany, but the orange juice and the fruit platters looked more authentic in California. I ate as much as an average rifle company and Summer ate more. Franz had already eaten. I fuelled up on as much coffee as I could take. Then I pushed back from the table. Took a deep breath.

'OK,' I said. 'Let's go do it.'

We went back to Franz's office and he made a call to his guys. They told him Marshall was already out on the range, but Vassell and Coomer were sitting tight in a VOQ rec room. Franz drove us there in his Humvee. We got out on the sidewalk. The sun was bright. The air was warm and dusty. I could smell all the prickly little desert plants that were growing as far as the eye could see.

Irwin's VOQ looked like it had been built by the same motel contractor that had gotten the XII Corps contract in Germany. There were rows of identical rooms around a sandy courtyard. On one side was a shared facility. TV rooms, table tennis, lounges. Franz led us in through a door and stepped to one side and we found Vassell and Coomer sitting knee-to-knee in a pair of leather armchairs. I realized I had seen them only once before, when they came to my office at Bird. That seemed disproportionate, considering how much time I had spent thinking about them.

They were both wearing crisp new BDUs in the revised desert camouflage, the pattern people were calling chocolate chip. They both looked just as fake as they had in their woodland greens. They still looked like Rotary Club members. Vassell was still bald and Coomer was still wearing eyeglasses.

They both looked up at me.

I took a breath.

Senior officers.

Harassment.

It could be you that goes to jail.

'General Vassell,' I said. 'And Colonel Coomer. You are under arrest on a charge of violating the Uniform Code of Military Justice in that you conspired together and with other persons to commit homicide.'

I held my breath.

But neither one of them had a reaction. Neither one of them spoke. They just gave it up. They just looked resigned. Like the other shoe had finally dropped and the inevitable had finally happened. Like they had been expecting this moment from the start. Like they had known for sure it was coming all along. I breathed out. There were supposed to be all kinds of stages in a person's reaction to bad news. Grief, anger, denial. But these

374

guys were already through all of that. That was clear. They were right there at the end of the process, butted hard up against acceptance.

I cued Summer to complete the formalities. There were all kinds of things from the Uniform Code that you had to spell out. All kinds of advisements and warnings. Summer ran through them better than I would have. Her voice was clear and her manner was professional. Neither Vassell nor Coomer responded at all. No bluster, no pleading, no angry protestations of innocence. They just nodded obediently in all the right places. Got up out of their chairs at the end without even being told.

'Handcuffs?' Summer asked me.

I nodded.

'For sure,' I said. 'And walk them to the brig. All the way. Don't put them in the truck. Let everybody see them. They're a disgrace.'

I got directions from a cavalry guy and took Franz's Humvee to go get Marshall. He was supposed to be camped out in a hut near a disused range target, observing. The disused target was described to me as an obsolete Sheridan tank. It was supposed to be fairly beat up. The hut was supposed to be in better shape and close to the old tank. I was told to stick to the established tracks to avoid unexploded ordnance and desert tortoises. If I ran over the ordnance, I would be killed. If I ran over the tortoises, I would be reprimanded by the Department of the Interior.

I left the main post alone, at nine thirty in the morning exactly. I didn't want to wait for Summer. She was all tied up with processing Vassell and Coomer. I felt like we were at the end of a long journey, and I just wanted to get it over. I took a borrowed sidearm, but it was still a bad decision.

TWENTY-THREE

IRWIN OWNED ENOUGH OF THE MOJAVE THAT IT COULD BE A plausible stand-in for the vast deserts of the Middle East or, if you ignored the heat and the sand, a plausible stand-in for the endless steppes of Eastern Europe. Which meant I was long out of sight of the main post buildings before I was even a tenth of the way to the promised Sheridan tank. The terrain was completely empty all around me. The Humvee felt tiny out there. It was January so there was no heat shimmer but the temperature was still pretty high. I applied what the unofficial Humvee manual called 2-40 air conditioning, which meant you opened two windows and drove at forty miles an hour. That set up a decent breeze. Normally forty miles an hour in a Humvee feels pretty fast because of its bulk. But out there in the vastness it felt like no speed at all.

A whole hour later I was still doing forty and I still hadn't found the hut. The range went on forever. It was one of the world's great military reservations. That was for sure. Maybe the Soviets had a bigger place somewhere, but I would have been surprised. Maybe Willard could have told me. I smiled to myself and kept on going. Drove over a ridge and saw an empty plain below me. A dot on the next horizon that might have been the hut. A dust cloud maybe five miles to the west that might have been tanks on the move.

I kept to the track. Kept going at forty. Dust was trailing behind me like a tail. The air coming in the windows was hot. The plain was maybe three miles across. The dot on the horizon became a speck and then grew larger the closer I got to it. After a mile I could make out two separate shapes. The old tank on the left, and the observation hut on the right. After another mile I could make out three separate shapes. The old tank on the left, the observation hut on the right, and Marshall's own Humvee in the middle. It was parked to the west of the building in the morning shade. It looked like the same shoot-and-scoot adaptation I had seen at XII Corps in Germany. The building was a simple raw cinder block square. Big holes for windows. No glass. The tank was an old M551, which was a lightweight armoured-aluminum piece that had started its design life as a reconnaissance vehicle. It was about a quarter of the weight of an Abrams and it was exactly the type of thing that people like Lieutenant Colonel Simon were betting the future on. It had seen service with some of our airborne divisions. It wasn't a bad machine. But this example looked pretty much decomposed. It had old plywood skirts on it designed to make it resemble some kind of previous-generation Soviet armour. There had been no point in training our guys to shoot at something our other guys were still using.

I stayed on the track and coasted to a stop about thirty yards south of the hut. Opened the door and slid out into the heat. I guessed it was less than seventy degrees but after North Carolina and Frankfurt and Paris it felt like Saudi Arabia.

I saw Marshall watching me from a hole in the cinder block.

I had only seen him once and never face to face. He had been in the Grand Marquis on New Year's Day, outside Bird's post headquarters, in the dark, behind green-tinted glass. I had pegged him then as a tall dark guy and his file had confirmed it. He looked just the same now. Tall, heavy, olive skin. Thick black hair cut short. He was in desert camouflage and he was stooping a little to see out the cinder block hole.

I stood next to my Humvee. He watched me, silently.

'Marshall?' I called.

He didn't respond.

'You alone in there?'

No reply.

'Military police,' I called, louder. 'All personnel, exit that structure immediately.'

Nobody responded. Nobody came out. I could still see Marshall through the hole. He could still see me. I guessed he was alone. If he had had a partner in there, the partner would have come out. Nobody else had a reason to be afraid of me.

'Marshall?' I called again.

He ducked out of sight. Just melted backward into the shadows inside. I took the borrowed gun out of my pocket. It was a new-issue Beretta M9. I heard an old training mantra in my head: *Never trust a weapon that you haven't personally test-fired.* I chambered a round. The sound was loud in the desert stillness. I saw the dust cloud in the west. It was maybe a little larger and a little closer than before. I clicked the Beretta's safety to *fire*.

'Marshall?' I called.

He didn't reply. But I heard a low voice very faintly and then a brief scratchy burst of radio static. There was no antenna on the roof of the hut. He must have had a portable field radio in there with him.

'Who are you going to call, Marshall?' I said to myself. 'The cavalry?'

Then I thought: *the cavalry. An armoured cavalry regiment.* I turned and looked west at the dust cloud. Suddenly realized how things stood. I was all alone in the middle of nowhere with a proven killer. He was in a hut, I was out in the open. My partner was a ninety-pound woman about fifty miles away. His buddies were riding around in seventy-ton tanks just below the visible horizon.

I got off the track fast. Worked around to the east of the hut. I saw Marshall again. He moved from one hole to another and watched me. Just gazed out at me.

'Step out of the hut, major,' I called.

There was silence for a long moment. Then he called back to me.

'I'm not going to do that,' he said.

'Step out, major,' I called. 'You know why I'm here.'

He ducked back into the darkness.

'As of right now you're resisting arrest,' I called.

No reply. No sound at all. I moved on. Circled the hut. Worked around to the north. There were no holes in the north wall. Just an iron door. It was closed. I figured it wouldn't have a lock. What was there to steal? I could walk right up to it and pull it open. *Was he armed?* I guessed standard procedure would make him unarmed. What kind of deadly enemy could a gunnery observer expect to face? But I guessed a smart guy in Marshall's situation would be taking all kinds of precautions.

There was beaten earth outside the iron door where people had made informal tracks to places they had parked. What an architect would call *pathways of desire*. None of them led north towards me. They all led roughly west or east. Shade in the morning, shade in the afternoon. So I stayed on open ground and got within ten yards of the door. Then I stopped. A good position, on the face of it. Maybe better than going all the way in and risking a surprise. I could wait there all day. No problem. It was January. The noon sun wasn't going to hurt me. I could wait until Marshall gave up. Or starved to death. I had eaten more recently than he had. That was for sure. And if he decided to come out shooting, I could shoot him first. No problem with that either.

The problem was with the holes in the cinder block. In the other three walls. They had looked the size of regular windows. Big enough for a man to climb through. Even a big man like Marshall. He could climb through the west wall and get to his Humvee. Or he could climb through the south wall and get to mine. Military vehicles don't have ignition keys. They have big red starter buttons precisely so that guys can throw themselves inside in a panic and get themselves the hell out of Dodge. And I couldn't watch the west wall and the south wall simultaneously. Not from any kind of a position that offered concealment.

Did I need concealment?

Was he armed?

I had an idea about how to find out.

Never trust a weapon that you haven't personally test-fired.

I aimed at the centre of the iron door and pulled the trigger. The Beretta worked. It worked just fine. It flashed and boomed and kicked and there was an enormous *clang* and the round left a small bright pit in the metal ten yards away.

I let the echoes die.

'Marshall?' I called. 'You're resisting arrest. So I'm going to come around and I'm going to start firing through the window apertures. Either the rounds will kill you or the ricochets will wound you. You want me to stop at any time, you just come on out with your hands on your head.'

I heard a burst of radio static again. Inside the hut.

I moved to the west. Kept low and fast. If he was armed he was going to shoot, but he was going to miss. Give me a choice of who to get shot at by and I'll pick a pointy-headed strategic planner any day of the week. On the other hand, he hadn't been completely inept with Carbone or Brubaker. So I widened my radius a little to give myself a chance of getting behind his Humvee. Or behind the old Sheridan tank.

Halfway there I paused and fired. It was no kind of a good system to make a promise and then not keep it. But I aimed high on the inside face of the window reveal so that if the round hit him it would have had to come off two walls and the ceiling first. Most of the energy would be expended and it wouldn't hurt him much. The nine-millimetre Parabellum was a decent round, but it didn't have magical properties.

I got behind the hood of his Humvee. Rested my gun hand on the warm metal. The camouflage paint was rough. It felt like it had sand mixed in with it. I aimed up at the hut. I was down in a slight dip now and it was above me. I fired again, high on the other side of the window reveal.

'Marshall?' I called. 'You want suicide by cop, that's OK with me.'

No reply. I was three rounds down. Twelve rounds to go. A smart guy might just lie on the floor and let me blast away. All my trajectories would be upward in relation to him because I was down in a dip. And because of the window sills. I could try banking rounds off the ceiling and the far wall but ricochets didn't necessarily work like billiards. They weren't predictable and they weren't reliable.

I saw movement at the window.

He was armed.

And not with a handgun, either. I saw a big wide shotgun barrel come out at me. Black. It looked about the size of a rainwater pipe. I figured it for an Ithaca Mag-10. A handsome piece. If you wanted a shotgun, the Mag-10 was about as good as it got. It was nicknamed *The Roadblocker* because it was effective against soft-skinned vehicles. I ducked backward and put the Humvee's engine block between myself and the hut. Made myself as small as I could get.

Then I heard the radio again. Inside the hut. It was a very short transmission and faint and full of static and I couldn't make out any actual words but the rhythm and the inflection of the burst came across like a three-syllable question. Maybe *say again?* It was what you heard after you issued a confusing order.

I heard a repeat transmission. *Say again?* Then I heard Marshall's voice. Barely audible. Four syllables. Fluffy consonants at the beginning. *Affirmative*, maybe.

Who was he talking to and what was he ordering?

'Give it up, Marshall,' I called. 'How much shit do you want to be in?'

It was what a hostage negotiator would have called a pressure question. It was supposed to have a negative psychological effect. But it made no legal sense. If he shot me he would go to Leavenworth for four hundred years. If he didn't, he would go for three hundred years. No practical difference. A rational man would ignore it.

He ignored it. He was plenty rational. He ignored it and he fired the big Ithaca instead, which is exactly what I would have done.

In theory it was the moment I was waiting for. Firing a long gun that requires a physical input before it can be fired again leaves the shooter vulnerable after pulling the trigger. I should have come out from cover immediately and returned lethal aimed fire. But the sheer stunning impact of the ten-gauge cartridge slowed me down by half a second. I wasn't hit. The spray pattern was low and tight and it caught the Humvee's front wheel. I felt the tyre blow and the truck dropped its front corner ten inches into the sand. There was smoke and dust everywhere. When I looked half a second later the shotgun barrel was gone. I fired up at the top of the window reveal. I wanted a tight ricochet that came down vertically and drilled through his head.

I didn't get one. He called out to me.

'I'm reloading,' he said.

I paused. He probably wasn't. A Mag-10 holds three rounds. He had only fired one. He probably wanted me to come out of cover and charge his position. Whereupon he would rear up and smile and blow me away. I stayed where I was. I didn't have the luxury of reloading. I was four down, eleven to go.

I heard the radio again. Brief static, four syllables, a descending scale. *Acknowledged, out.* Fast and casual, like a piano trill.

Marshall fired again. I saw the black barrel move in the window and there was another loud explosion and the far back corner of the Humvee dropped ten inches. Just dumped itself straight down. I flattened in the dirt for a second and squinted underneath. *He was shooting the tyres out.* A Humvee can run on flat tyres. That was part of the design demand. But it can't run on no tyres. And a ten-gauge shotgun doesn't just flatten a tyre. It *removes* a tyre. It tears the rubber right off the rim and leaves little tiny shreds of it all over a twenty-foot radius.

He was disabling his own Humvee and he was going to make a break for mine.

I got up on my knees again and crouched behind the hood. Now I was actually safer than I had been before. The big vehicle was canted right down on the passenger side so that there was a solid angled wedge of metal between me and him all the way to the desert floor. I pressed up against the front fender. Lined myself up with the engine block. Put six hundred pounds of cast iron between me and the gun. I could smell diesel. A fuel line had been hit. It was leaking fast. No tyres, nothing in the tank. And no percentage in soaking my shirt with diesel and lighting it and tossing it in the hut. I had no matches. And diesel isn't flammable the way gasoline is. It's just a greasy liquid. It needs to be vaporized and put under intense pressure before it explodes. That was why the Humvee was designed with a diesel engine. Safety.

382

'*Now* I'm reloading,' Marshall called.

I waited. *Was he or wasn't he?* He probably was. But I didn't care. I wasn't going to rush him. I had a better idea. I crawled along the Humvee's tilted flank and stopped at the rear bumper. Looked past it and scoped out my view. To the south I could see my own Humvee. To the north I could see almost all the way to the hut. There was an open space twenty-five yards wide in between. Like no-man's-land. Marshall would have to traverse twenty-five continuous yards of open ground to get from the hut to my Humvee. Right through my field of fire. He would probably run backward, shooting as he went. But his weapon packed only three rounds fully loaded. If he spaced them out, he would be firing once every eight yards. If he loosed them all off at the start full blast and unaimed, he would be naked all the rest of the way to the truck. Either option, he was going down. That was for damn sure. I had eleven Parabellums and an accurate pistol and a steel bumper to rest my wrist on.

I smiled.

I waited.

Then the Sheridan came apart behind me.

I heard a hum in the air like a shell the size of a Volkswagen was incoming and I turned in time to see the old tank smashed to pieces like it had been hit by a train. It jumped a whole foot off the ground and the fake plywood skirts splintered and spun away and the turret came off its ring and turned over slowly in the air and thumped down in the sand ten feet from me.

There was no explosion. Just a huge bass metal-to-metal thump. And then nothing but eerie silence.

I turned back. Watched the open ground. Marshall was still in the hut. Then a shadow passed over my head and I saw a shell in the air with that weird slow-motion optical illusion you get with long-range artillery. It flew right over me in a perfect arc and hit the desert floor fifty yards further on. It kicked up a huge plume of dust and sand and buried itself deep.

No explosion.

They were firing practice rounds at me.

I heard the whine of turbines in the far distance. The faint clatter of drive sprockets and idlers and track-return rollers. The muffled roar of engines as tanks raced towards me. I heard a faint *boom* as a big gun fired. Then nothing. Then a hum in the air. Then more smashing and tearing of metal as the Sheridan was hit again. No explosion. A practice round is the same as a regular shell, the same size, the same weight, with a full load of propellant, but no explosive in the nose cone. It's just a lump of dumb metal. Like a handgun bullet, except it's five inches wide and more than a foot long.

Marshall had switched their training target.

That was what all the radio chatter had been about. Marshall had ordered them away from whatever they were doing five miles to the west. He had ordered them to move in towards him and put rounds down on his own position. They had been incredulous. *Say again? Say again?* Marshall had replied: *Affirmative.*

He had switched their training target to cover his escape.

How many tanks were out there? How long did I have? If twenty tank guns quartered the area they would hit a man-sized target before very long. Within minutes. That was clear. The law of averages absolutely guaranteed it. And to be hit by a bullet five inches wide and more than a foot long would be no fun at all. A near miss would be just as bad. A fifty-pound chunk of metal hitting the Humvee I was hiding behind would shred it to supersonic pieces as small and sharp as K-bar blades. Even without an explosive charge the sheer kinetic energy alone would make that happen. It would be like a grenade going off right next to me.

I heard a ragged *boom, boom* north and west of me. Low, dull sounds. Two guns firing in a tight sequence. Closer than they had been before. The air hissed. One shell went long but the other came in low on a flat trajectory and hit the Sheridan square in the side. It went in and it came out, straight through the aluminum hull like a .38 through a tin can. If Lieutenant Colonel Simon had been there to see it he might have changed his mind about the future.

More guns fired. One after the other. A ragged salvo. There were no explosions. But the brutal calamitous physical noise was maybe worse. It was some kind of primeval clamour. The air hissed. There was deep brainless thudding as dead shells hit the earth. There were shuddering bass peals of metal against metal, like ancient giants clashing with swords. Huge chunks of wreckage from the Sheridan cartwheeled away and clanged and shivered and skidded on the sand. There was dust and dirt everywhere in the air. I was choking on it. Marshall was still in the hut. I stayed down in a low crouch and kept my Beretta aimed at the open ground. Waited. Forced my hand to keep still. Stared at the empty space. Just stared at it, desperately. I didn't understand. Marshall had to know he couldn't wait much longer. He had called down a hailstorm of metal. *We were being attacked by Abrams tanks.* My Humvee was going to get hit any second. His only avenue of escape was going to vanish right before his eyes. It was going to flip up in the air and come down on its roof. The law of averages guaranteed it. Or else the hut would get hit and collapse all around him first. He would be buried in the rubble. One thing or the other would happen. For sure. It had to. *So why the hell was he waiting?*

Then I got up on my knees and stared at the hut.

Because I knew why.

Suicide.

I had offered him suicide by cop but he had already chosen suicide by tank. He had seen me coming and he had guessed who I was. Like Vassell and Coomer he had been sitting numb day after day just waiting for the other shoe to drop. And finally there it was, at last, the other shoe, coming straight at him through the desert dust in a Humvee. He had thought and he had decided and he had gotten on the radio.

He was going down, and he was taking me with him.

I could hear the tanks pretty close now. Not more than eight or nine hundred yards. I could hear the squeal and clatter of their tracks. They were still moving fast. They would be fanning out, like it said in the field manual. They would be pitching and rolling. They would be kicking up rooster tails of dust. They would be forming a loose mobile semicircle with their big guns pointing inward like the spokes of a wheel.

I crawled back and looked at my Humvee. But if I went for it Marshall would shoot me down from the safety of the hut. No question about that. The twenty-five yards of open ground must have looked as good to him as they looked to me.

I waited.

385

I heard the *boom* of a gun and the *whump* of a shell and I stood up and ran the other way. I heard another *boom* and another *whump* and the first shell slammed into the Sheridan and bowled it all the way over and then the second hit Marshall's Humvee and demolished it completely. I threw myself behind the north corner of the hut and rolled tight against the base of the wall and listened to shards of metal rattling against the cinder blocks and the screeching as the old Sheridan's armour finally came apart.

The tanks were very close now. I could hear their engine notes rising and falling as they breasted rises and crashed through dips. I could hear their tracks slapping against their skirts. I could hear their hydraulics whining as they traversed their guns.

I got to my feet. Stood up straight. Wiped dust out of my eyes. Stepped over to the iron door. Saw the bright crater my gun had made. I knew Marshall had to be either standing in the south window looking for me running or standing in the west window looking for me dead behind the wreckage. I knew he was tall and I knew he was right-handed. I fixed an abstract target in my mind. Moved my left hand and put it on the door knob. Waited.

The next shells were fired so close that I heard *boom whump boom whump* with no pause in between. I pulled the door and stepped inside. Marshall was right there in front of me. He was facing away, looking south, framed by the brightness of the window. I aimed at his right shoulder blade and pulled the trigger and a shell took the roof off the hut. The room was instantly full of dust and I was hit by falling beams and corrugated sheets and stung by fragments of flying concrete. I went down on my knees. Then I collapsed on my front. I was pinned. I couldn't see Marshall. I heaved myself back up on my knees and flailed my arms to fight off the debris. The dust was sucking upward in a ragged spiral and I could see bright blue sky above me. I could hear tank tracks all around me. Then I heard another *boom whump* and the front corner of the hut blew away. It was there, and then it wasn't. It was solid, and then it was a spray of grey dust coming towards me at the speed of sound. A gale of dusty air whipped after it and knocked me off my feet again.

I struggled back up and crawled forward. Just butted my way through fallen beams and lumps of broken concrete. I threw twisted sheets of roofing iron aside. I was like a plough. Like a bulldozer, grinding forward, piling debris to the left and right of me. There was too much dust to see anything except the sunlight. It was right there in front of me. Brightness ahead, darkness behind. I kept on going.

I found the Mag-10. Its barrel was crushed. I threw it aside and ploughed on. Found Marshall on the floor. He wasn't moving. I pulled stuff off him and grabbed his collar and hauled him up into a sitting position. Dragged him forward until I came to the front wall. I put my back against it and slid upright until I felt the window aperture. I was choking and spitting dust. It was in my eyes. I dragged him upward and hauled him over the window sill and dumped him out. Then I fell out after him. Got up on my hands and knees and grabbed his collar again and dragged him away. Outside the hut the dust was clearing. I could see tanks, maybe three hundred yards to the left and right of us. Lots of tanks. Hot metal in the harsh sunlight. They had outflanked us. They were holding in a perfect circle, engines idling, guns flat, aiming over open sights. I heard *boom whump* again and saw bright muzzle flash from one of them and saw it pitch backward from the recoil. I saw its shell pass right over us. I saw it in the air. Heard it break the sound barrier with a crack like a neck snapping. Heard it smash into the remains of the hut. Felt more dust and concrete shower down on my back. I went down on my face and lay still, trapped in no man's land.

Then another tank fired. I saw it jerk backward from the recoil. Seventy tons, smashed back so hard its front end came right up in the air. Its shell screamed overhead. I started moving again. I dragged Marshall behind me and crawled through the dirt like I was swimming. I had no idea what he had said on the radio. No idea what his orders had been. He had to have told them he was moving out. Maybe he had told them to disregard the Humvees. Maybe that explained their *say again?* Maybe he had told them the Humvees were fair game. Maybe that was what they had found hard to believe.

But I knew they wouldn't stop firing now. Because they

couldn't see us. Dust was drifting like smoke and the view out of a buttoned-up Abrams wasn't great to begin with. It was like looking lengthwise through a grocery bag with a small square hole cut out of the bottom. I paused and batted dust out of the way and coughed and peered forward. We were close to my Humvee.

It looked straight and level.

It looked intact.

So far.

I stood up and raced the last ten feet and hauled Marshall around to the passenger side and opened the door and crammed him into the front. Then I climbed right in over him and dumped myself into the driver's seat. Hit that big red button and fired it up. Shoved it into gear and stamped on the gas so hard the acceleration slammed the door shut. Then I turned the lights full on and put my foot to the floor and charged. Summer would have been proud of me. I drove straight for the line of tanks. Two hundred yards. One hundred yards. I picked my spot and aimed carefully and burst through the gap between two main battle tanks doing more than eighty miles an hour.

I slowed down after a mile. After another mile, I stopped. Marshall was alive. But he was unconscious and he was bleeding all over the place. My aim had been good. His shoulder had a big messy nine-millimetre broken-bone through-and-through gunshot wound in it and he had plenty of other cuts from the hut's collapse. His blood was all mixed with cement dust like a maroon paste. I got him arranged on the seat and strapped him in tight with the harness. Then I broke out the first aid kit and put pressure bandages on both sides of his shoulder and jabbed him with morphine. I wrote *M* on his forehead with a grease pencil like you were supposed to in the field. That way the medics wouldn't overdose him when he got to the hospital.

Then I walked around in the fresh air for a spell. Just walked up and down the track, aimlessly. I coughed and spat and dusted myself down as well as I could. I was bruised and sore from being pelted with concrete fragments. Two miles behind me I could still hear tanks firing. I guessed they were waiting for a cease-fire order. I guessed they were likely to run out of rounds before they got one.

I kept the 2-40 A/C going all the way back. Halfway there, Marshall woke up. I saw his chin come up off his chest. Saw him glance ahead, and then at me to his left. He was full of morphine and his right arm was useless, but I was still cautious. If he grabbed the wheel with his left he might force us off the track. He might run us over some unexploded debris. Or a tortoise. So I took my right hand off the wheel and reverse-punched him square between the eyes. It was a good solid smack. It put him right back to sleep. *Manual anaesthetic*. He stayed out all the way back to the post.

I drove him straight to the base hospital. Called Franz from the nurses' station and ordered up a guard squad. I waited for them to arrive and promised rank and medals for anyone who helped ensure Marshall saw the inside of a courtroom. I told them to read him his rights as soon as he woke up. And I told them to mount a suicide watch. Then I left them to it and drove back to Franz's office. My BDUs were torn up and stiff with dust and I guessed my face and hands and hair didn't look any better because Franz laughed as soon as he saw me.

'I guess it's tough taking desk jockeys down,' he said.

'Where's Summer?' I said.

'Telexing JAG Corps,' he said. 'Talking to people on the phone.'

'I lost your Beretta,' I said.

'Where?'

'Somewhere it's going to take a bunch of archaeologists a hundred years to find.'

'Is my Humvee OK?'

'Better than Marshall's,' I said.

I found my bag and an empty VOQ room and took a long hot shower. Then I transferred all my pocket stuff to a new set of BDUs and trashed the damaged ones. I figured any quartermaster would agree they were deteriorated beyond reasonable future use. I sat on the bed for a while. Just breathed in, breathed out. Then I walked back to Franz's place. I found Summer there. She was looking radiant. She was holding a new file folder that already had a lot of pages in it.

'We're on track,' she said. 'JAG Corps says the arrests were righteous.'

'Did you lay out the case?'

'They say they'll need confessions.'

I said nothing.

'We have to meet with the prosecutors tomorrow,' she said. 'In D.C.'

'You'll have to do it,' I said. 'I won't be around.'

'Why not?'

I didn't answer.

'You OK?'

'Are Vassell and Coomer talking?'

She shook her head. 'They haven't said a word. JAG Corps is flying them to Washington tonight. They've been assigned lawyers.'

'There's something wrong,' I said.

'What?'

'It's been way too easy.'

I thought for a moment.

'We need to get back to Bird,' I said. 'Right now.'

Franz lent me fifty bucks and gave me two blank travel vouchers. I signed them and Leon Garber countersigned them even though he was thousands of miles away in Korea. Then Franz drove us back to LAX. He used a staff car because his Humvee was full of Marshall's blood. Traffic was light and it was a fast trip. We went in and I swapped the vouchers for seats on the first flight to D.C. I checked my bag. I didn't want to carry it this time. We took off at three o'clock in the afternoon. We had been in California eight hours exactly.

TWENTY-FOUR

FLYING EAST THE TIME ZONES STOLE BACK THE HOURS WE HAD gained going west. It was eleven o'clock at night at Washington National when we landed. I reclaimed my duffel from the carousel and we took the shuttle to the long term lot. The Chevy was waiting there right where we left it. I used some of Franz's fifty bucks and we filled the tank. Then Summer drove us back to Bird. She went as fast as always and took the same old route, down I-95, past all our familiar reference points. The State Police barracks, the place where the briefcase was found, the rest area, the cloverleaf, the motel, the lounge bar. We were timed in through Fort Bird's main gate at three in the morning. The post was quiet. There was a night mist clamped down all over it. Nothing was stirring.

'Where to?' Summer said.

'The Delta station,' I said.

She drove us around to the old prison gates and the sentry let us in. We parked in their main lot. I could see Trifonov's red Corvette in the darkness. It was all on its own, near the wall with the water hose. It looked very clean.

'Why are we here?' Summer said.

'We had a very weak case,' I said. 'You made that point

yourself. And you were right. It was very weak. The forensics with the staff car helped, but we never really got beyond purely circumstantial stuff. We can't actually put Vassell and Coomer and Marshall at any of the scenes. Not definitively. We can't prove Marshall ever actually touched the crowbar. We can't prove he didn't actually eat the yogurt for a snack. And we certainly can't prove that Vassell and Coomer ever actually ordered him to do anything. If push came to shove, they could claim he was an out-of-control lone wolf.'

'So?'

'We walked in and confronted two senior officers who were doubly insulated from a very weak and circumstantial case. What should have happened?'

'They should have fought it.'

I nodded. 'They should have scoffed at it. They should have laughed it off. They should have gotten offended. They should have threatened and blustered. They should have thrown us out. But they didn't do any of that. They just sat still for it. And their silence kind of pled themselves guilty. That was my impression. That's how I took it.'

'Me too,' Summer said. 'Certainly.'

'So why didn't they fight?'

She was quiet for a spell.

'Guilty consciences?' she said.

I shook my head. 'Spare me.'

She was quiet a moment longer.

'Shit,' she said. 'Maybe they're just waiting. Maybe they're going to collapse the case in full view of everybody. In D.C., tomorrow, when they've got their lawyers there. To ruin our careers. To put us in our place. Maybe it's a vindictive thing.'

I shook my head again. 'What did I charge them with?'

'Conspiracy to commit homicide.'

I nodded. 'I think they misunderstood me.'

'It was plain English.'

'They understood the words. But not the context. I was talking about one thing, and they thought I was talking about a different thing. They thought I was talking about something else entirely. They pled guilty to the wrong conspiracy,

Summer. They pled guilty to something they *know* can be proved beyond a reasonable doubt.'

She said nothing.

'The agenda,' I said. 'It's still out there. They never got it back. Carbone double-crossed them. They opened the briefcase up there on I-95, and the agenda wasn't in it. It was already gone.'

'So where is it?'

'I'll show you where,' I said. 'That's why we came back. So you can use it tomorrow. Up in D.C. Use it to leverage all the other stuff. The things we're weak on.'

We slid out of the car into the cold. Walked across the lot to the cell block door. Stepped inside. I could hear the sounds of sleeping men. I could taste the sour dormitory air. We walked through corridors and turned corners in the dark until we came to Carbone's billet. It was empty and undisturbed. We stepped in and I snapped the light on. Stepped over to the bed. Reached up to the shelf. Ran my fingers along the spines of the books. Pulled out the tall thin Rolling Stones souvenir. Held it. Shook it.

A four-page conference agenda fell out on the bed.

We stared at it.

'Brubaker told him to hide it,' I said.

I picked it up and handed it to Summer. Turned the light back off and stepped out into the corridor. Came face to face with the young Delta sergeant with the beard and the tan. He was in skivvies and a T-shirt. He was barefoot. He had been drinking beer about four hours ago, according to the way he smelled.

'Well, well,' he said. 'Look who we have here.'

I said nothing.

'You woke me up talking,' he said. 'And flashing lights on and off.'

I said nothing.

He glanced into Carbone's cell. 'Revisiting the scene of the crime?'

'This isn't where he died.'

'You know what I mean.'

Then he smiled and I saw his hands bunch into fists. I

slammed him back against the wall with my left forearm. His skull hit the concrete and his eyes glazed for a second. I kept my arm hard and level across his chest. Got the point of my elbow on his right bicep and spread my open fingers across his left bicep. Pinned him to the wall. Leaned on him with all my weight. Kept on leaning until he was having trouble breathing.

'Do me a favour,' I said. 'Read the newspaper every day this week.'

Then I fumbled in my jacket pocket with my free hand and found the bullet. The one he had delivered. The one with my name on it. I held it with my finger and thumb right down at the base. It shone gold in the faint night light.

'Watch this,' I said.

I showed him the bullet. Then I shoved it up his nose.

My sergeant was at her desk. The one with the baby son. She had coffee going. I poured two mugs and carried them into my office. Summer carried the agenda, like a trophy. She took the staple out of the paper and laid the four sheets side by side on my desk.

They were original typewritten pages. Not carbons, not faxes, not photocopies. That was clear. There were handwritten notes and pencilled amendments between the lines and in the margins. There were three different scripts. Mostly Kramer's, I guessed, but Vassell's and Coomer's as well, almost certainly. It had been a round-robin first draft. That was clear, too. It had been the subject of a lot of thought and scrutiny.

The first sheet was an analysis of the problems that Armored was facing. The integrated units, the loss of prestige. The possibility of ceding command to others. It was gloomy, but it was conventional. And it was accurate, according to the Chief of Staff.

The second page and the third page contained more or less what I had predicted to Summer. Proposed attempts to discredit key opponents, with maximum use of dirty laundry. Some of the margin notes hinted at some of the dirt, and a lot of it sounded pretty interesting. I wondered how they had gathered information like that. And I wondered if anyone in JAG Corps would follow up on it. Someone probably would.

Investigations were like that. They led off in all kinds of random directions.

There were ideas for public relations campaigns. Most of them were pretty limp. These guys hadn't mixed with the public since they took the bus up the Hudson to start their plebe year at the Point. Then there were references to the big defence contractors. There were ideas for political initiatives inside the Department of the Army and in Congress. Some of the political ideas looped right back and tied in with the defence contractor references. There were hints of some pretty sophisticated relationships there. Clearly money flowed one way and favours flowed the other way. The Secretary of Defence was mentioned by name. His help was taken pretty much for granted. On one line his name was actually underlined and a note in the margin read: *bought and paid for.* Altogether the first three pages were full of the kind of stuff you would expect from arrogant professionals heavily invested in the status quo. It was murky and sordid and desperate, for sure. But it wasn't anything that would send you to jail.

That stuff came on the fourth page.

The fourth page had a curious heading: *T.E.P., The Extra Mile.* Underneath that was a typed quotation from *The Art of War* by Sun Tzu: *To fail to take the battle to the enemy when your back is to the wall is to perish.* Alongside that in the margin was a pencilled addendum in what I guessed was Vassell's handwriting: *While coolness in disaster is the supreme proof of a commander's courage, energy in pursuit is the surest test of his strength of will. Wavell.*

'Who's Wavell?' Summer said.

'An old British field marshal,' I said. 'World War Two. Then he was viceroy of India. He was blind in one eye from World War One.'

Underneath the Wavell quote was another pencilled note, in a different hand. Coomer's, probably. It said: *Volunteers? Me? Marshall?* Those three words were ringed and connected with a long looping pencil line back to the heading: *T.E.P., The Extra Mile.*

'What's that about?' Summer said.

'Read on,' I said.

395

Below the Sun Tzu quote was a typed list of eighteen names. I knew most of them. There were key battalion commanders from prestige infantry divisions like the 82nd and the 101st, and significant staffers from the Pentagon, and some other people. There was an interesting mix of ages and ranks. There were no really junior officers, but the list wasn't confined to senior people. Not by any means. There were some rising stars in there. Some obvious choices, some off-beat mavericks. A few of the names meant nothing to me. They belonged to people I had never heard of. There was a guy listed called Abelson, for instance. I didn't know who Abelson was. He had a pencilled check mark against his name. Nobody else did.

'What's the check mark for?' Summer said.

I dialled my sergeant outside at her desk.

'Ever heard of a guy called Abelson?' I asked her.

'No,' she said.

'Find out about him,' I said. 'He's probably a light colonel or better.'

I went back to the list. It was short, but it was easy enough to interpret. It was a list of eighteen key bones in a massive evolving skeleton. Or eighteen key nerves in a complex neurological system. Remove them, and a certain part of the army would be somewhat handicapped. Today, for sure. But more importantly it would be handicapped tomorrow, too. Because of the rising stars. Because of the stunted evolution. And from what I knew about the people whose names I recognized, the part of the army that would get hurt was exclusively the part with the light units in it. More specifically, those light units that looked ahead towards the twenty-first century rather than those that looked backward at the nineteenth. Eighteen people was not a large number, in a million-man army. But it was a superbly chosen sample. There had been some acute analysis going on. Some precision targeting. The movers and the shakers, the thinkers and the planners. The bright stars. If you wanted a list of eighteen people whose presence or absence would make a difference to the future, this was it, all typed and tabulated.

My phone rang. I hit speaker and we heard my sergeant's voice.

'Abelson was the Apache helicopter guy,' she said. 'You know, the attack helicopters? The gunships? Always beating that particular drum?'

'Was?' I said.

'He died the day before New Year's Eve. Car versus pedestrian in Heidelberg, Germany. Hit and run.'

I clicked the phone off.

'Swan mentioned that,' I said. 'In passing. Now that I think about it.'

'The check mark,' Summer said.

I nodded. 'One down, seventeen to go.'

'What does T.E.P. mean?'

'It's old CIA jargon,' I said. 'It means terminate with extreme prejudice.'

She said nothing.

'Assassinate, in other words,' I said.

We sat quiet for a long, long time. I looked at the ridiculous quotations again. *The enemy. When your back is to the wall. The supreme proof of a commander's courage. The surest test of his strength of will.* I tried to imagine what kind of crazy isolated ego-driven fever could drive people to add grandiose quotations like those to a list of men they wanted to kill so they could keep their jobs and their prestige. I couldn't even begin to figure it out. So I just gave it up and butted the four typewritten sheets back together and threaded the staple back through the original holes. I took an envelope from my drawer and slipped them inside it.

'It's been out in the world since the first of the year,' I said. 'And they knew it was gone for good on the fourth. It wasn't in the briefcase, and it wasn't on Brubaker's body. That's why they were resigned. They gave up on it a week ago. They killed three people looking for it, but they never found it. So they were just sitting there, knowing for sure sooner or later it was going to come back and bite them in the ass.'

I slid the envelope across the desk.

'Use it,' I said. 'Use it in D.C. Use it to nail their hides to the damn wall.'

*   *   *

By then it was already four o'clock in the morning and Summer left for the Pentagon immediately. I went to bed and got four hours' sleep. Woke myself up at eight. I had one thing left to do, and I knew for sure there was one thing left to be done to me.

TWENTY-FIVE

I GOT TO MY OFFICE AT NINE O'CLOCK IN THE MORNING. THE WOMAN with the baby son was gone by then. The Louisiana corporal had taken her place.

'JAG Corps is here for you,' he said. He jerked his thumb at my inner door. 'I let them go straight in.'

I nodded. Looked around for coffee. There wasn't any. *Bad start.* I opened my door and stepped inside. Found two guys in there. One of them was in a visitor chair. One of them was at my desk. Both of them were in Class As. Both of them had JAG Corps badges on their lapels. A small gold wreath, crossed with a sabre and an arrow. The guy in the visitor chair was a captain. The guy at my desk was a lieutenant colonel.

'Where do I sit?' I said.

'Anywhere you like,' the colonel said.

I said nothing.

'I saw the telexes from Irwin,' he said. 'You have my sincere congratulations, major. You did an outstanding job.'

I said nothing.

'And I heard about Kramer's agenda,' he said. 'I just got a call from the Chief of Staff's office. That's an even better result. It justifies Operation Argon all by itself.'

'You're not here to discuss the case,' I said.

'No,' he said. 'We're not. That discussion is happening at the Pentagon, with your lieutenant.'

I took a spare visitor chair and put it against the wall, under the map. I sat down on it. Leaned back. Put my hand up over my head and played with the push pins. The colonel leaned forward and looked at me. He waited, like he wanted me to speak first.

'You planning on enjoying this?' I asked him.

'It's my job,' he said.

'You like your job?'

'Not all the time,' he said.

I said nothing.

'This case was like a wave on the beach,' he said. 'Like a big old roller that washes in and races up the sand, and pauses, and then washes back out and recedes, leaving nothing behind.'

I said nothing.

'Except it did leave something behind,' he said. 'It left a big ugly piece of flotsam stuck right there on the waterline, and we have to address it.'

He waited for me to speak. I thought about clamming up. Thought about making him do all the work himself. But in the end I just shrugged and gave it up.

'The brutality complaint,' I said.

He nodded. 'Colonel Willard brought it to our attention. And it's awkward. Whereas the unauthorized use of the travel warrants can be dismissed as germane to the investigation, the brutality complaint can't. Because apparently the two civilians were completely unrelated to the business at hand.'

'I was misinformed,' I said.

'That doesn't alter the fact, I'm afraid.'

'Your witness is dead.'

'He left a signed affidavit. That stands for ever. That's the same as if he were right there in the courtroom, testifying.'

I said nothing.

'It comes down to a simple question of fact,' the colonel said. 'A simple yes or no answer, really. Did you do what Carbone alleged?'

I said nothing.

The colonel stood up. 'You can talk it over with your counsel.'

I glanced at the captain. Apparently he was my lawyer. The colonel shuffled out and closed the door on us. The captain leaned forward from his chair and shook my hand and told me his name.

'You should cut the colonel some slack,' he said. 'He's giving you a loophole a mile wide. This whole thing is a charade.'

'I rocked the boat,' I said. 'The army is getting its licks in.'

'You're wrong. Nobody wants to screw you over this. Willard forced the issue, is all. So we have to go through the motions.'

'Which are?'

'All you've got to do is deny it. That throws Carbone's evidence into dispute, and since he's not around to be cross-examined, your Sixth Amendment right to be confronted by the witness against you kicks in and it guarantees you an automatic dismissal.'

I sat still.

'How would it be done?' I said.

'You sign an affidavit just like Carbone did. His says black, yours says white, the problem goes away.'

'Official paper?'

'It'll take five minutes. We can do it right here. Your corporal can type it and witness it. Dead easy.'

I nodded.

'What's the alternative?' I said.

'You'd be nuts to even think about an alternative.'

'What would happen?'

'It would be like pleading guilty.'

'What would happen?' I said again.

'With an effective guilty plea? Loss of rank, loss of pay, backdated to the incident. Civilian Affairs wouldn't let us get away with anything less.'

I said nothing.

'You'd be busted back to captain. In the regular MPs, because the 110th wouldn't want you any more. That's the short answer. But you'd be nuts to even think about it. All you have to do is deny it.'

I sat there and thought about Carbone. Thirty-five years old, sixteen of them in the service. Infantry, airborne, the Rangers, Delta. Sixteen years of hard time. He had done nothing except

401

try to keep a secret he should never have had to keep. And try to alert his unit to a threat. Nothing much wrong with either of those things. But he was dead. Dead in the woods, dead on a slab. Then I thought about the fat guy at the strip club. I didn't really care about the farmer. A busted nose was no big deal. But the fat guy was messed up bad. On the other hand, he wasn't one of North Carolina's finest citizens. I doubted if the governor was lining him up for a civic award.

I thought about both of those guys for a long time. Carbone, and the fat man in the parking lot. Then I thought about myself. A major, a star, a hotshot special unit investigator, a go-to guy headed for the top.

'OK,' I said. 'Bring the colonel back in.'

The captain got up out of his chair and opened the door. Held it for the colonel. Closed it behind him. Sat down again next to me. The colonel shuffled past us and sat down at the desk.

'Right,' he said. 'Let's wrap this thing up. The complaint is baseless, yes?'

I looked at him. Said nothing.

'Well?'

You're going to do the right thing.

'The complaint is true,' I said.

He stared at me.

'The complaint is accurate,' I said. 'In every detail. It went down exactly like Carbone described.'

'Christ,' the colonel said.

'Are you crazy?' the captain said.

'Probably,' I said. 'But Carbone wasn't a liar. That shouldn't be the last thing that goes in his record. He deserves better than that. He was in sixteen years.'

The room went quiet. We all just sat there. They were looking at a lot of paperwork. I was looking at being an MP captain again. No more special unit. But it wasn't a big surprise. I had seen it coming. I had seen it coming ever since I closed my eyes on the plane and the dominoes started falling, end over end, one after the other.

'One request,' I said. 'I want a two-day suspension included. Starting now.'

'Why?'

'I have to go to a funeral. I don't want to beg my CO for leave.'
The colonel looked away.
'Granted,' he said.

I went back to my quarters and packed my duffel with every-thing I owned. I cashed a check at the commissary and left fifty-two dollars in an envelope for my sergeant. I mailed fifty back to Franz. I collected the crowbar that Marshall had used from the pathologist and I put it with the one we had on loan from the store. Then I went to the MP motor pool and looked for a vehicle to borrow. I was surprised to see Kramer's rental still parked there.

'Nobody told us what to do with it,' the clerk said.
'Why not?'
'Sir, you tell me. It was your case.'

I wanted something inconspicuous, and the little red Ford stood out among all the olive drab and black. But then I realized the situation would be reversed out in the world. Out there, the little red Ford wouldn't attract a second glance.

'I'll take it back now,' I said. 'I'm headed to Dulles anyway.'

There was no paperwork, because it wasn't an army vehicle.

I left Fort Bird at twenty past ten in the morning and drove north towards Green Valley. I went much slower than before, because the Ford was a slow car and I was a slow driver, at least compared to Summer. I didn't stop for lunch. I just kept on going. I arrived at the police station at a quarter past three in the afternoon. I found Detective Clark at his desk in the bullpen. I told him his case was closed. Told him Summer would give him the details. I collected the crowbar he had on loan and drove the ten miles to Sperryville. I squeezed through the narrow alley and parked outside the hardware store. The window had been fixed. The square of plywood was gone. I looped all three crowbars over my forearm and went inside and returned them to the old guy behind the counter. Then I got back in the car and followed the only road out of town, all the way to Washington D.C.

*   *   *

403

I took a short counterclockwise loop on the Beltway and went looking for the worst part of town I could find. There was plenty of choice. I picked a four-block square that was mostly crumbling warehouses with narrow alleys between. I found what I wanted in the third alley I checked. I saw an emaciated whore come out a brick doorway. I went in past her and found a guy in a hat. He had what I wanted. It took a minute to get some mutual trust going. But eventually cash money settled our differences, like it always does everywhere. I bought a little reefer, a little speed, and two dime rocks of crack cocaine. I could see the guy in the hat wasn't impressed by the quantities. I could see he wrote me off as an amateur.

Then I drove to Rock Creek, Virginia. I got there just before five o'clock. Parked three hundred yards from 110th Special Unit headquarters, up on a rise, where I could look down over the fence into the parking lot. I picked out Willard's car with no trouble at all. He had told me all about it. A classic Pontiac GTO. It was right there, near the rear exit. I slumped way down in my seat and kept my eyes wide open and watched.

He came out at five fifteen. Bankers' hours. He fired up the Pontiac and backed it away from the building. I had my window cracked open for air and even from three hundred yards I could hear the rumble of the pipes. They made a pretty good V-8 sound. I figured it was a sound Summer would have enjoyed. I made a mental note that if I ever won the lottery I should buy her a GTO of her own.

I fired up the Ford. Willard came out of the lot and turned towards me. I hunkered down and let him go past. Then I waited *one thousand, two thousand* and U-turned and followed after him. He was an easy tail. With the window down I could have done it by sound alone. He drove fairly slow, big and obvious up ahead, near the crown of the road. I stayed well back and let the drive-time traffic fill his mirrors. He headed east towards the D.C. suburbs. I figured he would have a rental in Arlington or Maclean from his Pentagon days. I hoped it wasn't an apartment. But I figured it would more likely be a house.

404

With a garage, for the muscle car. Which was good, because a house was easier.

It was a house. It was on a rural street in the no-man's-land north of Arlington. Plenty of trees, most of them bare, some of them evergreen. The lots were irregular. The driveways were long and curved. The plantings were messy. The street should have had a sign: *Divorced or single male middle-income government workers only.* It was that kind of a place. Not totally ideal, but a lot better than a straight suburban tract with side-by-side front yards full of frolicking kids and anxious mothers.

I drove on by and parked a mile away. Sat and waited for the darkness.

I waited until seven o'clock and I walked. There was low cloud and mist. No starlight. No moon. I was in woodland-pattern BDUs. I was as invisible as the Pentagon could make me. I figured at seven the place would still be mostly empty. I figured a lot of middle-income government workers would have ambitions to become high-income government workers, so they would stay at their desks, trying to impress whoever needed impressing. I used the street that ran parallel to the back of Willard's street and found two messy yards next to each other. Neither house was lit. I walked down the first driveway and kept on going around the dark bulk of the house and straight through the back yard. I stood still. No dogs barked. I turned and tracked along the boundary fences until I was looking at Willard's own back yard. It was full of dead hummocked grass. There was a rusted-out barbecue grill abandoned in the middle of the lawn. In army terms the place was not standing tall and squared away. It was a mess.

I bent a fence post until I had room to slip past it. Walked straight through Willard's yard and around his garage to his front door. There was no porch light. The view from the street was half-open, half-obscured. Not perfect. But not bad. I put my elbow on the bell. Heard it sound inside. There was a short pause and then I heard footsteps. I stood back. Willard opened the door. No delay at all. Maybe he was expecting Chinese food. Or a pizza.

I punched him in the chest to move him backward. Stepped in after him and closed the door behind me with my foot. It was a dismal house. The air was stale. Willard was clutching the stair post, gasping for breath. I hit him in the face and knocked him down. He came up on his hands and knees and I kicked him hard in the ass and kept on kicking until he took the hint and started crawling towards the kitchen as fast as he could. He got himself in there and kind of rolled over and sat on the floor with his back hard up against a cabinet. There was fear in his face, for sure, but confusion, too. Like he couldn't believe I was doing this. Like he was thinking: *this is about a disciplinary complaint?* His bureaucratic calculus couldn't compute it.

'Did you hear about Vassell and Coomer?' I asked him.

He nodded, fast and scared.

'Remember Lieutenant Summer?' I asked him.

He nodded again.

'She pointed something out to me,' I said. 'Kind of obvious, but she said they would have gotten away with it if I hadn't ignored you.'

He just stared at me.

'It made me think,' I said. 'What exactly was I ignoring?'

He said nothing.

'I misjudged you,' I said. 'I apologize. Because I thought I was ignoring a busybody careerist asshole. I thought I was ignoring some kind of a prissy nervous idiot corporate manager who thought he knew better. But I wasn't. I was ignoring something else entirely.'

He stared up at me.

'You didn't feel embarrassed about Kramer,' I said. 'You didn't feel sensitive about me harassing Vassell and Coomer. You weren't speaking for the army when you wanted Carbone written up as a training accident. You were doing the job you were put there to do. Someone wanted three homicides covered up, and you were put there to do it for them. You were participating in a deliberate cover-up, Willard. That's what you were doing. That's what I was ignoring. I mean, what the hell else were you doing, *ordering* me not to investigate a homicide? It was a cover-up, and it was planned, and it was structured, and it was decided well in advance. It was decided

406

on the second day of January, when Garber was moved out and you were moved in. You were put in there so that what they were planning to do on the fourth could be controlled. No other reason.'

He said nothing.

'I thought they wanted an incompetent in there, so that nature would take its course. But they went one better than that. They put a friend in there.'

He said nothing.

'You should have refused,' I said. 'If you had refused, they wouldn't have gone ahead with it and Carbone and Brubaker would still be alive.'

He said nothing.

'You killed them, Willard. Just as much as they did.'

I crouched down next to him. He scrabbled on the floor and pressed backward against the cupboard behind him. He had defeat in his eyes. But he gave it one last shot.

'You can't prove anything,' he said.

Now I said nothing.

'Maybe it *was* just incompetence,' he said. 'You thought about that? How are you going to prove the intention?'

I said nothing. His eyes went hard.

'You're not dealing with idiots,' he said. 'There's no proof anywhere.'

I took Franz's Beretta out of my pocket. The one I had brought out of the Mojave. I hadn't lost it. It had ridden all the way with me from California. That was why I had checked my luggage, just that one time. They won't let you carry guns inside the cabin. Not without paperwork.

'This piece is listed as destroyed,' I said. 'It doesn't officially exist any more.'

He stared at it.

'Don't be stupid,' he said. 'You can't prove anything.'

'You're not dealing with an idiot either,' I said.

'You don't understand,' he said. 'It was an order. From the top. We're in the army. We obey orders.'

I shook my head. 'That excuse never worked for any soldier anywhere.'

'It was an order,' he said again.

407

'From who?'

He just closed his eyes and shook his head.

'Doesn't matter,' I said. 'I know exactly who it was. And I know I can't get to him. Not where he is. But I can get to you. You can be my messenger.'

He opened his eyes.

'You won't do it,' he said.

'Why didn't you refuse?'

'I couldn't refuse. It was time to choose up sides. Don't you see? We're all going to have to do that.'

I nodded. 'I guess we are.'

'Be smart now,' he said. 'Please.'

'I thought you were one bad apple,' I said. 'But the whole barrel is bad. The good apples are the rare ones.'

He stared at me.

'You ruined it for me,' I said. 'You and your damn friends.'

'Ruined what?'

'Everything.'

I stood up. Stepped back. Clicked the Beretta's safety to *fire*. He stared at me.

'Goodbye, Colonel Willard,' I said.

I put the gun to my temple. He stared at me.

'Just kidding,' I said.

Then I shot him through the centre of the forehead.

It was a typical nine-millimetre full metal jacket through-and-through. It put the back of his skull into the cupboard behind him and left it there with a lot of smashed china. I stuffed the reefer and the speed and the crack cocaine in his pockets, along with a symbolic roll of dollar bills. Then I walked out the back door and away through his yard. I slipped through the fence and through the lot behind his and walked back to my car. I sat in the driver's seat and opened my duffel and changed my boots. Took off the pair that had been ruined in the Mojave and put on a better pair. Then I drove west, toward Dulles. Into the Hertz return bays. Car rental bosses aren't dumb. They know people get cars messy. They know they accumulate all kinds of crap inside. So they position big garbage cans near the return bays in the hope that renters will do the decent thing and clear some of the crap out themselves. That way they save on wages. Cut out even a minute a car, and staff costs drop a lot over a whole year. I put my old boots in one can, and the Beretta in another. As many cars as Hertz rented at Dulles in a day, those cans were headed for the crusher on a regular basis.

I walked all the way to the terminal. I didn't feel like taking the bus. I showed my military ID and used my checkbook and bought a one-way ticket to Paris, on the same Air France red-eye Joe had taken back when the world was different.

I got to the Avenue Rapp at eight in the morning. Joe told me the cars were coming at ten. So I shaved and showered in the guest bathroom and found my mother's ironing board and pressed my Class A uniform very carefully. I found polish in a cupboard and shined my shoes. Then I dressed. I put my full array of medals on, all four rows. I followed the *Correct Order of Wear* regulations, and the *Wear of Full Size Medals* regulations. Each one hung down neatly over the ribbon in the row below. I used a cloth and cleaned them. I cleaned my other badges too, including my major's oak leaves, one last time. Then I went into the white-painted living room to wait.

Joe was in a black suit. I was no expert on clothing but I figured it was new. It was some kind of a fine material. Silk, maybe. Or cashmere. I didn't know. It was beautifully cut. He had a white shirt and a black tie. Black shoes. He looked good. I had never seen him look better. He was holding up. He was a little strained around the eyes, maybe. We didn't talk. Just waited.

At five to ten we went down to the street. The *corbillard* showed up right on time, from the *dépôt mortuaire*. Behind it was a black Citroën limousine. We got in the limousine and closed the doors and it moved off after the hearse, slow and quiet.

'Just us?' I said.

'The others are meeting us there.'

'Who's coming?'

'Lamonnier,' he said. 'Some of her friends.'

'Where are we doing it?'

'Père Lachaise,' he said.

409

I nodded. Père Lachaise was a famous old cemetery. Some kind of a special place. I figured maybe my mother's Resistance history entitled her to be buried there. Maybe Lamonnier had fixed it.

'There's an offer in on the apartment,' Joe said.

'How much?'

'In dollars your share would be about sixty thousand.'

'I don't want it,' I said. 'Give my share to Lamonnier. Tell him to find whatever old guys are still alive and spread it around. He'll know some organizations.'

'Old soldiers?'

'Old anybody. Whoever did the right thing at the right time.'

'You sure? You might need it.'

'I'd rather not have it.'

'OK,' he said. 'Your choice.'

I watched out the windows. It was a grey day. The honey tones of Paris were beaten down by the weather. The river was sluggish, like molten iron. We drove through the Place de la Bastille. Père Lachaise was up in the northeast. Not far, but not so near you thought of it as close. We got out of the car near a little booth that sold maps to the famous graves. All kinds of people were buried at Père Lachaise. Chopin, Molière, Edith Piaf, Jim Morrison.

There were people waiting for us at the cemetery gate. There was the concierge from my mother's building, and two other women I didn't know. The *croque-morts* lifted the coffin up on their shoulders. They held it steady for a second and then set off at a slow march. Joe and I fell in behind, side by side. The three women followed us. The air was cold. We walked along gritty paths between strange European mausoleums and headstones. Eventually we came to an open grave. Excavated earth was piled neatly on one side of it and covered with a green carpet that I guessed was supposed to look like grass. Lamonnier was waiting there for us. I guessed he had gotten there well ahead of time. He probably walked slower than a funeral. Probably hadn't wanted to hold us up, or embarrass himself.

The pallbearers set the coffin down on rope slings that were already laid out in position. Then they picked it up again and manoeuvred it over the hole and used the ropes to lower it down gently. Into the hole. There was a man who read some stuff from a book. I heard the words in French and their English translations drifted through my mind. *Dust to dust, certain it is, vale of tears*. I didn't really pay attention. I just looked at the coffin, down in the hole.

The man finished speaking and one of the pallbearers pulled back the green carpet and Joe scooped up a handful of dirt. He weighed it in his palm and then threw it down on the coffin lid. It thumped on the wood. The man with the book did the same thing. Then the concierge. Then both of the other women. Then Lamonnier. He lurched over on his awkward canes and bent down and filled his hand with earth. Paused with his eyes full of tears and just turned his wrist so that the dirt trailed out of his fist like water.

I stepped up and put my hand to my heart and slipped my Silver Star off its pin. Held it in my palm. The Silver Star is a beautiful medal. It has a tiny silver star in the centre of a much larger gold one. It has a bright silk ribbon in red white and blue, all shot through with a watermark. Mine was engraved on the back: *J. Reacher*. I thought: *J for Josephine*. I tossed it down in the hole. It hit the coffin and bounced once and landed right side up, a little gleam of light in the greyness.

I called long distance from the Avenue Rapp and got orders back to Panama. Joe and I ate a late lunch together and promised to stay in better touch. Then I headed back to the airport and flew through London and Miami and picked up a transport south. As a newly minted captain I was given a company to command. We were tasked to maintain order in Panama City during the Just Cause endgame. It was fun. I had a decent bunch of guys. Being out in the field again was refreshing. And the coffee was as good as ever. They ship it wherever we go, in cans as big as oil drums.

I never went back to Fort Bird. Never saw that sergeant again, the one with the baby son. I thought of her sometimes, when force reduction began to bite. I never saw Summer again, either. I heard she talked up Kramer's agenda so much that JAG Corps wanted the death penalty for treason, and then she finessed confessions out of Vassell and Coomer and Marshall on all the other stuff in exchange for life in prison. I heard she got promoted captain the day after they went to Leavenworth. So she and I ended up on the same pay grade. We met in the middle. But our paths never crossed again.

I never went back to Paris, either. I meant to. I thought I might go climb down under the Pont des Invalides, late at night, and just sniff the air. But it never happened. I was in the army, and I was always where someone else told me to be.